The Returning Tide

LIZ FENWICK

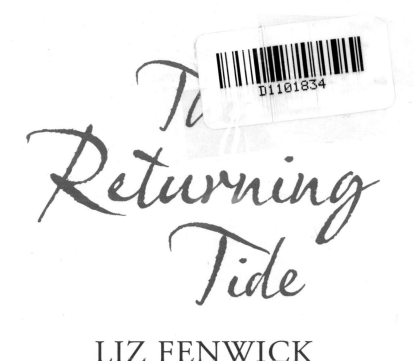

First published in Great Britain in 2017 by Orion Books,
an imprint of The Orion Publishing Group Ltd
Carmelite House, 50 Victoria Embankment
London EC4Y 0DZ

An Hachette UK Company

1 3 5 7 9 10 8 6 4 2

A CIP catalogue record for this book
is available from the British Library.

ISBN (Trade Paperback) 978 1 4091 6210 0

Typeset by Deltatype Ltd, Birkenhead, Merseyside

Printed in Great Britain by CPI Group (UK) Ltd
Croydon, CR0 4YY

www.orionbooks.co.uk

To my parents, Jim and Kay ... they have taught me that love isn't about saying the words but what you do

There is a tide in the affairs of men,
Which taken at the flood, leads to fortune.
Omitted, all the voyage of their life
Is bound in the shallows and in the miseries.
On such a full sea are we now afloat.
And we must take the current when it serves,
Or lose our ventures.

SHAKESPEARE, JULIUS CAESAR, ACT 4, SCENE 3

Ebb Tide

The tide rises, the tide falls
The twilight darkens, the curlew calls

H. WADSWORTH LONGFELLOW, THE TIDE RISES, THE TIDE FALLS

✳ One ✳

Windward, Mawnan Smith, Falmouth, Cornwall
12 September 1945

The marquee housing the wedding party was small, but it was not needed. Under the clear blue sky, the wheat in the next field rippled in the light easterly breeze, but the sea swelled like my sister's belly. The war was over. She had just married, and not too soon, for she was starting to show. Her groom, handsome in his US Army captain's uniform, stood awkwardly beside her with his arm resting against her back. He squinted into the distance looking for something, something that had been lost. Innocence, I should imagine. Eventually they would head to America and, if fate were kind, I would never see my sister again.

Touching the pearls at my neck, I turned away from the couple and my father came up to me with his camera. His hands shook. 'Take the photograph for me.'

I crossed my arms.

'Take it,' he barked, as if he were giving an order to the troops. His uniform demonstrated that he outranked me; he was a major in the Army while I had just been demobbed from the Navy. He had a role and I was adrift on the tide, ready to go where it would take me as long as it was away from here.

Holding the camera in the direction of the couple, I would not look through the viewfinder. I did not want to see them perfectly framed in the September sunshine. Instead I peered over the top of the camera at the house. Until recently Windward had been a place of happiness and refuge despite the war.

I pressed the shutter button, the camera clicked, I handed it back to Father then walked away. My duty was done. I'd had enough.

In front of me the waters of Falmouth Bay glistened. Below the tide was out revealing the rocks that threatened any boat without a chart trying to navigate onto the shore at high water. My sister had always been the romantic one. She never stopped talking about love. Love. How deluded I had been. One night in London at the Savoy, I had met the most handsome US lieutenant. Just one glance from his big blue eyes and I was lost without a map and my compass found a different north. Everything changed.

1 May 2015

I folded the hankie I'd used to wipe the moisture from my eyes and my fingers ran over the raised embroidered image on the corner. Lily of the valley. The scent of the just-opened bells floated on the warm air. No matter how many times I'd removed the rhizomes over the years, the flowers returned annually like an unwanted weed. In front of me my granddaughter Peta, her fiancé Fred Polcrebar and my grandson Jack marked out the lawn with stakes for where the marquee would be erected in a few months' time. They weren't to know the importance of the date. The promise of summer heat filled this May day, while on 12 September 1945 the sun, although warm, had spoken of cooler days ahead.

Peta was a radiant bride-to-be and Jack, her over-protective brother, was anxious and questioned every decision. He hoped this would change Peta's mind and make her see reason. Love clouded the brain he felt and she was too young. I knew well enough that these things would run their course. They always did. I could have stopped the events of years ago but what good would it have done me?

'How does it look from over there, Mrs Rowse?' Fred unbent and shrugged his broad shoulders.

'Fine, but please call me Elle.'

'I can't do that.' He walked towards me with a big grin, looking more boyish than his twenty-three years.

'Why ever not?'

'It just wouldn't be right, that's all.'

'Because I'm so old.' I laughed at his horrified expression.

'No.' He glanced away from my lined face.

'Liar. Call me Elle or Gran. Take your pick but not Mrs Rowse. You're family now.'

Jack coughed as he marched towards me. His beautiful mouth was twisted in a scowl and his hands were clenched into fists. He was so easy to read.

'Talk to her,' he whispered.

'You don't like the position for the marquee?' I raised an eyebrow, glancing at the stakes in the lawn.

'Don't tell me you're on her side.' He kept his voice low so that Fred and Peta couldn't hear him.

I suppressed a smile. 'I wasn't aware there were sides to take.'

'They are too young.'

'Many people marry even younger.' Twenty yards in front of me Fred was laughing at something Peta had said.

Jack thrust his hands into his pockets. 'That doesn't make it right.'

I frowned. He shouldn't be like this. Concern for his sister's happiness was one thing but that wasn't where this was coming from. It was deeper. It was his past, his parents.

'You don't believe in love either.' He expelled a short breath and I smiled at his frustration with me.

'I was happily married to your grandfather for twenty years.' I reached out to touch Jack but he'd moved too far away.

'Yes, but you were in your forties.'

'And that makes a difference?'

'It does.' He shook his head and walked into the house.

Peta hammered in the last stake with the mallet. Confidence oozed from her. She knew what she wanted and was moving towards it with a conviction that made me envious. Fred took her hand in his and kissed her forehead. Young love. True and pure. Could they make it against the odds?

I turned away from them towards the solid front of Windward that faced the bay. It had once been a house full of happiness. I'd thought things had turned around with Andrew and me, but darkness thrived in the unlit corners waiting to ambush the unsuspecting. Right now each granite stone seemed to be held in place with mortar made of pain and loss. Seeing Jack's outline through the drawing room window I knew it was not just my own pain and loss, but this generation's as well.

Peta stopped under the bank of trees and picked a shoot of lily of the valley. She breathed in the scent and her face lit up. She turned and walked towards me with the delicate stem adorned with pure white bells between her fingers. 'The return of happiness,' she said, handing it to me. It was far too late for that. Peace was the most that could be asked for.

5 May 2015

Peta cast me a repentant glance from across the room and I glared back. She knew this would be the last thing in which I would want to take part in any manner, but I sat on the sofa with a camera pointing at me. My ankles were crossed, shoulders held down, chin lifted, as my grandmother had demanded of us. Around me, Windward still felt like my grandmother's house rather than mine, despite the sixty-nine years since she'd passed away. In all that time, little in the house had changed.

The young woman from the BBC cleared her throat, looking fearfully excited about talking to me. 'Mrs Rowse, this is a picture of you taken on VE Day.' She held up a glossy print in the space between us. The image was of a woman wearing a WRNS uniform in the arms of an airman. The woman's smile would have lit up the London skyline if it hadn't already been properly alight behind the two figures, the first time it had been so in years.

I knew that face, the smile, those eyes.

'It's a wonderful shot,' the young woman said, 'and it captures the feeling of joy so well.'

I nodded. It was a silly picture and it irritated me that my hat was askew.

'Was that your boyfriend? Fiancé?'

'No.' I took it from her, my hand shook.

'Did you know him?'

'No. The war in Europe was over and like everyone I wanted to dance, to sing, to celebrate.' The happiness was palpable that night. Well, it had been for most people. The young woman studied the picture and I could see her creating a fairy tale, but the story the picture told was a lie. It simply captured a moment before everything altered. I breathed in, making an odd sucking sound.

'Such a wonderful photo.' She looked at me, trying to see the link between the jubilant woman in the photo and the old one in front of her. About the only thing the same after all these years was the nose. The eyes were no longer bright, nor as deep an amber. Time had altered all other resemblance.

'Photographs are rarely what they appear to be.' I handed the print back to her.

She frowned, placing it on the table. 'It's a picture of happiness on VE Day.'

'It is.' I turned away. On the table by the window in a small silver frame was a picture of my mother alone, sitting elegantly in Windward's garden. The photograph didn't reveal how broken she was – lost almost totally in a world in her head. The sunlight's angle at this time of day highlighted the thin layer of dust covering the patina of the table's walnut veneer. I couldn't remember when I'd last dusted or polished. Someone had to be doing it.

'It's obvious you were thrilled the war was over.'

'Yes.' I looked away.

'Now tell me about your war. It's so important to hear from those who lived through it.'

In a few days it was the seventieth anniversary of victory in Europe. It was history now, and they wanted to save it for future generations so that the past wouldn't be forgotten. But some things should be forgotten, and my war was one such thing.

'I believe you worked at HMS *Attack*.'

I nodded; she'd done her research.

'Can you tell me what it was like as a Wren and telegraphist?'

I straightened my back, remembering the ballet mistress hired by Grandmother to ensure my sister and I deported ourselves properly. We had done everything in unison. Our movements were so precisely matched when we were young, no one could tell us apart.

'You recorded the messages from the boats.'

I focused on the reporter, as images floated through my mind. They were fragments, really, snapshots of past times, as if I were flipping through an album – but then I frowned and shut the album, before it went further.

'I know this must be hard for you.'

The movement of the clock on the mantelpiece … *dit dah*, *dit dah* … •– / •– – the letter 'A' on continuous repeat. I opened my eyes wide. She had no idea.

'It's important that we hear your words. Have you spoken about your experience before?'

'Spoken about it? We couldn't.' Did they tell the young nothing these days?

'It's important you tell me, tell us, before it's forgotten, lost.'

'Some things are better off lost.'

She frowned. 'I know you were working during Exercise Tiger, on the day when the German E-boats came among the convoy of US forces that were preparing for D-Day.'

I closed my eyes. This was what she was after. 28 April 1944. This was my war – the last words of men dying. Even now they whispered in the back of my head, becoming louder. I had tried for years to keep them silent, not allowing them to be heard. This reporter thought I would want to recall it, bring it all back – their pain, their fear, and their dying words. *Help us*. I could hear it now. •••• • •–•• •––•/••– ••• My finger twitched, tapping out the Morse. Opening my eyes I stared at her. 'I don't want to talk about that.'

The reporter pressed her lips together. 'I'm sure the memories are painful.'

'You have no idea.'

'Post-traumatic stress disorder,' said the reporter.

I squinted at her. 'What?'

'Did you talk to anyone about it after that day?'

I raised an eyebrow. 'No.'

'Why not?'

Today's world. They talk about everything. The television and papers regale me with details of everyone's sex lives, as if I cared. Nothing is private and they keep trying to make themselves perfect, but nothing is. Nothing is meant to be. 'We didn't talk because of the Official Secrets Act and the threat of court martial.' I stood and walked to the window, catching my reflection in the glass. An old woman stared back at me. The clock spoke to me, bringing back all the Morse. That was the language of my war and I didn't want to hear it.

'I'm afraid I can't help you.'

Voices echoed off the tiled floor in the hallway. What had happened to the Turkish carpet that used to soften the entrance? That was one small detail that had changed. My grandmother had loved that carpet for its rich, colourful shades. The intense sunlight that filled the hall most days had bleached the depth from the tones. It had worn threadbare in places where many feet had walked over the years, including the paying guests. I smiled. That was how Andrew had walked back into my life, across that carpet.

The warmth of the carpet's colour had contrasted with the stark black and white floor tiles. It was not the most practical of floors for a country house surrounded by fields. Muddy footprints felt impossible to lift from the white tiles, once we no longer had help washing it daily. Grandmother had chosen those tiles without ever considering a life without hired help. I laughed and then remembered – I had tripped over the carpet recently and Jack had rolled it up and put it away. I understood why he'd done it, but I also hated having to give in to my frailties.

'Did you get what you wanted?' Jack's voice betrayed no

emotion as it drifted in from the hall. Since I had these new hearing aids it was harder to tune people out. There had been advantages to being quite deaf.

'No, not really.' The reporter sighed. 'I suppose with a bit of editing we can use it on the day. It would really help to have more, though.'

He laughed. It was the laugh he used to divert, the one I knew so well. He kept himself closed, off limits. His wry amusement acted to protect him. His mother's death had broken him and his father's death less than a year later had finished the job.

'She has so much valuable information. It's clear she's not lost her faculties.'

There was silence and I pictured Jack, eyebrow raised and disdain spread across his face. He was an ally. I understood him. No one else did, although many had tried. Women fell at his feet but he walked all over them. None that attempted to catch him for themselves had broken that solid steel cage he had put himself into thirteen years ago. He blamed love – and I could understand why; I did too, if for entirely different reasons. Only Andrew, Jack's grandfather, had chipped away at my own steel, making holes that had allowed me to breathe sometimes.

Love. For Jack, love equalled death. He would never risk it again. For me, it equalled loss.

'Can you have a word with her?' asked the reporter.

'I suggest you try again tomorrow,' Jack replied.

'Do you think that will work?' Her voice rose in excitement.

'No, but then you will have tried.'

Although I couldn't see them, I sensed her disappointment from here. Jack did try and bring joy and hope. Such a shame he wouldn't let it into his own life. It was a waste. That was what my mother had told me years ago in one of her lucid moments. *Let it go*, she'd said. *Make the best of what you've been given.* I could never let go, but eventually I had let someone else in, just a bit. Andrew had been a patient and kind man. I'd tried to be a good wife and stepmother.

'I think she's still suffering from what she lived through.' She coughed.

'She may well be but she won't tell you about that.' I heard the footsteps across the hall. 'It's not what that generation did.'

The door closed and Jack entered the library. 'You weren't very obliging.' A smile hovered around his mouth and touched his eyes. He was a handsome boy, like his grandfather in many ways, but fair where Andrew had been dark.

'No.'

He sat opposite me. 'She didn't mean any harm.'

'What good is it to tell her about my war?'

He picked up the photograph that she had left behind. He looked from it to me. 'You are so beautiful, Gran.'

'Was.'

'No, still are.' He looked over the top of it.

'I don't look like that anymore.'

He grinned. 'Yes, you do.'

'Pah.'

'Older, yes, but the smile is the same, the eyes, the nose.' He stood. 'Are you going to help the woman and record a few sound bites for her?'

'There is no need. It will all be there in the official records.'

'It's not quite the same, is it?' He bent down and kissed my forehead.

'You think I should do it.'

'Do only what you want to do,' he said.

'Hah.'

'It's your choice, Gran.' He headed to the kitchen. Soon there would be glorious smells wafting through the house. Right now, the light from the table lamp reflected off the glossy print. Everything worked in that photograph, even my crooked hat. The photographer would have been spoiled for choice with all the joyous images around London that night. But he had chosen me in the arms of an airman.

My war. The sun had left the south face of the house; although I couldn't see it, I knew it bathed the kitchen and study in its last rays before it dropped below the tall trees marking the boundary of the garden. When did my war begin? That was easy to pinpoint, but I don't think it ever properly ended. I still felt its effects every day.

We had moved to Windward, then my grandmother's summer home, just after the Blitz had begun in 1940. Mother's nerves had become too frazzled by life in London when a house three down from us was hit by a bomb and almost completely destroyed.

There had been no complaints from me when our summer retreat became a full-time one. Grandmother had later decamped here as well, when the Army requisitioned Uncle Reginald's house in Oxfordshire. I smiled. Grandmother had gone on and on about what an inconvenience it had been, when she could have stayed in the estate's dower house. But Cornwall was in her blood and it had been the perfect excuse not to do the right thing and watch over the estate, but to do what she wanted.

Looking out to Falmouth Bay, I remembered it, as it had been then, busy with naval activity – now, it was only filled with the occasional tanker and pleasure craft. I leaned on my cane, listening. The sound of Glenn Miller's 'In the Mood' played in the distance. Was I losing my mind? I closed my eyes. Those years were so far away but right at that moment they grabbed at my throat, cutting off the air. The sound of the air-raid siren filled the room. I looked left and right, trying to remember where the shelter was, but the siren stopped and I heard Jack's voice sing the words to 'Run Rabbit Run'.

I laughed. Silly old woman. It must be some programme on the wireless. Jack liked to listen to Radio Four while he cooked. Music was so powerful. I'd deliberately avoided listening all these years. It acted like a time machine. Being held in Bobby's arms listening to him whisper in my ear the words to 'I Only Have Eyes For You'. That was when I realised that I'd lost my heart forever. I shivered. He'd held me so close and when the music finished he whispered the words I'd been longing to say.

I love you.

The wind blew through the open window. I rubbed my arms. What hair was left on them was standing up. It didn't do to think about old memories. That damn reporter was at fault. I could have avoided all the fuss of the anniversary. Why would I want to look back? Why would anyone want to? We must live for now, not for the future or the past.

The smell of simmering onions drifted through the house. The lack of change in Windward over the decades had more to do with my laziness in recent years, but previous to that it had also been imposed by penny-pinching. And yet, it didn't look bad for it. Andrew had wanted me to spend his money on it, but by that time frugality was ingrained in me. Grandmother would be rolling over in her grave at the idea. The Hon. Agatha Davies, *née* Worth, had married well, but her children were a disappointment to her and her grandchildren had proven even worse. How the great had fallen – but it wasn't all bad. Andrew had been a good man, and now I was blessed with his grandchildren.

'Gran, dinner's ready. Do you want to eat in the kitchen or the dining room?' Jack stood in the doorway humming along with Bing Crosby to 'Don't Fence Me In'. His legs moved and he held a hand out in invitation to dance, with a grin spread across his handsome face. Yes, life had provided compensations along the way.

❋ Two ❋

Eventide, Falmouth Heights, Cape Cod, Massachusetts
15 August 2015

A fly bounced off of the window screen and disturbed Lara's vigil, watching her great-grandfather's chest rise and fall. Each time she saw him breathe, she wondered if it would be the last time. According to the nurse, he had not been awake or conscious since she'd gone to bed at midnight. It wouldn't be long now. The family had been called but no one was rushing. They had all said their farewells. Lara stood and walked to the window. Goodbyes. She hated them and this was one she definitely didn't want to make.

The dog days of August were living up to their reputation. What breeze there was wasn't even stirring the muslin curtains. The beach in front of Eventide, Grandie's home, was empty. Nantucket Sound was still and a heat haze hung above the water. The fly paused on the windowsill, then the only thing disturbing the heavy air was the rasp of Grandie's breath as he exhaled. Sitting on the bedside table were the flotsam and jetsam she'd picked up for him on her morning's walk. It was the treasure haul of a child. Each day this past week she'd strolled the beach as the sun was rising, bringing back something that she hoped would delight him. Two days ago, the last time he'd spoken coherently, he had explained the life cycle of the horseshoe crab while he held the skeletal shell she'd found in his hands. His mind was still so sharp. It was just his body that was giving up. His passion for the ocean and all things in it had been his life's work, and that life was nearly complete.

He was ninety-four. She knew that there was no chance that he would make his next birthday in September even though she wanted him to. Without thinking she picked up the clamshell and placed it in his open palm, helping him to feel the contours of it. His eyes opened and fixed onto her. There was love in them. She swallowed.

'Tell me what type of clam this is? You know me, I can never keep them straight. Is this a little neck or a top neck?'

The visiting nurse popped her head through the door. 'All OK?'

Lara nodded and waved her away. If these were his last hours she was going to be selfish and not share him. The shell fell from his hand onto the floor and she bent down to collect it. It had scudded under the bed to rest against an old metal box. Picking up the shell, she pulled the box out as well and placed both of them on the bed. 'What's this?' she asked, gesturing to the box.

He tried to lift his hand, but it fell back to the bed. The top of the box was covered in dust, which she brushed away revealing a yellowed label that said: *WWII*.

'May I open it?'

He blinked and she took that for a yes, knowing she or someone else would have to open it eventually. It wasn't locked, and only needed a bit of force for the lid to shift. At the top of the box were his military medals. Lara picked one up, surprised at its weight. A red and white striped ribbon held a medal with an eagle surrounded by words – Efficiency, Honor, Fidelity. There were so many others nestled on the tray.

She placed it in his hand and he smiled, but said nothing. Putting it back, she lifted the tray to see what was under it. A few black and white photographs of him in uniform sat on some loose papers.

'You were so handsome.' She held up a picture. 'Of course, I'm not saying you aren't now.'

He smiled.

'Where were you in this one?'

His eyes closed and Lara flipped the picture over. Something was written in faint pencil. She squinted, holding it closer. 'Helford River?'

There was no response from him. He had fallen asleep again. His periods of wakefulness were less and less. Placing the photos aside, she picked up the sheets of folded paper.

25 June 1944

My dearest love,

I cannot begin to say how relieved I am that you are alive. I've seen the dead and injured come in daily and I have prayed that it wouldn't be you, but was almost afraid to hope. I don't think my heart could take it. I don't understand how in such a short time you have come to be my world but you have. Please, please stay safe. You are my heart, you are my life. I can barely breathe when I think about you and the danger you must be in at the moment. I know I must be brave and I will be for you.

I love you.
Yours always,
A xxxxxxxooooo

Amelia, her great-grandmother. He had met her in England during the war. Lara opened another but stopped to check Grandie again, picturing him as he was in the photos, so young and so very handsome. She really shouldn't read these very private letters, but it was the first tangible contact she had had with her great-grandmother. Her name was rarely mentioned.

Darling,

Seeing you yesterday almost made things worse. To have you with me for a few hours makes being apart unbearable. I touch my lips repeatedly remembering the feel of yours on mine. I want you so badly it's all I can think about. When will this wretched war end so that we can be together?

I find I am jealous of every couple I see. It reminds me you are far away and I can't touch you or feel the warmth of your skin on mine. If you had told me a few months ago that I could feel this way I wouldn't have believed you. You are my obsession. Every time I shut my eyes I see you and I try to hold you close but at best you are nothing but a pillow. I cannot describe the coldness that crawls over me after the heat of my dreams.

All my love,
A xxxxxxxxxxxxx

P.S. My physical need for you is invading all my thoughts. I want to know you fully. I understand waiting but my heart and body do not. I dream of nothing but you – all of you – and I wake to the reality that you are not here in my arms touching me.

Lara blushed and folded the letter with care, placing it with the others. It felt wrong to read them. Grandie had never married again even though Amelia had died in 1950, four years after giving birth to their only daughter, Lara's grandmother Betty. His love for Amelia had lasted his whole life. These letters showed she had passionately loved him too.

Below them were several tiny books each embossed in gold with a year – 1943, 1944 and 1945. Flicking through the pages, Lara saw he had written a line or two at most on each day. He'd never spoken about the war, even though she and her twin, Leo, had asked years ago.

She paced the room, stopping to stare out the window over to the hazy outline of Martha's Vineyard – the vista so achingly familiar. Eventide had been as much a part of her life as Grandie. The view never bored her. With each tide the beach in front of the house changed. The sand shifted and creatures thrived. The house would go to her grandmother, Betty, who had already stated her plan to sell it. She had left the Cape years ago and her life was now in Florida where the winters were kinder.

It was time to let go. Lara turned back to the room. Her great-grandfather appeared so small on the bed with its tall,

17

carved posts, each topped with the pinecone filial. The trouble-some fly landed on his nose. Lara brushed it away again then stroked the thin hair across his brow. He'd been so handsome when young, and traces of those looks were still there in the structure of his face.

'I love you, and I know you are ready.' She sat down on the bed next to him and took his hand in hers. 'I'm trying to be ready too.' She sighed. 'Letting go is hard and, well, I've never been good at it. Or losing, for that matter.'

His eyes opened. He was listening.

'But that's what this year has been about so far.'

He blinked.

'More divorce stuff arrived in the mail.' She wasn't sure why she was telling him this. He wouldn't understand giving up. It wasn't what people of his generation did. You married and that was it.

'I know what you're thinking.' His glance didn't leave her face. 'I should stick it out. But ...' She took a deep breath. 'If it had been my choice alone, I would have.' She shook her head. 'But you aren't in a marriage alone.' She paused. 'And, well, that's what Pierre felt he was, in our marriage. Alone.' Her long hours had taken a toll on their time together. You didn't get weekends off in the restaurant trade. He didn't have days off in the week.

Grandie's eyes closed. Lara paused until she saw he was still breathing. Should they, or more correctly she, have done more to save the marriage? What would Grandie have done? 'We drifted apart.' Every day this past year she and Pierre had passed each other in the kitchen and in the hall, no longer touching, and she'd been too tired to notice. The wedding band on her finger caught the light from the bedside lamp. 'It was more my fault than his, if I'm honest.'

His breath paused and her heart tightened.

'I'm not sure if you can hear me or not but I need to know how you stayed in love with your wife all this time. Amelia has been gone for over sixty years. How do you make a love like that happen?'

His hand moved, searching out hers. She'd left it too late to ask these questions. If the nurse was right, Grandie might not utter another word.

Unlike modern houses the kitchen in Eventide didn't face the view, but the driveway. No doubt when someone bought the house they would alter it to meet modern ideas and not those of the late 1800s. Lara, however, liked the fact that when she was cooking she wasn't distracted by the view. In the kitchen the focus should be on the ingredients and what you were doing with them. This was a lesson she understood more today than she had all those years ago when she had made blueberry muffins with Grandie. Years at culinary school and in the kitchens of top restaurants had taught her this and more.

Behind her on the table were the final agreements of her divorce. Her marriage was almost finished. She hadn't really paid attention to the details. For years she'd worked twelve- to thirteen-hour days six days a week. On the seventh she slept. She hadn't known Pierre anymore, and hadn't really known herself outside of a kitchen.

Lara put the kettle on the stove and jiggled the gas knob. The flame burst into light under it and she watched it discolour under the metal base of the kettle. It was the same one that had always been there. Once it would have been something she would have wanted from the house. She would have prowled the kitchen grabbing the old mixing bowls along with the dog-eared copy of *Good Housekeeping's Best Recipes* and the battered *La Veritable Cuisine de Famille par Tante Marie*. Locating the French cookbook on the shelf, she picked it up and leafed through the pages, wondering when Grandie had acquired it. Lara had practised her high-school French while trying the recipes. What she'd loved most about the *Tante Marie* book were the handwritten notes in pencil in the margins, with ideas for alternative ingredients. In some ways she could credit the hours spent with this as the inspiration for her career.

Flicking through to the back of the cookbook, she reached the end papers, where there were many handwritten recipes inscribed in pencil. This wasn't Grandie's or her grandmother's writing so it had to be the book's first owner. Running her hand over the careful script she smiled at the recipe for rosehip syrup. Outside the window the garden was filled with sea spray roses. They produced beautiful hips. She wouldn't be here to harvest them this year. She had no idea where she would be come September and October.

She knew she wouldn't take any of these books now. They would be hauled off to the local charity shop for resale. Despite the memories, there was no point holding onto the past. She had nowhere to put them. Pierre was getting the house they had bought five years ago here in Falmouth. Lara was taking a bit of cash and not much more than the blurry memory of the hope she'd felt on their wedding day.

She shook her head. That had been ten years ago. The kettle whistled an uneven tune and she shut the gas off, watching the flame collapse into the burner. It disappeared so quickly once it was starved of fuel, a bit like her marriage. Love had died without daily care. She pulled the brown teapot down from the shelf. Grandie might have brought this back from England after the war along with his bride Amelia. The spout had a small chip but otherwise it was sound. Maybe this would be the one item from Eventide that she would ask for.

The screen door swung open and in walked Leo. Lara's eyes filled. Never had he looked so good nor had seeing him felt so welcome.

'Hello, Runt.' He dropped his bag on the floor and opened his arms.

Lara walked into them. 'You're just jealous you were second born.' This old joke never seemed to end despite their twenty-eight years.

'True.' Leo held Lara away from him to look into her eyes. 'How is he?'

'Leaving us.'

'At his age that's not a surprise.'

She frowned. 'I know.'

'How's the life of leisure going?'

She blew out an exasperated sigh.

'Face it, you needed a break.' He grinned. 'Alright, I'll admit that calling your boss an incompetent tyrant and then walking out was not the ideal way to do it.'

She laughed and rolled her eyes.

'Six months' paid leave isn't something to complain about,' he said.

'True, but . . .' She tried to find the words to express her worries.

'You're too good a chef not to be hired again.'

She looked up at him, briefly tearful that, as always, Leo understood. He threw an arm around her and they walked through the house.

'Enjoy the time off. You've had a lot to deal with.' He tugged on her ponytail. 'You've always been impatient.'

'True,' she laughed.

They met the nurse on the stairs. Leo continued up to Grandie and she watched him go. He would need his time alone with their great-grandfather. She turned to the landing window. Clouds had rolled in and the afternoon had become cooler than the blistering heat of the morning. There might be a thunderstorm before long. She picked up the picture on the sill. It was of Lara and Grandie on her wedding day. He was walking her down the aisle as her father had died ten years earlier when she was just eight. Grandie had done his best to fill the gap in their lives.

She squinted into the distance and saw a lightning bolt illuminate the leaden sky over the Vineyard. In the black and white photograph she held she could see his love for her, but he had behaved distantly on the day. Maybe he'd known the marriage wouldn't last. He'd made it plain he felt they were far too young to marry at eighteen. Lara had pointed out that he hadn't been much older when he'd married. He'd agreed, but had added that living through a war aged you in ways that normal life never could. She had asked him to tell her more but he had simply replied, 'I'll tell you someday.'

Someday was here, but Lara knew the time for words had passed.

The rise and fall of Grandie's chest was slower. Lara placed his worn rosary beads in his hand. Her heart told her that it wouldn't be long. She helped him to make the sign of the cross. She spoke the words and Grandie's eyelids fluttered. Every night he'd say the rosary before he went to sleep. Up until three years ago he'd done this on his knees. Permanent slumber was calling and maybe he couldn't go without saying his prayers. He'd taught her, and now the old familiar words came back.

As she finished the Hail, Holy Queen, she heard a step behind her. She brought the rosary beads to Grandie's lips then placed them back in his hands. His breathing was less laboured.

'Leo,' she whispered.

He stepped towards the bed. 'Soon?'

'Yes.'

He touched her arm and gave her an encouraging smile. 'Go take five minutes.'

Lara left Grandie with Leo and headed downstairs, knowing it was now only a matter of hours. When Grandie died there would be a huge hole in her life, and her life was filled with so many at the moment.

Outside the kitchen door she took a deep breath of the sweetly scented air. Maybe she should call her grandmother Betty or her mom but there was nothing that any of them could do. Life would go on somehow. In the meantime she didn't want to miss a minute with Grandie.

She dashed back upstairs, and as she came into the room Grandie's eyes fixed onto her. 'You're awake,' she said, pausing on the threshold.

'Yes,' Grandie whispered.

Leo looked at her from the far side of the bed. 'We've had a chat.'

She opened her mouth then shut it. Maybe she'd been talking too much and hadn't given Grandie the chance.

'Hold me so that I can see the bay.' Grandie's voice caught, but it was clear. With Leo's help she held him upright. He focused on a distant point. The dark sky met the darker sea, yet overhead the clouds broke and the blue seemed somehow brighter. The bay was still. In the distance Lara heard the ferry's engine as it began the journey to the Vineyard.

He sighed and his eyes focused on the horizon. She looked down the crescent of the beach. The tide was at its highest, almost obscuring the sand.

Her great-grandfather wheezed, 'Adele.'

Lara looked at him. Frowning, she met Leo's glance. Her brother mouthed, *Adele?* She shrugged, thinking they must have misheard him.

Grandie's breathing slowed but he remained focused on the eastern horizon. The surface of the bay went from still to ruffled, breaking up the darkness from the storm clouds with bright blue patches. The water had begun its journey back out to sea. He took a ragged breath and as his eyes closed he said it again: 'Adele.'

Then he was gone.

❋ Three ❋

Windward, Mawnan Smith, Falmouth, Cornwall
15 August 2015

'Gran?' Peta stood waiting, silhouetted by the sunlight flooding the drawing room.

I looked up from the crossword, catching the date on the top of the paper. VJ Day, a day that filled me with extreme sadness. It was best not to think, not to remember.

'I was wondering.' She stopped and came to sit beside me. This hesitancy was not normal.

'Yes?' I put the paper and pencil aside. I was stuck on 5 down, 'divided game'.

'Jeopardy.'

I frowned. She pointed to the crossword.

'Of course.' I filled it in before I forgot. 'You were wondering?'

'Years ago I used to go into the attic and …' She looked out towards the sea. Despite the fine weather the bay was covered in white horses racing towards the shore. It had been years since I had been down to the cove, but I could picture them breaking on the rocks that jutted out from the cliffs. Was the tide high or low? That would make a difference. Would the charging waters be bashing against the cliffs or dying on the sand? I'd always loved sunny days when the sea behaved as if a great storm was raging. With the water this tumultuous there probably was a storm, somewhere out at sea.

I turned to Peta. Why was she hesitating? 'Out with it.'

'I've just been in the attic.'

'And?'

'I was looking for—' She paused, playing with the seam of her jeans.

'For what?' She clearly thought whatever she was going to say would bother me.

'Well, when I was small there used to be a lace wedding veil in an old suitcase.'

I drew in my breath.

'I don't want to upset you but I would love to wear it for my wedding. It would be the something old – something that links me to you.' Her hand stilled and her eyes pleaded.

'It was my grandmother's, not mine.' My voice tailed away. It would have been wrong to wear it when I married Andrew in the registrar's office.

'Yes, I guessed. Your mother's too?'

I nodded.

'I can't find it.'

'No.' I had seen Peta playing with it when she was about nine or ten. Even then it represented what had been lost. Yet I hadn't thrown it out.

Peta's hand grabbed mine. 'Forget about it, Gran. It's too raw.'

'Stop using that hocus-pocus with me.' I pulled my hand away and stood up. A shiver ran across my skin. Peta and this 'seeing' gift of hers had always unnerved me. Maybe it was like the connection I'd had long ago with my sister, but if so the last thing I wanted was for her to use it on me.

'Sorry, I have no control over it.' She rose. 'I can't see anything much with you. It's more feelings. All I know is that you're in pain.' She bit her lower lip. 'No, not pain, anger even ...'

I interrupted her. 'Nonsense.'

'Gran.' She put her hand on my shoulder. I didn't shake it off.

'Come with me.' I picked up my cane and she took my hand, reminding me of her as a little thing who had clung to me when she lost her mother. More of the darkness this house held in its walls. Maybe it was right that the veil be used. I closed my

25

eyes for a moment, picturing my grandmother. I laughed. She would not approve of Peta with her nose stud and hippie ways. And that was as good a reason as any for Peta to wear the veil and change its fortunes.

The hot air of the attic smelled of dry timber. A thick coat of dust covered every surface. I fought the temptation to turn around and leave it undisturbed. But for the look of anticipation on Peta's face I would have done so. Her eagerness infected my reluctance, weakening it. At the far end of the attic stood a door and I held the key. The last time I had opened it was to store the veil away from Peta's playful hands. Why had I locked it away? To keep it from Jack and Peta? Or from me? More likely to have a real defence against the memories stored here, wrapped up in fabric and paper. When Andrew was with me it was easier not to think of the past and only hold onto what joy the present provided.

'Thank you,' said Peta, speaking softly as I unlocked the door and she followed me through. I tripped on a loose board and she steadied me.

'It should be in here.' I bent down. The battered leather case sat in plain sight among the school trunks, as if it held nothing more than cobwebs and yellowed linens. Tucked away in here was my past. I couldn't bring myself to throw it out, a choice that now felt foolish. Laying the case on the floor, I steeled myself then slid the catches.

On the top, wrapped in tissue, was the veil. When a child, I had played the same games that Peta had, parading down the wide staircase as the radiant bride. My sister had waited at the bottom holding a silk top hat, standing in for the man of my dreams. How foolish we'd been, how churlish to hold onto the anger for so long. But anger was better than grief. Both had left me less than before, no longer Adele but Elle.

'Gran?' Peta touched my shoulder. I shivered despite the heat. 'Yes?'

She picked up the delicate lace, handmade over a hundred years ago. Her eyes gleamed. 'Thank you.'

'A pleasure. May it bring you – no, may it crown your joy.' It hadn't brought happiness to Mother but at least Grandmother had had a happy if short-lived marriage. Grandfather had died in World War I.

She kissed my cheek. 'What else have you squirrelled away?' She peered over my shoulder and I dropped the lid before she saw the contents. The thump shook the dust from the rafters. The locks clicked.

'Nothing of importance.'

5 June 1943

'Are you sure about the Wrens?' Amelia stretched out on the grass at the edge of what was left of Windward's lawn, lying back to look at the sky. The day was warm but a fresh breeze blew off Falmouth Bay, tempering the heat and stirring her blonde hair.

I put down my book of poetry and looked at my sister. 'Yes, and thanks to Father we've had long enough to think about it.'

She rolled onto her side. 'Everyone but us joined at seventeen.' She wrinkled her nose. 'I don't think he refused permission because he felt we were too young. "Immature," he said.'

'Mother.'

She nodded. We looked at each other, understanding what neither of us wanted to express. She looked out to the bay. 'I can't believe they let me join the senior service.'

'Of course they want you. You can drive already, much to Grandmother's despair.'

'Don't know why you don't like driving.' She pursed her mouth just like Grandmother and I shrugged, thinking about the speed and Amelia racing along until she almost lost control.

'But I *was* in control.' She threw a daisy at me and I raised an eyebrow. 'Plus I love engines, thanks to Patrick.' Her eyes sparkled, full of mischief.

Again I raised my eyebrow, remembering Grandmother's handsome chauffeur. I also recalled the time Amelia had been kissing Patrick instead of learning from him how to drive, and I'd had to suddenly pretend to have an interest in flowers so I could lead Grandmother down the garden path and away from them. I don't think Grandmother had been fooled – Patrick had left her employment shortly after my moment of gardening enthusiasm. However, I'd been dying to know what kissing him had been like and I'd worried that Amelia would fall pregnant. She'd howled with laughter, explaining that she hadn't done *that*.

'But you'd be wasted as a driver,' said Amelia, 'far too clever. Father seems certain that you'll have a place at Cambridge.'

'That's because he went there.' I sighed. 'I want to go to Durham.' Looking up at the cloudless sky, I thought of the distance from here, not wanting that but craving a place where I would not be a twin and not be Father's daughter. Yet I did not want to be away from Amelia. I didn't know how to be apart from her, but it was about to happen regardless.

'Rebel.' She laughed. 'Miss Parsons's influence, no doubt.'

'Possibly.' I brushed the stray pieces of grass off my skirt. Neither my neat attire nor my behaviour gave any sign of rebellion. 'What time are we due on the beach?'

'Tide's on its way out now.' Amelia looked at her watch. It matched mine exactly. It was an early eighteenth birthday present from Grandmother. Even though we tried not to dress alike everyone still treated us as if we were the same person. Today Amelia wore a violet coloured blouse while I wore white. I knew I'd be cooler. Maenporth Beach would be a heat trap, sheltered as it was from the northerly winds. 'So if we leave in an hour.'

I nodded, plucking a blade of grass. Everything had been so slow in coming and now time was disappearing too quickly. Having passed the interview and the medical both of us had to wait until we'd reached eighteen. 'I hope I make it through training.' I held the grass between my thumbs and blew against it, making a squeaking sound. Telegraphy was so intricate that it required six months of training, while Amelia would be away for only one to become a driver. Father approved of my path, but like Grandmother he was less keen that Amelia was going into the Motor Transport division. I wouldn't have put it past them not to put pressure on people in high places to make sure she only drove officers and not transport vehicles.

'You will and, of course, I'll be green with jealousy over your months in London.' She looked at Windward. 'I'm not going far for training and only a month away. Lucky me gets to be the immobile Wren.' She wrinkled her nose.

I tried not to laugh at her expression. It wasn't fair that I was allowed to go and she had to stay. My parents felt I was the more stable. I should have been happy that they saw I was more responsible, but they only knew the half of it. We appeared and sounded the same but if people bothered to look closer our differences were obvious. Yet no one saw us as individuals except Amelia and me. We were simply written off as a pair and at times treated like a circus act.

'Who else would make sure Mother and Grandmother don't kill each other?' I asked. We both laughed at this, and I marvelled again at how the sound matched and merged into one.

'True. I'll miss you. Who will I laugh with?' she said, echoing my thoughts for the millionth time.

'Good question. I suppose letters will have to suffice.' I stood and squinted into the distance, counting ships out of habit. Amelia extended her hand and I grabbed it.

'You'll see plenty of Father and Aunt Margaret though.' She wrinkled her nose. 'Do you think she misses Uncle Reg as much as Grandmother thinks she should?' She raised an eyebrow.

My aunt, impossibly glamorous as she was, wouldn't let her worry show. It wasn't done. 'I suspect Grandmother's reflecting her own worries for her son onto Aunt Margaret, who isn't playing along.' We locked arms and walked back to Windward.

She turned to me. 'You will call and write often, won't you?'

I dropped my head onto her shoulder. I was as uncertain as she was about my leaving her. In all our lives we'd always been together. But recently I'd been longing for the chance to be just me – not me and Amelia, not twins.

'You'll know how things are even when I don't call.'

'That hasn't been too hard when you haven't been far away, but we've never tested distance before.'

'I know.' I hugged her arm closer to me. 'I suppose this is one way to find out.' We both laughed, catching each other's glance. Her pupils were pools of dark uncertainty. Looking at Amelia I saw my own fear. Swallowing hard, I forced a smile. As scared as I was, this was exciting and I was leading the way.

I stood with Mother in the kitchen. She always looked lost here. This was beyond her and anything she ever thought she would need to deal with, but she wasn't as bad as Grandmother. The kitchen was so far removed from Grandmother's life before the war, she barely knew how to cope with it. She'd had to learn to boil a kettle now that Mrs Tonks who had been the cook had gone to work on a farm. Fortunately Amelia had a flair for cooking and the evacuee children from Latimer School who had stayed here had not cared what it was so long as they ate. But they had gone back to London and the house felt empty without them. Mother had been low since their departure, and I suspected mine would not help her state of mind.

'What time is your train tomorrow?' She handed me a knife. Potatoes were abundant at the moment and seemed to make up a large portion of our meals. Not that I was complaining. It was food. I scrubbed off the clumps of soil and watched the grit slip down the sink.

'Midday.'

She frowned. 'Your grandmother has insisted you travel first class.'

I nodded.

'She doesn't want you mixing with the hoi polloi.'

'Indeed.' I laughed.

Mother squinted, peering out of the window. How would she fare with just Grandmother while Amelia was away most of the day? Mother and Grandmother hadn't seen eye to eye on things since my parents had married. Mother had wedded for love and, according to Grandmother, below her station. Nigel Seaton was a surgeon and worked for a living and this had taken us all over Britain. Grandmother's goal was to at least marry *us* well, but the war had interrupted her plans and Aunt Margaret wouldn't be presenting us at court.

Wrapping a tea towel around her hand she looked at me. 'You will take care.'

'Of course.'

She reached out and touched my arm. 'Yes, I can rely on you for that. But less so with your sister.'

'She's the fun one, I'm the sensible one.' I hid my own worries behind a smile. Who would help Amelia out of scrapes and who would pull me into them? Without each other I was far too serious and she too reckless. But she was the lucky one staying here, although she didn't see it that way. Windward was the home of my heart, from its granite quoins hewn from the nearby quarry to its vast seaward-facing windows. I loved it here and it was Amelia who missed London, our last place of residence.

'I know. And that's what worries me.'

I turned away from Mother. Her fear chilled me. 'She'll be fine and so will I.'

'This wretched war.' She paused, sighing. 'It will be the end of us.'

I frowned. 'We won't let Hitler win.'

'Whether he wins or not we are lost.' She walked out to the garden and I stared after her. She bent to Grandmother's vegetable bed and wrenched up some carrots.

'Daydreaming on the job?' Amelia tapped my shoulder then waltzed out to Mother.

Guilty. I sighed and put the potatoes into the pot of water, thinking about Mother's words. *We are lost.* I put the lid on the pot. Who knew what was ahead for any of us? I prayed that life would return to normal soon. The granite lintel above the range hinted at permanence. I touched it. It was a relic of the farmhouse that had stood here before Grandmother built Windward. This terrible war couldn't and shouldn't wipe away our lives. But it had changed them already. Excitement vied with fear, twisting my stomach round. Tomorrow I would be leaving Windward and Amelia.

The veil was stretched out on some old lace-drying racks that Peta had found in the attic. The years of dust had been washed away and the colour was now more of a bright ivory rather than that of weak tea. Her capable hands had begun to repair the damage the years had doled out. I walked around it in awe of its fine detail. At eight I hadn't noticed any of this. It was simply beautiful and would make the wearer feel happy and loved. It had for Grandmother and, at that time, I thought it had for Mother.

Having been wrapped with dried lavender, the withered grey flowers had fallen onto the carpet when Peta had opened it. I bent to sniff the fabric to see if any of the fragrance had remained after laundering, but it smelt of soap, nothing more. Here in the dining room it was far from harmful sunshine as it dried. Peta was keen to conserve this piece of history. I fought the urge to rend it apart. It had no magic power to make happiness or to change the past. We choose our own path.

I walked to the stairs. After yesterday's jaunt into the attic my joints ached more than normal. But the physical discomfort I could take. Strangely I welcomed it. It was real. My body was old and slowly it was failing. Last night as I lay in bed thinking about the suitcase and its contents, my heart opened. For so long I had kept it closed, but last night the pain of the past pinned me to the bed. Unable to move, I had felt my heart slowing until it stopped. I don't remember it starting again but it had. Hate and anger were bitter tastes in my mouth upon coming to consciousness, unlike the salty tang of my tears.

My vision blurred and I clutched the banister. I had to face the old demons. Breathing was hard but I walked the landing until I reached the stairs to the attic.

'What the hell do you think you're doing?' Jack's voice was more amused than cross.

'I'm going to the attic.'

'Well, I knew it wasn't a trip to the shops.' He walked towards me. 'You really think this is a good idea?' He raised an eyebrow and again I saw his grandfather's humour. Andrew never told me off as such, but humoured me until I came to his way of thinking, even about marrying him.

'So you think you will manage these old stairs with your cane and your dodgy hip?' He leaned against the wall. 'This I have to see.'

'I am nothing if not determined.' I placed the cane on the first step. Yesterday I had done this without a problem. But today was different. It was as if the trip through the locked door had set off a timer inside of me, counting down.

'This I know is true. But I think I've only seen you go in the attic once in all my life. What's so essential up there that you need it now?'

'That would be telling.' I looked away from his inquisitive glance. Since yesterday I'd been haunted by the other things I'd glimpsed in the suitcase.

'It would, and it might make more sense to tell me what you want and let me find it.'

'That would be boring.'

'Indeed, boring and sensible.' His smile transformed his serious face.

I made it up the first step, but wobbled.

'Gran ...'

I stepped to the second. A quick count told me I had twelve more to climb before I had to manage the tricky bit at the top. Why wasn't there a railing? I reached the third step and heard Jack move to the one below me.

By step five my head was nearing the opening at the top. I leaned forward so that I didn't hit the ceiling when I ventured in. The air was thinner. Dust filled my nose. I sneezed, lifting my hand to my mouth. Jack's arms grabbed my waist as I swayed.

'You're hard enough to manage without adding broken bones to the list.'

'True.' I climbed another step and then another. Jack's hand never left my waist until we reached the top and began to walk through the odd chairs, ripped lampshades and other bits of discarded junk.

'It had better be worth it.'

'That, I can't promise.' In truth I wasn't sure why I was doing this. If the letters were still there, would it help to look at them?

Placing the cane on the uneven floorboards, I teetered to the end. I hadn't relocked the door yesterday. It swung on its hinges. I searched for a draught or some other cause, but saw no source. Everything looked as it had yesterday. Old trunks, a discarded chest of drawers, a rolled carpet, broken tennis racquets and there among this junk was my old case. Yesterday I had removed only the veil and hadn't allowed Peta or myself to look at the rest of the contents, but they were there and would not be silent. My thoughts rang with their pleas. I clutched a rafter.

Jack stood still not saying a word. His unspoken questions were there in his posture. He stood with his feet far apart, hands on hips, and I knew he was waiting for an explanation. I turned from him and pulled on the light, which revealed the dust motes hanging in the air.

The boards cracked as I made my way to the case, staying in the middle where my head wasn't in danger of making contact with the beams. Jack followed silently until I stopped in front of the small tower of school trunks.

'Fancied a trip down memory lane, did you?'

'Not really, but I need to retrieve something.' I noted that my sister's trunk sat on the top of the pile. Why was it still here?

Jack studied the names. 'Ha, here's Dad's. Doubt there's anything worth keeping there, maybe the odd sock.'

'True, but he did like to keep it and wouldn't let us use it for your aunt.'

'Probably kept his lads' magazines in there.'

'No, those were under his mattress.'

Jack laughed. 'No secrets, eh?'

I smiled and looked away. 'None.'

He stopped at the one stamped on the top A.D. Seaton. He frowned. I tensed. 'Not your initials, Elle Seaton. I suppose this is some relative of yours?' He shook his head. 'Why do people hold onto these old school things?'

34

'Yours is at the other end of the attic.' I pointed to where I had seen several metal trunks.

'Just bin the damn thing.' He laughed. 'Shall I help you and then bring this suitcase to the sitting room?'

I pursed my lips. The sitting room was too public. 'My room. Thank you.'

※ Four ※

Maenporth Beach, Falmouth, Cornwall
5 June 1943

All of the rocks at the base of the cliffs were revealed along with the seaweed which was used to make penicillin and our reason for being on the beach. Only August would bring a lower spring tide this year and I wouldn't be here to see it, which I tried not to think about. It would be the first summer that I could remember that I hadn't spent at Windward. I stood up, leaving the bucket on the ground, and rubbed my lower back. The sand seemed to stretch for miles into the turquoise waters. Days didn't come much more beautiful than this.

Tonight was my last night at home, however, and I shivered despite the heat. Looking for Amelia, I found her across the beach near the first pillbox closer to the high water mark. On a day like today there was no hardship involved, but we'd been out here in foul weather too. Sweat rolled down my back and damp tendrils of hair clung to my neck. A swim would cool me off but there was no time for that. We had a job to do. Everyone played their part. I bent to work again, thinking of what would happen tomorrow. I was heading to training, but nothing was certain.

'You'll have a ball in London.' Amelia laughed as I jumped at her voice. She took the bucket from me and emptied it into a bigger one. I shrugged, taking mine back. 'You will,' she said. 'I know you will.'

Our glances met. 'Not without you.'

'We couldn't be together always, silly.' She looked out to sea.

'Ah, yes, you are going to marry ... was it Eddie, Philip or Angus?'

'Philip's yours, remember!' She hit my arm. 'Angus Lambert is for me. I want the one who'll take me away to far-flung places with strange-sounding names.'

I laughed. She was forever falling in love. I had liked Angus first, but I couldn't compete since she had kissed him before me. With trepidation I'd confessed my plans to her while sitting on a rock overlooking the cove, and then she'd just walked up to him on the beach and kissed him. I'd hated her for all of a day then laughed and asked for all the details. After telling me his mouth tasted of peppermint and cigarettes she'd told me he wouldn't know it hadn't been me. She swore she'd done it to stop me from messing it up and making it all awkward. She was right. I would have made a botch of it, but if I were honest, part of me was still a bit cross. However, she made flirting appear effortless. Even now, here on the beach, she had a young sailor hanging on her every word. How did she do it? We were so alike and yet when it came to men I was inarticulate and bumbling while Amelia radiated joy.

Pausing to stretch, I rubbed the salt off my hand and onto my hankie while I studied my sister as she bent to her work. She was so much better with her hands. Despite having spent more time kissing Grandmother's chauffeur than learning, she could take an engine apart and that knowledge would now be put to good use.

'Hi.' A young man came up to collect my seaweed. 'Amelia?' He grinned.

I looked up and tried not to frown as I corrected him. 'Adele.'

'Gosh, I always get it wrong.' He shrugged.

I silently added, you're not the only one. I just wished he didn't appear so disappointed. Without my twin around I had a chance to be seen.

'Anyway, we've enough today.' He held out a hand for my bucket, emptied it into the larger one and then searched for my sister. What was wrong with *me*?

I glanced down and saw some mussels clinging to the base

of the rocks. Maybe we could have them for dinner tonight. I began to collect some in my emptied bucket, and when I checked, he'd wandered off towards Amelia who was laughing and holding her hair off her neck. Her breasts lifted in the process and I wasn't the only one who had noticed. Was she aware of it? Did she understand the effect she had? Turning away from her I went further along the rocks. I should try and be more like her, more relaxed and flirtatious. She made it look so easy. If I attempted the same manoeuvre it would be awkward, blatant.

Over my shoulder I saw Amelia on her way to me. Her bucket was already full of mussels. Something told me she hadn't collected them herself. An open shell lay at my feet, its interior whites glistening until they silvered and blued at the edges. I picked it up as Amelia came to my side. One half fell away from the other and dropped onto the wet sand below.

'I'll do a fish stew or something with these.' She shook the mussels and I looked up at her as the sea washed over the dropped shell. The tide had turned. 'Or maybe I should let Mother do it.'

I smiled. 'They'll have to learn to do some of the cooking.'

'Mother's not too bad.'

'I know, and Grandmother is enjoying growing all the vegetables, but ...'

She laughed. 'When Mrs Tonks left to work on the farm, Grandmother's face was a picture.'

'Cleaning and cooking!' Just the thought of Grandmother peeling a potato let alone washing one was enough to send me into fits of laughter.

Giggling, we walked back to the others. I wanted to drink in every detail, for tomorrow I'd be gone and I wasn't sure when I would be back. Amelia would be here, so at least part of me remained.

She adjusted her hair then climbed on to her bike.

The sailor dashed up to her. 'So I'll see you tomorrow night at the dance?'

She laughed and touched his cheek with her finger. 'Only

if you promise to behave.' He grinned and gave her a salute before dashing off in the direction of Falmouth.

'You're incorrigible,' I said.

'I know.'

I took a deep breath, letting it out slowly.

She looked across at me. 'Please don't disapprove.'

I smiled. 'I don't. I …' I peered at her, noting a freckle appearing on her nose. 'I think I might be jealous.'

'Of course you are, ninny. But it's simple really.' She paused and slipped a hat on. 'All you need to do is smile and … don't think too much.'

I shook my head. This was where we were so different. She wouldn't remember that sailor at all until he appeared at her side at the dance, eager for her attention. What I knew and the sailor didn't was that if she spied another man before then that she deemed more charming, she wouldn't glance his way again. I wasn't sure I'd be able to do that.

'Shall I try and make moules marinière tonight with these?' she asked.

I rolled my eyes. 'We haven't got the ingredients.'

She smiled and glanced at my bucket. 'We have more than enough to trade with Mrs Long at the farm. Let's see if she can give me a bit of cream for your mussels.'

'And the wine?'

'I made cider with some of the apples in the autumn so I'll use that.'

'Garlic?'

She turned her head and looked into the wood climbing up the hill across from the beach. Wild garlic would be there, mixed with the last of the bluebells.

'Will it work?'

'Of course it will. Trust me. Besides, it's our last night before we become Wrens!'

'Indeed it is.' I set off up the hill ahead of her but stopped at the top, waiting for her to catch up. 'You will be careful?' I said, when she arrived at the hilltop.

She frowned. 'I'm not stupid.'

'No, you're not.' *Just reckless and never considering of the consequences*, I thought, but I couldn't say anything. She had sped off towards the farm, anyway. I just hoped she'd be safe without me around. Today we were eighteen, and tomorrow I left Cornwall and my sister.

Windward, Mawnan Smith, Falmouth, Cornwall
16 August 2015

'There can't be much in it. There's no weight to it at all and the leather is so brittle it'll disintegrate.' Jack tilted his head to one side. 'Once you've had a look for whatever it is, I suggest we put this in the bin.'

Out in the bay a sea fog was moving in from the north-east as I stood watching St Anthony's Lighthouse. Soon the lighthouse had disappeared from sight, along with Pendennis Castle. Sometimes I wished a mist would slip into my head and erase the memories like it did the landscape, only leaving vague outlines.

'Did you hear me?' Jack came to my side.

'I did. Thank you.' I turned towards him. 'Could you bring me a whisky?'

He raised an eyebrow. 'First up in the attic then drinking alone in your room. Should I be concerned?'

I laughed. 'Of course you should. Make it a healthy one, please.' He sent me a searching look and I smiled. The afternoon light caught the hint of strawberry in his blonde hair. Was it the touch of ginger that made him prickly? 'Go.'

He fled and I touched the suitcase. It was older than I was. It had belonged to my father and it was the one that left Windward with me on a bright June morning in 1943. Time hadn't been kind to it. My father's name was embossed under the handle: N.J.G. Seaton. I closed my eyes, remembering him as I had last seen him at Mother's funeral – thinner, paler and his teeth stained. Not the dashing man in uniform who had given me this when I'd joined the WRNS.

My back protested as I bent down. The latches stuck but came open eventually. Jack was right, there wasn't much in it.

Bundles of letters and a few photographs. My hands trembled as I held a faded picture of my sister and me in matching swimming costumes sitting on the rocks, and another one of us laughing, heads thrown back with Windward behind us. These things had no power now but still they stirred emotions. A pale piece of fabric rested under the letters. I frowned. A christening gown wrapped around her letters? I hadn't done that. Mother must have. Her misplaced anger travelled through the years. My hands clenched around the delicate fabric expertly mended by the nimble hands of Mrs Tonks. I had taken the blame and punishment for the ripped bodice when it had been Amelia who had torn it in a fit of anger when she'd discovered that as the eldest I had worn it not her.

I freed the gown. The fabric had yellowed and was fragile. The intricate lace trimming was still in perfect condition, only the rend in the lawn cotton ruined the appearance. It slipped through my shaking fingers and back into the case. How many children in the family had worn the gown? My mother and her brother Reginald had, but it was older still. Where was the gown Amelia had worn? I remembered seeing it years ago. That was the problem with touching an artefact; it made it all real again.

My fingers played with the green garden twine that held her letters. Over the years it had bled into the envelopes and possibly onto the paper contained in them. I turned them over in my hand then picked up the other ones bound in ribbon. My hand shook. What would they tell me? I'd never opened them.

I let them fall back into the case and picked up the letters she had written to me during the war. I was sure I knew what they said, but had my memory changed them? A memory alters over the years, each remembrance twisting it subtly, until it is no longer an accurate account of the past, more a reflection of the person trying to recall it. I didn't want to read her words, but the photograph unearthed by the girl from the BBC had stirred something inside me.

Jack appeared at the door with a glass in his hand. 'Not sure about drinking in your room, but I suppose you are old enough.'

'You could say that.' I placed the bound correspondence onto the chest of drawers and took the whisky from him. He peered into the case.

'No dead bodies?'

'No.' I took a sip, waiting for him to move on.

'Just the odd skeleton then.'

'Hmm.'

'So these are letters to your lover?' He cast me a mischievous smile then picked up the pile.

'No.' A memory. Letters from my lover. 'Don't you have something to do?'

'Right. I know when I'm not wanted,' he said, and backed away. I reached a hand out to him, but he was already at the door, and moments later he was gone. Jack was someone who needed to feel wanted and I had just pushed him away. I was sorry, but I also knew that venturing into the past was best done alone.

10 September 1943

Dearest A,

I don't like having you so far away, but even though you are I can feel your excitement. Your clever brain is thrilled by all that you're learning. I really do think you should go for a place at Oxford (it's closer than Durham and not Cambridge) when this beastly war is finished ... if it ever ends. I know Grandmother will never forgive you for becoming a bluestocking. She despairs of us. She becomes so cross when I wear trousers. But she is proud that you are in the WRNS. I heard her bragging about you to one of the ladies in the village. Doesn't say anything about me, though. I'm a lowly driver not a soon-to-be telegraphist. However I think she is secretly hoping I'll fall for some officer and marry quickly.

Yes, I'm still doing much of the cooking despite working long hours. Madame Pomfrey is a huge ally in the food stakes. I've learned so much from her and my French has improved far more than any tutoring would have done. Despite French cooking lessons and driving, life here still revolves around the dances. My world doesn't feel as glamorous as yours in London. I'm jealous that you are making it to the 400 Club. It doesn't seem fair. Are you making the most of being there? Somehow I doubt it. You need me to push you. I'd be slipping out every night.

Things are becoming more interesting though with so many visitors from across the pond arriving. I'd wink if I could. Grandmother won't stop saying how vulgar they are with their over bright smiles and chewing gum. The big excitement of course is the colour of some of the visitors. People stop and stare. In my travels I see all shapes and sizes of them. Things are changing. I can't say what but when you have leave and come home you will see.

The weather has been glorious and I long to swim but I never have time. I can't tell you anything of what I'm doing but I'm behind the wheel mostly and sometimes entertaining after hours. I can see your frown from here but seriously, who knows if we'll survive? Bombs fell the other day and didn't do any damage, thank God. In fact it was a bonus as there were so many stunned fish. Mother and Grandmother along with many others collected them. We practically fed the whole village and I've smoked many of them. That night we ate incredibly well on Grandmother's vegetables and the fish.

I've become very good at cooking fish of all types. There's no turning one's nose up at a lowly mackerel or a pollack. No fish is too plain including grey mullet. Grandmother has taken to fishing off the rocks. If you could see her in the gardener's old straw hat and her dress all rucked up. If I could sketch it I would ... of course, I hear you ask ... she was wearing her double strand pearls!

Mother has gone silent for the most part. She seems to live for Father's infrequent calls and sporadic letters. He is a beast to keep her so much in the dark, but then I suppose he has to. I do miss him too but I think she is really suffering. He was home on leave ages ago and she never knows where he is.

The house and the Red Cross work keep her very busy, thank

43

God. Otherwise I think she would completely collapse into depression. This threatens her constantly. If you see Father do press him to be better. I know what he's like wrapped up in his job, which is so important, but she needs him. I did suggest that she should move back to London but she shivered like I had walked on her grave. The night in the Blitz when the house nearby was hit still gives her nightmares. I remember it but frankly compared to what most people have lived through it was nothing.

I know I can hear you say I am being too tough on her and you are right. She is delicate and artistic. Thank God we are more robust like Father!

I'm so pleased you saw him when you visited Aunt Margaret. She seems to see more of him than anyone and certainly more of him than her own husband. Grandmother had herself all spun to pieces about Uncle Reg again. She ranted that he had no right to head off to war without an heir or two in the nursery. His volunteering at the start still bothers her.

How is Aunt Margaret? Did you say she was working for the Red Cross too? Is she still so glamorous? I long for some of her red lipstick.

I miss you so much and yes, I still hear you in my head, which officially makes me mad and you too. Love you so much.

Your other half,
XXXX

I took a large gulp of the whisky and lifted the letter to my nose. The softest touches of tuberose clung to the yellowed page. Tabu. It was funny how one note of the fragrance remained. It was all so real. Here in this room, Grandmother's room. Her pearls, minus one strand, hung on my neck. The other one was with my sister.

Truro Train Station, Cornwall
6 June 1943

The train was too crowded; even first-class seats were in short supply. I didn't have a uniform and wouldn't have one for the first month so I felt out of place on a train full of them. Everywhere I looked men and women were kitted out and perched on suitcases and standing where they could find space. First class wasn't much better but I finally found a seat next to the window in the last compartment in which I looked. A major smiled and helped me to store my bag.

'London?' he asked.

'Yes.' I smiled my thanks.

'Me too.' He grinned and I nodded, wondering what Amelia would do. No doubt she would chat to him, but that might lead him on and I wouldn't know how to handle that. The landscape outside the window was a safer option. It didn't expect anything from me.

The war had taken its toll on people, but as the train moved through the countryside I could almost forget that I was heading to London for training. I had no idea where I'd be posted after the six month course, and that was rather exciting, even though part of me was jealous of Amelia staying at home. It was good that she could play her part and still look after Mother. Someone had to and she was far better at it than me. I had less patience, but I loved Cornwall more.

The train stopped at St Germans Station and I remembered all the times we'd spent at Carvallek, Eddie and Tom Carew's home. I wondered how they were. Mother wasn't very good at keeping in touch. Maybe Aunt Margaret would know, as their mother Rebecca was a dear friend of hers.

The door to the compartment opened and I smiled, thinking of a game of hide and seek in the gardens.

'Well, hello, Delly. It is Delly, isn't it?' Eddie walked into the compartment. In surprise I stood to see the object of my thoughts standing in front of me in his uniform. The splash of freckles across his nose was the reminder of the boy I'd been

45

remembering. Eddie embraced me, shocking the major who'd been trying to get my attention.

'Right the first time, Flight Lieutenant.' I grinned, thinking how handsome he was in his uniform. 'Were you at home?'

'Yes, I had forty-eight hours' leave and Mother wanted to see her baby boy.' He sat opposite.

'How is she?'

'Fretting. With big brother Tom flying as well she figures she won't have any children by the end of the war.' He frowned. 'Tom has outlived the odds so far and I've always been the luckier of us two.'

'How's Sarah?'

'At school and thankful to be away from Mummy.'

I laughed. He always made me smile. Grandmother had hopes that either Amelia or I would marry Tom and put the family further back up the social ladder with a title, but Tom was dull whereas Eddie was full of fun.

'How are your mother and Amelia? I won't ask about the dragon – I know she'll be miserable if at all possible.'

'Actually Grandmother has taken to gardening well.'

He laughed. 'My mother has too. Who knew the flowerbeds could be so productive?'

'Ah,' I said, 'Grandmother wouldn't sacrifice her borders. Half of the lawn has been dug up instead.'

'Mother has a house full of children from London. I do think she missed her calling in life. She should have been a school mistress.'

I shook my head. I could not imagine Eddie's mother with a house full of children. Rebecca was always immaculate and my mother had always felt insecure around her. Father's response had been to tell her not to be silly, and yet his gaze had never failed to follow Rebecca.

'How's Amelia?'

'Excellent. Joining the Wrens like me.'

He looked out the window and his dark hair fell across his forehead. 'Do send her my best when you next speak to her. Where is she?'

'Off on training right now but she'll be living at Windward.'

'Lucky her.'

'Yes, but it's not the same now.' I glanced out of the window. The tide was high as the train crossed the Tamar.

'True. Nothing is.' He leaned forward. 'Heading to London?'

I nodded.

'Shame I'm not.' He sighed. 'Will you be there long?'

'Six months.' I clasped my hands together, feeling the sweat on my palms.

'Brilliant news. I'll see you, then. Will your aunt have your contact details?'

'Yes.'

His eyes lit up when he smiled. Although I knew Tom was the better catch, the better looking of the two, Eddie would still be my choice with his dark hair and laughing brown eyes. I had no plans to fall in love, but looking at his smile again maybe I could be tempted.

✳ Five ✳

Eventide, Falmouth Heights, Cape Cod, Massachusetts
15 August 2015

The sky was changing from solid grey to dark blue. The air was cool. Goosebumps covered Lara's arms. Standing on the porch she debated going to get a sweater, but was reluctant to leave Leo to venture upstairs. Grandie wasn't there anymore. Eventide was silent except for the sound of thunder over Teaticket. The storm had stalled above for a long time. Its noise raged while they called everyone including the doctor, the funeral director and, of course, their grandmother. Betty had been quiet in her response, which had surprised both of them. But, Lara thought as she rubbed her arms, becoming an orphan even in your seventieth year had to be a solemn moment.

'Penny for them.' Leo handed her a glass.

She swirled the wine then sniffed. 'We shouldn't be drinking this without food.'

'True, but it was his favourite and champagne was the only other alternative.'

Lara wrinkled her nose. 'He'd want us to celebrate.'

'Yes, but it wouldn't feel right tonight.'

The moon appeared above the horizon, half hidden by the storm clouds. 'Agreed.'

'To Grandie.' Leo raised his glass.

'The best of us.' Lara touched hers to his then took a sip, letting the richness play across her tongue. Grandie had said his appreciation of wine had come from his time in France after the war. She looked at the label on the bottle: Calon Ségur,

48

Grandie's favourite wine. He had told her that the Marquis de Ségur had owned two other vineyards, Lafite and Latour, and it was said that he had made wines in those two but his heart was at the Calon Ségur vineyard so their label had a heart circling the name. Grandie's Christmas table wasn't complete without it but Lara hadn't been able to spend a Christmas on the Cape since she finished culinary school years ago. The restaurant trade didn't respect holidays or family life. She sighed.

'Runt,' said Leo.

She looked up.

'He had a good life.'

She released her breath. 'I know.'

'Maybe your non-compete gives you the chance to reassess yours.'

Lara walked to the edge of the porch and leaned on a pillar. 'Will another top restaurant hire me after I behaved so badly?'

'They will.'

'How do you know?' She turned to him. 'I was so unprofessional.'

'They expect chefs to be divas.'

'That's because of reality TV shows which are nothing like the real thing.' She laughed. 'The restaurant world is tough and fickle. By the time six months is over all I have achieved will be forgotten and I'll end up as sous chef to someone less qualified than I am.'

'You don't know that.'

She smiled. 'Sadly I do.'

'Look at it this way. At least I helped with getting the non-compete halved. You could have had a year instead.' He walked to the opposite pillar and stared at the water.

'Yes, it helps having a top lawyer for a brother.' She sat on the old rocking chair. So many childhood summer nights had been spent here on the porch listening to adults chatting inside while she and Leo caught fireflies and dodged mosquitos. The world had been simple then and they had known all they had needed to know. Now it was filled with questions like what to do with her life. 'It was also a bit of luck that Stephan was in a good mood when they approached him.'

'Luck always plays a part.' He sipped his wine.

'Up until this year I would say I've been very lucky.'

He turned to her. 'You still are. It might just be a different type of luck.'

'No husband, no job and no plan?' She shook her head.

'Yes.'

She leaned forward. 'To me that equals no luck.'

'It depends on how you look at it, Runt.'

She laughed. 'OK, tell me how you would.'

Leo sat down next to her. 'Remember being out here watching the fireflies when we were ten, and we told each other what we were going to do?'

She nodded.

'Well, you haven't done anything on that list.'

She snorted. 'No, I haven't.'

'But I have.'

'Show-off.'

'No, not a show-off. I just didn't get side-tracked.' He raised an eyebrow.

'Not fair.' Pierre was what he was talking about. Grandie had been right. Marrying at eighteen had been a mistake. It hadn't worked out as she had planned.

'Fine. Maybe it's not fair, but right now you have a chance to do something you wanted to.'

Lara stared at him. For once she couldn't see where he was going.

'You always wanted to go to England, to trace the family history.'

She laughed. 'Yes, I did.' The idea had been discussed many times. They already knew all of the Irish and Yankee side of the family, but had nothing about their great-grandmother. Lara looked into the wine glass then glanced up. Leo's eyes met hers.

'Adele?' they both said at the same time.

A few moments of silence followed, before Leo leant across

and filled her glass. 'What do you think?' he asked. 'A long-lost lover?'

'Not likely. Grandie went to Mass everyday until he couldn't drive or walk.'

'True.' He swirled the wine. 'We didn't mishear, did we?'

'No.' Lara was sure that they hadn't. If only one of them had heard him then it was a possibility, but not both. 'Maybe Betty can shed some light on it when she arrives.'

Leo laughed. 'In your dreams.'

'We can hope. But I need some information from her if I'm setting out to find her mother. Amelia is the black hole in our family history.'

17 August 2015

Her grandmother's normally tanned skin had a grey tinge in the mid-morning light. Lara handed Betty a cup of tea, watching her as she turned the blue and white striped mug around in her hands. 'What am I going to do with all of this?' She looked at Lara then back at Eventide's sprawling kitchen filled with paraphernalia.

'I wish I could say I'll have it but ...'

'I know, dear.' She placed her hand across Lara's pale one. 'Is there anything in particular you do want?'

Lara nodded and lifted up the metal box she'd found under Grandie's bed. Betty frowned. 'Good lord, what on earth is that?'

'Grandie's military metals, World War II diaries and a few photos.' Lara placed it on the kitchen table. Betty opened it and rifled through the contents. Her hand shook when she saw the letters.

'From your mother?' Lara sat down.

Betty shrugged. 'I assume so.'

'What do you know about her?'

'Not much.' Betty picked up the photos. 'I was four when she died.'

'Do you remember her?'

'Truthfully, not really.'

Through the kitchen window, Lara saw her own mother Maeve in the garden talking with Leo, probably about the arrangements for Grandie's funeral tomorrow. Right then, she tried to imagine life without her mother in it, and couldn't – but then, she had eventually adjusted to life without her father after the motorcycle accident. She missed him, but her memories of him had faded too. 'I haven't found anything of hers other than these letters.'

'Thank you for doing so much in the house.' Betty smiled.

'I left the heavy stuff to Leo and I went through the paperwork for you.' Lara sipped her tea, wondering whether to press Betty further. 'Your mother?'

Betty sighed. 'I don't remember her.'

'Do you have any pictures, her passport, wedding certificate, anything?

Betty shook her head. 'Dad was in Europe when it happened. A neighbour found my mother washed up on the beach.' She picked up a photo of Grandie in uniform. 'He was different then.' She traced the outline of her father. 'Different from the man you knew.'

'How?'

'He was rigid.' She pursed her mouth. 'Well, he was and he wasn't. He was a military man who gave it all up to come home because of me.'

Lara tilted her head. 'You mean he didn't live with you?'

'No, he was posted to Europe.' She shook her head. 'My mother and I were here in Eventide.'

Turning the mug in her hand, Lara thought about how quiet it would have been here nearly seventy years ago especially in winter. 'Are there any pictures of you as a child? I didn't find any.'

Betty grimaced. 'There weren't many, and sadly we had a cleaner who took a shine to a box that held all the relics of my childhood, including pictures and paperwork.' She sipped her tea.

Lara opened her eyes wide. 'So you really don't know anything about her?'

'I was told she was beautiful.' Betty touched her hair. Lara looked at her grandmother's smooth face. It hadn't been achieved by good genes alone, but with the help of a surgeon in Florida where she lived. 'Leo tells me you're going to England?'

Lara nodded. 'I'm hoping to visit Cassie, you remember her?'

Betty frowned.

'Grandie worked with her father when he came on secondment to the institute,' said Lara.

'That rings a bell.' Betty looked into the distance. 'You two were inseparable.'

'She runs a catering company in Cornwall now, so I plan to see Cassie and to trace Grandie's steps during the war.' Lara pushed the diaries from the box toward her. Betty flipped through them without really looking.

'When will you work again?'

'I don't know exactly. Hopefully in the new year.'

'Well, you can't stay around here with Pierre down the road. You might as well go and see if you can find anything out about my mother while you trace my father's steps.'

'Thanks.'

'Sorry I have nothing that can help.' Betty stood up and put the mug into the dishwasher. She looked out at a window box filled with red geraniums in need of dead-heading. Her eyes darkened and she seemed to think for a moment. 'There used to be a picture of them together,' she said.

Lara sat up straight.

'I think it was taken on their wedding day.' Betty turned back to her and adjusted her belt. 'But I haven't seen it in years and if I remember correctly it wasn't a good photo.'

'Any picture is better than none.'

'Funny, that's what I used to think. I'm not so sure now.' She placed her hand on Lara's shoulder. 'I used to stare at it and dream she would come back from heaven. And the more I stared at it, the further the idea of her slipped from me until she was there no more.' Betty walked into the garden where

53

she approached Leo and spoke briefly before she turned around and came back.

'I do have two things of my mother's,' she said. 'I'll have Kevin bring them up.' She glanced at her watch. 'I'll give him a call now. He'll be leaving for the airport soon.'

Lara frowned. Kevin was Betty's third husband. He was nice enough but Lara had never seen the appeal. Of course, Lara wasn't a sixty-five-year-old widow, as Betty had been when she had married him a few years ago.

'These things won't help you find her but it's right that you should have them.' Betty smiled. 'I just asked Leo if he minded you having them, and of course he doesn't.'

Lara knew there had to be some value to them if Betty had checked with Leo. Betty had been rigorously fair in giving them attention and presents over the years.

'Yes, I think Dad would have approved.' Betty pulled out her phone and dialled. 'Kevin? So glad I caught you, darling. Can you be a dear and go into the safe and take out the blue felt bag? In it should be a single string of pearls with a diamond clasp, and the Tiffany diamond and pearl earrings.'

Lara's eyes widened.

'I'll be at the airport to collect you. Sorry about the long stop in Logan. See you tonight.' Betty tucked the phone in her pocket. 'There, that's done and it's probably something I should have done years ago. They will suit you.' She kissed Lara's cheek.

'Thank you.'

Betty smiled. 'I think it would be good if you can find out who my mother was. It was something I could never discuss with Dad. He just clammed up on the subject.'

Lara thought of the clamshell still sitting on Grandie's bedside table. Why had he been so silent about his wife? Love that lasted beyond death must have been very special. But how the hell was she going to find out about her great-grandmother when all she had to go on was her first name and her nationality?

✳ Six ✳

Hampstead, London
18 August 1943

Dearest,

It's so hot in London, I'm longing for Cornwall. I can't recall having spent any time here in August ever. How are you? Are you still enjoying being a driver or has the fun gone away? Me? The course is good. The girls are lovely but some of the sailors are awful, always saying 'Give us a kiss, Jenny.' I used to like the name Jennifer but after being called Jenny or Jenny Wren the whole time I've gone off it completely. No, I haven't fallen for any of them.

In case you are wondering, I haven't heard from Philip or any of them. Have you? Has Mother? How is she? I spoke with Father. He's fine and I may see him this weekend. If I don't then I will go to the cinema. Last weekend we went and it was the funniest thing. Not the film but what happened to me. In an act of rebellion I hadn't worn the regulation knickers but the ones Aunt Margaret had given me. Well, I stepped off the bus and they fell to the ground, the elastic had gone. I swiftly retrieved them and shoved them in my gas mask bag, trying desperately to keep a straight face as the girls walked ahead and an American GI whistled. We were all laughing so hard. Once we reached the cinema, I went straight to the ladies to tie knots in them to secure them.

I hear Morse in everything, like the hot water pipes and footsteps. Secret messages abound. Not that you and I ever needed code to communicate with each other, but it would have been fun with the boys. They could have tapped on the pipes and we could have met them at the cove. However it's now deadly serious and I'm working so hard to maintain the fastest speed in class.

Thank you for the stockings. Can I send you anything from London, not that there is anything in the shops?

Missing you terribly,
Xxxxx

10 September 1943

I adjusted my jacket and glanced quickly in the mirror. At times it still startled me. I looked like Amelia but not quite – everything was on the wrong side. We used to spend hours looking in Grandmother's mirror, just staring at the reflection. Sitting side by side we were the same, and yet when I looked at her I saw Amelia and not me. I adjusted my hat and took a deep breath. I was halfway through my training and I had leave. However, instead of going home to Windward I'd be spending it in London at my aunt's as Mother and Grandmother were on the train now. Today I had the afternoon to meet Aunt Margaret and catch up with her before Grandmother arrived and took over.

I wasn't sure what Aunt Margaret and I would be doing but I looked forward to not thinking in dots and dashes. I'd only realised recently that I was selected for telegraphy because of my fluency in French and Italian. I'd had no idea that Morse was taught as a language or that it would push the other languages out of my head. The other girls were the same.

Dit dit dit dah ··· **–** . Some days my head swam in the rhythm. Rhythm was everything in Morse, a bit like dancing. But unlike having a lovely song in my head my nights would be filled with SOS – *dit dit dit dah dah dah dit dit dit* ··· **– – –** ···· . I wasn't surprised we'd lost two of the class so far. They had cracked under pressure and gone 'dit happy', as we called it. I think it threatened us all and on top of the need to master Morse and increase our speed we were learning a bit of encryption so that we would understand what would happen before or after our transmission or recording. I confess I wished I had Amelia's brain when there were lessons on electricity and how it all worked. She would master that with ease, just as she had driving and engines.

At the sound of an automobile horn, I looked out of the bus window. Sunlight fell on the remains of buildings and glinted off broken windows. There were ruins everywhere, yet the woman on the opposite side of the road was sweeping up, doing what she no doubt had always done. London went on despite its altered state, the opposite of me. I looked different on the outside because of the uniform but was the same on the inside. I wasn't sure it was so with Amelia.

There was one definite change in me, though. A sense of power had arrived with my uniform and it hadn't disappeared despite the three months of wearing it. It had transformed me – I was somehow both invisible and noticeable. The only downside I'd found to the uniform was the stockings. Amelia had sent me a nylon pair but despite extra care I could repair them no more. Today I wore the dreadful lisle ones. They looked so awful I had to try and forget them but couldn't. They were too thick and made even the best legs look old.

Aunt Margaret had suggested we meet at Fortnum's so I stepped off the bus and strode down Piccadilly. I paused in front of Hatchards with its partially boarded up windows and peered into the small opening to see the display of books.

'Adele.' My aunt came up to me and kissed my cheek. 'Still so hard to adjust to you in uniform.' She walked into the shop and I followed in her wake. This is what we always did. My aunt was a law unto herself. Even Grandmother was under her spell. Or maybe it was just that Margaret was the only child of an earl, unlike Father, who was simply a clever consulting surgeon. Grandmother missed her life before the Great War when everything was clear to her.

'Reg is coming home and this is the list of things he requires.

I'll just drop it off and then it will all be ready for him.' She turned and smiled at me. 'Now let's go and have some tea at the Ritz and you can tell me all your news before the others arrive.'

Despite rationing, her clothes were immaculate. She exuded glamour with her red lips and almost black hair. As I watched her glide across the pavement now, heads turned to follow her progress.

Even back in the summer of 1939 when she'd picnicked on the beach with us, she had looked like she'd walked off the pages of a fashion magazine with her daring two-piece swimming costume. I could remember Grandmother's voice, muttering how scandalous the costume was, revealing her midriff for all to see. But Amelia and I had been full of envy. None of our large party could take their eyes off Margaret as she joined in our game of beach cricket. It had been a spring tide and the sand stretched forever before disappearing into the turquoise waters of the bay.

At the behest of Uncle Reg who suddenly fancied moules, Amelia and I with Eddie, Tom, Angus and Philip had scoured the rocks for mussels. As the group spread out in the search, Philip and I found ourselves alone in a small cave. The sand was cold and damp and the rock face was covered in barnacles, limpets and mussels. I set to work loosening the shells and slipping them in the bucket. He was close by and when I turned he was staring at me.

'You won't collect any lunch that way.' I smiled and tilted my head.

'True.' He stepped nearer with a big grin spread across his freckled face. His auburn hair had fallen across his brow and I resisted the urge to push it back into place.

'Adele?'

Looking up he was at least a head taller than me and his shoulders were broad. He'd filled out in the nicest of ways since the summer before.

He stepped closer. We were almost touching. My breath caught. Staring into his brown eyes I began to think I might be a little in love.

'I ... I want to kiss you.'

I drew in a breath. 'Yes.' His lips touched mine and he began to pull back but I moved nearer to him.

'There you two are.' Amelia stood in the entrance to the cave with a wicked smile on her face. I flushed as embarrassment spread through my body. 'We're taking these up to the house so Cook can begin making lunch.'

His fingers grazed mine as he took my bucket and handed it to Eddie.

I'd fallen a little bit in love with Philip that summer, or as in love as a fourteen-year-old could be. The following summer the holidays weren't quite so blissful. The boys including Philip had been practically counting the hours until they could join up. At the least, Philip and I had managed to steal away a few times to walk the coastal paths, talking books and dreams. Those carefree summers felt very far away.

I sighed, enjoying the warmth of the sun on my face. London was not Cornwall but the sun was the same. Was it as clear and bright at home?

'The weather is glorious, isn't it?' Aunt Margaret linked her arm through mine and looked up at the sky. 'I hope it remains fair for Reg's leave.' She glanced at me. 'I have to say the uniform suits you. The navy blue sets off that glorious blonde hair of yours with those amber eyes. I always hoped that my children would have your eyes.'

I smiled. Uncle Reg's eyes were close to the same colour but not quite. His hair had gone sandy and thin while thus far Amelia and I were still white blonde.

Once we arrived at the Ritz we didn't dawdle in the lobby, and my aunt whispered in my ear, 'I don't want to be caught by that dreadful bore Mrs Johnson. We came out together and she talks endlessly of her children.' She shivered. 'I think I shall simply adopt you.' She gave me a smile. 'I do think dear Amelia will be married off before long. The girl cannot wait.'

We were led to a table and Aunt Margaret waved at several people I recognised but couldn't put a name to. It was always this way with her, but thankfully we didn't have to pass their tables first to reach ours. My stomach was gurgling at the prospect of food. Hopefully she would chat with them after tea and not before.

As we settled I admired her hat, which she wore at a jaunty angle, tilting down, nearly covering one eye, while the other side swept up revealing her beautiful hair. I longed for her wardrobe. Everything she wore was so chic and she'd had most of her clothes made in Paris before the war.

'So, dear one, tell me, have you found a suitable boy? Or are you like your darling sister and keeping the troops happy?'

My eyes widened and my face coloured. It confirmed all I had been feeling about Amelia.

'I had a lovely chat with her the other night and she confessed all as your mother and grandmother were out.' She took a drag of her cigarette, leaving clear red marks on the white paper. 'An admiral proved a bit stuffy, but it sounds as if a few captains have been most amusing.' Her deep throaty laugh made me smile. She waved at a waiter and ordered for us.

I shook my head. 'I spend most of my time fighting off the able seamen who think I should be looking after their needs.'

'How dreary – unless, of course, they are beautiful, in which case you should be.'

I leaned back and frowned at her.

'Have I scandalised you?' she asked.

I nodded.

'Good. Who knows what will happen in this blasted war, and quite frankly we all need to find what joy we can.'

The tea arrived and I studied my aunt more closely. Did she really feel this or was it just talk? Was she finding joy without my uncle? I was horrified at Amelia's behaviour and I certainly wouldn't be 'finding joy', as Aunt Margaret put it. This was the first time my sister and I had differed on anything that mattered. How could things change so quickly? Or had I simply not noticed before?

A woman swept up to the table. 'Margaret, I'm so pleased I've seen you.'

'Sophia, you remember my niece Adele Seaton.' The woman nodded in my direction. I didn't remember her so I doubted she did.

'Sorry to interrupt you but I must speak with you. Can we go and find a quiet place?'

Margaret frowned but stood up. 'I'll be with you in a minute, Sophia.' She leaned over to me as the woman moved to the side of the room and waited, watching us. 'Sorry about this. I've been avoiding her but I can't wriggle out of it now.'

I shrugged.

'You are a dear,' she said. 'I'll sort out everything here. Just enjoy it and I'll see you later.'

I watched my aunt leave and wondered who Sophia was to command such a response from Margaret. My aunt was cowed by few people. A man joined them as they disappeared out of sight. I turned to study the others having tea. The place was full of the grand and the uniformed. I laughed as I realised that included me.

12 October 1943

Slipping off my shoes and rolling my neck from side to side, some of the tension left me as I looked around the cabin. I slipped onto my bunk and felt the counterpane wrinkle beneath me. Right now all I wanted was my own bed and Amelia to talk to. She would understand. I wouldn't even have to tell her what I'd written in the half-finished letter in the drawer. I rose and retrieved it. My flesh crawled just thinking about what had happened tonight – the man's eager face, his persistent words and even more pervasive hands. Maybe if I finished it I would feel as if she were here.

I wish I were more like you. It would make life easier. It's hard saying no and it feels endless. Tonight a pesky able seaman also on the course cornered me for the umpteenth time and tried to charm me into a kiss or more. He definitely wanted more. He backed me into a dark corner and rubbed up against me. I know you say it's all fun and I'm sure you are right, but you have to want it and I definitely don't. Certainly not with him.

'Come on, Jenny, you know you want to. I'll be off on a boat risking my life and you'll have a soft shore-based job.' His words echoed in my head. I shuddered at how he had tried to make me feel it was my duty to let him do what he liked to me. Eventually I'd pushed him away. 'Stuck-up bitch,' he'd snapped, before finally leaving me alone.

Tell me, how do you do it? Tell me how you separate love from a bit of fun.

Saw Uncle Reg. As always he makes me laugh but this time his humour was darker. For the first time I sensed some of Mother's depression lurking in the shadows of her brother's eyes. Aunt Margaret was over-bright. Dare I say it feels like his return has unsettled her? When I was out the other day with her she was relaxed but when with him she was brittle from the laughter to the smile. The number of cigarettes she consumed doubled, along with the gins.

Father is wonderful. I still have no idea what he does. I'm not sure why a surgeon is in an office most of the time and not in a hospital. But it's not me or any woman running this war. I think we might do it all very differently. Enough of that.

We had dinner and went to the 400 Club afterwards. How we laughed at the antics of a duke who was there without his duchess but with someone else's wife! Father and I danced into the small hours and Angus and Eddie appeared. Both were asking after you, especially Eddie.

I bit the edge of my nail then forced my hand away from my mouth. Grandmother's voice rang out in my head, telling me I'd never find a husband worth having with hands that looked as though they belonged to a fishwife. But did I want a husband? Yes, in theory, someday. Philip came to mind. I hadn't seen him in ages. But my stomach tightened just thinking about him. I longed to spend time with him in London and visit nightclubs like the 400. Sighing, I imagined us dancing in the smoky haze that filled the club so that it felt as if we were the only people there. Of course that was never the case.

How is Mother? When I finally reached her by telephone she sounded distracted, but it could have been because Grandmother came in during the call with a live rabbit asking how to kill it. Is she all right? Grandmother seems to be coping surprisingly well, but Mother I'm concerned about.

I miss you and Cornwall so much. It's not that London isn't wonderful. Seeing everyone is brilliant but I long to be near the sea and you. Mind you, there aren't many occasions to wear evening dress in Cornwall from what you say and I do enjoy it so much. Thank you for sending me your blue silk dress. I know how you love it. I promise to look after it and might try and pretend I'm you while wearing it. Who knows what will happen if I do!

Do fill me in on all the details. I don't want to miss a thing and I know you are keeping things from me.

Love you, miss you,
A xxx

P.S. Thanks for the stockings. Where did you get them? No, don't answer that question. Love you. Xx

I looked around at the cabin. Even after all these months I stumbled to call my bedroom a cabin, along with all the other naval terms like galley for kitchen, gangway for corridor, deck for the floor and gash for rubbish.

The cabin was more like a dormitory. Four bunks, two chests of drawers and one mirror – not homely at all, and I was beginning to count the days until we were finished. The accommodation in many postings would be much more basic than this but at least we would be doing something. The waiting was the main reason for my restlessness. Learning telegraphy was challenging but I was over halfway through training and while

I wasn't able to march well, I knew my Morse code. In fact I found myself dreaming in it and hearing it as if it was English being spoken. I smiled. A few nights ago I dreamed that Philip had declared his love for me, but in Morse – it was as if he was whispering to me and the *dit dahs* were as beautiful as English. I laughed at my own foolishness; first at the dream itself, and second that Morse had become so engrained I didn't have to translate it, I just knew. The switch had taken place, as French had the year we spent in France when we were ten.

Amelia would be proud. I was even mastering the technical requirements, never my strong point. Patience was hard. Right from the start Amelia was working productively, but then she already knew how to drive and take an engine apart. Not, it would appear, that she'd had to do much messy work. I had to be patient and I'd never been very good at that.

29 October 1943

Rain pelted down as I dashed to quarters. Ever since I'd seen Aunt Margaret and Uncle Reg at the beginning of October the good weather had disappeared. It had been all grey and dull. No sight of the sun or blue skies. All was bleak. I longed for tea and quiet. Of course there would be tea, but chatter would bounce off the mess walls. In the hall as I watched the scurry for the post I thought a letter from home might lift me out of this blue funk I'd slipped into. But I wasn't sure. The air felt heavy with dread. It might have simply been the days drawing in, or the fact that I was missing Amelia and jealous she was at home.

'There's post for you.' A fellow Wren handed me two letters, one from Mother and the other from Amelia. I smiled my thanks and walked to my cabin, which was blissfully empty. Despite gurgling complaints from my stomach I climbed onto my bunk and read Amelia's letter first.

28 October 1943

Dearest Half,

How the time is flying. I loved hearing about your exploits and I'm so jealous that you've seen both Eddie and Angus. Are you sure you're not a little in love with one of them? Do try and have fun. Despite your stories of dancing until the small hours, I can tell you are focused on work, which is right. I can't argue with that but don't miss the fun. No, don't lecture me. I am being very careful and very selective. They have to be handsome, very handsome! But I do see the way Grandmother looks at me and I know she knows I'm up to no good. But it is good – it lifts my morale and theirs, and it's fun.

Have you noticed Yanks in London? They are appearing everywhere and my God they are so good-looking. They are a lovely distraction from this endless war. It drags on so but the Yanks seem to smile in the face of it.

Mother isn't well. I don't mean physically – she is thriving that way – but when she thinks she's alone I've seen her crying. Her telephone conversations with Father sound so business-like and none of the lovey-dovey stuff we used to hear. I am concerned.

I know you've told me that Father is frightfully busy and very preoccupied when you see him and I'm sure he is but he needs to think of Mother. Of course Grandmother is having none of it. It's all 'don't be ridiculous' and 'get a hold of yourself'.

Last night at ten to six after Grandmother turned on the wireless in anticipation of the news, she turned to me. I knew it would be at least five minutes before the thing would be warmed up. She had a 'lecture' look on her face. I braced myself and thought of offering to get her sherry but she had anticipated that and I saw one on the table beside the sofa. However, she surprised me. It wasn't about my activities but about the Americans. She was absolutely scathing about them. Too many teeth, too much hair and too much sex drive – simply vulgar. She's been listening to the local gossip and my goodness is it working, and we don't even have that many of them here yet. I know you can picture her saying it took them too long to join our efforts. She ended just as the wireless came to life, warning that she would disinherit me if I engaged with them in any way!

I knew exactly what Grandmother meant. She was right. They were vulgar and London was beginning to fill with them. Surely Amelia wouldn't be that foolish. Grandmother was worrying over nothing. Amelia was a bit reckless, that was all.

She is really becoming more and more eccentric by the day but her vegetables are the better for it. She spends hours out there lecturing them. It does us no good at all, but the cabbages seem to love it!

   I miss you so much and I know you know that. Glad you're out dancing every now and then. Do remember that all work and no play makes Jill a very dull girl.

Best love,
Xxxx

P.S. Will send more stockings soon and yes, it's best not to ask.

P.P.S. Barbara in the village is pregnant and everyone is whispering because her husband hasn't been home for six months ... I'm remembering to be careful. xxx

P.P.P.S. I was out early this morning and met Jim Bolitho on the way back from his aeroplane watch. The poor man looked exhausted having watched the sky all night then off to tend the cows. He told me that his brother had thus far survived as a gunner on a Lancaster bomber.

P.P.P.P.S. We've just had awful news and I can't bear to write but Mother is

My heart stopped. I ripped open Mother's letter.

1 November 1943

Darling Adele,

It is with heavy heart that I write to tell you Philip is dead.

I cried out but couldn't take in air. The words blurred but wouldn't go away.

Patricia is devastated and could barely speak when she telephoned. He is her only child and she is beyond consolation. I know you liked him, possibly even more than liked him. Amelia gasped your name when she heard the news, confirming what I had always thought. Both Patricia and I had realised early on that you were a good match with both of you being the quiet, academic sort. Dare I say your father and I had hopes that he of all the boys could capture your finicky heart.

Had hopes. My hands shook. Philip. My dream.

I know this news will be particularly hard for you as you are so far from us. I've spoken with your father. He rang as he had seen Harold who confirmed Philip's death.

Death is everywhere at the moment taking all our best. I am so grateful that I have girls. I know I shouldn't say this but I am. This war is killing all that is good and I see no end in sight.

I wish I were there to hold you. I know you will be brave about it all. You are more like your father in that. I fear I'm not being brave at all. Amelia has taken it hard and isn't talking about it.

Everything else here at Windward is fine. The relentless rain is depressing as always. It feels as if all the mud in the fields has come into the house. Your grandmother forgets there is no one to clear her messy footprints off the hall floor but me. Sometimes I do wonder about her.

I have no other news and can't find any happy things to say. I am missing you desperately.

With love,
Mother

A lone tear rolled down my cheek. I wiped it away and looked to the window. The sky was dark and I couldn't see the rain, but I could hear it beating against the glass. ·· / ·—·· ——— ···— · / —·—— ——— ··—

❋ Seven ❋

Falmouth, Cape Cod, Massachusetts
21 August 2015

As 'Lord of All Hopefulness' faded, the crowd filed out of the church behind Grandie's coffin. Leo walked ahead with Betty, and Lara with Maeve, who squeezed her hand as she spotted Pierre standing in the last pew. Lara caught her breath as he smiled, slightly bowing his head. Light from the window gleamed off his jet-black hair. This was not the way things should be. He should have been at her side, not standing like an unwanted mourner at the back of the church. He looked up and his eyes said sorry in so many ways.

Sunlight blinded her as they stepped outside. Lara pulled her sunglasses out of her pocket and slipped them on. Her mother leaned closer to her. 'Are you OK?'

She nodded, even though it was too big a question to answer.

'It was good of Pierre to come.'

Again Lara nodded. Speech wouldn't be a good idea at the moment; tears were threatening.

'I don't think he'll come to the grave or back to the house,' said Maeve.

Lara helped her mother into the limo. 'No.' She knew he wouldn't because that would require them to talk; not that they hadn't been speaking to each other before the divorce, just not actually *talking*. They had both been very good at saying the right words at the right time to ensure that no one was angry. No voices had been raised, no other people were named in the divorce – they had simply grown apart. That somehow made it sound worse, on today of all days.

'It was a very good turn-out at the church,' her mother said, adjusting the seatbelt.

Lara nodded. 'Is Gerald going to come in the limo with us?'

The corners of her mother's mouth lifted. Gerald was the first man Maeve had allowed in her life since Lara's father had died so long ago. 'He's taking his own car. He didn't want to intrude.'

'Oh.' Lara looked out of the window as the hearse began to move and the motorcade fell into line, snaking behind Lara and her mother. Leo and Betty's heads were just visible in the limo in front. 'Did Betty ever get on with Grandie?'

Maeve shook her head. 'There was always a distance in that relationship.'

'That's one way to put it. Do you know why?'

'No, but I often wondered if it was because Amelia died when Betty was so little.' Her mouth lifted on one side. 'He made a brilliant great-grandfather but that was much later in life.' She paused. 'I sometimes wonder if his years in the Army had toughened him too much to be the only parent of a girly girl.'

Lara's mouth twitched. Her mother had nailed Betty with the 'girly girl' thing. Lara chuckled, thinking of how fastidious Betty was with her appearance.

'All right, chick?' Maeve placed her hand on Lara's as they pulled up at the cemetery.

'As all right as it's possible to be ... at the moment.' The limo came to a stop by a mound of soil and both Lara and her mother pasted on their public faces before walking to the graveside.

Following the burial, Eventide was full of chattering people just as Grandie would have wanted it. Lara smiled. She wished she could discuss it all with him, and hoped he was looking on from heaven, pleased with the turn-out. She was less happy with the canapés, and now regretted not organising the catering for Betty herself. At least Leo had been in charge of the drinks.

She turned the champagne flute in her hand, and watched as small bubbles rose to the top. When she was six Grandie had used the bubbles in a glass of champagne to explain souls rising to heaven leaving the body behind, an image she'd never forgotten.

This champagne was excellent, and had been his favourite. She remembered her first glass of Pol Roger at the age of fourteen on New Year's Eve. It had a lovely dryness to it and it had remained her favourite sparkling wine all these years, even though she'd enjoyed the best that France and the world had to offer. She leaned against the balustrade. Manhattan seemed a long way away at the moment. Closing her eyes for a second, the noise of the hushed conversation around was reminiscent of being back at the restaurant.

Lara watched her brother talking on his mobile. It must be Deborah, his girlfriend, who was out in Beijing on business. She hadn't been able to make it back for the funeral and Leo missed her. He finished the call, picked up a bottle of champagne and came over to fill up Lara's glass. 'Here's to Grandie and his good taste in drink.'

Lara raised her glass to his, letting them touch lightly. 'What did he always say about it?'

'He'd quote Churchill. Something about how a single glass imparts a feeling of exhilaration.'

'Yes, I remember now. And that a bottle produces the opposite effect.' Lara twisted the thin stem. 'I may have had too much already, then.'

'Is that the first time you've seen Pierre since the divorce was final?' He raised an eyebrow.

'Yes.'

'How have you escaped it, being around here?' He waved a hand.

'By being very low key and avoiding going back to our house – along with just about everywhere we used to go.'

'How long will you be able to continue this?'

She shrugged.

'Look, sis, you need to do something.'

71

She tilted her head. 'I've spoken to Cassie and I've booked my flights.'

'Excellent.'

'I'm just not sure what comes *after* I've had a month or two away, that's the problem.' She winced.

'And you don't fancy working in a greasy spoon diner after hitting the heights of the Michelin stars so young?'

She frowned. 'Not really, but then you know that.'

'You've climbed so swiftly.'

'You're a fine one to talk.'

He chuckled. 'Fair point – but maybe you should set your sights a little lower to build your reputation again.'

Her shoulders fell and she closed her eyes for a moment. Her dreams of her own restaurant and life with Pierre were all gone. It was time for a big rethink. Hopefully a stretch with her best friend away from here would provide it.

25 August 2015

As the morning sun rose higher, Lara breathed in the fragrance of the cedar shingles as the dew baked off them. It was a smell that always reminded her of home. She slipped onto the beach in front of Eventide and stopped to look out on the water. The nine o'clock ferry was already making its way toward Oak Bluffs.

A shell hit her on the head. 'Hey, you.' It had been thrown by Leo, who was standing at the edge of the beach, tapping his watch. 'Time to get back,' he called out to her.

'I know.' Looking towards Eventide and beyond the sea grass dune separating them from the house she could see Betty and Kevin chatting by their rental car. They would be heading off shortly.

'It's been great having you around.' Walking to her, he picked up a pebble and weighed it in his hand.

She looked up. 'You're normally working so hard that if I was here, I'd never see you.'

'True.'

'I feel like I'm running away,' said Lara, as she skimmed a stone.

Leo paused and looked out to the Vineyard. 'You're taking a sabbatical.'

'Is that what you call it?' She skimmed another stone.

'Well, I must speak the truth.' He grinned.

'You are a shit-hot lawyer. I thought you never spoke the truth.'

He laughed and linked his arm through hers. 'You need to think about your future. You gave Pierre the house, and, well, I advised against it at the time but you didn't listen to your little brother.'

She looked up at him. Leo had received the height as well as the academic genes. 'I know,' she said, 'but it was my fault the marriage failed.'

'It takes two for one to fail.'

'I'm not so sure.' She glanced out towards the Vineyard.

'I am. Trust me, I'm a lawyer.'

'That's every reason not to trust you!' They both laughed and looked up at Eventide.

A gentle wave pulled the last bit of water from the sand, revealing a startled crab and the fragments of a jellyfish while returning the seaweed to the sea. The tide always revealed new treasures – the odd bit of sea glass, a scallop shell, and now sadly more than ever before the debris of modern life, like plastic bags. She bent to pick up a jingle shell, glistening gold in the early morning sun, but it was so light it slipped through her fingers. She left it where it fell. Together with Leo, she walked slowly back to the house to say goodbye to their grandmother.

The low tones of the foghorn sounded through the night air thick with moisture. It felt much later than eight o'clock. The blurred light coming from the windows of the British Beer Company welcomed them. Moisture beaded on Lara's face and her shoulders were covered with ever-growing drops of water, which were forming a critical mass and seeping through the

Harvard sweatshirt she was wearing. It wasn't hers but one of Leo's she'd found when clearing things out.

'You OK?' Leo threw an arm over her shoulder and marshalled her across the street and into the bar.

'Yeah.'

'Liar,' he said, and gave her a reproachful look. 'You said you wanted to come.'

'I know.' Lara took a deep breath before she pulled open the door. 'It's a place I associate with Grandie, but also with Pierre.'

'Mixed, I get it.' Leo led the way and Lara watched him scan the bar to make sure the coast was clear. It wasn't that Lara didn't want to see Pierre at all, but right then she would rather avoid it – everything inside her was too emotionally raw.

'Hey, guys. You here for the quiz?' asked one of Grandie's colleagues from the institute. Lara had spoken to so many of them earlier this week. She shook her head.

'Can I get you a drink?' the woman asked. This scientist had been one of Grandie's many mentees over the years.

'Thanks.' Lara smiled. 'A small IPA.'

'That's kind. I'll have a pint of the same.' Leo peered around to the restaurant area where tables were full of people enjoying their vacations.

'Fancy joining our team?' the woman asked after she'd placed the drinks order.

'We'd only hold you back,' said Lara. 'Besides, Grandie always played on the opposing team, so it wouldn't feel right.'

The woman laughed. 'They'll have a tough time beating us without him on their side.' She handed Lara a glass then one to Leo. 'We all miss him.'

'Thanks.' Lara perched on a stool, putting a folder next to her glass.

Leo sat beside her and cradled his beer. 'Love this place. It always feels like home.'

'True. We both put enough hours in working here.' She looked at the bottles lining the back of the bar, remembering her first job clearing tables and Leo washing dishes.

He picked up the folder. 'Is that your itinerary for the trip?'

She nodded. 'That, plus Grandie's diaries, photos and letters.'

She took the folder from Leo, opened it and laid the contents carefully on the bar, making sure the surface was clean and dry. Picking up Grandie's 1943 diary, she turned to the first entry and ran her fingers over the writing, wishing he were still here.

November 25, 1943

On plane to London – an odd way to spend Thanksgiving

November 26, 1943

Report to HQ

'We know he graduated West Point in the spring of 1943 and was on a plane to London on Thanksgiving Day.' She put the diary down, frowning. 'Interesting that he flew. From what I remember from history class, most of the troops went on ships.'

'Maybe he had a reason to reach London quickly.'

She sighed. 'Why didn't we ask these questions years ago?'

'I did ask about the war but he never wanted to talk about it.'

'True. We know so little.'

He nodded then sipped his beer. 'So you fly to London.' He looked at her e-ticket. 'And hopefully you'll discover more.'

'Hopefully.' She drew wiggly lines in the condensation on the side of her glass. 'But I have so little to go on.'

'You always liked puzzles.'

'Yeah, jigsaws. This is a bit different.' She lifted her glass and studied the beermat. 'It's funny how Cassie lives near this Helford River.'

He nodded. 'I bet she's excited to see you.'

'I think so.' She took a long sip of her beer then pulled out the photo of her grandfather standing alone on a headland with an expanse of water behind him. Leo took it from her, peering at the faded writing on the back. 'It looks like there might have been a date on it but the pencil has rubbed away.' He handed the photo back to her. 'I guess if you're going to be close, that'll make tracing his footsteps easier.' He sorted through the photos then picked up the letters, while Lara turned to study the bar. It was all so familiar. The guest beer might change and the tourists smelled of a different brand of sunblock but the bar was a constant for her. She had had her first sous chef job here.

'These letters are pretty explicit,' he paused, 'for the time.' He put them back in the folder.

'Agreed – it feels wrong to read them but we have nothing else.' Lara looked at the diaries, wishing they provided an easy clue or even stated the answer outright. But from her quick study of them they were more like a travel journal, noting places and names in some sort of code. She supposed Grandie had used it more as an aide-memoire. 'It's so strange that there are no pictures of her.'

'Do you think Grandie destroyed them?'

'Possibly. Could have been too painful. Maybe there weren't any to destroy.'

'Are you OK with doing all of this?' Leo finished his beer.

'Yes.' Lara put her empty glass down. 'It will keep me out of trouble and out of the kitchen for a while.' She gathered her things and as they left the bar he flung an arm across her shoulder.

'You'll find a way.'

She snorted doubtful laughter. 'Glad you have faith in me.'

'I do.'

They walked along the beach towards Eventide in silence as the fog began to lift. By the time they reached the house the sky was clear, with stars scattered across the black expanse. Lara just wished her future were as easy to see.

❉ Eight ❉

Windward, Mawnan Smith, Falmouth, Cornwall
25 August 2015

I walked to the end of the terrace and squinted into the distance. Another tanker was heading towards Falmouth. Was it coming to reside in the bay or did it have actual business to do? I hoped it was the latter. Although the bright orange and green hulls added contrast to the view on a dull day, I preferred the bay filled with moving ships and boats. On a mizzly summer morning such as this there was still activity from the small craft making their way out.

The top of Nare Head to the south was just visible. The old air defence battery was still there, and was now used by the coastal watch. Much better to be counting basking sharks than trying to pretend to be Falmouth. But it had lured the bombers away from their real target with fake train tracks and false lights. The last time I walked that stretch of coast the ruts from the tracks were still clearly visible. Closing my eyes, I recalled them finding a 700 kilogram parachute bomb just off Durgan beach a few years ago. It seemed impossible that it had lain there untroubled for seventy or more years with countless holidaymakers swimming above it. It made an almighty blast when they set it off in the bay – explosions like that were rather spectacular to watch when there was no threat to life, unlike others I had seen and felt.

Looking through the mist that morning, I lowered myself onto the stone wall. Why did it all feel so close right now? The key anniversaries were over and I'd survived another year. Jack had found a frame for the photo of me on VE Day and placed it in the sitting room. He seemed to think it was good for me to see the past but I ignored it, and would not talk of it. It was best to let the ghosts sleep.

But it wasn't the picture, or even Peta wanting to wear the veil. My war had never left me, despite my desire to forget. I'd known where the letters were and they'd never troubled me as they did now. Those years felt so close I could touch them. Turning from the bay, I looked at Windward, Grandmother's house, built in 1911 on her family's land. It was fortress-like in some ways, but that wasn't surprising considering its position facing the easterly winds. My grandmother had loved the freedom this house provided her. It was hers wholly and not entailed in my grandfather's estate, which Uncle Reg had inherited at the age of nine on my grandfather's death in 1917.

'Gran, you'll get very wet if you stay out there much longer.' Peta held out a hand, smiling. I hoped the weather wouldn't be like this for her wedding. Accepting her help I linked my arm through hers and we went into the breakfast room where the wedding details were spread out on the table. Jack stood with a coffee cup in his hand and a frown on his face.

'Wouldn't it just be easier to live with him?' he said.

Peta glared at him. 'I'm not going to bother to answer that question. Why don't you make some fresh coffee for Gran while I show her the final seating plan?' She picked up a plate with crumbs on it. 'And please bring some more of that lovely cake.'

He rolled his eyes and left while Peta pulled out a chair for me. I didn't need to see the wedding details, but Peta never let that deter her. She'd always look at me and see more than I'd want. I'd no choice but to continually turn away from her.

'So, Gran, let's pray for decent weather so that the sides of the tepee can be up.' She looked up from the papers on the table. 'It would be such a shame to have a day like today when you can barely see the view.'

'True.'

'But even if it totally chucks it down, they promise that the tepee can take it.'

Tepee. I pursed my mouth, looking at the picture Peta slid in front of me. It had very little resemblance to the small tepees shown in old films. This had a vast expanse and three main peaks. Good selling on their part, but I knew well what Mother Nature could hand out on this exposed bit of land. Despite being three storeys, the house sat lower into the hillside than many other houses built early in the 1900s. The ceilings were high but not as high as you would expect in an Edwardian country house. The architect had spent his summers nearby and understood the landscape with the effects of the winds. The tent company did not, of that I was sure.

'I've sketched out the table plan and for you I've made sure that there is a seat with a back on it.' She smiled at me. 'Everyone else will be on benches.'

I nodded. What was I supposed to say? Everyone else would be much more comfortable on chairs as well, not just an old woman.

'We wouldn't fit in a hundred people if we seated them that way.'

I shook my head. It was uncanny how Peta could read my thoughts. Fortunately she understood that some things should remain private. For all her careless appearance she was a sensible child, but she had given Jack and me a very hard time during her teens.

Jack carried a tray into the room. 'Madam, your coffee.' He bowed slightly after he had placed it on the table.

'Thanks, bro.' She winked. 'Now, Gran, I want to make sure you'll be sitting with people you want to talk to as opposed to people you feel you have to.'

'You've found some, have you?' I smiled.

She laughed. 'Working on it.'

Jack chuckled as he handed her a cup.

'You won't be on the top table.' A furrow appeared between her brows. 'It would be too confined there. I think you would be happier closer to the open side of the tent.'

'Assuming the weather is fine.' Jack smirked and Peta hit his arm with the pencil in her hand. She moved bits of sticky yellow paper around the large diagram. 'If I put you on the table with Victoria and Sebastian Roberts and, of course, Eddie, that would definitely give you a few people to talk to, about gardens if nothing else.'

I nodded, thinking of Eddie sitting with me at a wedding. At least he would understand. Tightness closed around my heart and squeezed, but I smiled at Peta. Her happiness was infectious.

'Where are you putting me?' Jack leaned against the table cradling his cup.

'You're not as lucky as Gran. No quick escape routes for you.' She looked up at him. 'You're on the top table.'

The colour left his face and he closed his eyes. He would do anything for Peta but I knew this was pushing him close to the limit. First she'd asked if he would give her away. Reluctantly he'd agreed. She above anyone knew what he thought about love thanks to their father's behaviour, but she'd pushed further. She'd asked if Jack would make a speech. He'd said no, that she should pick someone else. She pointed out that there was no one else. They were family. Aside from me they only had each other. Peta had had enough sense not to ask me.

Placing my coffee on the table, I pushed myself up. 'I'll leave the rest to you.'

Peta kissed my cheek. 'Thanks. And I don't think I've said it, but thanks for letting me have the reception here.'

'No thanks needed. It's mine, so it's yours.' I waved my hand, dismissing her gratitude, realising that that wasn't quite true. The house had been left to both my sister and me.

Hampstead, London
5 November 1943

Dearest Half,

My heart is broken for you and for me and for Philip's parents. I know you will tell me that you didn't really care for him. But I know you did. Besides, it's simply awful. Bloody Hitler. Sorry about the language but it's the only word that expresses my anger.

Mother is not doing very well. Grandmother is beastly to her and I'm working longer hours. Both of them have to fend for themselves.

I don't know what to say. I feel you pulling in to yourself but please don't. You have to live. I'm too tired to write anymore. I'll post this in the morning. I want you to know I know and that you can't hide.

Always yours,
Xxxx

Throwing my sister's letter down, I jumped down from the bunk. It was as if upon hearing of Philip's death part of me had closed down. She was right. It was foolish to think myself in love because of a few stolen kisses. There was enough else to think about. Training was nearly finished. Soon a sparker's badge would adorn my sleeve and we were supposed to select two locations for placement. Of course my first choice was St Merryn. I missed Cornwall – the air, the sea, the people. Although having lived in London for the six years before we went to Windward, these six months had showed me that I didn't belong here. When in Cornwall I had never missed London and now I longed for a star-filled sky and the cry of the curlew on the evening breeze. I wanted my days to be filled with the scent of wild honeysuckle in the hedges and the smell of Mrs Tonks's pasties coming from the kitchen at Windward ready for our picnics.

Camilla, a fellow rating with uncontrollable curls, walked into the room. 'We're off to the cinema, would you like to join us?' She smiled and her hair continued to move even though she stood still.

I forced a smile. 'Yes.' I didn't want to but Amelia was right. I had to live.

'Wonderful. We're meeting downstairs in twenty minutes.' She disappeared from view but then popped back in. 'Did you hear that Paula Thompson has gone?'

81

'No.' I frowned. 'Dit happy?'

She nodded. 'See you downstairs in a few minutes.'

To crack at this point so near the end was hard luck. So many had fallen out early. I'd been close myself a few times despite achieving the highest speed on the course. Morse had become a second language for me, sometimes overtaking English in my thoughts. It had startled me when I realised I had begun to think in *dit, dit, dit, dah* during daylight hours and not just in my dreams. I straightened the counterpane on my bunk and put Amelia's letter away, knowing I needed to embrace the now – just not as zealously as she did.

12 November 1943

Dearest,

You'll never guess who was home on leave and came to visit us. Yes, it was Eddie. His mother Rebecca has been staying with us so this was where he spent his leave. He told me all about seeing you in London and how you had spoken about Philip. I know he too has taken Philip's death badly. He's the first and hopefully the last of our gang to die. I hate this beastly war.

But for a few days we had the most wonderful time. His mother isn't terribly well as you know so it fell on me to entertain him. Fortunately I had some leave as well. The weather has been glorious for November so he and I were off on bikes all around the area. We had a lovely evening down at the Ferryboat Inn and also went to the pictures up at Barbary's Garage at Penwarne. There was even ice cream. Mrs Barbary used custard powder supplied by the Americans.

You wouldn't believe some of the changes taking place now that the Yanks are here. I can't say what but you'll see when you come next. The first ones to arrive in Falmouth were called Seebees but lately there are soldiers around. Even Negros. Grandmother is in an uproar because of what she heard on Wednesday at Carwinion at the working party. While the knitting needles clacked the tongues wagged. No one around here had seen a black man in person before and now there are so many. There were two major scandals. The first, it appears, is that the white soldiers don't get on with the black ones and there was a big fall-out when they were all invited together to a social nearby in a school hall. Secondly, and even more scandalous, it appears that Ginny Smith is involved with one of the Negros. I have to say he is a handsome chap.

Yes, I know I'm not telling you all, but it's so hard to try and convey everything as so much has been happening since Eddie's mother arrived here. Oh, I can hear you wanting to know more about Eddie and me. Well, yes of course I kissed him and may well have done more.

No, I can't lie to you. We did a lot more and it was wonderful. I think I'm in love.

I can hear your voice telling me not to be foolish and saying not to lose my heart but it's too late. I have said those words to myself. But I was lost the moment his eyes met mine. When he next has leave he will come down to Windward. Of course, I was heartbroken when he left and I catch my breath every time I hear a plane overhead even though I know he's nowhere near here. If you see him, tell me ... no, don't. I don't want to know if he's with another woman. I'm so lost already. I'm even turning other offers away. All it took was one look. It said it all. He saw me for who I am. He hasn't said he loves me nor have I told him. It's too soon but yet it isn't – for there may not be another chance. I hold close our embraces and hope that the war ends soon.

I can't stop thinking about him.

Is it possible that you'll have leave over Christmas?

My thoughts are everywhere and I must sign off and go and collect a rear admiral. I'll post this today. Do write. Although I can hear you, it's distant and I long to have you close again.

With all my love xxx

P.S. Mother is better with Rebecca here, which I didn't think would be the case as she was always awkward when we went

to their house. I'm also learning so much more about French
cooking. Mme Pomfrey is merveilleux. *As I'm working longer*
hours, she is doing much of the cooking and she is a wonderful
seamstress.

P.P.S. I know you are thinking about Philip's death and are
scared that my heart will be broken in the same way. I have
to believe it won't be. I have no choice in loving him, I just do.
xxxx

I put the letter down. So that was what I'd been feeling. She
said she could hear me, but I *felt* her. That shimmery excitement tied up in my stomach, clenching with dread – that was
all from her. We *were* different. I paced the cabin. Outside rain
tipped down. Drops on the window raced each other, merging,
separating and merging again.

The last time I'd seen Eddie he was dancing with a WAAF
and he was laughing. Now Amelia had fallen in love with him.
What should I say to her? This talk of love was everywhere.
My fellow Wrens were love-struck whether with new flames
or old ones. War made everything uncertain. I hadn't been in
love with Philip but had considered it. His death still took my
breath away. It was unfair.

Sighing, I sat on the bunk. Loneliness. Despite having people
around me all the time, I was alone. I missed Amelia so much
it physically hurt. I wanted to cling to her. Maybe she was right
to love and I was simply jealous.

Despite the pain in my stomach, I forced my body upright. I
needed to be on parade in five minutes. My reply to her would
wait until this evening. I was pleased for her. Eddie was wonderful. They would be happy once the war was over. Hopefully
they wouldn't have to wait too long.

'Peta's stored her stuff in the library and filled the garage with what seems to be tons of junk.' Jack rubbed his left shoulder. 'Not sure how she managed to fit all of it into her flat in Falmouth.'

'It will be strange having her on the other side of the river when she moves into the house with Fred.' I looked up from the newspaper, although I'd been failing to read it. My thoughts had been back in the war. I couldn't escape from it. I even woke sobbing in the night, and was thankful that I'd so far disturbed no one but myself.

'She will still be close at hand.'

I smiled. 'The other side seems a long way away.' I looked out to the bay. As the crow flies, the opposite side of the bay was so close and it was quite a quick journey with a boat. But in a car the route twisted through tiny lanes up and down the undulations of the landscape. Despite the proximity the geology of the south and the north of the Helford was different.

'Not sure why's she's getting married.'

'She's in love.'

He humphed. 'What good does love do?'

'Plenty.'

'My parents were a shining example.' He ran his fingers through his hair.

'They loved each other.' I tilted my head to the side. If I kept this light, I might reach him. The loss of his mother and aunt had hit us all hard. But when his father George ignored his doctor's warning and continued drinking, he all but gave himself the heart attack that killed him. Jack had pleaded with his father to slow down, to stop drinking and to remember that Peta and Jack needed him, loved him. George hadn't heard. Grief had made him deaf to all but his own pain. In 2002 Jack had buried both his parents and his own heart shortly thereafter.

'That's my point. Too much love and look what that produced.' His piercing blue eyes stared at me. They hadn't missed much over the years. Always perceptive and sensitive when young, it distressed me to see them so hard now.

'You and Peta.'

He laughed and despite his cold veneer I knew falling in love was exactly what he needed. However I doubted he would ever let that happen, which saddened me. At least for a brief moment in time I too had known love and had swum in its all-encompassing waters. I knew from watching others that it could have been lifelong. The war had made short work of long term, the same way it had made short work of life and of death. But I had had love, at least, with all the fireworks.

I looked at Jack. He was a good if contained man. His grandfather had had that same manner, which had hidden his passion. Andrew had loved me far more than I him. He'd never asked from me more than I could give. It had worked, but then we had been past the first flush of youth when we had married.

I walked to the window. Despite being August, the weather had other plans. Guilt ran around me like the raindrops racing down the window. When Andrew – or Commodore Rowse, as he was then – had come to stay in Windward in 1964 with his family, I'd been keeping the roof above it by taking in bed and breakfast guests. My world shook when he walked through the door with his children. He was so much a part of the past I'd tried to forget. But by the end of their three-week visit he'd convinced me to marry him. I'm still not sure how. My heart had been locked tightly away. It might have been the way this gentle widower behaved with his two teenagers, and was so clearly devoted to them. He'd wanted their time on holiday to be special yet he'd dragged me out on picnics with them and reminded me that laughter was possible again – especially with games of beach cricket.

'What's making you smile?'

'Thoughts of your grandfather.' I touched his hand. 'It may not have been the state of passion that Peta is in with Fred, but it was good and it was worth having.'

'If you say so.' He flexed his shoulders. 'I've got some work to do.'

I frowned. He didn't need to work – he had plenty of money from selling the accountancy widget thing he'd created. And yet, for the hell of it, he played with numbers doing the accounts for a few local firms. He should have been focusing on living, but he wouldn't be told.

❊ Nine ❊

Eventide, Falmouth Heights, Cape Cod, Massachusetts
26 August 2015

Walking back into the kitchen, Lara straightened the cookbooks on the shelf. Comfort food. She knew the recipe by heart for the Jordan Marsh blueberry muffins. It was a hot day to be baking but she didn't care. The house would smell wonderful and she could eat the results. She preheated the oven, greased the tins and then began to measure the ingredients.

Leo walked through the back door carrying a newspaper as she was creaming the butter and sugar together. He stuck a finger into the bowl and she slapped his hand.

'Oi.' She dipped her own finger into the bowl and tasted the mixture. The butter melted in her mouth. She sighed.

'What's up?' he asked.

She frowned. 'Am I that transparent?'

'To me.' He watched her measure out the dry ingredients. 'You've always cooked when you are worried.'

She stopped mixing, dusted the blueberries in flour and then added a pinch of cinnamon to the mix.

'Spill.' He sat on the counter not far from where she was working.

'If I'm honest, I think I'm afraid to leave here ... that it will be gone when I return.'

He stuck his finger in the batter again. 'It will be.'

'You're so matter of fact.'

'It makes it easier.'

'Does it?' She tilted her head to one side and studied him.

'You need to move on. We all do.'

'True.' When she'd filled the tins she handed the bowl and mixture-covered spoon to Leo before she put the muffins into the oven.

'Afraid of travel?'

Wincing, she said, 'A bit. Of flying, at least.' She set the timer. 'Also the irrational fear that we shouldn't dig into Grandie's past.'

'Adele, you mean.' He polished off the batter on the spoon and began on the bowl.

She nodded.

He took a breath. 'We all have secrets.'

Lara laughed. 'Yeah, I know, but he was so ... straight.'

'True.' He sighed. 'I doubt you'll find anything out about either Amelia or Adele, whoever she was. But you'll have a good break with Cassie and return refreshed.'

Lara smiled. 'Thanks.'

'A pleasure. And now on this glorious day, let's take a trip down memory lane once the muffins are done.' He put the finished bowl in the sink.

Shaking the sand off her towel, Lara climbed into Leo's car. They hadn't spent a day on the beach together in years. And this one, Craigville, had been a favourite of Grandie's. It had been an inspired choice on Leo's part. With the car door still open, she brushed the sand off her feet, slipped her flip-flops on and breathed in the scent of suntan lotion carried on the breeze. Leo made his way through the families spread across the beach to join her.

'Now for an ice cream,' he said, climbing in and starting the engine.

'Perfect.' Lara leaned back and pulled her salt-crisped hair into a ponytail. This whole day had been a healing one.

'Four Seas.'

Lara smiled. A trip to the ice cream parlour had always been Grandie's way to tempt them off the beach. According to him

Four Seas had the best ice cream on the Cape, and the full parking lot as they arrived confirmed this. Lara looked to see if the board still hung outside listing the flavours. As a child her favourite had always been peppermint stick but as an adult she'd learned to appreciate the perfection of vanilla. Some might call it boring but the subtle balance of the sweet with the spice was a hard-won thing. Too much of either and the ice cream was over-sweet or overpowering. She appreciated both the quick all-in method of making a light vanilla and the richness of a custard-based one. It depended on what if anything it was being paired with and what had come before. People had so little appreciation of how their main course could affect their enjoyment of their dessert. They would often be better off experiencing a set meal where the chef was aware of the blending of flavours.

She shrugged away her thoughts and pulled open the parlour's screen door. Right now she was famished.

'Shall we grab a table and enjoy being here rather than just taking a cone away?' Leo gave her a questioning glance.

'You read my mind.' Lara smiled and followed him to the bright blue booths. Once seated, she saw a sign above the door advertising banana splits. She must have been twelve the last time she'd had one. Her mouth watered.

A waitress arrived and placed glasses of water on the table. 'I'll give you a minute.'

'No need. I know what I'm having.' Lara looked at Leo. He grinned.

'Great.' The waitress pulled out her pad and pencil.

'I'll have the banana split with vanilla ice cream.'

'Do you want strawberries too?'

Lara thought about the sweet stickiness of the berries with the chocolate sauce, the vanilla and the banana. 'Yes, please.'

'Anything else?' she asked.

'A black coffee, thanks.'

The waitress turned to Leo.

'Could I have the same, please?' He smiled and glanced at Lara. 'Well, you didn't look like you'd share.' She laughed. He took his sunglasses off the top of his head. 'So let's get down to important stuff.'

Lara looked up, worried.

'Are you OK for money?'

Before she could answer, their coffee arrived, giving her time to think. 'Well,' she said at last, 'I don't have a mortgage any more and I'm still being paid. So I should be fine for a while.'

'Good. And you're smiling.'

'It's been a great day.' She grinned. 'Thanks.'

'It was obviously the salt water.'

She laughed. 'Grandie said that about everything from cuts and bruises to a cold.'

'I know. But he was right. We're both better for today.'

'We are.'

The waitress brought their banana splits. Leo picked the cherry off the top and offered it to Lara. She didn't hesitate and ate it immediately. It was childhood all over again. She took up the long spoon and dug down deep to capture a bit of all the flavours.

'So now is a good time to tell you something.' Leo looked serious despite his words. 'I know it's all been rough – the divorce, Grandie's death – and I know how tough you are.' He looked at her. 'But you need to go easy on yourself.' He gave her a lopsided smile. 'You've just lost two of your greatest loves.'

'Thank you for reminding me.' She peered at the melting mess at the bottom of the bowl. It was a good representation of her life.

'Sorry. But on the upside, Grandie has left you some money.' He took a sip of coffee.

'What?' Her head shot up.

'So it's time to plan your life while you're away.' Leo leaned back and studied her.

'I didn't expect anything.' The ice cream was almost melted and she took another mouthful. The mix hit her taste buds with the sweet sharpness of the berries and the buttery richness of the chocolate sauce.

'I know, and he wanted it kept a secret.'

'Why?' She pushed the dish away. She could use another coffee to help her think.

'At the time I helped him to update the will I thought he was just being discreet, but now I'm beginning to think Grandie liked secrets.'

'You mean like Adele?'

Leo nodded, then looked up from her, and his mouth broke into a big smile as he stood. 'Why, if it isn't Judith Warren,' he said.

'Leo.' A tall dark-haired woman kissed him on both cheeks. 'Let me introduce you to my husband, Tristan Trevillion.'

Leo shook his hand. 'Why don't you join my sister Lara and me?'

'Would love to, but we haven't got the time. I'm trying to show Tristan the highlights. It's his first trip to the Cape.' She took Tristan's hand and Lara envied the happiness radiating from them both. Tristan's eyes reminded Lara of the sea and their gaze barely left Judith.

'Here for John's wedding?' Leo asked.

'Yes.' Judith blushed, looking slightly awkward, and Lara made a mental note to ask Leo more about John. She wondered if he was a friend from the law firm.

'I'm so happy for him.' Judith smiled.

'Me too.' Leo raised an eyebrow. 'How's life in England?'

'Love it. I can't begin to say how much Cornwall suits me.'

Lara's eyes opened wide.

'I'd forgotten that's where you went.' Leo turned towards Lara. 'Lara will be there soon to do a bit of family history research.'

Judith pulled a card out of her bag. 'How wonderful. You'll love it. If you find yourself near the Helford River, give us a call.'

'Thanks, that's exactly where I'll be staying.' Lara smiled, tucking the card into her own bag.

'Then definitely call.' Judith turned to Leo. 'See you next week at John's wedding and congrats on your news.' She glanced at Lara. 'I know it's a secret but I hear congratulations are in order for you. I saw Deborah last night at her parents'. She looks so happy I guessed the news and she confessed.'

Lara's glance shot from Judith to Leo. His face filled with colour as he nodded.

'Thanks,' he said.

Leo remained standing until Judith and Tristan had reached the counter. Lara glared at him the whole time, giving him the full death-stare, until he finally looked back at her, his expression awkward and tense.

'Sorry,' he said. 'I was about to tell you.'

Lara took a few deep breaths, fighting back the tears.

'Seriously I was. In fact the next thing I was going to say was that I needed you back in December for the wedding. Will you be my best man?'

Lara opened her mouth to speak, then shut it again. Of course she would stand up for her brother. Deborah, his girl-friend – *fiancée*, she corrected herself – was great, but it hit her that now more than ever she was truly alone. 'Of course.'

'I'm sorry you heard this way.' He reached across the table. 'We only decided after the funeral.' He picked up her hand. 'Losing Grandie made me realise I didn't want to waste another day.' His grip tightened. 'Today was all about us having some time together so that I could tell you.'

'I'm thrilled for you both.' Lara looked into her brother's eyes, so like her own. They were filled with happiness. She wanted that kind of happiness for herself, but she'd blown her chance.

'You'll be OK, Runt. Pierre wasn't the right one. You'll find your soul mate.'

A tear wobbled on the corner of her eye and she blinked.

'Do you remember the scandal when a friend of mine was left at the altar?'

Lara nodded, wondering where this was leading.

'It was John who was left and Judith was the woman who ran away.'

Now Lara knew why the reference to John had made Judith

blush. She scanned the crowd at the counter but Judith and Tristan had gone. 'She doesn't look the type.'

'No, but she did the right thing, although it didn't seem that way at the time.'

'The right thing?'

'Yes, she knew it wasn't right and she didn't do what everyone expected of her.' He stared at her and Lara looked away. Leo knew her so well.

Lee Tide

But no Man moved Me – till the Tide
Went past my simple Shoe –
And past my Apron – and my Belt
And past my Boddice – too

EMILY DICKINSON, 656

❈ Ten ❈

London
1 December 1943

Dearest Half,

I'm so sorry you couldn't get leave to meet me in London. I missed you.

I'm in love, I'm in love, I'm in love, I'm in love! I don't know how we managed to both have leave at the same time, but I was with Eddie in London. From the moment he met me at the station and pulled me into his arms and covered me in kisses I was lost. In some ways I felt like I was living your life in London except I wasn't sneaking out to go to the 400. What an evening we had. Aunt Margaret loaned me a dress and we danced, how we danced. Just to be in his arms was enough. But it wasn't, of course. He told me he loved me. I'm in heaven but you know that. We only had forty-eight hours and I don't think I slept at all until I was on the train. I didn't want to miss a minute with him.

I placed the letter down, ignoring the pang of jealousy. It couldn't be real love. It was too quick. Surely it was infatuation like Philip and me. Love was a slow thing. It had to be if it was meant to last a lifetime. That's what I'd always been told. I touched my lips, wondering what the kisses had felt like. Those few innocent embraces with Philip had only hinted at more. Amelia's excitement was with me. I shivered. She'd been so near.

There was a thump from the floor below and a happy shout.

97

Tomorrow training finished. I looked around my cabin. The others were all out. I would miss their chatter and silly pranks. It had been a bit like boarding, except the work was much more important, if boring. I paced the floor. Excitement bubbled in me, as did worry. Eddie was wonderful and in truth perfect for her, but … I picked up a pen and sheet of paper then settled on my bed with a book to use as a desk.

Dearest Half,

Have you lost your mind? It's madness to fall in love now. Your heart will be broken, especially with a pilot. But Eddie is wonderful, no argument. And I have seen him as you know and he has eyes for no other.

I thought of Philip. I hadn't been in love with him. But with his death a part of me had died too.

Wait for love after this war. Someday it will end and then it will be safe to love. I have to believe it will. I can hear you saying you don't intend to put your life on hold and that we may all be dead tomorrow.

I put my pen down and looked at the photograph on top of the chest of drawers that I shared with Sue. We were only allowed one picture and hers was of George – George of the heavy spectacles and lopsided grin. I'd become rather used to having him there next to my photograph of Mother and Father that Amelia had taken at Windward two summers ago. Although the picture of them was in black and white, it had caught the rays of the setting sun falling on the bark of the old pine tree, and even now I could remember the almost-red glow on the trunk.

Sue popped her head around the door. 'Fancy a cup of tea?'

'Yes.' I stood up. 'I'll meet you downstairs.' I tucked the letter under my pillow, figuring I'd finish it later. I was distracted and wasn't really focusing on it, mainly because I was half wondering where I would be posted. We would find out tomorrow.

Downstairs I listened to the chatter and was surprised to find Sue standing in the galley alone. We had left HMS *Pembroke* in Mill Hill and this private home in Hampstead where we were now quartered felt like a girls' dormitory combined with a grand house. The months here had flown by, lost in the dots and dashes of Morse.

'Excited?' Sue turned from the teapot as I entered.

'Yes.'

'Scared?'

I bit my lip. 'A little, but I'm also desperate to start doing something worthwhile.'

'Hmm.' She handed me a cup. 'Do you think we'll get leave?'

I shrugged. I hadn't been back to Cornwall since I'd left six months ago. It had been early summer then and now it was almost Christmas. I didn't feel quite whole away from my home, but that was what the war did. It took parts of you and only if you were lucky would they come back. Maybe that's what Mother had meant when she'd said we were lost. After all, the Great War had taken many of their generation. Mother had been lucky that Father had survived. 'It would be good to go home for the holidays,' I said, 'but they may want us to relieve others.'

'True.'

'Heard from George?' I saw the letter on the counter.

She smiled. 'Yes. All was well as of ten days ago.'

'I don't know how you bear it.'

'You do. We all do.'

I sipped my tea. 'My aunt makes light of my uncle being gone, but I can see the worry in her eyes.' I blew on the surface of the tea. 'I see it in your eyes too. A letter arrives and your spirits lift but then there's a long gap and although you smile I know you're worried sick.'

Sue laughed. 'You can't always choose when to love. It chooses you.'

'Pah. You have a choice in everything.'

99

'Do you?' She stroked the outside of the envelope. I knew there was no sense having this discussion with her.

'Just you wait, Adele,' she said. 'When you aren't looking, someone will steal your heart, and then, only then, will you understand. I can't wait to see it happen.'

I laughed. 'Not likely.'

We stood to attention as our Chief Wren came in. 'Ready for tomorrow?' she asked.

We nodded. Tomorrow was the passing-out parade and the Duchess of Kent would be there. Despite the general excitement, I didn't think this would go well. I was supposed to lead the parade, having achieved the highest marks in telegraphy, but marching was still not my forte.

HMS *Attack*, Portland, Dorset
6 December 1943

I emerged from the tunnels and dragged fresh air into my lungs. Even though the tunnels were ventilated, I couldn't help thinking the atmosphere inside them was as tired as I was. However, it made the end of my shift more of a delight as I felt the wind on my face and smelt the tang of the sea. HMS *Attack* in Portland hadn't been my choice at all, but none of us had been sent to posts that we had selected. The war had needs of its own and had dictated our transfers. At least, like Cornwall, the water was everywhere in Portland. Although not a ship, in some ways with the sea surrounding the peninsula it did feel like a boat, especially with the harbour filled with so much activity. Just days ago I'd come on the train across the long, narrow stretch of land that connected Portland to Dorset. Chesil Beach lined the west side of this strip and the east side curved around the harbour as Portland rounded outward and upward from the water like a tassel dangling off the south coast of England.

From the base of the hill on this grey December day, I looked across the rough expanse of water to the chalk cliffs that marked the Dorset coast. None of Cornwall's dark dramatic rocks were here, only clean bright ones. I needed to write to Amelia, not that I could tell her much. I longed to describe where I worked. With each shift I entered the tunnels at the base of the hill behind HMS *Attack*. The wall curved up and around, echoing the shape of the almost circular metal plate that held the door at the entrance. I imagined it was like we were large moles when I walked up the corridor. Each room off the hallway, which bent around in a squared-off U, was a hive of focused activity. It was so different from training. Distraction was everywhere, from someone's footsteps to a sneeze. The signals never seemed to be clear. My head hurt from trying so hard to listen. There was no room for mistakes now.

The wind was bitterly cold, reminding me of standing in the garden looking out over the bay. I wouldn't be home for Christmas. It would be the first time Amelia and I had been apart for it. I wasn't sure how I felt. Loss, yes, but also a sense of freedom. I was sure that as Christmas Eve came I would long to be with my family, but right at that moment I felt a purpose that I'd never felt before.

The wind tugged at my hair and threatened my hat as I walked up the steep incline to our quarters, a Nissen hut built into the sloping base of the cliffs. All the cabins were named after ships and housed six girls in double bunks. The five others in mine had all had been welcoming, despite the cabin's name being 'Tormentor'. But it was early days, and I'd only just finished my sixth shift. Straightening my shoulders, I took a deep breath then another before I walked into the building. The blur of voices chatting sounded loud compared to the Morse tapping I had been listening to for the past hours in the tunnels.

Georgette, one of my room-mates, greeted me as she looked up from the letter she was reading. I nodded in her direction. Judging from the red flush on her cheek, it must be from her fiancé. His picture rested on a chest of drawers. He had a kind face that I didn't mind looking at when I went to get my clothing. However, another one of the girls, Pat, had taken up with one of the Americans, and his smile irritated me as it beamed from the photograph beside her bunk. I couldn't say why except that it was just too big and brash. I'd thought there were lots of Americans in London, but they were *everywhere* here. I couldn't avoid them even though I tried. They were our allies, of course, and I knew we needed them, but that didn't mean we had to like them.

I shook my head. I sounded like my grandmother sometimes.

Georgette glanced at her watch. 'I'd lost track of the time.' Folding the letter, she tucked it in her bra, above her heart. I watched her walk away and said a silent prayer for the opportunity to be alone, but then Pat arrived and slipped some stockings into her drawer. Without her telling me, I knew where they were from – the Yanks. I couldn't say that I wasn't jealous about the stockings – that would have been a lie – but I just didn't like the thought that there might have been some payment in kind for them. The Americans were oversexed and over here. On the train the other night, one of them kept running his hand up and down my leg, but it was hard to confront someone in the dark. No matter how many times I pushed that hand away, it came back, along with his beery breath.

'Adele.' Pat stood up. She was a good head taller than me, dark and exotic. Her eyes smiled when she spoke and despite her choice of boyfriend I liked her. She worked on the docks, doing maintenance in the electrical workshops. In her overalls and headscarf she didn't look glamorous, but it was all there in her full mouth and almond-shaped eyes. 'Going down to eat?' She straightened.

'In a moment, need to collect myself a bit.'

'It can all be a bit much to start.' She smiled and slipped out the door. I sank on to my bed and pulled my writing pad from under the pillow.

Made it through my sixth shift. It feels so different from all the training – so important. Not surprising but still a shock. I can't say much except that sometimes it's so boring and then at other times I haven't a moment to think. What I do has to be automatic and I pray I don't make a mistake. I don't think it breaks any rules to tell you I work underground. The ceiling curves around you and you can smell the damp, the odour of bodies and something that could almost be adrenaline. But I miss fresh air and daylight. When working it's like I slip into another, endless world.

While I think about it, can you have a word with Mother? She seems to be under the illusion I am on a boat. I tried to tell her Attack was a shore establishment and it was just a Navy thing to call them after old warships. She just wasn't listening and went on about the war going so badly that they were putting women on ships. She worked herself into a real state.

I paused, then scratched out the last three sentences.

Right now I would like to collapse on the bed drinking cocoa until I fall asleep, but I'll head to the mess hall and be sociable for a while. In some ways you would have been more suited to this type of life, a bit like when we boarded. You thrived on the busyness and the camaraderie while I hid in the library. I miss you right now. I would send you to be in my place, to be the social butterfly, but down to the mess I must go.

I placed the pad and pen back under my pillow. I would finish the letter tonight and post it tomorrow. Maybe it was being so close to the sea, but I was homesick for Cornwall, for Windward. The trees would be bare, so the vistas normally hidden from the house would be on view. I swallowed, missing home and missing Amelia.

London
20 December 1943

I stood in the lobby of the Savoy waiting for Father. He was late but that wasn't unusual these days. The world was upside down, or at least London was, but it did at least feel a bit like Christmas, especially with the decorations in the window displays I had peered into on my journey here. This opportunity to come to London had happened at the last minute. I wouldn't be home for the holidays, but it would be wonderful to see Father and at least have some contact with my family. I'd thought I would be fine about being away for Christmas, but as it approached I couldn't deny the longing I felt.

Elegant women swayed in on the arms of men in evening dress. I was still in uniform. I had hoped to change at Aunt Margaret's but there hadn't been time. My overnight bag with my dress in it sat at my feet. I longed to change, as dinner at the Savoy was a treat. Looking up, I saw a tall American lieutenant watching me. A smile hovered on his lips and there was a gleam in his eyes.

I couldn't help myself. My mouth lifted in response then I looked at my watch. Father had been due half an hour ago. The American walked over to me.

'Is your date late, ma'am?' he asked. His voice was deep and his eyes blue. My nose crinkled. Father and 'date' didn't quite go together.

'Yes, he is.'

'So is mine. I think I've been stood up.'

Over six feet, with broad shoulders, I doubted anyone would stand up this dark-haired officer even if he were American. 'I'm positive I haven't been.' My smile was prim. I knew it. Americans were so forward. I scanned the people milling through the lobby, looking for any familiar face.

'I like confidence in a woman.'

Laughter burst out of me. I could be confident that my father wouldn't stand me up, but not so confident had it been a real date. Then I frowned. I'd never been on one.

'What have I said?' he asked.

'Nothing. Sorry.'

'What are you sorry for?' He tilted his head to the side and I could see yellow flecks in his blue eyes. They were intelligent eyes, and not frivolous as I had supposed.

'"Sorry" is the English way of avoiding the subject or filling a gap in conversation,' I said.

'I see.' The corners of his full mouth lifted. 'I know this is forward, but shall we give them both another ten minutes, and if they don't appear, may I take you to dinner?'

I glanced again at my watch, as if that would somehow make my father waltz through the front door. A polite way to say 'no' hovered on my lips. How would Amelia handle this? I needed her right at this moment. Looking up, I saw the American was smiling, but not in a cocky way.

'Yes, that would be fine,' I said.

'Fine?'

'Yes, fine.'

He chuckled and it seemed to come from deep within. My grin widened and to my surprise I found myself hoping my father would be late – maybe because of a sudden emergency that required his medical knowledge. At eight thirty in the evening that would be unusual, but it was the war and nothing was out of the ordinary any more – even accepting dinner invitations from strange American officers.

'I'm Bobby Webster.' He held out his hand. It appeared strong and showed signs of having been outdoors a great deal. A large gold ring stood out on the tanned skin. It wasn't a signet but worn on his left ring finger.

'Adele Seaton.' He clasped my hand in his. My skin looked so pale in comparison to his, but then I'd been working inside for weeks on end. I imagined he might have been training outdoors – somewhere in the southern States possibly.

'Lovely to meet you. May I call you Adele?'

I squinted. The Americans were so casual. How the world had changed in the past few years. I pressed my lips together. He was far too familiar, yet he had asked, and it would seem churlish to say no, so I nodded.

Then I looked up and saw my father enter the lobby, closely followed by a sour-looking major. Father spotted me immediately, and I turned to the lieutenant. 'Thank you for the kind offer, but my date has arrived. Goodbye.' I extended my hand. The American held mine for a second too long and disappointment flashed in his eyes. My heart raced and I knew I felt the same way. He released my fingers and I dashed towards Father, away from the temptation of the lieutenant with beautiful eyes.

'My darling girl.' Father swept me into his arms and held me close for a moment before setting me back onto my feet and indicating to his right. 'Let me introduce you to Major Percival Parkes.'

'Major.' I nodded and waited for him to respond, but he turned to my father, and as he did so I saw Bobby Webster slip past us, out of the lobby and into the darkness.

'I haven't long,' said the major.

'Yes, sorry.' Father took my hand. 'I hate to do this but I need to have dinner with Parkes, as we ran out of hours today. I'll meet you day after tomorrow for lunch. Come to the office, yes?' He gave my arm a squeeze.

'Of course.' I tiptoed and kissed him on the cheek. I could see he didn't want to do this but had no choice.

'Thank you, darling,' he said. I watched as they walked towards the basement, where the restaurant had been located since the Blitz, before I turned back to the main doors and left the lobby.

Out in the darkness I strode to the Strand, hoping there wouldn't be an air raid. As I allowed my eyes to adjust, I wondered if Aunt Margaret had any food in the house. My stomach growled, reminding me I'd been cheated out of a dinner at the Savoy. I could have had supper with Lt Webster had I known. It was always the way. My luck always ran to what could have been. Had it been Amelia here and not me, she would have accepted the handsome American and left Father without a companion. She was a law unto herself. Yet that was the thing. I was not my twin. I was Adele and I needed to be just me without her. It was hard but I hadn't told anyone since I began training in June I was a twin. Over the years I had learned that if that fact came out, everything focused on the circus show of being identical twins and not on anything else.

In the distance I heard a bus and hoped it was the number 9, which would take me to Kensington. A long bath might just make up for the missed meal, if there was enough hot water when I reached my aunt's. I adjusted my hat and walked towards the bus stop, trying not to think about food.

Sadly it was not the right bus, but the evening was mild so I strolled along, hoping I'd find a café where I could at least get a cup of tea. My mind raced through the possibilities of what could be so important that Father had to spend the evening talking to the major. Yes, doctors were important but I found it hard to believe that my father was organising things. It was Mother who had always kept our lives on course. But maybe the war had brought something out in him that he hadn't needed before. It certainly had with so many others, including me.

I stumbled when my shoe caught on a raised bit of pavement. Hands steadied me. 'Sorry,' I said.

'Careful how you go, love,' a man said.

'I will.' I moved forward, glancing between my feet and the darkness in front, telling myself to be extra careful how I proceeded. What had I been thinking accepting an invitation from a stranger? Was that me or had Amelia snuck into my head? Or for a mad moment had Lt Webster swept all logical thoughts from me? I stopped walking and smiled. It was certainly the latter.

❋ Eleven ❋

Windward, Mawnan Smith, Falmouth, Cornwall
27 August 2015

I cursed the confusion of the recycling pile. Instead of last Saturday's papers, which I'd wanted, I'd picked up the one from two weeks ago and it was filled with nothing but the anniversary of VJ Day. First VE day, now VJ Day. I tossed the papers aside. My world had altered on both days. My memories of that time would remain mine and no one else's. I picked up the letters from the old suitcase and brought them with me to the garden. The sun was warm and the breeze westerly.

A slight haze hung above the sea, but on shore it was clear. I was sad for Peta that the roses were finished. Roses blooming for a wedding always spoke to me of happiness. However, she had collected the blooms earlier in the summer and saved them for throwing. On her dress she had sewn silk petals to the bottom half of the skirt. It glistened when she turned around. The clever girl had designed it herself. It was all so different from the wedding day seventy years ago. During rationing, a remade dress had had to do. It shouldn't have mattered, but nothing had been how it ought to that day, including the bride and groom.

With my cane I batted away a fly resting on the arm of the chair. The chair rocked with the force. Pain radiated up my arm. I took a deep breath, suddenly remembering Mother's pearls, the ones with the diamond clasp. She had worn them when she'd been presented at court. Somewhere there was a picture. Those pearls, I wondered where they were. They suited young skin, not old. Maybe I should find them and give them to Peta.

I sat down and fingered the strand of pearls around my own neck. South Sea, and very beautiful. They were from Andrew, a wedding present. I had been forty-two then, still young in many ways.

'Gran?' Peta waltzed out to me. 'Are you hiding?' She sat on the low wall that divided the garden from the vast expanse of lawn.

'No. '

'I was looking for you and I tried everywhere,' she said.

'I often sit here.'

'True, but not normally at this time of day.'

I nodded. 'Why were you looking for me?'

She frowned. 'I could feel you. You felt unhappy, angry even.'

'Peta, please, please don't use that mumbo jumbo on me.'

'I have no control over it. I was working on the finishing touches of your outfit and I felt pain, so I downed tools and decided to find you.'

'Well, you have, and I'm alive and enjoying the afternoon in the garden under the Monterey.'

Peta's hand reached out and touched the letters. I knew if I stopped her it would make her more curious so I let her stroke them and forced myself to think about the beautiful blue dress she had designed for me to wear for her wedding. She was talented and should do more with her skills than she was at the moment. All this falling in love had stopped her.

'Gran, you are pleased about the wedding?'

'Yes, dear.' I turned to the sea. A gull rose on a thermal before diving down out of view.

She looked up from the letters, straight at me. 'Don't lie.'

'It's the polite thing to do.'

'You're not polite.' She tucked a wayward strand of hair behind her ear. 'Actually you are, but you're wicked sometimes too.' She chuckled. 'Oh Gran, you had a wonderful marriage to Grandad so why are you worried about me getting married? It's not Fred, is it?'

'No, Fred is kind.'

'That sounds dismissive.'

'It's not meant to be.' I paused, thinking. 'You're very young.'

She took one of my hands in hers. 'This is a problem?'

'No.'

'Gran. Something obviously *is* a problem. And I'd rather you'd said it than silently disapprove.'

I laughed. 'What about your work?'

'Ah, I see.'

'Do you?' I looked out to the bay and watched a yacht tack. 'How will you live?'

'Fred is about to become a partner in his father's business. I will continue to design dresses for the bridal market.'

'Will it be enough?'

Peta smiled. 'I can provide for myself.'

'Can you?'

'Yes.'

'Then don't worry about the thoughts of an old woman.'

Peta touched the pile of letters again. 'But I do.'

'No need.'

She stood, then bent to kiss my cheek. She smelt of lily of the valley, a scent from another time.

Falmouth Docks Train Station, Cornwall
28 August 2015

The small train pulled into the station and Lara could see Cassie talking on her mobile, standing by a white van with *Cassandra's Catering* emblazoned on the side. Cassie waved to her and pointed at the phone, then the smile fell from her face as she continued her conversation.

Lara disembarked from the train and made her way across to the van, arriving just as Cassie finished her call, flung out an arm and hugged her close. 'I can't begin to say how good it is to see you,' she said.

Lara grinned. 'Same.'

'Although I can see you're jet-lagged.' Cassie chuckled and

took Lara's bag, stowing it in the rear of the van. 'Hope you don't mind, but I have to stop at a client's to drop off a cake.'

'No problem.' Lara had climbed into the van and sat down before she realised she was in the driver's seat, the steering wheel in front of her. Being in England was going to take some getting used to.

'You may want to try something a bit smaller for your first drive here,' Cassie laughed.

Lara grinned apologetically and went to the passenger's side. Briefly, she wondered when she would begin to feel human again. Despite having slept a large portion of the train journey and consumed vast quantities of water, she felt worse than when she'd landed.

'You'll see what I mean as we head off.' Cassie drove out of the parking lot and came to a small circle on the road. She hadn't been joking: the roads seemed far too tiny for all but the most compact of cars.

'Is this a rotary?' Lara took a large swig from her water bottle.

'Haven't heard that word in years, but yes. This one is a mini roundabout.' Cassie cast a glance in Lara's direction as she navigated the car up a steep, narrow street. 'Good flight?'

'Good?' Lara tried to focus on the scenery. 'Well, we arrived.'

Cassie laughed. 'You always hated flying.' She turned the van down a road that Lara was positive was far too small for the width of the van.

'Give me a train any day.' Lara frowned, then gasped as a large expanse of bright blue water appeared in front of her. 'What's that?' She pointed.

'Falmouth Bay.' Cassie shifted down a gear. 'Do you remember that trip to California with my parents?'

Lara nodded. 'I was sick on both flights.'

Cassie laughed. 'It was a great trip despite that.'

Lara nodded, noticing the scenery becoming more breathtaking as the road grew narrower and more rural. 'Now on to a different subject. Grandie and World War II.'

Cassie slowed down as they came towards a beach. 'If you pay attention, there are signs of the war everywhere around here.'

Lara could see only a beautiful sweep of sand covered in families, but Cassie continued: 'Look over your shoulder then up from the rocks and you'll see two pillboxes.' Lara squinted, but they were almost up the hill before she spotted what she assumed were the pillboxes, low-built concrete structures with small rectangular windows. 'You'll find more evidence on the Helford.' Cassie reversed to let an oncoming vehicle pass. Lara held her breath, thinking that there was no way the car would be able to get by them. There was barely enough space for one vehicle let alone two.

At the top of the incline she glimpsed the bright expanse of sea in the gaps between some houses. 'These properties have a spectacular setting.'

'They do. We'll be heading to one of them in a minute to drop off a wedding cake.'

'You do wedding cakes?'

'I make them when asked but I don't ice them – I mean, frost them.' She smiled and Lara knew she was thinking of the time they'd tried making frosting with chocolate spread.

'Well,' she said, 'you remember how our last attempt came out.'

'I do, but it did taste good.'

'True.'

They pulled between granite gateposts. Lara read the sign – Windward – and thought it was a good name for a house in this position. The drive wound through large rhododendrons until it opened out into what looked like a small orchard.

'I'm catering a wedding here in just over two weeks' time.' Cassie smiled as she pulled up by the house. 'It's for a mate, Peta, and should be fabulous.'

She turned off the engine and her phone rang. 'Sorry, I need to take this. It's about the event tomorrow night. Can you grab the large box at the back and take it to the side door? It's normally open. Just walk in and drop it off.' With that, she turned and answered the phone. 'Hello, Cassie here.'

Lara took a deep breath as she walked to the rear of the van. She could smell cut grass and the scent of the sea. The cake box was large and carefully secured at the back. It was also heavier than she had expected, but then she remembered the preference in the UK for fruit cakes.

As she rounded the side of the imposing grey building, Cassie's voice faded away. Lara's glance travelled up the stone walls to a tower that topped the house, reminding her of a fort. The room in the tower had windows on all sides and she thought it must have the most amazing view. All the windows had stone surrounds that made the building look older than she guessed it was.

She tried to watch her step on the slate-covered path. The surface was uneven and the box blocked her view. As Cassie had said, the door to the kitchen was open. Lara paused on the threshold. She may have been told to just walk in, but it wasn't how she'd been raised.

'Hello?' She leaned through the doorway, blinking. As her eyes adjusted, she saw a large open fireplace filled with a massive range cooker and a table big enough to seat eight or more at a pinch. 'Hello?'

When she still didn't get a response, she hesitated with one foot on the step and the other one out.

'Who the hell are you?'

Lara jumped backwards, missing the step and bashing her hand against the doorframe. 'Shit.' The cake box fell, and she tried in vain to stop it from hitting the ground. The lid popped open, revealing several layers of cake broken in half. When she looked up, piercing blue eyes and a scowl were inches from her. She swallowed.

The man picked up the box, swearing under his breath. After he put it on the counter, he turned to her. She'd seen that aggressive look before. More than a few chefs along the way had bawled her out, and a key skill was learning how to take it and not fight back. Unlike what she had done when she quit her job a month ago.

He lifted his gaze from the broken cake and stared at her. 'You haven't answered my question.'

'I'm Lara … Pearce.' She knew it had been a mistake to

hesitate. His eyes narrowed as if he thought she was lying. She should be practised at saying Lara Pearce by now, but her instincts kept trying to make her say McNulty, her married name.

'Are you sure?' He placed a hand into his jeans pocket and leant against the counter. Lean and tense, he was about Leo's six foot two, and she felt small in his presence. The dropped cake couldn't be the source of his hostility.

'Yes, I'm sorry about dropping the cake.'

'I bet you are.' He stepped closer. Lara didn't budge. She knew it wasn't all her fault, but in dealing with customers it always was. They would ask for medium rare and yet would complain about too much blood. There'd been many times she'd wanted to head into the dining room and give a lecture on how to cook meat.

'I'll replace it.' She smiled despite the pain in her hand where she had hit it.

'Where's Cassie?' His voice was deep and now sounded less angry.

'On her cell.'

He shook his head. 'Bloody Americans think they can fix everything.'

Lara bit her lip to stop herself answering back. She was more than capable of making a cake.

He lifted half of the top layer of the broken fruit cake. 'Just don't bother, alright? No one will notice when it's iced. The marriage is going to end up like this anyway.'

Lara gasped at his comment. Was he the groom?

He looked up from the cake. 'Don't worry Cassie about it. She's a perfectionist and I don't want you to lose your job.'

Lara opened her mouth then shut it. There was no point in correcting him. It would just prolong the encounter. He watched her, expecting her to say something. 'Thanks.' She turned and strolled back to the van, thinking what a strange man he was. Good luck to this Peta in dealing with him.

Lara climbed into the van and waited for Cassie to finish her call. Once she was finished and had clambered back behind the steering wheel, Lara expelled a long breath. 'I have a confession to make. Also, that's one interesting groom.'

'So Fred was there?' Cassie beamed as she started the van and headed back down the drive. 'He's the nicest guy you'd want to meet. He and his father, Anthony, renovated the barn for me.'

Lara frowned, studying the view down the drive to the fields glimpsed over the top of the hedges. 'I wouldn't say nice at all. Bitter seems closer to the truth.' Out of the window, the scenery changed as they moved away from the coast through a village. 'Surprised he's getting married at all, considering he thinks it'll fail.'

Cassie laughed. 'That wasn't Fred.'

Lara turned to her, frowning.

'Was he tall, moody, beautiful eyes and a body to die for?' asked Cassie.

Lara nodded. Despite her anger, she couldn't dispute any of those things.

'That's Jack, Peta's brother.'

'Really?' said Lara. 'Well, he's got one hell of an attitude and he hates Americans.'

Cassie frowned. 'Didn't know about the dislike of Americans, but he's . . .' She shifted gear and picked up speed as they left the village behind and drove through impossibly contorted lanes.

'Yes, he's . . .?' Lara knew it would take some time for her to find her way around. The lanes twisted so much, if it weren't for the position of the sun above, she'd have no idea which direction they were heading.

'I was trying to think of the right word.'

'And?' They stopped at an intersection of sorts and turned almost back on themselves. Lara tried to read the quaint signpost painted in white with black lettering.

'"Broken" is probably best.'

Lara turned away from the scenery towards Cassie. 'That tells me nothing.'

'He lost his mum and his aunt in a tragic boating accident, and his dad later that year.'

'That's awful. What happened to his father?'

'I heard it said it was a broken heart but I don't really know what happened.'

'So he was ...' Lara squinted, looking out the window again.

'About seventeen, I think.' Cassie manoeuvred the van down an even smaller track with tree branches meeting each other above. 'Awful, really.' The track ended and an open yard appeared. 'Welcome to my domain.'

Cassie shut the engine off and grabbed Lara's bag from the back. Lara stepped from the van and stood looking at a small white bungalow with beautiful blue agapanthus lining the whitewashed walls. To her left was a massive barn, twice the size of the bungalow. Through the vast glass doors Lara saw a spotless commercial kitchen.

'Impressive.'

'I know.' Cassie linked her arm through Lara's. 'I was going to offer you a cup of tea, but I think you need something a bit stronger. Then you can tell me what you have to confess.'

Lara winced.

Windward, Mawnan Smith, Falmouth, Cornwall
28 August 2015

I studied the thin sheet of paper in front of me. The writing was compact, to fit the maximum amount on the smallest sheet. Rationing had touched everything. The spikes and the curves moved swiftly across the paper. Looking at the writing alone, it would be impossible to know which one of us had written the letter. Only the content was a clue.

Dearest,

My heart is aching. Eddie's letters and calls aren't enough. I can only say this to you. Grandmother frowns at me so and Mother is no use, but she is pleased about the relationship. I heard her say to Grandmother that it is a good match and Grandmother agreed, although you know she would have preferred it if it had been Tom. He has the title, but he doesn't have Eddie's heart. I don't need to tell you that or of my misery.

You haven't told me about Portland or the Wrens you are with. Were any of your friends from training posted with you? What can I tell you about here? There was another bomb dropped in the bay the other night and Grandmother was down on the beaches with everyone collecting the stunned fish. I wish I could have seen it but I was working. However I came home to find sea bass on the counter. I made a delicate sauce with chives and just a bit of cream. We have fewer eggs now that all of them have to go through official channels but Anne at the farm still manages to occasionally give us some extra.

Last Friday night I was driving behind Mr Wellbrook, the furniture man from Falmouth. You know, the one who deals in extra food on the side. Well, he was pulled up because his headlights were showing too much light. I watched the whole thing, waiting for him to be caught with black market goods. But you know how he uses a doctor's bag. It was sitting on the front seat and they waved him through. The smile on my face was so wide it should have cracked and the commodore in the car had no idea why I found the whole situation so amusing. You have to love life here.

Having said that, I miss London terribly. Maybe I should request a change. If I were in London I would see Eddie more. I hear you saying that if I requested a change I'd probably end up in Scotland and further away! You, as always, are right – and besides, Mother needs me. I can see the smile on her face isn't reaching her eyes. I think it's Father but I can't say for sure. His calls are shorter than necessary and they don't say much to each other, not like before. Do tell me how you find him when you see him again.

Missing you terribly and so longing to see you. I can't believe we won't be together at Christmas. We'll be having some of the Americans. Grandmother isn't pleased at all, which is why I had Mother issue the invitation. You know I'm a devil.

Love you so.
Xxx

My hand shook. Closing my eyes, it all felt so close, like it could be happening now. Windward was little altered except for the bathrooms, which had been done at Jack's insistence and his expense. The lawn was restored – replanting it was the first thing Grandmother had wanted to do when the war was over, but she kept growing vegetables. I laughed. Rationing had lasted a long time and those extra things had helped.

My joints creaked as I stood and the letter fell from my hand. Where was my sister now? I hadn't felt her in so long. I had blocked her and maybe she had done the same for me. At ninety there was a good chance she was dead. We weren't a long-lived family so I wasn't sure why I was still alive.

'Gran.' Jack strode from the drive towards me. The easterly breeze caught his fair hair. 'Can I give you a hand?' His glance fell on the letter. 'Still delving in the past, I see.' He studied me then took my arm. 'Looking at the scowl on your face, I'm not sure it's a good thing.'

'Dwelling in the past never is.' I looked hard at him. 'You have to let it go and move on.'

'Ouch.' He leaned back. 'Whatever was in that letter has made you grumpy.'

'Seriously, Jack.' I stopped walking. 'You only have one life. Don't waste it.'

He dropped his arm from mine and stepped back. I braced myself for the explosion. I'd overstepped the line we'd established years ago. He stared at me. His pupils disappeared to pinpricks, then he turned and marched off. I looked for something to lean against. His silence was worse than anything.

He couldn't keep holding himself apart from the world. He had to open up or it would kill him one way or another. This I knew too well.

✳ Twelve ✳

HMS *Attack*, Portland, Dorset
22 December 1943

I looked at the letter I'd started ages ago in London but had never finished. Since then I had received several from Amelia and everything I'd written was out of date and unimportant.

London is crawling with Americans. Of course they are here in Portland and Weymouth but they make more sense in a military setting. They are everywhere. I even had one try and pick me up tonight while I was waiting for Father.

However, paper was precious. I put a strike through it and chewed the end of my pen, puzzling why I could still see the American lieutenant's blue eyes and his dark brown hair.

I even had to deal with one at the Savoy while I was waiting for Father. He had the cheek to ask me to dinner and call me by my first name. You would have loved him. Tall, dark and bold. Of course your heart is spoken for. Have you heard from Eddie? Has he been through Cornwall again?
  Father looked well but I only saw him for moments. He had to have dinner with some major and I was sent home hungry. I'm sure Father felt terrible and I'm supposed to meet him for lunch tomorrow but it will be a quick lunch as I'm due back on duty at six.
  How are Mother and Grandmother? Or should I say, is Grandmother behaving? Aunt Margaret was much more

cheerful despite new people lodging in her house. She spent a long hour gossiping with me about their antics.

Will write more after I have seen Father for lunch. Missing you and hoping all is well.

I sat back and thought of Cornwall. I tried to picture the lanes and landscape crowded with jeeps and tents. It didn't fit and I didn't want Americans with their chewing gum in my Cornwall.

Everything I have written above is old news – sorry. I'm adjusting to life here. The Wrens in my cabin are a good lot and there is a friend of Angus's that we met a few years ago. It's good that I'm beside the water. It makes Cornwall feel closer. I try and imagine that on a clear day I can see Rosemullion Head and know that Windward stands nearby.

My lunch with Father was disappointing and short. He was with me physically but his mind was elsewhere. I would like to say it was on the war but

I paused mid-sentence, not sure if I should write what I thought. He was behaving like he was in love. I thought of Aunt Margaret's offhand comment. Was he seizing joy where he found it? I couldn't help but think so. Poor Mother.

I'm not so certain. It was as if he would have rather been lunching with someone else. I'm not sure with whom though. I had hoped it would be my Christmas but I came away feeling empty. I'm so jealous of your Christmas at Windward even if you do have Americans at the table. Do you still have that French refugee, Mme Pomfrey? Does Mother miss the children from Latimer School still?

I chewed my nail. Despite the lack of material pleasures, Christmas the past few years had been so jolly with the children, and Father having leave. Now I was preparing to spend my first Christmas away.

I will miss you so much. Do tell me everything, especially how Grandmother deals with the Americans.

All my love
Xxx

HMS *Attack*, Portland, Dorset
25 December 1943

'Happy Christmas, Adele,' a rating called as I left the bunker.

I waved and made my way out into the darkness. It took a moment for my eyes to adjust and I blew on my hands as I walked. Chilblains were a problem. In the distance I could hear the sound of a carol being sung. I stopped for a moment as 'God Rest Ye Merry, Gentlemen' carried on the cold air. It was Christmas Day and there was no peace on earth.

I felt for the men on the boats. It was bad enough to be here away from home, but they were under constant threat in the Channel. It had been quieter in the wireless room. It was as if we all knew that we should be elsewhere with our loved ones. I sighed. Christmas lunch had taken place while I was on duty. The hymn finished and I continued my walk back to quarters, hoping there was soup or something warming. The north wind had an icy bite to it and there would be a hard frost tonight, but no snow. However much snow might lift the spirits, it would just make everything more difficult.

I sang 'O Little Town of Bethlehem' as I went, pausing only when I heard footsteps behind me

'I know the words, but not the tune,' a deep voice said.

I jumped and turned to see an American who in the darkness seemed as broad as he was tall. 'Is the tune different in America?'

'Yes, ma'am. It goes like this. "O little town of Bethlehem, how still we see thee lie ..."' His baritone sounded out the hymn on the still night air. 'See. Same words, different tune.'

'You have a lovely voice.'

'Thank you, ma'am.'

I flinched. I knew he was being polite, but it was almost too much and that was the problem with Americans. Too much smile, too much teeth, too much good humour and, finally, too much here. But I did accept that we needed them.

We reached the mess and he stopped. 'You have a merry Christmas, ma'am.'

'Thank you, you too.' I dashed inside as fast as my frozen legs would let me, with the American tune playing in my head.

Sitting down with a bowl of stew and a mince pie, I thought, *Happy Christmas*. At home no doubt the Americans would have provided ingredients that would have allowed Amelia to make a meal to celebrate. Stew didn't quite compare. But I was hungry so I ate it, trying to pretend it was goose with all the trimmings. I was picking the last crumbs of the mince pie up with my finger when I saw Pat enter the mess and head straight for me. 'Not much of a Christmas dinner,' she said, and frowned.

'True.' I stood up.

'We're going on shore in half an hour.'

I smiled, thinking of the peace that would fill the quarters with most of the occupants out. 'Good luck.' I cleared my plates and began walking to our cabin.

'No, no, no – you're joining us.' Pat kept pace with my steps as walked through the cold night air.

I rubbed my aching wrist. Tension travelled up my arm to my neck. 'I'll pass.'

'I'm not taking "no" for an answer. It's Christmas and you are coming to the dance, Adele.' She stood in the doorway to our cabin.

'Look, Pat, I've been on duty all day and all I want to do is put my feet up, not go dancing.'

'It's Christmas, there aren't enough women and life is too short, as we know only too well.' She frowned again and looked at the picture of Sally's husband. He had been shot down two weeks ago. 'I'm heading downstairs and I expect to see you on the liberty boat. No bah humbugs allowed.' She went out of the door and I slipped off my shoes. I didn't want to do this, Christmas or not. A dance hall filled with smoke and false happiness. I would much rather fall into bed.

I turned and sat there with my presents at the bottom of my bunk. I glanced at my watch; there was enough time to open them and still make the liberty boat on shore. The name 'liberty boat' made me smile. It was a battered old bus and the name caused much amusement among the Americans. But then everything about us caused amusement, our quaint ways. Maybe that was what really bothered me. I felt they were laughing at us, at our warm beer and our gardens not yards. I rubbed my temples. This was not going to help and I was in danger of becoming a Scrooge or, worse, a total spoilsport. Amelia would be kicking me at this point. Maybe that was the problem. Without my twin I wasn't whole. I didn't feel like joining the party – or, if I was honest, life. God, I missed her and I knew she felt the same.

I opened my mother's present first. She'd given me a scarf in bright red wool. Grandmother's turned out to be a copy of Jane Austen's *Pride and Prejudice*. There was another package wrapped in newspaper. I smiled as I read the tag on the bottle:

Take a spoonful of this, dear, to keep Cornwall in your bones and keep you fit and well. Rosehip syrup, 1943. Happy Christmas, Mrs Tonks.

Trust Mrs Tonks to be worried about me. She always had been over the years we visited Windward, fussing whenever she could. I opened the bottle and took a deep breath. Cornwall. The scent transported me there. If only the feeling would last. I sighed and opened Amelia's present – a pair of silk French knickers that she'd made with the help of Mme Pomfrey. In her note she promised me that the elastic wouldn't give, as there was none. My mouth lifted into a smile as I stroked the fabric. They would be wasted under my uniform. Tucking them into the bottom of my drawer, I wonder what she thought of the book of poetry I'd sent her. I was trying to enlighten her, while she was trying to lighten me up. I chuckled.

The final present was from Aunt Margaret. It was large and as I opened it I knew immediately what it was: a dress in emerald-green satin. It was one I had admired on her. Her note fell on to the bed.

My darling Adele,

Sorry to give you a hand-me-down but clothes are in such short supply and you had admired it so. I found so little to buy for Christmas and then inspiration struck. I hope you bowl over all the men you must be meeting. Plus green is your colour!

With love,
Aunt Margaret

I stroked it. The fabric gleamed, becoming almost like the sea in the way the light and shadow played across the surface. It was beautiful and I was touched by her generosity, but I was not sure when I'd wear it. Wrapping it in its tissue, I placed it with the extravagant knickers from my sister. Then I changed my blouse to try and feel fresher for the dance hall that I didn't want to go to. Merry bloody Christmas.

The liberty boat was full of laughter as I climbed on board and squeezed into the last empty seat. Sitting beside me was a Wren who worked in Supply with Angus's friend. Dot struck me as quite sensible and just a little bit older than me. Her eyes saw everything and had a bit of mischief about them that lit up her neat face.

'Happy Christmas,' I said as we set off. The moon was up and I could make out the high bank of Chesil Beach as we bumped along the causeway. I heard rather than saw a vehicle pass us. So many accidents and deaths had happened since the blackout. I wouldn't want to drive, let alone in the dark without lights. I didn't know how Amelia did it.

'Looking forward to the dance?' Dot's soft voice could be barely heard above the noise.

I turned to her. 'Truth, no.'

'Tired, homesick?'

'Both.'

'It'll be good for you. We have to grab life while we have it.'

'Yes,' I agreed, but I honestly didn't feel it. The bus stopped and we all filed into the dark streets. At home the fire would be lit, the wireless on, while Grandmother slept in her chair. Would Amelia be playing charades with our guests or would they all be singing around the piano? Normally it would be Father who would play but he wasn't there. I wasn't sure where he was – he'd never said.

Dot tapped my shoulder and I followed her as a group of Yanks strolled up. 'Hello, Dot. Merry Christmas.'

'Happy Christmas all.' She took my arm. 'This is Adele and she's missing home.'

'Aren't we all, honey.'

My back straightened with disdain. *Honey*, I thought. *Really.* Then I slowed my steps. I thought nothing of a bus driver in London calling me 'darling' or a stranger in Cornwall calling me 'my lover', so 'honey' might not be any different, yet I still bristled. Maybe it was the tone and implied intimacy. I shivered as I walked along the street in darkness. Music could be heard spilling out of the hall each time the door opened. I braced myself for the noise, the forced joviality and the smoke.

Once we were inside, Dot touched my arm as if she sensed my desire to turn and run. 'Seriously, this will lift your spirits. Nothing like a bit of dancing.'

Under my breath I muttered, 'Bah humbug,' but I put a smile on my face and hoped I could find a quiet corner away from the Yanks.

Dot didn't let me slip away. She led me across the crowded hall filled with American servicemen towards a group of men in RAF uniform. 'Adele, this is Johnny. He's home for Christmas with a few friends.'

'Adele.' He smiled and his face coloured slightly. 'Dance?'

I liked his bashfulness and the way he looked in his flight lieutenant's uniform. 'Yes.' I took his hand, walking with him and ignoring the Americans. Tonight I would make it my duty to be sure all our own boys were partnered, especially the very sweet but quiet Johnny. It was a joy to be led about the floor with someone who could dance and wasn't trying to get too close. There was enough space between us so that I could actually look up at him and not be pressed against him. He hadn't assumed the immediate intimacy as so many did at these dances. He was a breath of fresh, English air.

The evening flew by and I even danced with a few Americans. I secretly hoped that Johnny would ask me for the last dance. I was afraid to look for him as I might catch another man's eye, so I stared into my teacup.

'May I have this dance?' Johnny stood in front of me, smiling.

'Yes.' I took his hand and he swept me onto the floor, this time holding me a bit closer but not too tight. Grandmother would approve. I smiled at the thought.

'Penny for them?'

I shook my head. 'Nothing important.'

'Well, I'm happy for it as it made you smile.'

I grinned, looking into his hazel eyes. 'It did.'

'Will you be here in two weeks?' he whispered in my ear.

'I don't know.' I glanced up at him. 'I'm not sure what shifts I will be on.'

He nodded. 'If you are ... will you save the last dance for me?'

'Yes.'

He pulled me a little closer and Christmas didn't feel so lonely all of a sudden.

HMS *Attack*, Portland, Dorset
10 January 1944

Opening Amelia's letter, I paused. Part of me wanted to know that they had had a wonderful Christmas and the other part of me didn't. For whatever reason she had taken a long time in sending it. I turned it over in my hands then settled on my bunk to read.

New Year's Day

Darling,

*What fun we had but I felt so guilty without you. Christmas
was divine, and even Grandmother enjoyed herself. Inviting the
Americans was inspired. First they came bearing gifts in the
form of food and spirits, so immediately we began plying drink
into Grandmother. What a difference that made. I then took the
gifts of tinned peaches and custard powder. The trifle was to die
for and while I worked in the kitchen the boys amused Mother
and Grandmother. I wish I could have recorded the laughter for
you. They had put the gramophone on and you won't believe it
but they were teaching Grandmother the jitterbug. It was magic,
as if Father Christmas himself had spread fairy dust on the old
bat. She looked years younger in the arms of a captain.*

*No one cared that the main meal was roasted rabbit instead
of goose. It was a Christmas to remember and the only things I
longed for were Eddie, you and Father. Eddie called and that
made me fall in love with him all over again. Do let yourself
fall in love. It makes the world worth fighting for and I know
you – once you give your heart it will be forever.*

*Last night I saw in 1944 at the Ferryboat Inn. Well in truth,
we all stood on Bar Beach singing Auld Lange Syne badly, but
it was memorable for the stars and the utter lack of light. I could
hear and feel the bodies around me but for that short moment I
stood in the darkness and somehow felt the world.*

*Do tell me you will have some leave soon. Maybe if you
haven't enough time to come to Cornwall we could try and meet
in London. Write to me! What was your Christmas and New
Year like? Who did you kiss to see the New Year in?*

Xx.xx

*P.S. Thank you for the book of poems ... are you trying to
'improve' me? Well, it's working. I'm reading a poem a day but
it's the same one, Elizabeth Barrett Browning's 'How do I love*

thee?' I think I have it memorised. It sums up exactly what I feel for Eddie.

P.P.S. Remind me when I see you to tell you about the handsome Dutchman who tried to woo Mother. She came to the Ferryboat with me one night and this charming man took a fancy to her. I don't believe she would have escaped except for his gammy leg!

Xxxx

Leicester Square, London
21 January 1944

We'd tumbled out of the 400 Club and onto the street. I knew my breath was coming out in little puffs even if I couldn't see it in the blackout. The ground was slippery underneath my shoes. The emerald silk of the dress I'd been given by Aunt Margaret offered little protection against the bitter wind. I pulled my wrap tighter and Angus threw his arm around me.

'Sure you've had enough dancing? It was a lot warmer inside.' His boyish grin spread across his face, revealing the gap between his two front teeth.

I smiled. 'Absolutely, but don't let me stop you from heading back in. I have to be on duty tomorrow so some sleep tonight is essential.'

He drew closer to me in the darkness. 'Always the serious one.'

'Absolutely. You drew the short straw tonight, finding this twin in London.'

He laughed. 'Nonsense. Although, truth be told, I've never been able to tell you two apart, even when you are side by side. But then, you both like to confuse me.'

'So true. You still don't know which one of us kissed you all those years ago.'

'Well, you could kiss me now and I'd know.' He tilted his head with a slow smile spreading across his face.

I laughed and gently pushed him in the direction of the

nightclub door. 'Go and enjoy yourself. You've earned it, and thanks for a lovely evening.'

'You don't mind?'

'I mind standing here when you could be in there sweet-talking another girl.'

He studied me in the moonlight then kissed my cheek. 'I know it was you.' He dashed in the door before I could deny it, and I thought back to those sun-drenched holidays at Windward.

Laughing I picked my way along the street, hoping that I'd find a bus or taxi. I hummed a little of 'Moonlight Serenade' as I went. Not that I was afraid, more to warn people that I was there. It was silly, as I was sure my footsteps were loud enough.

I'd reached Piccadilly when the air raid siren sounded, sending adrenaline through me. Looking around, I fought the urge to run. People came from all directions, moving swiftly as the noise of chatter increased. I joined the crowds heading into the underground station. Everyone was good-natured about it considering the hour, until a drunken man pushed into me as we walked down and called me a tart. My skin crawled as his beery breath filled the space between us. I kept my head lowered and continued moving, but he followed me, getting closer all the time. I looked around, seeking an escape route, but there were just too many people to move on the stairs.

'Leave the lady alone,' one man shouted. But he was too far away to actually help. All my muscles tensed – I wanted to flee, but the weight of people pressed me closer to the drunk.

'Mind your own business,' he slurred. 'And she's no lady.' He reached out for me and I leaned away as far as I could. I could see the platform down in front of me filled with more people. I didn't know what he was going to do. A scream began to rise in my throat as his hand neared the top of my strapless dress.

Suddenly there was a Yank in uniform removing the drunk's hand from my arm. 'Leave the lady alone,' he said quietly.

'Bloody Yanks. Think you own the bloody world, don't you?'

'Mind your language. There are women and children all

around you.' The crowd kept moving us forward onto the platform but sadly not away from the problem. I kept staring down, hoping that by ignoring the whole situation it would just go away.

'No Yank is going to tell me anything.'

'Fair enough.' The Yank's voice was very quiet. I could barely hear it over my pounding heart but it was clear that the drunkard had, and he took a step back.

'Bloody coming over here and taking our women.'

'Enough.' The Yank's voice was lower still – and it was then that I realised I knew him: Bobby Webster, the lieutenant who had asked me to dinner in the Savoy in December. Right now his blue eyes were not smiling with mischief but icy and focused. He took my elbow and manoeuvred me through the slow-moving crowd to the far end of the platform while a few other people thankfully distracted the drunk.

Taking off his overcoat, the lieutenant placed it on my shoulders. I hadn't noticed I was shaking. Shock had set in. Sinking onto the platform floor in a small open space among the families trying to soothe children, I was grateful for the warmth and for his silence. He sat down beside me, but not too close, while the noise of the people around me drowned out my racing heart. Throughout the war I had heard of these incidents but not once had I experienced such unpleasantness or raw hatred.

A child started crying not too far away. I listened to its mother croon softly and let her gentle voice work its magic on me too. I turned to the lieutenant. 'Thank you.'

'I won't say it was a pleasure but I'm happy to have been here to help.'

We sat in silence as the floor shook. I wondered how close a miss we'd had, and hoped that no one had been killed or injured.

'Emerald green suits you.'

I looked up at him, liking his slightly lopsided grin.

'Thank you.'

'You're welcome. I hope you had a good evening before this.'

I smiled. 'Yes, I did. You?'

'Acceptable.'

That wasn't what I'd been expecting. Acceptable. Normally when you asked the Americans anything, it was all superlatives. Intriguing.

Finally, after what seemed like a long time, the rising and holding tone of the 'all clear' signal sounded and people around us began to shift.

'May I escort you home?' he asked.

I scanned the platform, looking for the drunkard. 'Yes, thank you.'

Sirens filled the air as we walked along the darkness of Piccadilly. I tried to give him his coat back but he wouldn't let me. 'You'll catch a cold,' he said.

'What about you?'

'Winters are a lot colder in Massachusetts.'

'Is that where you are from?' I tried to make out his face in the distant light from a burning building.

'Yes, south of Boston on the coast.'

'Sounds lovely.'

'It is.'

I slipped and he steadied me. He continued to hold my arm as we went past Hyde Park along Kensington Gore. 'Where are you from?'

I smiled. 'Good question.' A taxi went past but it was occupied. 'A few places.'

'How so? Military family?'

'Not then.' I shook my head, thinking of Father. He'd taken to the service well and I think enjoyed the company of men, which he didn't have when he was with the family. Maybe it was refreshing.

'But now?'

'Yes. But aren't most people these days?'

'True,' he said. 'So. Are you going to enlighten me?'

'I was born in Cornwall, but that's not where we lived. My parents were on holiday at my grandmother's at the time.' I smiled, remembering Windward.

'Where did you grow up?'

'All over. Father is a consulting surgeon so we moved a bit until we settled in London before the war.'

'Never Cornwall again?'

'No, but we stayed there every summer without fail.'

'Beautiful place, but tiny roads.'

'You've been?'

He nodded but didn't say more. Was he one of the Yanks tearing up and down the lanes near Falmouth? But then there were Americans everywhere. Earlier today my walk down Cadogan Gardens had been accompanied by wolf whistles. It was something I'd become used to with the growing number of them on the south coast. We needed them for the war but we didn't have to like them.

The lieutenant and I dodged a group of people making their way in the chaos. With all this darkness I kept thinking there should be silence, but the night was full of noise.

'A good night, love?' asked a man walking in the opposite direction.

I laughed. Hardly the night out I'd expected.

'Why were you out alone, or did you lose your date in the raid chaos?'

I turned to him. 'I left him dancing. I have to be on duty today and need to catch an early train back.' I chuckled. 'So much for getting some sleep.'

'He let you leave without him?'

'He's a dear friend.' I thought of Angus and the stolen kiss.

'So you are free?'

'I guess so.' I smiled. 'As free as anyone is in this crazy world when we don't know who will be alive tomorrow.'

'*Carpe diem.*'

I squinted in the darkness to try and read his expression but couldn't. 'It all depends on how you want to seize it.' I paused. 'I mean, everyone wants something different.'

'Do they?'

'I think they do.' A person bumped into me. I'd been so

focused on the lieutenant and our conversation that I wasn't paying attention to what was around me.

'Don't we all want happiness?' he asked.

'Fair point, but what makes people happy is unique.' As we walked, the moon appeared from behind a cloud, casting a silvery light over the street.

'I would argue that the search for love is universal.'

'True, but what people think love is is very different.'

He laughed. 'I think we may have to agree to disagree.'

'Scared of continuing the argument?'

'Absolutely not. I'd love nothing more, but didn't you mention that you were heading to Kensington High Street?'

'I did.' As I said this, I could just make out the steeple of St Mary Abbots, which meant Aunt Margaret's house was close. 'Thank you for walking with me.'

'It's been a pleasure.' I held out my hand and he took it, but then frowned. 'Surely you're not staying here?'

'No.'

'Well then, I intend to see you home.'

'There's no need.'

'There's every need. My mother would never forgive me if I didn't walk a lady to her door.'

'Then it's just up the hill a bit.' I realised that he was still holding my hand in his. I wasn't quite sure how to pull it away without appearing rude. And part of me was enjoying the warmth through my glove. There was something different about this Yank. He was quiet for one, he wasn't chewing gum and unlike the others did not seem prone to forced joviality. If all Americans were like this polite lieutenant then having so many of them around might not be so difficult.

As we reached Aunt Margaret's house, he asked: 'How much time do you have before your train?'

'Not much. Just time to change our of my finery and back into uniform.'

'Well, a pleasure to meet you again, Adele.'

'And you too, Lieutenant.'

'Bobby, please.'

'Bobby.'

'Until we meet again.' He gave my hand a squeeze and released me to walk up the steps. I turned when I'd opened the door and for a moment I thought I could still see him standing on the pavement. I waved into the darkness, unsure if he was really there, but I was thankful that I'd met the polite American lieutenant again.

✳ Thirteen ✳

Weymouth, Dorset
5 February 1944

We were sitting on the wall that ran alongside the promenade, enjoying some unexpected sunshine. The bright, spring-like day had made me almost feel lethargic, but then a loud rumble of tyres stirred me back to wakefulness.

A convoy of jeeps filled with American GIs came driving past. I frowned. More of them. Pat waved energetically and they called out to her. She leaned over to me. 'The dances will be crowded out with men. You'll have to come more often now. It's your duty to keep morale up.'

I smiled. 'Their morale looks just fine to me.'

'Give them a few days on a wet field and they'll need your bright smile to tell them not all is bad in England.'

I laughed and looked back at the convoy. The Americans didn't need me. More vehicles came in sight as the convoy slowed to a halt – and suddenly, sitting in one of the jeeps right in front of me was Lieutenant Bobby Webster. Our eyes met, and then he smiled and tipped his cap.

'Now there's a handsome man.' Pat nudged me.

'Good to see you Adele,' he called out.

'The same, Lieutenant,' I said, just as the jeep started moving forward again, carrying him away.

'You know him?' Pat stared open-mouthed at me.

'We've met.'

'You didn't say. *And* you haven't fallen immediately in love?'

She refused to look back at the rest of the convoy, despite their calls of 'Hello, ladies', instead staring hard at me.

'I said we'd met, not had an affair.'

'You're a dark horse.' She laughed. 'He was certainly pleased to see you.'

I flushed. 'Not at all. And now that they've passed, we'd best head back to *Attack*.'

'Spoilsport. I want to know how and where you met him.'

'All I'll say is that it was London.'

'He wasn't the bloke who helped you in the shelter, was he?'

I grinned and began a brisk march towards the train station while Pat trailed in my wake, continually glancing over her shoulder at the troops. I turned to tell her to keep up – and accidentally walked straight into Commander Rowse. 'Sorry, sir.'

He smiled. 'Quite the sight.' He tilted his head towards the troops and I found myself thinking how lucky his wife was. I knew through the grapevine that he was married and didn't so much as look at another woman in the wrong way. That was what I wanted from a man, but only after the war. In the last week, I'd heard that the lovely Johnny I'd danced with in January had 'caught it', in the words of his friends. Another life snuffed out. There was no chance I would risk falling in love.

HMS *Attack*, Portland, Dorset

1 February 1944

Darling,

How I missed you last night. You would have seen the funny side but I couldn't at the time. We arrived at the Embassy Club and the first person we see is Commander Tommy Pinkerton-Smith who I had a merry time with while I drove him for three months. And I don't regret a moment of it but I was with Eddie and I could see mischief in Tommy's eyes as he glanced our way.

My hand shook sensing Amelia's embarrassment and fear. I stuffed the pillow on my bunk against the wall to be more comfortable.

I nearly died and hoped the floor would open when he made a beeline for us. He could drop me straight into it. It's not that Eddie thought I hadn't had other lovers, but it would have been most unpleasant to be faced with one. But Tommy, the dirty stop-out, waltzed up to us and immediately kissed me. I held my breath. It could go badly wrong.

However I had worried needlessly as he held out his hand to Eddie. 'I hear you are the luckiest man in Bomber Command, Lieutenant.' He smiled at me. 'Because Amelia has agreed to be your wife.' I nearly fell to the floor at this point. They shook hands vigorously. It turns out that Eddie had been a friend of Tommy's brother at school. Tommy winked at me as he went to the bar. After that point I knew it would all be fine. Eddie swept me into his arms as the band began to play, and time flew but I didn't want it to end. We walked through Hyde Park back to Aunt Margaret's to change as dawn was breaking. Everything sparkled with the dew and I just wanted to hold onto the moment forever.

Wife? She was engaged and she hadn't told me. The letter fell from my hand. I don't know how long I sat there, looking at the paper on the floor, before I bent down and picked it up again.

'Engaged' I hear you say? I'm not, or I wasn't when Tommy said that. I pulled him aside later. He said we'd both looked so happy, that had to have been the reason. When he returned me to the table he said, 'If you don't propose to this woman here and now, I will.'

Eddie replied, 'Funny you should say that.' Then he pulled a box out of his pocket. I nearly swooned as he fell to one knee and asked me to be his wife. Earlier he had held me in his arms while we danced and whispered those magic words properly for the first time. The delicate diamond ring says it all. I'm watching it sparkle in the daylight right now as the train makes its way to Cornwall. I will put the ring away once I get there because we both want to tell the family together. He will speak to Father first before we break the news to the mothers. I am over the moon.

I hate the leaving part so much. Despite the pain of it, I have never known such highs. Every time he leaves my side I die a little knowing there is a chance he won't return. So many don't. I'm secretly hoping that I'm pregnant so that I will have his child, even if he is gone. Is that wrong?

I can hear your voice telling me my life would be ruined. But would it? Don't be too hard on me in your thoughts. Remember I can hear them.

xxxx

P.S. Will write tomorrow with an update on family. Aunt Margaret sends her love. With great restraint I have kept the news from her. Can you imagine Mother's reaction if the aunt knew first!! Call her if you get a chance. She needs a lift. She hasn't had a letter from Uncle Reg in ages. She's keeping her spirits up but I can see how much it is costing her.

P.P.S. I drove the most delightful admiral yesterday, the old rogue. He knew Father well, so he behaved with me – just. Do you think Father acts in this way? Most of these men are married but they don't half try it on. I push the married ones away. However the night before last I met a divine major who knew Tommy Pinkerton-Smith. They'd been at Eton together. He was off to the Far East so I said I'd go dancing with him the following night but fortunately he cancelled.

I've enclosed a small bottle of scent. Don't ask how I got it but you know I don't favour Muguet des Bois. Wear it and remember your sister when you do.

Putting the letter down, I knew life would never be the same again. It was normal that this had happened, and it was what she had dreamed of ... finding love. But the tears in my eyes were both of joy and unspeakable sadness.

12 February 1944

In my cabin, I opened the small perfume bottle and carefully placed a finger over the opening, tipping it gently, not wanting to spill even the smallest amount of fragrance. I had been without perfume for months and Muguet des Bois was my favourite. It reminded me of May in Cornwall when the garden would be filled with lily of the valley. I scented both my wrists and behind my ears. Holding my inner wrist to my nose I took a deep breath. I was grateful that Amelia never felt that it was her fragrance. I shuddered to think where and how she had acquired it. Her letter didn't quite say, leaving me to fill in the blanks. I didn't like what I thought it might be. I didn't approve but there was little I could do from this distance. And I tried to understand, I really did, but didn't it make it worse having something briefly, tasting its sweetness, then having it ripped away? Philip and Johnny were gone. Wouldn't I be better off not knowing how sweet it tasted than forever after longing for it but never having it again?

I glanced at my watch. It was time to meet the others and head ashore. Despite HMS *Attack* being on land, everyone here always referred to Weymouth as 'ashore', and even after months here it still sounded funny to me. It was a dance night and I reminded myself that there were so few women it was my duty to keep the morale of the men lifted. Part of me wondered if Bobby – Lieutenant Webster – would be there. It had been a week since I'd seen him arrive in Weymouth.

Despite the jovial mood of the crowd on the bus, I stared out of the window thinking about my family. I longed to see them and I was missing so much of their lives. My sister was engaged. Father was preoccupied by the war and seemed somehow disconnected from us. Mother was depressed but Grandmother was on good form. How this damn war changed us inside remained to be seen, but the signs on the outside were more than visible on everybody. Some wore uniforms and others held on to whatever they could from life before the war. For Grandmother it was sherry before dinner and her pearls, even when fishing. Mother was caught in the crossfire, keeping Grandmother's routine in place but longing for Father and trying to pretend that it was all fine. Would the changes fade away when the war finished? As I stepped off the liberty boat, I hoped so, but I suspected things had moved on too far for that.

The street was in darkness and my eyes took a few minutes to adjust while I followed the sound of the music. Excitement bubbled within me and it was a strange emotion to feel in the middle of desperate times. Yet as I took further steps towards the dance hall that Christmas feeling of anticipation sat in my stomach. I knew the cause – Lieutenant Bobby Webster. I'd heard through Pat that the troops were camped about two miles away at a farm in Burton Bradstock, but it didn't mean that he was there. He could have been passing through – after all, he'd mentioned having been to Cornwall in the conversation we'd had as we walked through London. He hadn't said what he did, but then no one did these days. All I knew was that he was a first lieutenant in the US Army and he wore a big ring on his left hand. Nothing more.

I paused at the threshold of the dance hall, wondering if this anticipation would deflate as soon as I entered. If he wasn't there it would be worse than …

Than what? I asked myself, and stepped inside.

The room was filled with mostly US Army boys. Dare I hope he'd be here? As always the atmosphere was thick with smoke but the mood was bright. The Mills Brothers' 'Paper Dolls' was playing and the dance floor was crowded with couples. I searched for the lieutenant's broad shoulders and dark hair, but there were many tall dark-haired men. My spirits dropped. I was being foolish. There were things that could happen tonight that would be far worse than not seeing Lt Webster. We were at war, I lectured myself while squinting through the crowd trying to locate my friends.

Joining Pat at the table, I saw Bobby wasn't here. Relief and disappointment filled me in equal measure. I assured myself that I was only disappointed because I couldn't thank him again for his kindness. Despite this, I continued to scan the crowd as someone put 'A Nightingale Sang in Berkeley Square' on the gramophone. Pat was whisked into the arms of one of the American officers I'd just been introduced to and I looked down at the teacup on the table, noting the chip on the rim. It could do with being filed. I hummed quietly as the song came to an end.

At that moment, a deep voice whispered in my ear: 'Would you honour me with this dance?'

A shiver went up my spine. I looked up into Bobby Webster's intense blue eyes.

I couldn't speak, so instead just nodded and held out my hand. As his fingers made contact, my legs lost the ability to move. He smiled. Time stopped. The music, 'That Old Black Magic' by the Glenn Miller Band, began. It was like we were both caught in a spell, unable to move.

'Take the lady onto the dance floor or I will,' said a nearby voice, and the corners of Bobby's mouth twitched. He swept me up into his arms and somehow we managed the dance. The feel of his hand resting on my waist and the curl of his fingers holding mine cast a spell over me. Time and place were lost and it was just me and him in this hall of crowded people.

It was torment – one moment being so close to him, and then the song finished and I was handed into another soldier's arms without being able to say no. I felt Bobby's glance from across the room, and wanted him to cut in, but there were so few women here, I knew I be would lucky to have the opportunity to be in his arms again.

When I was finally able to leave the dance floor after too many dances for me to remember them all, I couldn't see him. Pat handed me a glass of water. The hall was warm despite the cold weather outside. Sweat beaded on my brow and I worked at keeping a smile on my face while Pat gave me one of her knowing looks. The next song began – it was 'I Only Have Eyes For You'.

'Would there be a mutiny if I held you in my arms for a second time?' Bobby was at my side and his words lifted my heart. It was the last dance of the evening. The one everyone reserved for someone special.

I turned, grinning with my stomach all a-flutter. 'There might be, but I'll take the chance if you will.'

✳ Fourteen ✳

Falmouth, Cornwall
31 August 2015

Seagulls called out as Lara walked along the quayside, looking out at the evening light on the opposite shore. Falmouth Harbour. This Falmouth was completely different yet somehow familiar. Gone were the cedar shingle houses, their lovely woody scent replaced by little alleyways and crooked buildings. Everywhere she looked was filled with surprising twists, turns and startling views of the water. Buildings were mostly old but not all. History loitered around every corner.

Studying the harbour again, she tried to picture it as it had been during the war, filled with naval vessels and people. Reading through all the information on the Internet, it appeared that most people here had welcomed the arrival of the American troops but that wasn't the case everywhere. Already her perceptions of World War II were changing. Grandie's first trip to Cornwall had taken place in November 1943, and then he was transferred back here in May 1944 in the run-up to D-Day.

His entry of 29 November 1943 read:

I thought I knew what green was but then I arrived in England. Ireland may be greener but I'm not sure my eyes can see that many shades. It's fall. I'm missing the colours. Although the trees here have turned, it's not to the same brilliance.

And two days later:

We are staying in a grand house for the night. Tomorrow we will be surveying. I have never seen roads so small or so twisted.

Lara totally agreed about the roads. She'd rented a car this morning but was terrified to drive it anywhere. The short distance from the rental agency back to Cassie's had been frightening for both her and Cassie, who had driven along behind her. Cassie was working tonight, and had kindly dropped Lara off in town on her way so she had the chance to explore on foot. Lara knew she needed to be brave and get used to driving herself, but she wasn't ready just yet.

A seagull cried while the smell of French fries mingled with the scent of seaweed and sunblock. Following the smell of food, she walked up the hill away from the harbour, the aroma finally leading her to the line for a take-out. The dusk was beautiful so she would head back to the waterfront and enjoy her first fish and chips on this side of the Atlantic. It was such a signature meal for so many restaurants on the Cape that it would be good to taste it here. The take-out place was obviously a relaxed establishment catering to plenty of tourists, from the looks of the customers' sunburn and bright clothes, but she had only expected cod and haddock to be on the menu, and was impressed with the possible choice of fish.

There were only three people in the line ahead of her when a deep voice at the take-out counter said: 'Three large cod and one portion of chips, please.'

Lara knew the voice instantly. It was the bride's brother.

After a quick discussion with Cassie, Lara had made another cake that morning to replace the one she'd dropped. It had been fun to be in a kitchen with Cassie again. Cassie hadn't revealed what had been said on the phone call about the damaged cake. But there had been a great deal of laughter, so Lara had to assume she hadn't been speaking to the man in the queue in front of her. He stood to the side waiting for his order. With his back to her, she could observe him. His fair hair was cut short and he stood tall with ease. The line moved forward again and she shuffled to the front, debating which fish she wanted and hoping that he wouldn't look her way. However, her glance met his as he turned from the counter holding his order. Lara blinked at his glare of recognition.

'The clumsy cook.' He moved towards her. She almost stepped back but overrode the instinct.

'Not clumsy at all. Just unlucky.' Lara forced a polite smile onto her face.

'I hear you're making a new cake, not Cassie.'

Lara blinked. 'It's already done.' She'd enjoyed it, playing around with the recipe that Cassie had provided. Following a recipe exactly had always been the toughest part of attending school. It had been essential to do so, but she had always longed to alter even the most simple of them to reflect the time of the year, or what was of interest to her taste buds at that moment.

His eyes narrowed. 'It had better be good.'

She looked up at him. The fluorescent light created shadows on his face, making it appear classical, carved and cold. 'Well,' she said, 'it will be better than providing the couple with a broken cake.'

He laughed, but not with amusement. 'A waste of time.' He turned and walked away. Lara shook her head. Was he talking about the cake or the marriage?

'What will you have tonight?' the man behind the counter asked.

'Cod and fries, please.'

'Vinegar?'

Lara wrinkled her nose. She might try it another time but tonight she didn't like the idea of the sharpness covering the taste of the fish. 'Just tartar sauce, please.'

'In the fridge beside you.'

Lara nodded, grabbed two tubs and paid. She studied the people enjoying the same food as the takeaway, but seated at tables overlooking the harbour. Her order arrived piping hot and she wandered for a bit before deciding to head back to the waterside.

Sitting with feet dangling over the quayside, she unwrapped her food, broke open the batter and watched the steam rise.

The cod flaked perfectly and the flesh was sweet and moist. The freshly made sauce was not overly sharp. It was a beautiful balance between batter, fish and sauce with the bite of the capers coming through. She leaned back and tried a fry. Not too thin and perfectly crisp on the outside, while soft on the inside … success. The only thing lacking was a glass of wine.

Cassie had mentioned that fresh local food was a big thing in Cornwall and this was right up her street. Lara could tell the fish was cooked on the day it was caught. It melted in her mouth.

Seasonal, local food was wonderful. Asparagus in November tasted like sodden stalks compared to the asparagus grown in Hadley, Massachusetts in spring. The season was short and just this year Lara had made a trip to visit the farms in May to cook and eat the asparagus within hours. It was then she truly understood the difference that fresh and local food could make in the dining experience.

So while spending time with Cassie and researching, she would enjoy Cornwall's food offerings. It was strange but, as she looked across the harbour at a small Navy vessel tied to a quay, she could sense Grandie here. It was probably just her grief taking another form, but nonetheless it was comforting, in an odd way.

Ferryboat Inn, Helford Passage, Cornwall
1 September 2015

'You have to have the oysters to start.' Cassie sat at a picnic table while Lara stared at the view. Grandie had mentioned both the pub and the river in front of her. A shiver ran up her spine as she looked across the water through the many moored yachts to the pretty village on the other side.

In a way it reminded her of parts of the Cape. Not the quaint cottages but the boats and the vibe in the pub. 'It's the first of September so I suppose it's all right.' Lara turned to Cassie then glanced at the row of whitewashed cottages lining a small lane that hugged the river. 'So this is the Helford River.'

Cassie nodded.

'It doesn't really look like one.'

'It's a tidal estuary.'

'Ah, that explains the beach.'

'Yes, and although it's changed since the forties I'd imagine the view looks pretty much the same.'

Lara joined her at the table and picked up the menu. 'What else do you recommend?'

'I'm having the special.' Lara frowned, and Cassie pointed. 'It's on the board behind you. Grilled mackerel.'

'Sounds good,' said Lara, 'but I'm tempted by the crab.'

'Can't go wrong with that here.'

'Hmm.' A few children splashed about in the water on the beach in front of the pub, reminding Lara of past summer holidays. The waiter came to take the order. Lara followed Cassie's lead on everything including the wine – after all, this was her turf and she would know best.

'Right. Now that we have a quiet moment, tell me all.'

'That's a big ask.'

'I know.' Cassie took a sip of wine and then stifled a yawn. 'Sorry. You're not boring me, I promise.'

'I know.' Cassie had every reason to be tired – she had been working flat out, all while Lara had been enjoying a few lazy days of not doing much of anything, except for lying in the garden and reading a book on Cornwall's involvement in World War II.

'Why don't you start with Grandie?' said Cassie. 'He was such a lovely man.'

Lara grinned, thinking of him. 'He was.' She pulled out the picture of him taken on the headland and passed it to Cassie.

'O-M-*G*. He was handsome in his eighties but in his twenties he was … devastating.'

Lara nodded. Clean cut, clear skinned, broad shoulders and slim waist all emphasised by the belted uniform. Classic heart-throb of the 1940s.

'So fit. He could be Captain America.'

'Enough.' Lara laughed. 'Do you recognise where the photo's taken?'

Cassie considered it. 'I'd say somewhere on Rosemullion Head, down at the mouth of the river.' She pointed to her right. 'You can't see much from here but if you walk on to the beach you can see out towards Falmouth Bay.' She looked over her shoulder. 'The tide's on the way out so after lunch we can go explore a bit.'

The oysters arrived and with one taste Lara felt she knew the river – the salt, the minerals, its wind and its waves. She and Cassie didn't say a word as they savoured each oyster with just a squeeze of lemon.

'So. Pierre?' Cassie looked up as she wiped her hands.

Lara shrugged. 'Well, I was a failure.'

'Nonsense. He was the failure. He couldn't take your success.'

Lara laughed. 'I always liked the way you looked at things.'

'Seriously, Lara, you're a brilliant chef.' Cassie sipped her wine.

'Brilliant or not, I blew it.' Lara shook her head. 'The job and the marriage.' She twisted her glass, looking at the condensation on it. 'I was so stupid.' She sighed. 'It doesn't look good to walk out on a two-starred Michelin chef. Or a marriage for that matter.'

Cassie studied her. 'You wouldn't have walked out for no reason. I know you, and it was Pierre who wanted out.' Lara flexed her fingers and Cassie touched her hand. 'You need a break. Enjoy being here and hopefully you can find out more about Amelia.' She raised her glass. 'Here's to you being head chef of your own restaurant – but only after a good break.'

Lara tapped Cassie's glass, wondering what she really wanted. For the moment it was to discover more about Amelia. That would be enough for now.

✳ Fifteen ✳

Constantine, Falmouth, Cornwall
2 September 2015

The large package sat on the kitchen table. Lara recognised her mother's writing. Puzzled, she picked it up and carried it through to the living room – but then stopped in surprise.

From the sofa, large yellow eyes watched her.

'And where did *you* come from?' she asked.

It was a cat – although 'cat' didn't seem to cover the size, grandness and fluffiness of the creature sprawled comfortably on the sofa. Lara suspected it might even object to being described as 'fluffy', and would probably prefer something like 'magnificent'. Cassie hadn't mentioned a cat and Lara hadn't seen one in the past few days. She wondered where it could have come from, until she registered that the terrace door was open, which meant it must have just wandered in. Lara wasn't sure whether the cat was a he or a she, but the lion-like mane of white fur and the disdainful stare made her think it could be a he. With his golden eyes he was regal, and scrutinised every move she made as she placed the box down on the table in front of the sofa.

She turned from the cat and read the customs form on the box. After that she pulled at the tape until she had one side of the box partially open. She tugged at the rest of the box but it wouldn't open without a knife, and by now she had collapsed beside the great white cat who was refusing to move from his prime position on the couch.

'What do you think Mom has sent me?' she asked her feline companion.

The cat replied by beginning to clean his paws while Lara stuck her left hand into the box to investigate the contents. Underneath the layers of paper and bubble wrap, it felt like two – no, three books. Her fingers then brushed a letter, which she pulled out and opened. It was from her mother, Maeve, and she carefully read it, thinking how strange it felt in these days of email to be receiving a letter.

August 25, 2015

Darling Lara,

As you know, Eventide has been sold and it's all moving rather quickly. Betty is being ruthless and much of the contents have been auctioned. I have saved a few things for you in Gerard's garage, but I suspect they're probably not the things you might have liked, as they had to be small. I did manage to grab the Cornishware but Betty had thrown out most of the cookbooks. Here are the few I salvaged. I don't know if you want them but I couldn't bear to see them thrown away, knowing you had used them so much. Also I found another picture of Grandie in his uniform. I knew you would treasure it and Betty didn't want it. I have never understood their relationship. She's dispensed with the past without a glance.

The rest of the pictures are from the local antique dealer who returned them to me. You remember the Winthrop desk? When they were cleaning it up they found these photos wedged at the back under the bottom drawer. I thought they might be of interest.

Am missing you more than ever. The sense of relief has arrived here on the Cape, with Labor Day around the corner and the weight of summer visitors gone. You know I love that freshness that arrives on the breeze, yet the heat of the sun is just as intense. Love you, my darling, and I hope that you are enjoying your adventure and a rest. Send Cassie my best wishes.

Hope to Skype soon if we can sort out this five-hour time difference.

Mom xxx

Lara dropped the letter on the top of the box, thinking of the scents of fall on the Cape, the slow turning of the leaves. She longed to walk the beach in front of Eventide. The cry of a seagull outside reminded her she wasn't far from the water and she could easily reach a beach. She wished she had enjoyed Eventide more when it was hers to use, but then wasn't it always the way to look back with longing?

She went out to the stone terrace, all the while feeling the cat's eyes upon her. Lara didn't know where the feline had come from, but her limited knowledge of them told her that if she didn't feed him he would disappear soon. Cats were creatures of comfort and Lara had to agree with him the couch was comfy – plus, it must have been bathed in sunlight most of the afternoon. Now the sun was behind the converted barn and out of view. However, golden light still hit the tops of the trees and turned everything softer. Because Cassie was so busy, tomorrow Lara would face the dragon, as she'd begun to think of the bride's brother, and deliver the new wedding cake.

The phone rang, and moments later Lara heard Cassie answer it. Lara went back inside and picked up a knife to properly open the box. On top of three old cookbooks – one of which was the beloved *La Veritable Cuisine de Famille par Tante Marie* – she found a small collection of oddly sized photos. Her hand stilled as she came to one. It was an out-of-focus shot of a couple on their wedding day, but there was no mistaking Grandie. His erect posture, uniform and broad shoulders were clear despite the fact that the camera was focused on the building. The couple were off to the right of the photo with the sea behind them and a bit of lawn in front. Strangely what was in clear focus was the side of a bay window made from grey stone to the centre left.

This must be the photo Betty had mentioned. Lara stared at it, running her finger over the image of her great-grandparents. She could see it was most likely Cornwall from the vague outline of the ocean and the headlands in the background. She had to be close to finding Amelia. She squinted at the picture, hoping she could perceive more detail, but all she got for her trouble was a mild headache.

Lara drove with both hands on the wheel, leaning forward slightly as she tried to see around the hedges that blocked her view of the road. In spite of having driven a little bit every day, she still hated it and walked everywhere if she could. But there was no possible way that she could carry the cake to Windward, so here she was, inching her way along tiny lanes towards the house. Roads narrowed without warning, bends appeared out of nowhere and people drove as if they had plenty of room.

Although the cake was well secured in its special box on the back seat of the car, Lara still took each turn with caution and had already been passed by four drivers frustrated at her lack of speed. She didn't care. This cake would be delivered whole.

Passing a small Catholic church on the right, she thought about Grandie. He'd been dead three weeks. The pain of his absence hadn't abated as she'd expected. Of course, being in an area that he had visited and trying to find out about her great-grandmother hadn't made it easy to forget. She wasn't sure she wanted to either. He was a huge part of her life. Losing him, her job, and her husband all at once had left her wondering who she was without them. She had no idea. She was empty. Only when she was cooking did she feel whole.

Windward's gates finally appeared and she breathed a sigh of relief. One part of the ordeal was over. Now all she needed to do was to put the cake into the kitchen without dropping it. She flexed her shoulders, parked the car and carefully collected the cake from the back seat.

The wind came whistling around the house and held the chill of autumn. Lara could tell that despite today's blue skies the house needed the strength of the grey stone that made up its walls. It was a beautiful setting but Windward obviously took the full force of the weather on a regular basis, sitting as it did high above the bay.

However, the garden showed no signs of the approaching colder days or damage from the prevailing wind. Roses were coming into flower again. She turned from admiring it, making sure she didn't lose her footing. Just like the last time, the kitchen door was open and the room in darkness, but unlike the previous visit, it was filled with the sweet scent of tomatoes cooking.

Lara hesitated on the threshold, waiting to speak until her eyes had adjusted to the gloom. 'Hello?' No response, so she ventured forth and put the cake on the large table that dominated the room. She ran her fingers over the bleached wooden surface while she noted the Mason jars lined up on the counter by the Aga. A butcher's block was covered in chopped onions and herbs with large containers of vinegar standing by. It was an impressive setup for preserving and someone was being industrious with a glut of end-of-season tomatoes.

'Hello?' Lara looked around. It was clear someone was home but nobody was in sight. 'Hello?' she called again. When no answer came she spied a pencil and a pad of paper by the phone. Quickly she wrote a note and then fled into the sunshine before she encountered anyone.

Once out in the garden she slowed her pace and slipped her sunglasses on. The vegetable patch was large and she saw still more bright red fruit weighing down the tired stems. They were at their sweetest at this time of the year, in many ways wasted on sauces and chutneys. Served with a lunch of cheese – preferably goat's – alongside fresh sourdough bread, the achingly ripe tomatoes would be perfect. Her mouth watered. Walking towards the car, she stopped to admire the orchard. The trees were heavy with fruit. A lazy wasp circled her, and she waved it away before slipping into the car.

Her delivery done, she carefully departed from Windward and made her tentative way towards Trebah Garden. Grandie had embarked from there for the D-Day invasion. She was halfway there when her cell phone rang, Cassie's number flashing on the screen. She pulled over into an entrance to a field and answered it.

'Hi.'

'Sorry. Two of the waitresses have gone down with flu. Can you come back and give me a hand?'

'Of course. See you soon.' Lara sighed. She could just make out the blue of the river. Trebah would wait for another day.

Windward, Mawnan Smith, Falmouth, Cornwall
5 September 2015

Peta was on her knees with a mouth full of pins adjusting the hem of my wedding outfit while I tried to stand upright without the support of my cane. This was becoming harder to do recently. The weather had been good, but what dampness there was always seemed to find its way into my hips and knees. My other joints didn't suffer in quite the same way.

'Shouldn't I hold the cane so that you know where it's catching?' I asked.

Peta shook her head and mumbled something that might have been 'Be still.' But that was the problem. At the moment neither my mind nor my body would be still. It was only a week to Peta's wedding and my thoughts kept returning to the same day seventy years ago. And because I didn't want to remember it, I kept myself busy.

I had dug out my will. It was worrying me. My heirs were Jack and Peta, which was what I wanted, but the difficulty arose from my sister. Her name was on the deed of the house. She owned half but it was for my sole use for my lifetime. I should have contacted her years ago, but some things went too deep and couldn't be undone.

The pain had been locked away for so long, but nothing could keep it away forever except death. And there was the rub. I wasn't dead, despite my aching bones and advancing age. The doctor insisted I was in good health, but it wouldn't last indefinitely. I didn't want it to. I had to sort things. My sister could be dead for all I knew. I hadn't felt her for so many years.

'Keep still.' I felt the prick of a pin as Peta's hand slipped.

It wasn't fair to leave the mess for Jack and Peta. Was Amelia still alive? I sighed and tried to focus on her but there was nothing. It was the way I had wanted it for so long.

There was probably a way to find out now. If I asked Jack he would look into it for me, but then there would be questions. Assuming that Amelia's children or grandchildren would want or even have any interest in Windward, of course. But everyone had an interest in money.

'There, that will be better.' Peta rose from her knees and placed the last pin into the pincushion. She touched my arm. 'Come back from those dark thoughts.'

I focused on her, frightened that she could see into my mind.

'No, Gran, I can't see details. Just pain, and that you've never shared it – but recently you've spent a lot of time delving into it, haven't you?' She lifted the dress carefully over my head. 'And that worries me.'

'It's because you are happy.'

'No, that's not it. Darkness isn't good, Gran.'

I smiled ruefully. No, darkness wasn't good but I couldn't escape it any more.

'Think of something happy – like the fact that Eddie will be here in a few days. It's been ages since we've seen him.'

I smiled. Eddie.

'That's much better. Although I do detect sadness there as well. Focus on the happiness, Gran. Think of my grandfather, or even another lover's kiss, or your first kiss.'

I laughed, remembering while she helped me into my clothes and handed me my cane.

'I hadn't realised you kissed quite so many frogs.' Peta chuckled.

'There are many things you don't know about me.'

'I know.' She smoothed my cardigan over my shoulders. 'It's best that way.'

'Yes, a bit of mystery is good as long as you don't dwell on it. I have to go and meet Cassie, my caterer. Is there anything you need?'

'No.'

'Fine. Keep thinking kisses – the good ones, that is.' She tucked my wedding finery over her arm and flew down the stairs. Before long I heard her car leave.

Kisses. Even now I still remember the first time he kissed

me in love and not just in passion. That one action had taken my heart forever with its tenderness. I knew then that I would never be in love with anyone else.

Windward, Mawnan Smith, Falmouth, Cornwall
8 September 2015

The bottom drawer of the desk was filled with papers that I hadn't looked at since my grandmother died. I wasn't sure I wanted to sort it but if I didn't, Jack or Peta would have to, and I didn't know what they would find. It was only when lying awake last night that I realised one of the biggest gifts I could give them was to be ready for the end. And that meant clearing everything out. They didn't need the fragments of my past that would raise more questions than provide answers. To them I was the widow of their grandfather who had no family except for them.

The black bin liner lay empty on the floor beside me and somewhere I could hear music. I think Peta was meeting with the man who would be the disc jockey at the wedding when the band finished. As my bedroom overlooked the bay I hadn't a hope of getting a wink of sleep in a few days' time, not that I'd had much sleep this week. My dreams were filled with the past – not as it had happened but as I wished it had. The pain was so great when I woke and realised that it hadn't been real, that it was just the power of the mind creating what it wanted to have happened.

Pulling a pile of papers out, I flipped through the fragile newspaper cuttings and smiled. It was Grandmother's engagement announcement in the *Times*, alongside both Mother's and Uncle Reg's birth announcements. There was a thin photograph album of her debutante year. She had been a beautiful woman. From minor aristocracy to middle class in no time at all. The money had gone and so had the gloss. All that remained were a few pieces of jewellery, and Windward. It hadn't been the First World War that had broken the family but the Second.

I tucked the clipping into the photo album. Peta might like

to see the dresses that Grandmother had worn. I dug through the back of the drawer and it appeared to be mostly the paperwork regarding Windward. Grandmother had left the house to my sister and me. To my mother she had given the jewels but by then it was the last thing Mother had needed. All the best ones had already gone to Aunt Margaret.

'What's brought on this bout of activity?' Jack sauntered in and peered over my shoulder. 'First you venture into the attic and now the bowels of the desk. Is there a lost treasure I don't know about? Is this where the map is?'

I laughed. 'Sadly no, but have you thoroughly checked the caves on the beach below?'

'Checked, and rechecked more times that I can count.' He shook his head. 'That looks like a title deed.'

'It is. It's the original paperwork on this place.' I held it up to him.

'Don't bin it. I'd love to look through it but I've got to head out to meet a client.'

I raised an eyebrow.

'Yes, I know, in person.' He kissed the top of my head. 'I'll be back in time to cook dinner though. I don't fancy one of your burnt offerings. Get some rest while I'm out. You've been very pale the last few days, like you've seen a ghost.'

My breath caught. I was living with my ghosts now, more than ever. 'I'll take a nap.'

'I won't be long.'

While I put the paperwork on the house back in the drawer, I contemplated whether this meeting with a client was a fluke or a new direction. Jack didn't do people unless he had to. Numbers were his thing and had been for years. He understood them.

✳ Sixteen ✳

HMS *Attack*, Portland, Dorset
17 February 1944

K atherine handed me yet another cup of coffee. I nodded
my thanks while slipping the headphones off one ear
and watched her walk back to her headset at the end of one
of the long tables lining both sides of the room. She fiddled
with the dial while listening through one ear. Daytime shifts
were normally quiet and more a case of keeping track of vessels
coming in and out. Mostly it was general broadcast stuff, which
could be tedious and hard, sometimes writing down more than
200 blocks of four- or five-letter codes. There was just another
hour to go before this shift was finished. It had been peaceful
except for one operator who had cloth ears, meaning we'd gone
back and forth for ten minutes repeating the same message.
Eventually he received it correctly. I was sure I'd dealt with him
before; he had a way of writing Morse that was like a signature.
I supposed I did too.

Yawning, Katherine put her headphones on fully. 'So quiet.'
She lit a cigarette. It was one way to stay awake but I wasn't
that keen. Yet the ashtray beside me held two butts, more out
of boredom than anything else. In a weird way I preferred the
midnight-to-eight shift. I was often sleepy but there was more
happening.

'So tell me about your American.'

My eyes opened wide.

She smiled. 'I'm assuming that's what you've been daydreaming about because most of this watch you haven't been here.'

I laughed. 'He's not mine.'

'Could have fooled me. He didn't dance with anyone else and the last two Saturdays he's saved the last dance for you.'

'Lieutenant Webster is a friend.' I pursed my lips. Even to my ears that was feeble.

She laughed. 'Just be careful. Don't lose your heart. Poor Jane found out the American she'd fallen for had a wife and three children back home.'

I blinked. 'How did she find out?'

'She overheard one of the GIs talking to another about her and him and how he'd ...' She dropped her voice to a whisper. 'How he'd had his way with her.'

My eyes widened.

'So be careful.' She smiled. 'You're a sensible one but we can all be foolish in love.' She took a long drag on her cigarette. 'I should know.' Katherine was a divorcee, after finding out her husband had another wife three towns away.

Dah dit dah dah dah dah dit dah (- ·-- --·-) came through my headphones. Our call sign, and it was just like someone was speaking my name. My back went straight, my pencil at the ready quickly recording a stream of code. Within minutes a sheet was filled, torn off then handed on to the coders to take away and decipher. A steady stream of messages came in for the remainder of the shift and I didn't think of Bobby again until I came off watch an hour later. He wouldn't be having his way with me any time soon. I stopped walking. Had people talked about Amelia that way? I hoped not. I looked out to the harbour, where there was another US vessel. How would I find out if Bobby had a wife at home? Maybe that was why he hadn't tried anything.

3 March 1944

Inside the tunnels it was always the same – a haze of smoke and stale air, whether it was night or day, warm or cold. It was a relief to be outside, and the sun shone down on me as I filled my lungs, pausing on the threshold of the tunnels. The days were becoming longer and the promise of spring showed on the hillside behind me. Dot waved from the distance and I walked to meet her. She'd been to Weymouth.

'Shopping?' I spied the bag in her hand.

'As usual there was nothing.'

'Then what's in there?' I asked, pointing.

'Toothpaste and soap.' She opened it to show me the contents, then jabbed me in the ribs. 'Isn't that your American?' Ahead of us stood a group of men. Bobby was there, looking out towards the docks away from me, and next to him was a US general, along with two majors, an admiral and Commander Rowse. My glance darted between the commander and Bobby, both handsome men. I walked a little taller as we headed towards the mess. We would have to pass right by them. Why was Bobby here? No, I told myself, I shouldn't be thinking of things like that. Just seeing the officers together told me whatever was happening was big. Admirals and generals equalled important, and Bobby was with them.

As we approached the group Commander Rowse looked at us and we saluted. Bobby turned and smiled. My breath caught. Dot and I quickened our steps as we passed them and entered the mess.

'He only has eyes for you.' Dot winked and I tried to think about food instead of Bobby. I hoped I'd be able to see him soon. It was foolish, but I couldn't stop it. I dreamt about him and when I wasn't focused on listening to *dit*s and *dah*s he was in almost every thought. I had it bad. Amelia would say it was about time. But surely I couldn't be in love? Lust, yes. All emotions were riding high. When life was so perilous everything was more intense.

Waiting for me was a letter from Amelia. Guilt needled at me. I hadn't written to anyone. The last time I tried to it was to congratulate her on her engagement. But I couldn't find the words. Her thoughts were filled with happiness, high like I had never known. I wasn't sure if I wanted to read about it.

1 March 1944

Darling,

*Something has changed. I can feel your excitement from here.
Why won't you share it with me? You are exhilarated. It's
buzzing around inside of you. You are in love and you haven't
told me. I'm trying not to be crushed, really I am. Hopefully it's
simply that you've been too busy to write. Please let that be all.
I'd never want to feel that you felt you couldn't share things with
me. I hope it's not because I would say I told you so because, of
course, I couldn't be mean. I wouldn't and I am only ever happy
for you. Are you silent because he's an American? You wonder
how I know it, but you are forgetting I can sometimes hear your
thoughts. Not always, though, and less so now.*

*I shall let it go and tell you about Eddie coming down and
the celebration we had. Father was here too. I hated that you
weren't but then you did know before everyone. We drank
champagne, ate oysters and danced to the gramophone – even
Grandmother. Eddie's mother was happy, happier than I have
ever seen her, but that could have been the telephone call from
Tom to wish us the best. He, like you, wasn't with us.*

*Don't hesitate to love. Don't hold back. You remember Kitty
in the village? Her fiancé is dead. She is dealing with it bravely,
saying at least she had known love. Don't waste your life. I
know what you're thinking but I hope you take the chance while
you have it.*

*Love you always,
Xxxx*

I held her letter in my hands. How could I forget that she
knew my thoughts? These feelings were all so new and unsure I
didn't know what to think. Her way was so tempting. Footsteps
sounded in the passage. Pat walked into the cabin.

'Oh, you're here. I thought you were in the mess. You've just
had a call from Lieutenant Webster. He wonders if you might

be free tomorrow.' She grinned. 'I told him you were because we were supposed to go ashore together so I said you'd meet him at ten.'

'You did?'

'I did. You may thank me later.' She ducked as I threw my pencil at her.

I swallowed, looking at Amelia's letter. My sister was telling me to take a hold of life now.

Pat handed me my pencil. 'Oh, he said to dress warmly.'

The weather had been bitterly cold the past few days, but just thinking of him had warmth spreading through me.

'Thanks.'

'Go and have fun – just not too much.' She winked and waltzed out the door chuckling. I glanced at my watch. How would I ever fall asleep now, thinking about Bobby?

4 March 1944

The morning was crisp and clear. Frost covered all surfaces and they sparkled in the low and golden morning sunlight. As the train made its way past Chesil Beach I thought about Amelia's letter. She and Eddie were lovers. I didn't want to believe it yet I was consumed with curiosity at the same time.

The train slowed for a moment and I looked up at the mound made of stones and pebbles dividing us from the sweep of beach I knew was on the other side. It was like this war. It blocked our path, kept us from living our lives. I tried to tell myself that it wasn't stopping Amelia – but what if Eddie was killed? In truth, it was quite likely to happen. How would she cope? The odds for Bomber Command were not good – he'd beaten them so far, but what if he didn't? What would she do if she fell pregnant? Grandmother would never forgive her.

I shook my head. I was right. Better not to risk anything at all until the war was over, and that included love. It was the only way to come out of this dire thing intact – or at least as intact as one could be. I wasn't sure if anyone would ever be whole again.

I stepped off the train. Scanning the platform I didn't see Bobby so I walked towards the exit, and finally spotted him standing at the edge of the crowd, searching for me. I studied him – so tall, so strong and so sure. My mouth went dry. He saw me. His serious face broke into a smile that felt brighter than the sun. He headed over to me, his pace quickening and he stopped just before we collided. 'You made it.'

'You doubted me?'

'Not you, but—' He stopped and looked behind him as some troops passed by in the distance. 'Right now nothing is certain.'

I nodded. We walked out of the station, where a jeep stood waiting. I tilted my head.

'I thought it might be good to escape on this beautiful day,' he said.

Escape. What a thought. I climbed in and noted the wicker picnic basket in the back.

Within minutes we were heading west towards Burton Bradstock where the Americans were camped, but before we reached Abbotsbury we turned off the road and onto a dirt track. HMS *Attack*, routine and duty felt a long way away. My hair was whipped out of its hold by the wind and lashed across my face as I turned towards Bobby. He wore a leather jacket and sunglasses and looked like something out of a Hollywood film. We wove through the narrow roads, getting occasional glimpses of Lyme Bay, and for that moment I felt far away from the war, even with the barbed wire on the cliffs. I knew if I looked behind us I would see the warships and military build-up on the beaches, but instead I studied Bobby. It was too noisy to speak until he turned onto a small side road that climbed up a hill.

'Where are we heading?'

He grinned and tapped the side of his nose.

'Or should I really be asking how on earth would you even know this spot existed, wherever it is?'

Bobby laughed as the jeep climbed further up the hill until the track ran out. He switched the engine off and pulled the basket from the back. 'I'll afraid we have to walk from here.' He took my hand and we headed up the hillside towards a small church-like building. 'What is it?' I squinted.

'St Catherine's Chapel.' We reached the top of the hill and there below us was the sweep of beach all the way to Portland – painfully beautiful and frightening at the same time. From this viewpoint the reality of the war was totally visible. Bomb defences covered the beach and the expanse of water that separated us from France was fully visible. Yet the air was warming with the sun while daffodils had bloomed near the church. At any other time it would have seemed perfect but the equipment cluttering Chesil Beach told another story.

'Beautiful,' he said beside me, his breath caressing my cheek. I turned and his lips were so close to mine. I shivered and he pulled me nearer to him, but then I stiffened, thinking of Katherine's warning. He stepped back and the wind from the sea cooled the air between us.

'Hungry?'

'Yes.' I couldn't believe the delights he'd obtained as he set out a blanket and organised the picnic of two chicken legs, some cheese and a beautiful loaf of bread. My stomach growled loudly. He laughed as he put out yet more food including some ham and a can of tinned peaches. My mouth watered at the thought of them.

'Do you know the history of the chapel?'

He nodded and tucked his hands behind his head, lying back with his eyes closed. His lashes were black and long. My fingers reached towards him but instead I picked up another piece of cheese, enjoying the creamy sweetness with the salt.

'It was part of an abbey destroyed by Henry VIII. Local knowledge says the chapel was built as early as the 1300s for the monks to retreat.' He opened his eyes and studied me. 'It was built in honour of St Catherine of Alexandria.'

'Of the Catherine Wheel?'

'The same. They say that local girls come here to pray to find a husband because St Catherine is the patron saint of spinsters and virgins, or at least locally she is.' A smile crept across his face.

I frowned. 'How do you know all this?'

He sat up and opened the peaches, offering me a bowl. 'I had a good chat with a local farmer and the vicar in the village church.'

I cut a peach with a spoon and slipped it into my mouth. The sweet taste hit my tongue and I closed my eyes with the pleasure of it. Bobby leaned back again and watched me as I caught the juice escaping on my fingers then quickly licked them. Even with the embarrassment of an audience it was too good to waste. His smile lit up his blue eyes. Amelia thought all Americans looked like film stars, which I knew wasn't true at all, but this one did. His quiet good manners belied all the brash antics of so many of the ones I'd met, including the ones who became too friendly on the train back to *Attack*. The imposed darkness of the blackout seemed to give them more license than they already felt they had. Bobby was different, and I couldn't say why.

'Tell me about where you come from and about your family,' I said, eyeing the last peach in the tin. He pushed it towards me. I didn't refuse.

'Not a lot to say,' he said. 'I'm from Massachusetts. I grew up south of Boston in a place called Situate.' He handed me a napkin. 'I have a younger sister who's training to be a teacher. My father is a lawyer and my mother was a nurse.'

'That tells me very little.'

He smiled. 'True.'

'Secretive?' I raised an eyebrow and studied his features: they were defined, clean-cut and very American somehow but there was something in his glance that hinted at more. He wasn't all on show, and I could see there were depths, especially in those eyes.

'I am what you see.' He waved his hand from the top of his head down to his feet.

I laughed. 'Just like me then.'

'Now we are on to an interesting subject.'

'Boring.' I glanced at the building and view. I presumed he knew this spot because it was used for surveillance.

'Tell me anyway.' He rolled to his side and rested propped on his elbow.

'Like you I have a mother, a father and a sister.'

He grinned. 'The similarities are astounding.'

'Indeed. My father is a major and a surgeon while my mother is in Cornwall running the local Red Cross and helping my grandmother. The Army took over my uncle's house, where my grandmother lived, so she had to move to her summer house in Cornwall.' I paused, thinking of home and feeling the normal twist of loss. 'Grandmother is doing wonders with knitting needles and has taken to fishing and gardening remarkably well for a woman who didn't know how to boil water.' I paused. 'Actually I'm not sure she can boil water even now.'

He laughed but then his face went solemn. 'It can't be easy having your home taken over.'

'No.' I looked at the view, picturing Grandmother as she supervised with Aunt Margaret the salvaging of the most precious items to the dower house on Uncle Reg's estate in Oxfordshire. Then deciding that even that was too close to 'the hordes' as she called them. Although she had known some of the officers, it had been too much for her to take.

'It was your father you were waiting for the night we met.'

I grinned. 'Yes, he was to take me to dinner, but in the end he arrived with another major and had to cancel.'

'So you should have taken me up on my invitation?'

'Yes.' I looked at the feast we had picnicked on. This was far better than dinner in the Savoy.

'Tell me more,' he said.

I plucked a piece of grass and ran it through my fingers. 'Not much to tell. My sister is in the WRNS and seems to be enjoying herself immensely.' I frowned, deciding not mention that I was a twin. 'She's gone and become engaged to a pilot and now lives on the edge of despair from letter to letter.'

'You don't approve of her choice of fiancé? Or is it his role?'

I tilted my head and studied him. 'I hadn't thought of it that way,' I said, and twisted the blade of grass in my hands. 'No, Eddie is the right man for her but I don't see sense in falling in love now.' I glanced up, wondering what his reaction to this statement would be. 'There is too much to lose. Any one of us might not be here tomorrow.' I looked at the chapel. 'Unlike the local maidens I won't be praying to St Catherine until the war is over.'

'You don't believe in seizing the day – a bit of *carpe diem*?'

'Yes, and no. Seizing a glorious day like today and enjoying it, by all means. It's something to hold onto. But letting your heart go and then suffering the loss is unwise.'

He studied me. 'And you are wise and clever.'

I threw the blade of grass at him. 'You're making fun of me.'

'Not at all. Just surprised to find someone who thinks so much like myself.'

'Really?'

'Yes.' His glance connected with mine and despite my words I felt my heart slip sideways for a moment. He picked up my hand and traced my fingers with his. I stopped breathing. Caught in a trance as his light touch against my fingers sent messages across my body, I lost the ability to think or speak. I could only feel.

He leaned forward and kissed me – his mouth just touching mine. I leaned in, keeping the contact. My head was telling me to stop and my body was urging me closer.

Suddenly, he pulled back. 'We can't risk you getting back late.'

Or risk my heart, I added silently – although I feared it might be too late on that account.

❃ Seventeen ❃

Constantine, Falmouth, Cornwall
10 September 2015

It had been a manic few days while some sort of twenty-four-hour bug had made its way through all of Cassie's staff. Lara and Cassie had been the only two not to succumb, and Lara hadn't had a moment to consider Grandie or Amelia, or anything else for that matter. Now though all was quiet, so she propped up all the photographs against the wall on the far side of Cassie's kitchen. It wasn't a lot to go on – a name and a blurry photograph. Her grandmother Betty wasn't interested in her own past – while she had loved Lara's father and cared deeply for Lara and Leo, she had always had an odd relationship with her father, one where there was respect but no warmth. Lara thought back to her conversation with Betty and wondered if Amelia's untimely death had caused the rift between them, or if they were just two relations who had never really liked each other. It was sad, but it did often happen.

In the fridge Lara pulled out a bottle of Margaret River wine she'd found in the shop in Constantine when she'd grabbed some groceries for dinner tonight. She had been stunned by the excellent collection of wines available, including many from the Stuart Vineyard. These had been stocked at the restaurant where she'd worked in Manhattan. It had been one of her favourites, and finding it in a rural shop so far away was a complete surprise. Opening the bottle, she took a sniff and could smell the eucalyptus that grew around the vineyard. While chopping a few radishes for salad and tomatoes for an omelette, Lara studied the blurry wedding photograph, searching for something that was distinctive. It was the only clue she had, a bay window.

There was a loud meow and the cat brushed against her legs. Cassie had made enquiries about the cat but thus far hadn't found an owner. They had both agreed that he should be called Snowy, and he had already made himself right at home, spending plenty of time on the sofa.

Lara turned as a gust of wind blew all the photos, scattering them across the kitchen floor. She picked them up and stared at the wedding photo again. Just out of focus, it haunted her. She saw herself in her great-grandmother's outline, but she couldn't see much more. The woman's features were blurred and it was more Lara's understanding of the fashion of the day that filled in the details. The veil and gown would have been white and she knew from films what the colour of Grandie's uniform was. It was clearer in her head than on the glossy paper.

Outside, a van with 'Boscawen Cyder' written on the side pulled into the drive. A man and a woman emerged together and headed to the barn. Cassie was working late and Lara had almost finished making their meal but she would wait until these new arrivals had gone before serving up. She switched on her computer and searched for the national archives to see what she could discover now that she was pretty certain the marriage of her great-grandparents had taken place in Cornwall. This led her to another site where she typed in the details that she already had but came up with nothing. Maybe if she knew the district she would find a better result? She stood and stretched. Out the window she could see Cassie and the couple talking as they headed towards the house.

'Lara, come and meet Sam and Demi,' Cassie called from the hall as she walked towards the kitchen. 'I see you've found Sam's wine.'

Lara frowned.

'My family's vineyard in Margaret River.' He smiled. 'Sam Stuart.' He held out his hand and Lara took it.

'Lara Pearce.' She liked the look of the tall, strongly built Australian.

'Hi, I'm Demi Williams, Sam's business partner,' said Demi.

'Wines?' Lara asked, noting how beautiful the petite blonde was.

'No, a boutique hotel not far from here, in Boscawen. Plus a cider business,' Demi said. 'Cassie tells me you're a chef. And she's also told me you've worked in some of the best kitchens on the east coast of the States.'

Lara nodded, and gave Cassie a look.

Demi smiled. 'Well, I'd love your input on a restaurant we're building.'

'Happy to have a look. Not sure what I can add. Surely you'd want the chef who will be working there to advise?'

Sam coughed. 'That's the problem. Thus far we've had no luck finding a chef who's willing to come to the wilds of Cornwall to an unknown restaurant – especially one of the calibre we're hoping to find.'

'Ah, I see.'

'Cassie has our number, so give us a ring when it suits you.' Demi pulled her keys out of her pocket.

'Will do.'

'See you at the wedding, Cassie. And I'll look forward to showing you around, Lara.' Demi waved and they disappeared out the door, back towards their van.

'Interesting couple.' Lara poured Cassie a glass of wine and began the omelettes.

'Very, bright and clever too.' Cassie rubbed her lower back. 'They're providing the wine for the wedding. Demi is also great friends with the bride and groom.'

'Sounds like this is a big wedding.'

'It is, in a way.' Cassie took a sip of wine. 'It's a linking of the north and the south sides of the river.' She laughed. 'In fact I think that's why they've bought a house in Gweek, so they sort of straddle both sides.'

Lara frowned at this.

'Gweek sits at the end of the Helford,' explained Cassie.

'Ah.' Lara put the salad bowl on the table and served the omelettes.

'You should go and see Boscawen.'

Lara nodded, thinking she was here not to look at hotels and kitchens but to try and track down her great-grandmother.

'Seriously, it's wonderful and the restaurant is going to over-look the river.' Cassie looked up from her glass. 'I'd say it's right up your street.'

Lara sighed. 'I can't work for months.'

Cassie laughed. 'It won't be open for months.'

Lara made a face.

'Just saying.' Cassie picked up her fork. 'Anyway, when the wedding's over we must head up to my parents in north Cornwall.'

'That would be brilliant. I'd love to see them.' Lara grinned but again wondered when she'd track down Amelia if she kept being distracted. 'By the way, what district of Cornwall is this?'

Cassie looked up. 'This is Carrick. Does this relate to your great-grandmother?'

'Yes.'

'Also worth checking Kerrier too.'

'Will do that.' Lara closed her eyes and once again wished she had more to go on.

11 September 2015

A paw hit Lara's face. She opened one eye. Light flooded the room. Snowy sat staring at her. Lesson one in living with Snowy would be to close the window at night but the weather had been so mild she would have been too hot. Why the English didn't have screens on their windows she didn't know. They were useful for keeping out insects and lonely animals. Lara stroked Snowy's head and stretched. Today she was heading to Trebah and would be back on the research path. All of Cassie's team had returned to full health.

After a quick coffee and piece of toast Lara drove carefully along the lanes. Coping with the tiny Cornish roads was getting easier, but not by much. Yesterday she'd taken a wrong turn along narrow, winding lanes and ended up near Port Navas, terrified she'd meet a car coming the other way and have to reverse for miles. This morning the roads were clear and she arrived at the Trebah Garden parking lot before it was open. Standing by the entrance gate, she studied the pictures displayed of the 29th Infantry Division preparing for D-Day. It seemed hard to believe that this peaceful place had played a key part.

The cool air was scented with eucalyptus and pine as she walked under a tree fern into the reception of Trebah Garden. She bought her ticket then stopped to read the wall plaques about the 29th Division. 7500 men had embarked on ten 150-foot flat-bottomed boats on 1 June 1944, and then onto Omaha beach on 6 June. Lara scanned the few pictures looking for Grandie but didn't see him. These men had been busy preparing for D-Day by widening the road from Penryn to here, which she had appreciated when she drove it a few days ago. It seemed unnaturally wide compared to the others she'd driven on. The disruption to this remote part of Britain must have been huge but there would have been no way to get their big vehicles to the river without doing it.

The garden, full of beautiful hydrangeas, occupied the sloping valley. The array of colour and varieties distracted her from her thoughts of Grandie, yet she could feel him here. What would have been in bloom in the garden then? Not hydrangeas. The plaque had said they had dug trenches and stored ammunition, so maybe nothing had bloomed except fear. Years ago Leo had felt Grandie was just being grumpy not talking about the war, but now, considering it, it might have been so traumatic he may not have wanted to remember, let alone discuss it. She walked on, enjoying the plantings, but thoughts of what her great-grandfather and all the other soldiers had experienced seemed so far from the tranquillity surrounding her.

Crossing from the tree-covered valley onto the beach, Lara was almost blinded by the light. She stepped down expecting to sink into sand but instead found the resistance of concrete. It covered the beach to where the water rolled in with the on-shore breeze. Standing in the middle of the concrete, she looked down the river trying to imagine it covered in GIs full of nerves and possibly excitement. This would have been the first action many of them had ever been in, including Grandie. Despite his military training it had all been theory and no practice, and bashing squares at West Point wouldn't have prepared them for what these men were about to face. Even the training they had done here was scant preparation for Omaha Beach.

Aside from the gentle sound of the waves crashing against the concrete it was peaceful. A few sailboats tacked across the river but the quiet was astounding. In spite of the few visible houses, the place appeared timeless. How had people reacted to seeing large landing craft filling this area? Despite the pictures in the ticket hall it was hard to imagine. Right now it was postcard-perfect with whitewashed cottages above a beach in the distance. The contrast of what she saw here with what those men had faced days later after being tossed about in boats was unthinkable. Her stomach turned. Those boats had not been made for high seas or comfort.

She slipped off her shoes and rolled up her jeans. The water was startlingly clear and equally cold – colder than that of the inner Cape. She stood ankle deep, letting her feet numb while she pulled her sweater closer. She looked out to the mouth of the river. Somewhere towards the bay was the spot where the photo of her great-grandfather had been taken. She could see the coastal path that she could take along the river.

Her phone rang, and she answered it right away. 'Cassie?'

'Lara, I need you.'

'OK.'

'It's Mum. She's in hospital and Dad's a wreck.'

'Oh God, I'm so sorry.' Lara realised what Cassie needed right then, and didn't hesitate. 'Go now. I'm just on the beach at Trebah. It won't be long before I'm back.'

'But Peta's wedding – it's tomorrow, and there's so much to—'

'I can handle it. I'll handle it all. Don't worry. Just get to your parents now and call me later.'

'Yes, thanks.'

'What are friends for? Now go, and drive carefully.' Lara took one last look down the river then headed back into the garden. A sadness followed her despite the beauty on view. She wondered how many of the men who'd been here had survived and were able to return home.

Mawnan Church, Mawnan Smith, Falmouth, Cornwall
11 September 2015

The scent of lilies filled the church. I looked at the handiwork of Victoria Lake – no, I had to remind myself, Victoria Roberts now since she had married the lovely Sebastian. She was with stalwart of the community Jane Penrose who always knew everything. They had done a marvellous job using lilies from the florist and what was in bloom in the garden – fuchsias, sedum, late roses, goldenrod, hydrangeas and Japanese anemones. The effect was warm and rich and I knew would go with Peta's dress and that of the bridesmaids. Peta's hair, now its normal blonde, would be threaded with soft pink rosebuds. She had included me in all the planning although I told her she knew best. I was interested but it all cut too close to the bone. Bar the lilies, these were the same flowers that had adorned this church in 1945 and this was almost like reliving it again. How could I want to be a part of it? As much as I loved Peta she had no idea what she was asking me to do, even with her second sight. She stood by the altar with Victoria who was clutching a bunch of laurel shoots in her hand. Peta was so like Jack yet so different. Eight years separated them and a lifetime of experience.

Jane came up to me. 'I wasn't sure about Peta's plan but I have to say the church looks stunning.'

'It does. But with so many people coming will anyone even notice the flowers?'

She laughed. 'I always do but then I would.' She adjusted one of the posies on the end of the nearest pew. 'Your mother had a way with flowers.'

I nodded. Of course she would remember that. Mother had

done the flowers for the church until it was physically impossible for her, not that she was infirm in that way. I had often wondered if that would have been easier to deal with rather than mental infirmity. Her talent with flowers was the last thing to disappear, and it had been a solace to her when nothing else could reach her. God knows I had tried.

'Did you hear my question?' Jane touched my arm.

'Sorry. I didn't.'

'I was just saying I remembered your sister's wedding. Of course, not much of it, as I was so young at the time. The goldenrod with the hydrangeas brought the memory back.' She paused. 'But there was also honeysuckle as well.' She looked about. 'Your mother had woven tendrils around the pillars. The scent was heavenly.'

I nodded and moved away, remembering that the wedding dress had been remade from Aunt Margaret's. The baby bump was mostly disguised but if you looked closely it was visible. My legs wobbled and I sat when I reached the front pew, as I had all those years ago. Except then the wobble had been caused by grief; now it was old age and sadness. My chest tightened and it was hard to breathe. I looked at Peta who suddenly turned away from Victoria and rushed the few steps to my side.

'Come on, Gran, a few proper breaths, please. You're not allowed to kick the bucket a day before I marry.' Her hand made slow circles on my back and slowly the tightness passed as air filled my lungs. 'Let's get you home.' She helped me to my feet and escorted me outside to her little red car. 'I need to grab my phone. I left it on the altar. I'll be right back.' She walked ten feet and turned. 'Think about now, Gran. Not the past.'

I watched her slip into the church and wondered how much she knew.

❋ Eighteen ❋

Weymouth, Dorset
11 March 1944

When the lights dimmed and the news reel began, Bobby took my hand in his. With his fingers encircling mine the world felt safe despite the images on the screen. I looked forward to seeing *Casablanca*. He slipped his arm around me as the opening credits began and I rested my head against his shoulder, feeling his strength. But before long I was caught up in the plight of Rick and Ilsa.

At the end of the film, he gave me his handkerchief as I watched Rick walk away with Captain Renault. I knew it was the right thing, but my heart would never be the same again. Bobby leaned down and kissed me before the house lights came on. I was still crying as we walked out into the darkness. He stopped and wiped the tears from my face. 'It was just a film.'

'I know, but it was …' My words were swallowed in tears. 'Love,' I finally mumbled.

'Yes, he loved her and he did the right thing.'

'But—'

'No buts. It was the right thing.'

I nodded. Rick and Ilsa would never have a future but they would have Paris. Would that ever be enough?

Soon, we arrived at the Golden Lion, the pub frequented by the Navy and the Americans. But my mind wasn't in Weymouth but Casablanca. The pub was so crowded I couldn't see much, but eventually I found a seat while Bobby went to the bar. I gazed through the smoke, wishing Sam was at the piano, but instead I saw a mass of uniforms and heard the sound of laughter.

Bobby smiled as he walked back to me. 'I'm slowly coming to enjoy this warm beer.'

I laughed and shook my head. 'I can't imagine cold beer.' I made a face.

'One day I'll show you the delights of an ice-cold beer on a hot summer's day and you'll look back to this moment and wonder why you ever thought this tasted good.'

'Is that a promise?' My mouth twitched, fighting a smile.

He looked me in the eyes and raised his glass. 'Most definitely.'

Just then another American approached us. 'You know you can't trust these West Point boys.' He winked. 'They're all full of themselves and far too smart for their own good.'

'You should know,' Bobby laughed.

'Indeed. Now introduce me to this English beauty.'

'Adele Seaton, this is Captain James Tucker of Houston, Texas, just in case you couldn't place the accent.'

Commander Rowse entered the pub and walked towards us. I shifted in my seat. Although many times I'd seen our officers in the pub, this was the first time I'd seen Commander Rowse.

Captain Tucker turned. 'Here's my date. I'll leave you two in peace.' He grinned. 'I have to say, Webster, you have wonderful taste.' He looked at me. 'If you get tired of him, I'm free.' He winked as he joined Commander Rowse, and together they drifted off to the far end of the bar.

'Pay no attention to him.' Bobby put his pint down.

'Why not?' I tilted my head, trying to see the two men.

'Because I'm jealous.'

I laughed, still watching Tucker and Rowse in deep conversation over their pints. 'Why?'

'I wouldn't want to lose you.' He touched my hand and I looked up to see the sincerity on his face.

'He wears the same ring that you do.'

'Yes, it a US Military Academy class ring.' He turned the large ring on his finger and I pulled his hand across the table. It was gold and onyx with West Point and 1943 embossed with a seal.

'Were you there together?'

'He was two years ahead of me.'

'Sir.' A soldier came up to Bobby and stood rigidly avoiding my glance. 'Are we playing tomorrow?'

'Yes, Army versus Navy at 0900.'

'See you then, sir.' He saluted and left the pub.

I glanced at Bobby, frowning.

'Football,' he said.

'Football?'

'American football. Do you want to come and watch?'

'I'd love to but I'm on the eight-to-four shift tomorrow.' I gave him a rueful grin.

'I could ask the commander.'

I frowned.

He tilted his head to the side and grinned. 'It would help with cultural understanding.'

I laughed. 'Are you playing?'

'Yes, I'm the quarterback.'

'And that is?'

For the next half-hour Bobby tried to explain the intricacies of American football to me. I understood nothing but the sound of his voice and his excitement about the game. The bell rang for last orders and he stood to walk me back to the train. Outside, the night was cold and dark without a moon or stars.

'What are you thinking about?' he asked, as we reached the train station. 'You've been so silent.'

'You,' I said as we stepped onto the platform.

'Me?' He stopped just short of the queue.

'Hmm, yes. You seem to fill most of my thoughts when I'm not working.'

'Excellent.' He pulled me into his arms. 'Here's something to be thinking about.'

His mouth touched mine. Warmth spread though me as he left a trail of kisses across my cheek to my ear lobe.

Just then, the guard called, 'All on board!' and Bobby helped me into the carriage. I leaned out of the window.

'Wish us luck.' He grabbed my hand.

'But I'm in the Navy,' I said as the train began to pull away.

'I know, but we're on the same side in the war.'

'Yes,' I called into the darkness, laughing.

12 March 1944

I stood on the side of the field with Dot, hardly believing that I'd been able to swap shifts around at the last minute. It did mean I would be on the midnight-until-eight shift, but seeing the delight on Bobby's face made the thought of a sleepless night worth it. There would be time for sleep later.

'Look at that grin. Someone's happy to see you.' Dot gently elbowed me.

'He's always smiling.'

Dot turned from the field to make a face at me. 'No, he's not. I've seen him around when you haven't been near and I would say he's a serious soul.' She laughed. 'You bring out the smiles in him. And, for that matter, he does in you.' We watched the coin toss, after which the ball was handed to Bobby. 'You're two of a kind. Serious and hard-working but lightening each other up. He's just not the same when you aren't around.'

The whistle blew. Bobby kicked the ball and both teams converged into action. I didn't know where to look. The ball was thrown forward and I expected to hear a whistle but there was none. I watched bemused, flinching each time Bobby was tackled despite the padding he was wearing.

I tried to remember the things he'd told me about the game the previous night but I apparently hadn't taken in a word because it made no sense. I'd expected it to be like rugby but it wasn't at all. Bobby caught the ball when one of the Navy players threw it and ran towards the goal.

'Go, Army!' I jumped up and down.

Dot nudged me. 'You are standing here dressed as a member of the British Navy … shouting "Go, Army". It might not be what you want to be doing.'

I blushed.

Dot laughed. 'Just because you're in love doesn't mean that you can support the Army.' She arched an eyebrow.

'I'm not in love.'

'You could have fooled me,' she said, and laughed again at my indignant expression.

HMS *Attack*, Portland, Dorset
9 April 1944

As was frequently the case when Easter was in April, the weather was foul. Christ may have risen but everything else was being battered down by the rain as I stood outside the church following the service. Just as I decided to make a dash for it across the road, a horn blared at me and there was a squeal of brakes.

'Do you need a ride?' Bobby leaned out of the jeep that had just come to a halt. His smile caught my heart. I ran over and hopped in. Raindrops rested on his long eyelashes and rolled down his cheeks. I lifted my hand to wipe them away, my fingers stilling on his cheekbone. A horn sounded behind us and I drew my hand and my glance away.

'Where are you headed?'

'Just off to a meeting, but I have time to drop you off.' His hand reached out for mine for a second before he changed gears and set the jeep in motion.

'Thanks,' I said. 'I thought you might be heading to church.'

'The padre held a sunrise Mass in the camp this morning.'

'Mass – do you mean communion service?' The jeep bumped along the road, avoiding the other vehicles.

He smiled. 'I'm Catholic.'

'Oh.'

'Is that a problem?'

I looked out at the rain. The visibility was deteriorating and I could barely make out the buildings on the quayside as we passed them. 'No, it's just another difference.'

We arrived back at the quarters and he pulled the jeep to a halt. 'I don't think the meeting will take long. Are you free?'

I nodded. 'Not sure what we can do.'

'Certainly not go for a walk, but I'm sure we'll find something. Shall I meet you here in an hour and a half?'

'Yes.' I was about to leave but then I turned to him. 'You're not married, are you?'

His face was a picture. 'No.'

'I just wanted to be sure.'

'Well, be sure,' he said.

'Good.' Smiling, I ran to the door and watched the jeep speed away, sending water flying in all directions. Within moments he was lost in the rain, and I steadied myself as I turned around and brushed the beaded drops off my shoulders. He was Catholic. Another gap had opened in front of us, just when I'd begun to find my way around his nationality.

14 April 1944

It had been almost a week since I'd last seen Bobby, with nothing more than messages and one telephone call in between, and I was restless. The atmosphere around us was fraught as more ships arrived and the harbour became an even busier hive of activity. Everyone except me was smoking almost continuously and the amount of coffee consumed had doubled. Hands practically shook with the effects of the caffeine and the will to stay alert and listening in the long hours of the night. It was funny how you could almost drift off – and then, like a lover whispering your name, adrenaline ran through your body with the - ·-- ---·- of the call sign. Everything tensed and all energy focused on listening, writing and responding. I'd come to realise that during those long hours my mind moved totally into Morse, my thoughts converting every sound without even thinking about it. Coming off a shift, it wasn't until I had taken in the fresh air that my brain reverted to English, but even after that there would still be traces, as something like the click of the train on the tracks nearby would tell me something. Morse code had become the language of my subconscious, especially after an eight-hour shift when the tension was high.

Tonight was no different. It had been filled with faulty

transmitters and crowded wireless frequencies. My head was swimming. I tried not to nod off during the breaks, but it did happen. Suddenly my head would fling up with the *dah dit dah dah* … And suddenly I barely had enough time to tear off the message and carbon copy for the coder before the next message began.

As I stood outside the tunnels I realised that this past week everything had become tenser. We had begun to make guesses as more American troops had arrived. HMS *Attack* and HMS *Boscawen* in Castletown were swamped with Yanks. Beyond me, the land sloped gently down to the docks and I could just make out Henry VIII's fort at the edge of the harbour. This place had been vital for the defence of England for a very long time. Mulberry harbours were lined up in view and battleships dotted the sea. It all spoke of readiness.

Commander Rowse had left a message for me to see him when my shift was finished. I was slightly in awe of him. The commander was a naval man through and through; it ran in his blood. His face was stern and darkly handsome. One could, in a flight of fancy, picture him as a pirate off the coast of Cornwall, which was where he originally came from.

Even the blast of fresh air as I'd emerged from the tunnels hadn't blown the cobwebs away. Only some sleep would. Yawning, I sat outside Commander Rowse's office with my hands folded neatly on my lap and my ankles crossed. To the best of my knowledge I'd done nothing wrong; if I had, it wouldn't be the commander speaking to me but the WRNS first officer.

In the background I heard footsteps – *dit dah dit dah dit*. My finger began tapping on my knee.

'They will see you now.' A Wren clutching files hurried down the corridor. I wiped my palms on my skirt, wondering who *they* were, and walked into the commander's office.

'Seaton.' WRNS First Officer Smith spoke and I stood to attention in front of the three people in the room, one of them an American captain.

'As you are aware, the Americans are here in force now.'

Commander Rowse nodded to the squat captain who stood by the window while First Officer Smith was seated by the desk. 'And it's our job to make sure that things work smoothly.' He stood and moved towards the chart on the wall. 'After discussions with First Officer Smith and Captain Harris, you have been selected to work with the American telegraphists who are arriving as we speak.'

The captain smiled. 'There has been nothing but praise for your work.'

I nodded, unsure how to respond.

'You are being promoted to a leading Wren.' First Officer Smith didn't show any emotion. I couldn't tell if this was being done with her approval or not. I wanted to smile, thinking of the killick – the anchor – embroidered in bright blue thread against the navy of my sleeve. I would now outrank my sister and I would have been lying to myself if I hadn't admitted this gave me a thrill.

'Tomorrow you will report at 0800 hours to Captain Harris, where you will begin working with the new telegraphists and accustoming yourself to their equipment.' He picked up the phone. I nodded and left the room. Gone was the coming excitement of an evening with Bobby tomorrow, and in its place was the fear of the overwhelming task ahead of me.

Weymouth, Dorset
15 April 1944

'Congratulations, Leading Wren Seaton.' Bobby was waiting slightly apart from the others when I stepped off the liberty boat.

'Thank you.' I glanced at my sleeve. It was still a surprise to see the anchor. 'Not used to it.'

He laughed. 'From what I hear, you're the top telegraphist.'

I frowned. I knew I was fast, and most importantly accurate, but how did he know?

'Don't look so concerned. I heard from Commander Rowse.' He slipped my arm into his. 'He thinks very highly of you.'

'This secondment to your side says that.' I stopped walking. 'Did you have anything to do with it?'

He bent down and whispered, 'No, I have nothing to do with the Navy. I'm just a messenger. But the commander has seen us together so it came up in polite conversation.' He chuckled. 'Or maybe not so polite. He told me to behave myself and – in short – that you were not that type of girl.'

I pulled back, trying to read the expression on Bobby's face. I'm not sure what I was more shocked by, the commander's comments or Bobby's.

'I told him that I would take very good care of you.'

'Thank you.' I moved closer to him again and breathed in the scent of soap and mint. His warmth travelled through the fabric of our uniforms.

'You've gone quiet.'

I nodded. It felt strange to be heading to the dance hall in daylight. When I'd arrived in December the journey had been in darkness, but now I could see the boarded-up shopfronts and blacked-out houses. I didn't have to navigate by sound but could see the way. In the twilight the effects of the war were visible. In front of a bombsite, daffodils bloomed in a pot as if in defiance, a splash of cheerful colour in the landscape. But war wasn't normal. We'd been at war for so long, I wondered if I remembered what normal was. 'Do you think this war will ever end?'

'Yes, I do.' He stopped walking, letting the others move further away from us. 'I have to believe that we will win and all that everyone has given their lives for will return.'

'I hope you're right.'

'Have faith.' He pulled me into his arms and I rested my head against his shoulder.

'I try, but sometimes it's so difficult.'

'That's true of all of us.'

'Come on, you two.' Pat and her American had emerged out of a side street and gestured to us. I frowned at her, but we walked with them to the dance hall. I'd come to love and loathe the Saturday dances. If Bobby was here then it was magic to be in his arms, dancing to anything. If he was away, which happened more and more, then they were a trial. I didn't want to dance with other men. Time was too precious.

'Fools Rush In (Where Angels Fear to Tread)' was playing as we entered. Bobby took me onto the dance floor and sang along to the words. Dot was right – I was in love. But was he in love with me? Or was I just someone to pass the time with, to make the war less harsh? How could I tell?

The song ended and we joined Dot and Bobby's fellow officers at a table. I tried to study him, but I was swiftly taken to the dance floor by another American – a Californian who was missing his wife and son terribly. He rarely let on, but I'd seen it when he showed me a photograph of them. How hard the separation must be. Would I be strong enough to bear it when it was my turn?

He led me back to the table and Bobby was missing. I couldn't find him in the crowd but I did see some of the women I'd be working with. They were grouped together with a bevy of men around them. I knew it was my duty to go and speak to them. Straightening my jacket, I set off across the hall, avoiding men's eyes. If I met their glance I'd be dancing before I could speak.

The women looked up and smiled shyly before they stood straighter. I cringed. I'd ruined their evening by coming over. 'Hello.' I forced a bright smile onto my face. 'Hope you're having a good evening.'

'Yes, thank you.' The one I pegged as the leader spoke with such a thick accent I struggled to understand her if she went too quickly. I believed she said she was from New Jersey.

'I imagine it's all a bit different from home.'

'Yes, it is,' said one of the quietest, and I hid my surprise.

The music began and I felt Bobby's hand on my shoulder. 'Excuse me, ladies. I'm stealing her away for this dance.'

It was 'I Only Have Eyes For You'. I thought of it as our song. Bobby's deep baritone sang along quietly as he swept me around the floor, avoiding the other couples. I closed my eyes and tried to forget my new team and the thick smoke filling the air. I tried to pretend it was just the two of us. But despite his hand resting lightly against my waist and the feel of his heartbeat under my cheek, the world intruded. I found myself thinking about the space that had been made in the tunnels for my team. It was more cramped than the wireless room next door but somehow we had managed to fit all the equipment in. It hadn't taken me long to adjust to it.

Bobby pulled me closer. 'You're not here with me,' he whispered. His breath tickling my neck brought me back to the here and now, away from the logistical nightmare in front of me. It was hard not to think about it – I had spent the past two days going through things with Captain Harris and my team, and I now had so much responsibility, not just for my own work but for that of others. I swallowed.

'Sorry.' I tilted my head up and smiled.

'Hmmm.' He held me a little tighter. 'Anything I can help with?'

Sighing, I rested my head against his shoulder as the music changed. 'Sadly no.'

'Should we take a walk?'

The thought of the clear night and the cold breeze was far more tempting than being in a smoky hall with so many other people. Admittedly, being alone in the darkness with Bobby was not conducive to logical thought, but all the noise and motion was muddling my thoughts. I needed clarity, not the jitterbug.

Bundled into our coats, we left the noise of the hall behind and walked arm in arm down the street towards the esplanade. I tried to picture it as it was before the war, without the barbed wire and other defences, but couldn't.

As we passed other military personnel and heard the sounds of aircraft overhead, I knew I needed to focus on the here and now, or at least on Bobby. 'What are your plans when the war is over?'

'Now that's a provocative question,' he said.

'Is it?' I tilted my head to the side and squinted into the darkness. I couldn't see his expression.

'Are you talking concrete plans or dreams?'

I stopped walking. 'Both, I think.'

'Ah.' He turned and pulled me close to him. 'Now, my dreams all involve you, a house by the sea and at least three children.'

My breath caught. What he was saying was madness but my heart beat faster, as if it was trying to escape and join with his. His thoughts so matched my own but I wasn't sure how we had come to this point so quickly. 'You're teasing me.'

'No.' He shook his head. 'It's what keeps me focused. The dream that after this nightmare is over I could have a normal life with you.'

'What would you want with a woman like me?'

'A long life to enjoy it all with you.' He leant down and I knew what was about to happen. I stood on tiptoes, bringing us closer together. A cold breeze swirled around my ankles. I shivered as his mouth met mine. Our bodies locked together against the icy wind and the world. A hunger grew in me, so great. I wanted him, all of him.

'Evening, you two lovebirds.'

'Tucker.' Bobby held me closer. 'Terrible timing as always.'

'True, my gift in life, I'm afraid. Have to drag you away.' We began walking and Captain Tucker joined us along the esplanade, our pace quickening.

Bobby turned to me. 'Shall I take you back to Dot at the dance hall?'

'No, I'll make my way back to the train. I have the impression that Captain Tucker needs you urgently.' I stood on tiptoe and kissed him. 'See you soon.'

❊ Nineteen ❊

Windward, Mawnan Smith, Falmouth, Cornwall
11 September 2015

Jack paced the terrace, next to the low stone wall with the lavender appearing over the top. I could tell he wasn't seeing the beauty of the September garden around him. Roses had come back into bloom, the hydrangeas were still putting on a valiant show and the sedum were just beginning to reach their peak. In his hand he held paper and pen. His whole being was focused and his hair was in disarray, just like when he had been a small boy working out the solution to his maths homework. That work had been a struggle until a brilliant teacher had unlocked the numbers for him – after which we couldn't hold him back – but right now his expression was exactly the same. He couldn't see the logic or the way through.

Every so often he would squint and look out to the bay. His whole life changed out there when his mother and his aunt died in a terrible boating accident. I hoped he wasn't looking backwards. I knew that never helped and he needed to get this speech right for Peta. Above everyone, she believed in him and loved him. Her love for him had helped him heal, and his had done the same for her.

'He doesn't look happy.' Fred's voice intruded into my thoughts. I turned.

'No, he doesn't,' I said.

'I did say to Peta that it wasn't fair to ask him to give a speech.' He glanced about looking for his fiancée. He was a good-looking boy, strongly built yet still lanky, showing his youth. Half man, half boy. I remembered so many like that, and how many of them had never filled out into adulthood.

'No, it's not fair, but who else would she ask?'

'True.' He wiped his hands on his jeans. He had a pencil stuck behind his ear and a few bits of wood shavings on his shoulders. He and his father had been constructing a raised platform for the top table. They were doing it to save money, but it seemed a waste of time. However, Peta wanted everyone to be able to see them and not feel excluded if they weren't sitting close enough. 'Maybe I should have a word?'

I raised an eyebrow.

'You think not?'

'He has to work this out himself,' I said.

Fred shook his head. 'Maybe Peta should then. He doesn't have to do this.'

'Yes and no.'

Fred frowned.

'He loves her.'

'True.' He smiled.

'Ah, there you are.' Peta appeared carrying a tray filled with mugs.

'You read my mind.' Fred kissed her then took the tray from her. 'Shall we sit over there in the shade?'

'Of course.' Peta tucked her arm through mine and led me to a table placed out of the way under a large Monterey pine. The day was hot and unnaturally still. The water in the bay looked motionless but I knew it was an illusion. Just like Peta's calm. Nerves must be surging through her. She was so young, just twenty-two.

Big dark clouds crept above the bay. I listened to the chatter behind me. Peta was positive that the weather for tomorrow would be perfect. The view in front of me told otherwise. But wasn't rain on your wedding day supposed to be an omen for success? It had mizzled as only the Cornish weather could on the day I'd married Andrew. It had been a simple affair with only his children and two friends as witnesses. We held our wedding breakfast at the Green Lawns Hotel nearby and had a lovely time. Andrew and I then caught the train to London where we spent our honeymoon before returning to Windward and a season of summer guests. That had also been the last summer I had to use Windward as a B&B. Andrew insisted it was unnecessary, saying that I had made it his home and he could afford both it and me. I smiled. He had looked after me very well; I had enjoyed watching his children grow and even more enjoyed Jack and Peta. They felt more mine somehow, although no blood linked us. George and Pamela were teens when they had moved into Windward. I was merely there for them, but with Jack and Peta I'd played a bigger role. Now all I wanted was for them to both find happiness. Looking at Fred and Peta, I could be sure that at least one of them had succeeded.

✳ Twenty ✳

HMS *Attack*, Portland, Dorset
27 April 1944

Exercise Tiger had gone to plan last night and I woke this afternoon with a sense of excitement that hadn't left me. Now an hour before my midnight shift I breathed in the clear air while I walked from my quarters to the tunnels. The first part of the exercise had gone smoothly – not even a dropped signal, which was unheard of. We were going to win this war, I just knew it.

I looked up to the sky. Thousands and thousands of stars were above me. My heart lifted. One more night of practice and then I imagined they would be looking for good weather for an invasion. Not that anyone said as much, but with exercises on this scale it had to be what they were moving towards. The American girls I was working with had proved to be not as bad as I feared, just a little nervous. But I supposed if I were that far away from home and everything was different, I wouldn't be my calm self either. It was that way with the troops too. When they had first arrived they had been excitable, but weeks in a muddy field had dampened their enthusiasm as it would anyone's.

Tonight's shift would mark the end of this round of exercises. I hadn't heard from Bobby in days. I imagined he was involved but didn't know for sure. Work was something we never spoke about.

'Well handled last night,' said a voice behind me as I strolled, still staring at the night sky.

I started in surprise, and turned to find Commander Rowse. I immediately stopped and stood to attention and saluted. I hadn't seen or heard him walking towards me in the darkness. 'Thank you, sir.'

'I knew you were the right person for the job.'

I nodded, feeling the colour rise in my cheeks. Everything was going so well, even the war for once. I began walking again.

'The conditions are good.' He matched his pace to mine.

'Yes, sir.'

He nodded and turned towards the docks while I dashed the rest of the way to the tunnels. I wanted to make sure everything was ready for my watch as it had been last night. This was an American operation and I was there to make sure it went smoothly.

Inside the tunnels, I approached the wireless room, saw the team waiting for the change of shift and could feel their restlessness. A quick head count told me they were all there. Susan, the youngest of the team, came forward.

'I'm so glad you're here. Dolores is afraid to say that she isn't feeling well.' She pointed at her stomach and mine tightened in sympathy.

'I'll have a word with her.' I looked through the door to the eight women currently working at the two long tables lining the walls of the narrow room. Their weariness was apparent in the hunch of their shoulders. Listening required intense focus and I knew the convoys were underway by now.

'Dolores?'

She nodded.

'Are you unfit for duty?'

'I'll be fine.'

I raised an eyebrow. 'Are you certain?'

'Yes.'

The decision was made, but I hoped it was the right one. I walked into the room to speak to the officer in charge. It was five minutes to midnight.

*

The clock on the wall read 0300 and the convoy was making good progress. The radios were relatively quiet and Captain Harris had stepped out of the room. I took a deep breath. Silence filled the air along with cigarette smoke and the smell of cold coffee except for the occasional tap on a straight key. Another few hours and this would be finished. I would see Bobby tomorrow, I hoped. His smiling blue eyes appeared in my mind, then vanished as my call sign began. Pencil poised above the paper, my finger hovered above the lever. The sound of chairs scraping on the floor nearly drowned out the signal. Around me the team sprang into action, barely keeping up with the pace. The silence had been replaced by the fierce sound of tapping.

Across the room I saw heads lifting up from the desk and making eye contact with each other with puzzled frowns on their faces. Something was happening. I shut out the noise around me and concentrated on listening to the messages coming in. As I scratched out the Morse on the pad I realised it wasn't encoded. It was plain language.

'Oh my God. They're being fired on.' It was Dolores who spoke. She was as white as a sheet.

'It's practice,' said one of the girls. 'Just like last night.'

I'd overheard that live rounds were being used to ready the men. So many of them had so little experience of anything, let alone battle. I thought of the fresh and eager faces standing on the side of the dance floor or walking along the street smiling.

'No, no, they've been hit and the boat is going down. They're not using code.' Dolores's head was back down as she continued to write and tap.

'Remind them to use code,' I called above the furious noise of metal tapping metal. The women's quick glances to each other spoke of panic, and I couldn't deny that I was feeling it too.

I adjusted my headphones, listening to be sure of what I was hearing. Writing at speed. Yes, they were hit. It wasn't encoded. The man transmitting was using plain language. I replied, telling him to use code. The stream kept coming in plain language. The fear flowed with each word, almost stuttering.

We're twenty miles off Portland Bill. Send help.

SOS ••• – – – ••• *The ship has been hit.*

I looked at the women around me, and they were all caught up in what was happening. The boats didn't know where the fire was coming from. I was listening to the dits and dahs revealing their confusion.

Why are the Brits firing at us?

I replied to use code.

No, no, it's not the Brits. There are E-boats. Not sure how many. Send help.

Are you sure it's not U-boats? I asked, my finger swiftly tapping out the question.

E-boats, they replied. *Three, maybe more.*

My hand could barely keep up with the flow recording their words. It wasn't just *dits* and *dahs*, it was fear. That didn't need translation.

Why is no one helping us?

Another glance about the room and to the door revealed that Captain Harris hadn't returned. Had he slipped out in the quiet moments to confer? Where was he now? Men were dying and we needed to do something. He could help. We were safe in an underground tunnel while E-boats destroyed the convoy. Somewhere quite close there was a battle raging. Where were the ships that were supposed to be protecting the landing craft? What was happening in the rooms down the hall? What were the UK ships saying? Did they know what was happening?

The boat is going down. We're lost. Christ. Bill's caught shrapnel through the chest.

This is Ensign Peter Crown. Please tell my wife I love her. Tell my mother I'm sorry. Tell my—

The transmission ended. I glanced around. The white faces around me told the same story.

Dear God, I prayed. *Help them.*

I picked up another signal. Again the telegraphist on the boat wasn't using code but plain language. They *had* to use code. The E-boats would be picking up these signals as well. His words put every hair on my body on edge. They were dying.

Where is help? We're being shot at from all sides.

There are three E-boats. Men in the water dying. SOS ... --- ...

My hand shook as I wrote it all down. I could no longer see the women around me. I was with the men on the boats with the explosions going off all around them. They told me everything. With each *dit* and *dah* I heard them die. Without the protection of code their pain was mine.

I stood with earphones still on, looking at the ashen faces about me. Were they hearing the same thing? Why was no one helping these boats? There were boats in the harbour. They could do something. We could stop this. We had to.

Christ, they're drowning, all these men with their packs on ready to land on the beach. They can't swim.

Please use code, I frantically typed, but that was not what they wanted to hear.

We're dying. The ship's been hit again. SOS ... --- ...

I'll see what I can do, I transmitted. My finger hovered over the key. What else could I say? I looked for the officer in charge as I tore off another sheet. Still no sign of him. Did he know what was happening? Had he gone for help?

Please.

What could I say? My fingers tapped swiftly. *You just have to do the best you can for yourself.*

They are not coming. God, someone please help us.

One of the team looked up. 'What can we do?'

'Just log everything, absolutely everything.' I took my head-phones off. I had to do something. I signalled for the women to continue to work. The coders were as puzzled as I was. They had nothing to do, there was nothing to decode. I tried to stand fully straight but walked as if the world had tilted. Where was the captain? Where had he gone? These men needed help. They were within distance of Portland. We could have boats to them in minutes. Why weren't we doing something? Last night all the powers that be were here and tonight it was only my girls and me.

Outside the telegraphy room, I looked down the narrow

tunnel and the walls seemed to close in. What was happening? Were we being invaded? I shivered. No one was in sight. I did not know what to do – abandon my shift and go in search of aid, or stand with them and record the massacre? I had taken a few steps down the hall when I heard a cry from one of my operators. I returned to my post. I would witness this with them. I lifted the headset to my ears and sank down onto the chair.

Hours passed. No help came to us or to them. The officers were nowhere to be found. I felt the numbness about me. The anger of earlier had abated. The horror remained, hour after hour. I heard their pain, my ears rang with the tone of their deaths.

Finally, the clock on the wall showed 0800. The next shift arrived and we handed over in silence. I collected the sheets from everyone. We'd lived a lifetime in eight hours and provided the last contact with many men who would never see the morning light. I avoided my operators' eyes. I would only see my own anger, my powerlessness and my pain reflected in theirs. One of them reached out and touched my hand. I stilled, then took a deep breath. Our glances met and then I turned away, marching down the hall to hand the sheets over.

The door was open to the office but no one was there. *Abandon ship* rang through my mind. They had all escaped, leaving us powerless. It was a massacre. I had no idea how many men were dead. But all I could think of was Bobby. Was he one of them?

Eventually I found Captain Harris coming out of the operations room. I thrust the sheets at him. If I could have hit him with them I would have. I was about to stumble away when I saw Commander Rowse emerge behind Harris.

The commander nodded at me as First Officer Smith suddenly appeared at my side, leading me out of the tunnels with the officers following behind. Fresh air slapped me in the face but it didn't revive me as it normally did. Both Rowse and Harris were speaking, but I barely registered what they said. My head was filled with the dying men's words, the thick smoke of the cigarettes mixed with the aroma of strong coffee in the telegraphy room, all of which had been consumed in the small hours of the night watch. We let them die and did nothing. I was dimly aware of Commander Rowse instructing Smith as I was led away.

The next thing I knew, I was in Smith's office and she was pouring a large whisky, despite it only being just past eight o'clock in the morning.

'Drink this.'

My hands trembled as I took the glass. The liquid burned the whole way down and my stomach complained. Everything was numb except for the tight knot inside, holding me together. At least the burning of the whisky meant I was still able to feel something. The world around me was out of focus. Nothing was right. No one had done anything. No one had behaved as they should. The boats had been fired upon from the land by the Allies and they had been intercepted by the Nazis. Confusion and inaction had ruled. It was criminal.

'I understand you have been through an ordeal.' Smith's eyes said much more than her words.

I didn't respond. The men who died had been through an ordeal, a trial by fire and death, by drowning in the icy waters of the Channel, far from their homes and loved ones. I raised the glass to my mouth, looking with unseeing eyes over the rim.

'Pull yourself together, Seaton.'

I nodded. This wasn't supposed to have happened. We weren't supposed to let them die just off our coast.

Commander Rowse came in. He looked as terrible as I felt, pale and shaken. The superintendent poured him a whisky too and then she topped up mine. He knocked his back in one.

'There will be a meeting at 12.00 p.m.' He looked directly into my eyes. 'You will be there. I know I am stating the obvious but do not say a word to anyone about what you have heard or think you have heard.'

I focused on him. He was supposed to know what to do, and instead he was looking at me and pleading with me not to break. How was I supposed to hold this in? I could already feel myself fracturing, the cracks growing, everything inside ready to spill out. I followed his lead and drank the whisky down in one, as the superintendent arched her brows.

'Go and get some sleep,' she said.

'Thank you.' Even to my ears the words were slurred, but whether it was from drink, exhaustion or despair I didn't know and didn't care.

When I reached my cabin, I was grateful no one else was there. I stumbled into the bathroom and splashed my face with water. My stomach roiled. I retched into the sink, but but nothing came up. Again and again my stomach spasmed uselessly. Nothing would come out of me. Nothing was allowed to. My face looked no different than it had this morning but I knew I would never be the same.

✳ Twenty-One ✳

Falmouth, Cornwall
12 September 2015

The coffee was dark and Lara needed every atom of caffeine in it as she flipped through the notes for the wedding. When Cassie had called her back yesterday from the hospital, saying that her mother had had an aneurysm, Lara hadn't hesitated – she had told Cassie to stay with her dad, and that she would take care of the wedding. On Cassie's instructions she had called Peta Rowse, brought her up to date on the situation and assured her things would be fine: everything was ready, Cassie's team knew everything they needed, and Lara would be there to supervise. The bride had been remarkably unperturbed that her caterer wouldn't be there, instead showing more concern for Cassie and her mother.

Lara scanned through the paperwork. One hundred and fifty guests and three courses. The first course would be served in the form of canapés while everyone was drinking champagne and the official photographs were taking place. During that time the main course of local beef and lamb would be cooked on site on barbecues. The vegetarian provision was a quiche made with local Cornish cheese, a white Stilton, and caramelised onions; these would be made this morning and served warm. Fresh salads and vegetables including new potatoes would be served on platters distributed on the long tables. Going through the pages again, she looked for the diagram of the seating plan in relation to the cooking and service areas.

The reception was being held in a tepee. The information

included a picture of one used for another wedding. It was certainly different. Lara tried to picture a tepee in the setting but memories of her own reception by the sea kept blotting the images out. Hopefully Peta Rowse and her future husband would be luckier than Lara had been, but she didn't hold out much hope for any marriages these days. Something was different in society as a whole. Life was more disposable.

The brownies she'd help to make yesterday were cut and packed and she checked all the fridges and supplies twice before heading back into the bungalow to change. Cassie had insisted that once everything had started Lara was to change out of chef's whites and mix among the guests to make sure things were happening correctly. Her team knew what to do but Cassie had said she would feel happier if Lara was on hand.

Opening the wardrobe in her room, Lara stared at her available clothes, but saw little to no option for what to wear. She hadn't packed to go to an Indian summer wedding. Snowy snaked around her legs as she continued searching and tried to decide on a solution. Finally, she admitted defeat: she would have to see if Cassie had anything suitable. They were the same size but even as kids their tastes had been very different.

Snowy followed her through the kitchen, knocking off the wedding photo of her great-grandparents perched on the kitchen table. She bent down and placed the picture back, wishing there was more she could uncover about it. With the little information she had, there was virtually no chance of discovering more, unless someone was still alive who remembered Grandie. Leo was making enquiries through Grandie's West Point connections, so maybe something might come up that way.

'Well, Snowy, what do you think Cassie will have in there?' Lara opened the closet in Cassie's room and looked at the array of floral dresses. They suited Cassie so well but Lara didn't see herself as a flowery sort of girl. However, she was drawn to a vintage rose-covered print on a sundress that reminded her of the forties. She took it out and found a lovely pair of red shoes with a strap across the ankle that matched the roses in the print.

The heel was quite chunky and not too high so that would work on the lawns. There was nothing worse than being at an outdoor event and having your shoes sinking into the grass.

'This'll do, Snowy. Don't you think?' Lara held the dress up in front of herself and looked in the mirror. She'd sweep her hair up in a 1940s roll to complete the picture. Wind rattled the glass in the window behind her. She wondered if she was being too optimistic with a sundress, but Cassie must have a small cardigan that would go over it.

The cat followed her while she did her hair then she located a cardigan before pulling on a pair of black trousers and tee-shirt to be worn under her chef's white jacket. She would change into the dress once she was confident that all was running smoothly.

She had time for one more cup of coffee before the team arrived, then they would set off to Windward. Snowy walked along the sofa and rubbed up against her as she went to the kitchen. Lara stroked his long white fur head to tail. He definitely seemed like he'd moved in permanently. She knew she should take him to the vet or something to see if he was microchipped – his owner might be worried about him. Cassie had asked around, and the grapevine had come back with no one missing a cat. Snowy meowed and jumped down before wandering to the kitchen where he stood expectantly in front of the cupboard that Lara had recently filled with cat food. She was aware that she had possibly gone completely mad over this cat, but at least he seemed as happy as any cat could be.

Windward, Mawnan Smith, Falmouth, Cornwall
12 September 2015

The setting took Lara's breath away. On her previous two visits she'd never ventured to the side of the house facing the sea. The lawn stretched out to a cliff that then dropped to a beach below. She walked through the set-up while Cassie's catering team assembled the barbecues to the side of the house. In the middle of the lawn was a massive damp tepee. It was huge, with three peaks from which the structure was formed. Everything was dripping from the night's rainstorm and she was grateful she'd remembered to throw some wellington boots into the car at the last minute. Although the sun shone brightly, it would need to build up some heat to dry everything out. She looked out into the bay. The sky was clear of the clouds that had arrived yesterday. Things were so sharp she felt she was watching high-definition television. Raindrops clung to the needles of the pine tree and the light shining through them cast a rainbow onto the fabric of the tepee. Was it a promise of good things to come? She hoped it was for the bride and groom.

The refrigerated van was parked close to the kitchen. Lara took a swig of coffee as she surveyed the site, noting the bank of restrooms discreetly placed a small distance from the house, behind the cover of a few trees. It was all laid out well and thus far didn't look overtly 'weddingy'. Cassie had mentioned that Peta was a dress designer. Lara's appreciation of the bride's talent grew as she caught sight of one of the bridesmaids dashing through the kitchen in a burgundy dress that faded to soft pink on the floaty skirt about her. It wasn't your average bridesmaid dress. She then saw another whose dress began with a soft pink flattering her skin tone until it became burgundy by her ankles. As more bridesmaids passed the window, she saw that each dress was different – some were strapless and sophisticated but others were more in the style of a 1950s diva. Lara was impressed, and wondered what the bride had chosen for herself.

Tipping the remains of the coffee out, she ventured into the tepee to be met by a steely-haired woman creating wonderful little flower arrangements at regular intervals on the long tables. The effect was charming and would beautifully complement what Lara had seen of the dresses.

'Hello, are you Cassie?'

'No, sadly her mother's in hospital. I'm Lara.'

'Victoria Roberts,' the woman said as she stuck another anemone into a small vase. She stopped then stood straight. Her bearing was impressive and Lara wondered if she was about to be yelled at. 'How disappointing. Nothing too serious, I hope.' Before Lara could reply, the woman asked, 'Does Peta know?'

Lara nodded. 'I spoke to her yesterday.'

'Good. You don't need extra stress on your wedding day.'

'True.' Lara counted the tables, noting the dance floor at one end of the tepee and several sofas at the other. 'The flowers look wonderful.'

'Thank you. Bride's choice.'

Lara left the woman completing her task and walked to the table that held the wedding cake. The smooth royal icing was covered in delicate autumn leaves and wrapped in tendrils of honeysuckle and jasmine. It was a work of art. She turned back to the dance floor. By the time the music was on and the floor filled with happy wedding guests, she would be long gone.

Peta stood in my bedroom in front of my grandmother's tall mirror, just as my sister had on this day seventy years ago. My mother had insisted I be there at the wedding, but she hadn't seemed to understand how hard it had been. Even then her mind was slipping from reality. Only six people on that bright beautiful September day knew the whole truth and each had been scarred by it in different ways. All these years later, I only knew what had happened to my father, my mother, my grand- mother and me.

Today, the photographer clicked away and I tried to ignore him while I placed my grandmother's veil on Peta's head. Somehow this antique worked beautifully with the dress she'd designed and made. She was the picture of innocence and love despite the thin gold ring in her nose and graduated pearls going up her ears.

I secured the last hairpin in place and she covered my hand resting on her shoulder. 'Thank you.'

'For what?' I smiled, looking at her happiness. That was what would take me through today.

'For everything.'

I fussed with the fall of the veil, noting the holes that created the pattern and made it both beautiful and delicate. 'It was nothing.'

'That's not true.' Her finger lifted my head. 'You have always been here for me.'

I swallowed. 'I love you.'

'I love you too and I don't say it enough.'

I turned from her happy beauty. I would not let the past cloud today.

'I don't know what's causing you pain but I feel it.' She gave me a hug and wiped a tear from the corner of my eye. 'I don't know if you are thinking about my parents. And that makes me sad too, but we will both come through this.' She kissed my cheek. 'And look. I was right about the weather.' The morning had broken dry and blowy, but as if by magic the air had stilled. It was as fresh as if God had wiped the day clean, and the sun was shining intensely. If a breeze didn't stir up soon it threatened to become steamy, but I knew nothing would make Peta wilt. She looked as fresh as a breath of sweetly scented air.

'So lovely.'

'Thank you. I feel it too.' She looked at her reflection in the mirror, her eyes smiling at me.

Her chief bridesmaid tapped on the door. 'The little ones are ready.'

'Great, thanks. All set, Gran?'

I nodded and let her friends do the final adjustments, putting the flower crown in place before Peta turned and walked out into the hallway. She looked like a fairy goddess, so far from my sister's fragile visage seventy years ago. Back then I couldn't look at how frightened Amelia had been about marrying a man she barely knew. Her eyes had shown that worry but my own pain blocked it out. Peta's showed nothing but radiance.

The scene out on the landing was chaos. Small children darted in and out of the adults. The grown-up bridesmaids were doing their best to marshal the children into order on the stairs for a photo. Jack stood quietly in front of his bedroom. He wore an expression of grim determination and I longed to dash across the landing and tell him it *would* be all right. But that wasn't possible and I had no idea if it would be all right. What was certain was that everyone looked beautiful.

The young girls were in multi-coloured tutus and the little boys in patchwork waistcoats. In fact, Jack wore a similar waistcoat under his morning coat. He wasn't too different from these little energetic boys. It was easy to remember him at this age, forever presenting me with birds with broken wings and lost kittens. He had always wanted to fix everything – I'd assumed he'd become a vet or a doctor. Where had all that need to fix things gone? I sighed, realising it had died with his father. Jack had tried to make him see that he was still loved but George hadn't been able to see anything beyond the loss of his wife.

Peta looked up from the chaos and held out a hand to her brother. He smiled at her and my heart leapt just a little. The little boy was still in there and he would do anything for his sister, even this.

⁕ Twenty-Two ⁕

HMS *Attack*, Portland, Dorset
28 April 1944

There was a tap on the cabin door and Pat walked in with a cup of tea. 'Hi. The superintendent sent me up with this.' She squinted at me. 'I think you might need it.'

I nodded, my head throbbing. Bright sunlight was streaming through the cabin window, and every time I looked at it a sharp pain seemed to cut my head in half. Death might be preferable to this. The taste of the whisky was stale on my tongue.

'I don't know what has happened.' Pat shuddered. 'But there have been bodies of young Americans brought onto shore all morning. It's awful.' She sat on the end of my bed as I closed my eyes, trying to block out the image that her words had created.

Bobby.

'Thankfully I heard from Joe.' Her hand flew to her mouth. 'God, I'm sorry. Have you heard from Bobby? Joe didn't mention him.'

I opened my eyes and took the cup and saucer from her, blowing on the tea to cool it down. The oily puddles on the tea's surface moved around. 'No.'

Pat glanced at her watch. 'It's ten fifty.'

I nodded, and my brain crashed against the sides of my skull. I winced.

Pat looked at my uniform on the floor where I had cast it off. 'Do you need a hand?'

'No, thanks, I'll be fine in a minute.'

206

'Sure?'

'Yes.' I placed the cup and saucer on the floor and tried to revive myself. I wouldn't think about how much my head hurt. It was minor. Somewhere out there so many were dead and their families would be without them. I might have lost Bobby, and that pain would go deeper than anything whisky could inflict. I rocked myself back and forth until I found the strength to put on my uniform then straighten the counterpane on my bed.

Once I was outside, I could hear the lament of a lone piper. As I neared the dock I saw a convoy of US military trucks lined up. I kept walking although I feared what I would see, my heart breaking with each step. The rear admiral and Commander Rowse were on the rescue motor launch watching the bodies of the dead being taken off as the piper played each soul ashore. Tears flowed down my face. Were these the boys I had heard dying last night? God forbid, was Bobby one of them?

Commander Rowse looked up, his face ashen but resigned. Such a loss of life. He saw me and I knew I had to pull myself together. I turned from the scene and took in great gulps of air to chase away the cobwebs that were clogging my brain. We'd let those men die last night. I knew it. They were close enough to Portland that help could have reached them. Their deaths were unnecessary and on our hands. I paced. Anger pumped through me until suddenly there was nothing and it was time to go to the meeting.

An American sergeant with a clipboard stood on duty outside the door to the meeting room. He looked me up and down. 'Name?'

'Leading Wren Seaton.' I bit the words out. My hands clenched into fists.

He stepped back after he had ticked my name off the list. The room was already full. Unfortunately there was only one seat left, right in the front row. If it hadn't been for my pounding head I would have stood at the back, but I ventured forward to take the seat, scanning the crowd, hoping against hope that I would see Bobby or at least someone I could ask about him. As I sat, I wondered if this was how Amelia felt when she didn't

have news of Eddie. But no, she was better than me, more positive. I had to hold onto hope. Bobby could be in London, or
anywhere. I prayed that he was not one of the many bodies I
had seen being piped off the boat as I walked to the meeting.
Those were the men I'd heard last night. I knew I would always
hear them.

I turned my attention to the American general standing at
the front with a chart on an easel and a pointer. Beside him
was an admiral from the US Navy as well as the rear admiral. I
could see Commander Rowse at the side with a worried frown
on his face. The rear admiral stepped forward.

'I can see that we are missing a few people but we need
to proceed.' I studied him as he looked around, making eye
contact with many people. 'Everyone knows why we are here.
But I will make it plain now: everything said today is classified
and covered by the Official Secrets Act. If anything leaks it will
be court-martial, no questions asked. This is genuine and not
simply a threat. I am relying on the highest integrity from all of
you.' Again he slowly scanned the room, leaving no one out of
his glance, including me.

'What I need from you is to focus on your own key roles.
There are lessons to be learned from what has happened and it
is important to all those men who have lost their lives that we
do learn.'

The US admiral stepped forward. 'If you are here, you know
that for the past few nights there have been practice landings
on the Dorset beaches. What is clear from last night's tragedy
is that there were mistakes made. Everyone and everything will
be investigated and tighter security will follow.' He cleared his
throat. 'It is imperative.' He stared at the faces looking at him.
'I want to thank you all for doing your best in a dire situation,
particularly the medics. Many lives were saved thanks to them.'

Despite his polite words I could see his anger, yet they
hadn't told us anything. I probably knew more than many of
the people around me. There had been friendly fire as well as
enemy, or at least that was what the men had said.

'No stone will be left unturned until we discover exactly what occurred.' The US admiral turned and walked to the side of the room. 'You will each be questioned, and remember that you must not say anything to anyone except Commander Rowse or myself.'

I looked at the commander. He stood straight but his eyes were weary. I doubted whether he'd been able to grab a few hours of sleep, as I had done.

The meeting was over. People began to move and when I turned I saw Captain Tucker. His glance met mine before he left the room. I found him waiting for me in the passage outside.

'I have no news.'

I nodded. It told me what I feared most. Why hadn't I told Bobby how I felt about him? Now I'd never have the chance. Outside I walked into the thick fog that was rolling in off the sea. 'No news' didn't have to be bad, but it was hard to hold onto hope.

30 April 1944

Dot walked beside me to our quarters. We'd been to church. I tried to pray but sat in silence and mouthed the hymns. Two days had passed, and the weather was still grim – I hoped the sun would arrive soon to burn the mist away. Despite being late April, it felt like it was winter. Not even the hymns could lift the gloom inside me.

'This is the second day the flag's been at half-mast.' Dot looked out to a boat in the harbour. 'Do you think it's because of all the young Americans that were brought in the other day?'

I shrugged. There was nothing I could say. I wished I didn't know. There had been no word from Bobby.

'Are you all right?' she asked as we entered our cabin. 'No – stupid question, isn't it?'

I nodded. She'd heard from her flyboy yesterday so all was fine in her world. Mine was focused on my job. My heart veered from one side to the other. Had I listened to my own advice and not fallen for Bobby then I wouldn't be in this position. I wouldn't know what love was or about its loss. Once we reached the common room, I opened the letter I had received from Amelia. I hadn't had a chance to look at it before.

28 April 1944

Dearest Delly,

Eddie's last leave was cancelled and he hopes he can get leave in the middle of May. Hopefully we can be married then. I know it's insanity but I just want the security of knowing he's mine, truly mine. He thinks I'm mad and that we should wait until this wretched war is over but he says he's happy to marry me today or tomorrow or any old day if that's what I want. Mother is quiet about it and I'm concerned about that, but Grandmother is all for a wartime wedding.

I smiled as I looked out the window. Yes, Grandmother would approve of Amelia marrying Eddie Carew. She might even think the match improved my chances but my heart belonged to one man. There would be no one else.

I am worried about Mother. She is very distracted and doesn't want to talk to Father when he calls. I think she's beside herself with worry. Do call her if you have a chance. I know you will say that it's me she listens to, but believe me when I say she's not listening.

If you can get some leave and see her that would be wonderful.

Other news – I still adore my job although everyone is tense. I spend a lot of time with a rear admiral and when we began he was chatty but now he sits in the car in silence. That says it all.

I went to a dance in the village last night. The Americans are charming and it provided some light relief from the tension at home. Yes, I'm talking about Mother again. She is fine when she is focused on things for the Red Cross but once that is done we lose her. I don't know what to do.

Aunt Margaret rang and was very chatty. Uncle Reg seems to

*be fine from what she had to say but there was something odd in
her tone when speaking about him.*

    *I miss you terribly. With you here this wretched waiting could
be bearable but it's not. I feel your fear. Won't you share it with
me?*

*I love you
Xxx*

I folded her letter. Tonight I would ring Mother. I might be
able to get some leave in May. It was unbearable to even think
about missing Amelia's wedding. It was hard enough when
they had their engagement celebration without me. Of course I
understood, but that didn't stop the disappointment. So much
of our lives recently had happened without each other. The
separation felt wrong yet I knew in my heart that this would
widen as time moved on. Amelia and I would be apart. It had
to happen but I hadn't really considered it before. I took a deep
breath and felt a stab of something like fear.

    I hadn't heard from Bobby. Anyone that knew him seemed
to be avoiding me. The casualty figure was high and I had to
accept that Bobby was dead. The pain cut through me as I took
out some paper and started to write.

Dearest Half,

*I haven't told you much about the man I love and now I'm writing
to tell you he's dead. I can't say more because, well, I can't.*

    *I don't know where to put my grief so I focus on work and I
walk and walk. My friends are worried but they are giving me
a wide berth, sensing that I don't want to talk about it. Why
didn't I listen to my own words and not even look at a man until
this wretched war was over? What am I going to do? Why does
love hurt so much? How do you bear having Eddie so far away
and never knowing if he's safe or not?*

    *I want to write to his family but I can't. I long to make some
connection but we haven't even spoken of our feelings to each*

other properly. I doubt he'd even mentioned me in a letter home. What if they don't know yet? I can't say any more but I feel broken in two from the inside. Pain is seeping into everything that once held happiness.

I'm sorry to hear Mother isn't well. She was always prone to be blue. It must be hard for her to be so far from Father. In hindsight she should have opted to spend the war in London with Aunt Margaret, who seems to be having a marvellous time despite Uncle Reg being so far away.

Missing you but you know that.
Love you xx

HMS *Attack*, Portland, Dorset
6 May 1944

'I won't take no for an answer.' Pat stood by my chair in the galley. 'You're coming ashore and going to the dance. It's your duty.'

I glared at her but she wouldn't leave. I looked at the book and tea beside me. She was right. I needed to do this. Bobby wouldn't want me to just sit in my room. Besides, it was here that my every quiet moment was haunted by dreams filled with the words of dying men. I had to assume that Bobby was one of them. 'Fine,' I said. 'I'll come.'

'That's better.' I made a face at her but she ducked around me. 'Right then – we'll catch the liberty boat and you *will* have a good time.'

'I will have a *time*,' I said. 'I'm not sure "good" will be a part of it.'

Swearing drifted up through the floorboards of the galley. The language of the sailors imprisoned on the floor below had enlarged my vocabulary. Many times I'd had to ask Pat the meaning of a few of them, which was most embarrassing. We smiled at each other and Pat tucked her arm in mine as we set off. The evening was warm and clear and the hillside was covered with gorse.

Sitting by the window on the liberty boat I looked at the sliver of the moon appearing from behind a cloud. I needed to be positive. Even if my world had died with Bobby, I still had to go on. Scenery blurred outside the window but I would not cry.

On reaching Weymouth the crowd coming off the liberty boat was full of high spirits. I lingered towards the back, looking at the beach. The tide was out and I longed to walk its length. My glance caught Captain Tucker's. He was waiting for his latest conquest. He smiled at me. It was the first time he'd made eye contact since he'd told me he had no news of Bobby. I began to walk with the crowd. A breeze swept down the narrow street from the sea and stirred my hair, loosening a few tendrils. I shivered, then stopped when I felt a hand touch my arm.

'Adele.'

Bobby's deep voice moved through me. For a moment I was rooted to the spot, willing my heart to beat. Tears filled my eyes.

I turned.

'You're ... here,' I whispered.

He had a large scar across his forehead. My hands reached up and made contact with his skin. It was real and warm and not just the workings of my imagination in the dark hours of the night.

He brought my fingers to his mouth. 'Yes, just in time to dance with you.'

My chest contracted. To be in his arms again. I closed my eyes for a moment then opened them wide, not wanting to miss a second of seeing him. I could barely breathe let alone speak. 'Yes.' I threw my arms around his neck and pulled him close before I kissed him like I never had before.

Twenty-Three

Mawnan Church, Mawnan Smith, Falmouth, Cornwall
12 September 2015

The shade from the tree provided relief. The air was steamy from the intensity of the September sun. Guests were milling about and I took comfort from their number and their attire. There was no similarity to my sister's wedding other than the date, the location and the sunshine. Fred's brothers were making light work of fitting all the people into the church. I rather suspected it would be standing room only at the back.

The car filled with the bridesmaids, young and old, had just arrived. Happy chaos ensued with the children running free among the gravestones – dashes of bright colour spinning round and round. Yes, it was so different from seventy years ago, when all had been solemn and there had been only a few guests to witness the event. Today would be wonderful.

The car carrying Peta and Jack arrived shortly after. He stepped out, so handsome and so serious. Opening the door for his sister, he held out a hand to assist. Her foot shod in a glittering blue shoe appeared, followed by the beautiful smiling bride. Peta radiated something beyond happiness – contentment. She stood beside her brother and kissed his cheek, leaving bright marks that she wiped with her fingers. With a hankie he cleaned her hand then his face, giving her a lopsided grin. My heart released. Today would be fine. I breathed easier.

A squeal emerged from one of the young bridesmaids and Fred's youngest brother took my arm then led me from the safety of the tree into the church. The sweet perfume of the lilies mingled with the quiet chatter as everyone waited for Peta. Fred stood by the altar with wide eyes, only looking at the door. The organ began its first tentative notes and the congregation rose. The energy of the young attendants burst through the door followed by the more sedate parade of the bridesmaids, all four of them looking beautiful, especially Peta's latest acquisition, Demi. Her beauty almost eclipsed the bride but as Peta walked through the door, tall and proud at her brother's side, nothing could dim her loveliness or her peace. Peace was a funny word to come to mind but there was a serenity to her that couldn't be denied.

Fred's smile lit the church brighter than the sunlight streaming through the window. I caught sight of Tamsin, Fred's mother, on the other side of the aisle, dabbing her cheeks. Her husband Anthony was moved as well. Tears slipped down my face, too. I wished Andrew were here.

Someone slipped into the pew beside me and grabbed my hand. It was Eddie. God, he was a sight for my tired eyes. Ninety-four years old and he was still trim and dapper in his morning suit. He leaned forward.

'Hello, Delly. Looking beautiful as always.'

'You old rogue,' I whispered back, smiling at his use of the endearment. It had been a long time since anyone called me Delly.

He kissed my cheek as Peta and Jack passed us. Jack was pale but a fleeting smile hovered on his mouth. When he handed Peta to Fred, his shoulders dropped down a bit – one of his tasks today completed. He slid into the pew beside me and grabbed my hand. Surrounded by men I loved, some of Peta's peace reached my heart.

The ceremony had gone beautifully and the singing from the young soprano, Hannah, hadn't left a dry eye in the house, except for Jack. It was good to see local talent flourish. I understood she was off to university next week to study history but would continue her singing as well. Jack had remained restless throughout the service. His nerves were palpable. When I tried to speak to him on the short journey to the house, he wasn't listening. All he needed to do was raise a glass and toast them, no more.

People were spilling out across the lawn clutching their champagne glasses and sampling Helford oysters. Peta had wanted to make the whole event as local as possible. I understood the beef was from the farm next to us and the lamb came from another one near to the RNAS Culdrose. Everything looked as it should. Jack wandered off, probably needing a moment of peace. His sister was now a married woman. He was no longer responsible for her, not that Peta had ever let him believe he had been. He'd tried to watch her every step since the moment George had died and left them orphaned.

'Mrs Rowse,' said one of the pretty little bridesmaids, 'the photographer would like you down by the garden wall for pictures.' She glanced about. 'Have you seen Jack?'

I pointed in the direction of the old stables. He would appear when he was ready but there was no point in telling that to this bright thing. She'd been tasked by Peta and would do her job.

Grabbing a flute of champagne, I made my way through the guests, smiling but keeping my distance. The sooner these pictures were taken the better, then I could find my seat and simply watch the proceedings. I was like Jack, waiting for the moment when I could fade into unimportance – although I knew this was easier for an old woman than a handsome and eligible man of thirty.

Twenty feet in front of me stood the happy couple with the backdrop of Falmouth Bay behind them. Their carefree ease with each other was so different from the stiff formality of the previous wedding here. Peta and Fred were laughing at something one of the children had said and their hands were linked – no doubt like their hearts. Mine tightened. Once I'd known such happiness.

'Let's get this over with.' Jack put a hand on my elbow. The bridesmaid had done her job well.

'They are happy.'

Jack stopped walking and looked closely at them. 'Yes, yes they are.'

I followed his glance. The wind picked up and the full skirt of Peta's gown curled around her body. My breath caught. Was she pregnant? I blinked. No, my eyes were playing tricks on me.

'Great, you're all here. Mrs Rowse and Jack, could you stand either side of the couple?' The photographer parted me from Jack and placed me close to Fred. I looked up to see the Polcrebar clan being led in our direction by Tamsin. For one so small she clearly ruled them all with an iron fist. She had married young and stayed that way, raising three fine sons. She would be there for Peta. It would all be OK.

'Now, Fred, let's get a shot of the bride with her brother and grandmother, then we'll roll in your family for the next one.'

Peta kissed my cheek as she slipped an arm around my back. 'It's all good, Gran. Thank you for everything.' Looking in her eyes I saw her happiness. I was wrong to worry. I had to keep my concerns to myself and hope Jack would as well. One of the pageboys attempted a handstand on the grass behind the photographer, causing laughter as his father swept him up by his feet and carried him to his mother.

'Can't keep control of your kids, Mark,' Fred called.

The man who'd carried the child turned back with a big smile. 'No, he reminds me of you, Fred – full of wicked energy.'

'Great, now you tell me!' Peta called as the child squealed in delight and his mother came along holding a little girl in her arms.

'You wouldn't have listened to me anyway,' Mark called over his shoulder, setting his son on his feet and ruffling his hair. He placed an arm around his wife and they walked back towards the tepee.

The photographer sighed. 'Can you all look this way? We'll get these done and you can all go to the party.'

'Hear, hear,' said Fred's father Anthony. I tried to appear happy; this was a joyful day after all. I looked at the two people who loved me without question. I'd always been a part of their lives. Of course, that wouldn't be the case for much longer. At ninety there were a limited number of years available. And to be honest, there was only one thing left that I would like to see. I turned to Jack. The smile on his mouth did not reach his eyes.

In the distance the photographer was trying to organise the family but it didn't look like he was getting the cooperation he wanted. Lara smiled then turned to check everything. More canapés were at the ready and the champagne bottles were cooling in large metal troughs. The waiting staff were busy. Her job was almost done. She double-checked the heat from the barbecues and tasted the seasoning in the salad dressing. No worries there. Cassie had a finely tuned team. Lara walked to her car and pulled out the clothes carrier. She would slip into the dress and move among the guests checking things as unobtrusively as possible.

The sundress was ideal for the heat of the day. Now that she had it on she could see it was truly in a 1940s style, with a belted waist and full skirt. The light in the bathroom off the kitchen was not ideal for refreshing makeup, but she made quick work of it, touching up the red lipstick and tucking a few loose strands of hair back into their roll. The overall effect of the hair and the dress worked well. Digging into her bag, she pulled out the necklace and earrings that Betty had given her. She wondered if Grandie had given them to Amelia as a wedding present, but they looked older. Adjusting the string of pearls around her neck, she walked back to the car to put her chef's clothes out of the way.

The sound of happy voices floated on the light breeze. Coming around the outside of the building, Lara stopped. The view out across the sea was impressive, but it wasn't that which had brought her to a halt – it was the large bay window of the house, juxtaposed with the view. It looked very much like the one in her great-grandparent's wedding photograph. She pulled out her phone and snapped a picture. She told herself it was probably more likely that this style of window was common in Cornwall, as were the stunning views, but it would be worth a check, at least.

In the distance she could see the photographer was still taking pictures of the wedding party. The bride was wearing a cream flapper dress covered in leaves that progressed in shades, reaching the bottom in a full blaze of colour. Somehow this modern twist worked well with the classic style and a veil that swept around her feet. The veil must be a family one. Peta's brother Jack held himself away from the group and Lara could see the photographer trying to encourage him back into the fold. Viewing the group from this distance, she saw how beautifully Peta had designed each outfit to suit the wearer, down to the vivid silk vests on the men. The whole gathering was a stunning array of colour with the sparkling blue bay as the backdrop.

She walked back towards the tepee and turned her attention to the guests. The champagne flowed freely and the band played jazzy numbers from the fifties and sixties. The voice of the singer had a distinctly Sinatra feel. The sun was warm while the breeze was both cool and in the right direction to keep the smoke from the barbecues away from the tent. If it all went this well she would be home soon and curled up with Snowy while the bride and groom were dancing the night away. She just hoped they didn't plan on watching the sunrise and taking a dip in the sea like Pierre and she had. She sighed. It wasn't fair to compare her disastrous marriage with the one taking place today, but the bad taste of failure still lingered.

Lara hovered by the opening of the tepee. Everything was proceeding to plan – dinner was cleared, and according to Cassie's schedule it was time for the speeches. If Lara hadn't seen several British films, she would have been puzzled by this item on the event plan. In the movies the best man always gave a short humorous account of the love affair between the bride and the groom, and today Fred's brother had been funny and light-hearted. She was tempted to try the same at Leo's wedding in December.

Now Jack stood with a microphone in his hand, his face solemn. His eyes were the colour of a summer sky and the curl in his blonde hair refused to be totally tamed. Maybe it was his stance or the set of his mouth, but Lara felt for him. The crowd hushed as he cleared his throat.

'I know that I'm not the best person for this task but Peta has asked me to thank the bridesmaids and the children.' He paused and looked at a piece of paper in his hands. His Adam's apple bobbed visibly. 'I want to thank my grandmother on Peta and Fred's behalf for the use of her beautiful home. Elle Rowse has been a huge part of Peta's and my life, just as much a parent to us as grandmother, and sometimes all at once.' He picked up his glass and looked into the crowd until he spotted her. 'Thank you, Gran,' he said, and the crowd responded with a polite 'Hear, hear.'

Then he turned to the bride and the groom and paused, a bit too long. Lara willed him to continue. She saw the people directly in front of her fidgeting on the bench and a few people leaned in to whisper. She frowned. Jack looked down at Peta and Fred and cleared his throat.

'I don't believe in love,' he said. 'It makes you do stupid things. You lose all perspective and things go wrong.'

Lara could hear the gasps throughout the crowd, and saw the groom's father shift in his seat as if he was about to stand and hit Jack. A man directly in front of her said in a stage whisper, 'Get him off!'

'But if I did believe in love and marriage,' continued Jack, ignoring the hubbub of discontent, 'then what these two have ... just might be it.'

Lara looked at the happy couple. Both appeared shell-shocked, and understandably so, yet she knew what Jack meant. She didn't believe in love anymore, but as much as she agreed with him, his sister's wedding was not the right time to air his views. Life today didn't work as it had in the past. Love and marriage belonged to a time when things were mended not thrown away. She mentally raised a glass to his braveness as he asked everyone to toast the bride and groom and their future life together. As they all returned to their seats, the atmosphere in the tent had changed from joyous to angry. People began moving. Lara rushed the waiting staff to get the coffee and brownies on the tables. Maybe a little sugar would calm everyone. Otherwise a fight might start and no newly-weds deserved that, even if the perfect ideal of married love no longer existed.

Despite the high-backed chair I had been given, my body complained bitterly as I stood. I wanted to shout at everyone to be quiet and forget what Jack had said, but with these damn hearing aids I could hear the loud whispers, and could read the thoughts expressed on Tamsin and Anthony's faces. Peta was paler than she'd been earlier, but she placed a hand on her brother's arm and kissed his cheek when he sat down next to her. No matter what he said she would still love him, but that speech would put some strain on their relationship. I hadn't thought his anger and bitterness had gone so deep that he'd be unable to stop it coming forth at a time like now.

Eddie took my hand once I reached my feet. 'Well, that will be discussed for years to come.' He shook his head. 'Sometimes it's best when people don't say a thing.'

A wry smile formed on my mouth. 'Indeed.' Both he and I knew bitter disappointment but it was not our way to speak of it. Our generation didn't talk about such things for many reasons, and one of them was that we thought to spare other people's pain. Silence might wreak havoc with your insides, but it made for a calmer, quieter existence. I thought of the reporter wanting me to talk about the war. My war, as she called it, was best left locked inside of me, where it had no power to harm anyone else.

'I'm off to find a whisky,' Eddie said. 'Will you join me?'

He still had charm even at ninety-four. He was a gentleman through and through. 'I need a bit of fresh air first.' I took a breath. 'A stiff drink does appeal though.'

'I'll see if I can shepherd young Jack away from the angry wedding party and bring you one.'

'Thank you.'

'A pleasure, my dear.'

He hobbled one way while I went the other, towards the opening of the tepee. The setting sun was catching the tops of the pines in a golden glow and falling on the open ground beside the house. I shivered; the heat had left the day as the sun lowered in the sky. The catering staff had been superb, always there with the correct food or drink, sometimes before people had even realised they needed it. Their white shirts were almost yellow in the light as they moved with their trays towards the tent. At least something had run smoothly. I just hoped the band would begin playing again and defuse the tension. The breeze had turned. The weather would soon change.

As I looked across the view, my eye was caught by a floral skirt billowing in the breeze. The woman wearing it was walking beside the house, and the pattern of the dress reminded me of one I had once owned. I paused, trying to see which guest had wandered to the working part of the house – and then I saw her properly. Caught there in the golden light stood a vision of myself, young again, with my grandmother's earrings catching the evening sun.

I was rooted to the spot. I barely registered Eddie as he walked towards me, a drink in his hand and a concerned expression on his face. 'Have a good sip of this, put some colour in your face. You look like you've seen a ghost.' He followed my gaze and a second later he had dropped the glass in his hand. It didn't shatter as it hit the grass, which was more than I could say for Eddie. His face crumpled in front of me.

'Good lord.' He cleared his throat. 'It is an uncanny resemblance.'

We stood shoulder to shoulder, watching her. I was relieved. If he could see her, my mind wasn't playing tricks on me. I didn't want to think about it, but it was all I could do. How could that woman look identical to myself and my sister? There was only one answer and I couldn't believe it. Why now?

I closed my eyes and counted through the years, guessing that the doppelgänger was in her mid-twenties, maybe thirty. It was hard to tell these days and yet she wore clothing that spoke of the past. I recognised the fabric pattern. But it wasn't the clothes or the hairstyle. It was like the years had melted away and I saw what I wanted to remember. It was that last summer before we'd turned eighteen and our lives went their separate ways.

Moments later the vision moved into the house and out of sight. The woman was gone.

'I tell you,' said Eddie, 'it gave me a shock to see my old fiancée just as I remember her.' He placed a hand on his heart.

'Yes.' I looked at Eddie, knowing his pain must be as sharp as mine. He was of a more forgiving nature, yet still he'd never married. His heart had broken and never healed. Dwelling on the past wasn't helping things.

'Need a drink by any chance?' He coughed. 'I do.'

'Yes, I definitely do.' I squinted at him. Maybe that was the way to go, to drown all the memories and the pain in alcohol. But unlike my father, I hadn't chosen that route.

I stopped. I was being unfair. Father had seen things that he couldn't forget, from the beaches of D-Day to the death camps. He'd tried to block it out, indulging in women and wine until Mother had broken completely. It was as though the pain of his war couldn't be contained within the body; its damage had to spread. My war had been different. Unlike my father, I didn't crack in the aftermath of everything that happened – I became solid, unbreakable. And, thankfully, Andrew had known that. We had never spoken of the war, except for general references.

Eddie, too, never spoke of what happened. He would regale the willing with the joys of flying, the excitement, the daring ... but not how he lived with the fact that he had killed thousands of civilians. I could see those ghosts in his eyes; they spoke to the ones in mine, despite the fact that I'd never pulled a trigger or dropped a bomb.

Rip Tide

Make haste! The tide of Fortune soon ebbs.

SILIUS ITALICUS, PUNICA, BOOK IV, LINE 732

❊ Twenty-Four ❊

Windward, Mawnan Smith, Falmouth, Cornwall
12 September 2015

I settled on the sofa in the sitting room, comfortable at last.
The fairy lights lined the flaps of the tepee and they twinkled
in the darkness. The night had drawn in so quickly that in the
bustle of the celebration I hadn't noticed until a chill had settled
on me and Eddie suggested we retire to the house.

'Do you think the girl could be connected to Amelia in some
way?' Eddie handed me a drink. In the tepee, the music continued and the dance floor was already crowded. 'It was a shame I
couldn't find her. I did look and I asked about her.' He shook
his head. 'But she disappeared like a vision.' He looked at me
closely. 'But she wasn't one, Delly.'

'I know,' I said, and frowned. His question reflected my
thoughts but I didn't want to talk about it. It was too painful.

'She was the caterer.' He laughed. 'A cook like Amelia.' He
took a deep sip of whisky. 'Do you know what happened to
Amelia in America?' he asked.

I swung around, the loud beat of the music pounding in my
head. 'Do you?'

'You know I don't. How could I?'

I closed my eyes. I couldn't lash out at him. It wasn't fair.

'Thought you might,' he said. 'She's your sister.'

I sighed and Eddie placed a hand on my shoulder.

'You never told me what happened.'

I shook my head, unable to reply. Even when Mother died
I'd refused to have contact with her. Father had stepped in, not

227

that I wanted to engage with him either, but for once he did all that was necessary including informing my sister. He had tried to talk to me, to explain I guessed, but I had refused to listen to him.

'I knew whatever it was it … had to be bad. You won't even speak her name. Had Robert Webster been yours?'

I gasped.

'I see.' He took a sip of his drink. 'She had been quite loose when I pinned her down but …' His voice trailed away. 'She was a good person, the best really. I don't think she would have done it deliberately. I know she thought I was dead.' He shook his head. 'It was the only thing that kept me from walking off a cliff.' He laughed grimly. 'That and the fact that walking was very tricky at the time.' He tapped his prosthetic leg.

He looked at me as if willing me to speak. I pressed my lips together.

'I can only make guesses if you don't tell me,' he said.

I turned to him. 'We don't talk.'

'No, this is true. Putting the pain into words doesn't make it go away. It makes it more real because, then, you have to look at it, you can't step around it anymore. Yet …' He took a long drag of his whisky. 'I have found that I've had to talk as I've become old. The bottling it up, the denying it didn't make it go away. It simply came out at night when I was alone. I'd wake screaming out names of people that were long dead.'

It was my turn to reach out to him. My war had been bad but it was nothing compared to what he'd lived through. Having survived the European arena he went to Asia, where he was shot down and captured. When he'd come home he was half the man he had been when he left, and his fiancée was somebody else's wife. How he could find any good words for her at all was beyond me, but then he had always been kind.

The piles of unopened letters sitting upstairs might answer his questions – I had originally thrown them away, but Mother had retrieved them, hoping I would reach out to my sister and see reason. She thought I was taking the moral high ground but she had no idea. I couldn't know about Amelia's life. Reading the details would only make the pain cut deeper. Ignorance should have been bliss, if only my imagination hadn't always tried to fill in the blanks.

'Delly, let it go now.'

I flinched. Elle, that was who I had become. The wedding and the baby had taken the future from me, so I had changed myself. Elle defined the new me, the me I'd carved out of the pain so I could embrace any future I could find.

I doubted Mother ever wrote to Amelia of what had happened afterwards, when Father didn't even bother to return anymore, not even for the holidays. She wouldn't have burdened my sister with that. She would have written only the positives. I could almost hear her voice, as if she was sitting in her favourite armchair in the corner: *It's been a lovely spring with the weather so mild it's brought on the roses early, and your sister has stepped in and taken over your grandmother's garden. Who knew she had it in her?*

I actually glanced over at the armchair, just to be sure Mother wasn't in fact sitting there. It had been sixty-four years since a bad bout of pneumonia took her that bitter November. With the appearance of the woman in the dress tonight, I felt the presence of the past in a manner that I hadn't in years. The way she had walked and turned her head was identical. And yet my mind refused to believe what my eyes had seen. I knew that she must be related; there had to be a link.

However it was one aspect of her that had unsettled me most – her hands, with their graceful fingers. Turning my own hand over in front of me, I saw the fingers were still long but graceful no longer. Age had bent them, the once-clear skin coloured by the sun. Youth was a memory, but in my head I was still young. It was my body that had aged. All these memories should have disappeared. I didn't want them, and once opened they were not easy to close again.

'Delly, where have you gone?' Eddie stood in front of me, but I barely saw him. I had gone back to a time of promise. But now both Eddie and I were relics of the broken past.

HMS *Attack*, Portland, Dorset
10 May 1944

Dearest Half,

*After writing of my despair, I hope you knew that it had turned
to pure joy. It's been four days since I've seen my love. The sun
shines and my heart sings. I keep pinching myself. He's alive
and that's all that matters. I'd thought I'd never feel his arms
around me again and had steeled myself to live in this world
without him but now I don't have to. I thought what I felt for
him could never be stronger but I was wrong.*

*You are wondering what happened to him. I honestly don't
know. He has had stitches on his forehead, that is all I know.
We held each other on the dance floor not daring to speak.
Today I am counting the hours until this afternoon when I can
go ashore and see him. We will only have four hours but it will
have to be enough for now.*

*I don't know how you can live without Eddie. I'm obviously not
as strong as you are and all these years I thought I was the strong
one. Hah! Silly me. I can hear you chuckling as I write this. Will
Eddie be able to come home on leave? I hope you can marry then.
If it looks likely give me as much warning as you can. Will you
marry in Cornwall or elsewhere? What will you wear?*

I can't sit still any longer. I'll write to you after I've seen him.

I stopped writing, put the letter away and straightened my
bed, after which I paced the room. All I knew right now was
that I wanted to be in Bobby's arms, not here. I couldn't afford
to waste any more time. If nothing else, what had happened
on 28 April had taught me how important it was to live in the
now. I had today with Bobby. I might not have tomorrow.

After dinner Pat and I walked towards the tennis courts. I
hadn't knocked a ball around in a while but a few Wrens were
playing as we passed.

'Out with it, Adele.' Her words sounded abrupt but she was
smiling.

I flushed. There was no easy way to ask what I needed to know. 'Um, can you tell me ... you know ... how it's done?'

She looked at me closely then laughed. 'No wonder you looked so uncomfortable all through dinner.' She raised an eyebrow. 'So you want to do the dirty deed with your Yank?'

I nodded, not liking the way she said it.

'I didn't think you had it in you. But maybe you have. Maybe we all have because of the blasted war.' She sighed, looking out to the white cliffs in the distance. 'You've lived in the country and seen animals do it.'

I nodded, swallowing.

'Don't worry, it's much better than that but the action's the same.' She put her arm around me and whispered details in my ear. I felt my face flush with heat. I was both excited and revolted at the same time.

'Judging by your expression – and your resemblance to a beetroot – you might not be ready.' Pat smiled. 'But better to plunge in than be like my old aunt after the last war. There may not be many men left once it's over, and she still hasn't had one.'

Weymouth, Dorset
11 May 1944

As the train slowed and I peered out of the open window, I could see Bobby in the distance, standing waiting on the platform. Everything in me rejoiced. The sun beat down on his head and as the train brought me closer I could see highlights in his brown hair. When he was a child living near the sea he would have been fair. Would our children be fair-haired like me or dark like him? I caught my breath, shocked at what I had just thought – but I knew that was what I wanted more than anything. My head told me it was too soon to think like that, while my heart was already there, feeling how it could happen.

Impulsively I leaned out of the window and waved. In the past I never would have shown emotion so publicly but now I couldn't hold it back. I needed Bobby to know exactly how I felt about him. We might not have much more time. The train slowed further and I pulled back from the window and dashed to the door. Not a second could be wasted. My stomach was in happy knots of anticipation. I'd made a decision and Amelia was right. *Carpe diem* – we might not have a tomorrow but I needed today.

Once the train had come to a halt, Bobby opened the door and I flung myself into his arms, nearly knocking him off his feet.

'That's quite a hello,' he said, laughing.

'Hmmm.' The touch of his sun-warmed skin against mine reassured me he was real, not just a memory. He studied me. I stared back, trying to convey everything that was in my heart. Smiling, he took my hand. The afternoon was beautiful, with the sea so blue and the cliffs in the distance so bright. Everything had a golden glow, and even the barbed wire on the beach didn't look as threatening.

The jeep stood by, which meant we could escape inland and forget the madness of the war for a few hours. I intended to make the most of them.

Bobby was quiet as we left town. Swathes of tight blue buds caught the sunlight that was falling through the trees as we drove into one of the many large areas of woodland.

Parking the jeep under a tree, he pulled a basket from the back and held out his hand for mine. Like other times when our fingers touched, my heart raced; it knew of my plans. I intended to make Bobby fully mine today. My conversation with Pat was fresh in my mind. Fear and excitement knotted my insides.

As we walked up the hill I noticed the set of Bobby's mouth. There was no smile as he squinted against the sun, scanning the horizon. I squeezed his hand. 'All right?'

He stopped and kissed my forehead. 'Sorry, I have something to tell you.'

I looked up, trying to read him, and knew I didn't want to hear what he would say. 'Yes?'

'Let's eat first.'

I frowned. The food would taste of sawdust with this hanging over me, but his face was set so I tiptoed and kissed his cheek. He smiled, and once we reached a beautiful field he spread out a blanket and unpacked the food. It was filled with treats. Things I'd taken for granted in the past were to be cherished now, like the sweetness of butter on fresh bread.

And with that thought, I was suddenly certain what Bobby was going to tell me. *He's being transferred*, I told myself. It seemed the only possibility.

Waiting for his announcement made this feel like it was my last meal. I should have been savouring the experience but I couldn't. I lay back on the blanket with the wool scratching through my blouse while the heat of the sun warmed my face. My whole body called out to the man not three inches from me, but I didn't know how to close the gap. I thought of my sister. She would know how.

He pushed a stray lock of hair off my cheek. My breath stilled. He leaned over me, blocking the sun from my face. His lips touched mine. The salt of the ham and sweetness of the peaches was on his lips. The kiss deepened. I felt the length of his body along mine. I pushed against him and heard his gasp. He pulled me closer. Although I knew what I needed to do, part of me was still afraid, unsure. As his lips travelled to my neck and along my collarbone, sensations built and I moved under him.

My fingers explored his back, making their way down to the base of his spine, then hesitated before going lower. His hand travelled to my breast. Proper thought disappeared as his mouth soon reached the top of my bra. There was a groan – from me or him, I couldn't tell. The fabric was pushed aside. His thumb brushed my nipple. My heart stopped and started again when his mouth replaced his fingers. My hands slipped around his torso while our hips moved with their own rhythm.

A crow cried above and suddenly Bobby pulled back.

'This isn't right.'

Cool air circled my flesh where his lips had just been. 'Don't stop.' I kissed his cheek, working my way to his mouth.

'No, we mustn't.' He sat up and shifted uncomfortably.

I lay back shivering. He leant forward and pulled my bra and blouse back into place. 'I'm so sorry. I lost control.'

'No.'

'It's not right.' He stood up and took a couple of steps away, scanning the horizon.

I closed my eyes. I wanted him so much and he'd just pushed me away. Opening my eyes, I stood and went to him. 'It *is* right. I love you.'

He turned to me, his eyes wide. 'I love you too.'

'Then what's wrong?'

'I want to marry you.'

'Yes, please.'

He pulled me into his arms and whispered in my ear, 'That's why it's wrong. I want to do this right. I want to be with you forever and I don't want us to look back and regret anything.'

I sighed. 'We may not have tomorrow.'

'I know. But –' he kissed me '– I love you so much that I never want you to think I didn't ...' He paused. 'It's not easy to explain.'

I looked up at him. 'Try?'

'My parents.'

'Yes?'

He shook his head. 'They came from very different backgrounds. It caused problems.'

'But they are together.'

'Yes, it worked but not without ... a lot of pain on all sides. My father wasn't Catholic, but my mother was.'

I frowned. 'I don't understand.'

He sighed. 'My father came from a very wealthy family. My mother was an immigrant.'

'Oh.' I ran through what the implications of that would mean here, but I knew so little about America.

'His parents forbade him to marry.' He turned from the view and looked at me. 'They did anyway and they disinherited him.'

'I see.' But I didn't at all. His parents loved each other. Surely that was enough?

'I don't want this to happen to us. I want to do this properly.'

He took my hands in his. This I could understand, even if it was frustrating. 'You might become pregnant, then if something happened to me ...' He shook his head. 'We have to be strong.'

I swallowed. I didn't want to be strong. I wanted to make love to him right there and then. My body was shouting: *We have today, we may not have tomorrow.*

He kissed me before I could protest.

'I'm being transferred.' He trailed a finger down my face.

I nodded. I hadn't wanted to hear the words. Once he left Weymouth, who knew when I'd see him?

'Can you say where?'

He closed his eyes. 'No, but ... you know it. You love it.'

Cornwall.

He stroked my cheek. 'Say you'll be my wife.'

'Yes and yes and yes again.'

'We'll make this happen.'

I nodded. I knew somehow we would.

❋ Twenty-Five ❋

Bodmin Moor, Cornwall
14 May 1944

I pinched myself and it hurt, so this must be happening. I was
in a jeep, driving through Cornwall with Bobby, heading
to an empty Windward. Mother and Grandmother were in
London on a long-overdue visit to Father. I wasn't sure where
Amelia was for I hadn't had a letter, but no doubt she was
having fun. And, just for a change, so was I.

The hours passed in a blur and off the A30 we found a quiet
spot to have tea and a sandwich. The sky was cornflower blue
and not a cloud dared mar its surface. I lay back on the grassy
hill and closed my eyes, trying to contain the excitement of
having Bobby to myself for three days. I had no idea how
long it would be before I would see him again. It was simply
wonderful that we would be spending the time in Cornwall.
My two loves together. My heart would be whole.

My breath caught. Amelia. I turned to the man at my side.
Everything in me called to him. He was my life, and Eddie
was hers. Something twisted inside me and I knew part of me
would never be complete without her.

'Why the frown?' He turned and leaned on his elbow.

I squinted. I couldn't tell him about the hole that my future
would have without my sister. 'I haven't been home since I
went into training almost a year ago.'

'This worries you?'

'Things will have changed.'

'True. Nothing remains the same.'

'Those are wise words.' His eyes were a deeper blue than the sky as they stared into mine. His love would fill every gap in my life and make a new whole. I wouldn't worry about the future but only think about the now. I didn't want to rush ahead – I wanted to slow down time so that each minute would be the equivalent of an hour or a day. I took a deep breath and closed my eyes, enjoying the warmth of the sun and the touch of his fingers resting on my arm.

'A penny for them?'

'Wishing today could go on for ever.' I opened my eyes and stared into his.

'Lying here by the road?'

'No, just lying in the sunshine with you.'

He kissed me and filled my entire view. I traced his lips with my finger, wanting to remember their feel. Three days to make memories to hold onto. Big things were about to happen. I sensed but didn't know for certain. Although Bobby appeared relaxed, he wasn't.

He stretched out next to me, our sides touching and our hands entwined. 'We have hours of driving in front of us.'

'I know.'

'We should be moving.'

'If you insist.' I pushed up onto my elbow and stared at him. His mouth, full and firm, had a smile hovering on it. His eyes were half closed against the sun. The scar on his forehead had healed. I leaned down and kissed it. He groaned and pulled me on top of him. Kissing, we rolled over. 'I want you so much,' he whispered just below my ear, sending shivers through me.

'Yes.' I squirmed with pleasure and we rolled again, this time over and over, gaining momentum until we landed in a heap at the bottom of the hill near the jeep, both of us full of laughter.

He held out his hand to pull me up and into his arms. 'That was a close shave.'

We looked out across the moor with Rough Tor in the distance. He laced his fingers through mine, and we climbed back up the hill, collected the picnic basket then set off again.

*

237

The black sky was filled with stars as we arrived at Windward. The pines scented the soft night.

'You're home,' Bobby whispered.

And I was. Windward was the constant in my life and as I looked at its silhouetted mass against the evening sky I felt a pull to it that had always been there. Amelia and I had been born here, with the sea air in our lungs and the tang of salt in our mouths. Poor Mother had gone into labour early while walking on the beach below the house. The local farmer's wife had come to the rescue and delivered us. I let the evening wrap around me and embrace me in the feeling of home, of Cornwall.

Bobby grabbed the bags then took my hand. We crossed the lawn already covered in dew. Walking into the kitchen, all was in darkness. I switched on my torch, and the beam picked out the familiar shapes of the range and the table. There was so much to show him and so little time. I longed to take him down to the beach where we could lie on the cold sand, stare at the night sky and look for the phosphorescence in the sea. But the beach was off limits, as was the whole coast, covered in defences of varying types. The best that I could do would be to take him halfway down the cliff to my old hiding place. From there we could experience the still of the night and listen to the waves coming ashore.

We went past Grandmother's room and climbed the flight of stairs to the turret room, where we dropped off his bag. This was the best room in the house, although not as large as Grandmother's. It had sweeping views across the bay as far as Dodman Head in the north to the Manacles in the south. In many ways I was surprised the house hadn't been requisitioned for the view of the coastline. The hotel nearby had a similar outlook and the Dutch cadets were using their beach house, while the Home Guard had built a base just along the coast. A notebook by the window confirmed my belief that Grandmother kept a record of all the marine activity that she saw.

Coming to my room, Bobby placed my bag on the bed and then I took his hand and tugged.

'Where are you taking me?' he asked.

'To a special place.'

'Sounds intriguing. Would we be able to have a drink there? It was a long drive.' He let go of my hand and pulled a bottle of whisky out from behind him.

I smiled. 'Yes, we'll grab two glasses on our way out.'

Back in the kitchen, I jumped when I found someone there. I'd forgotten about Madame Pomfrey, the French refugee.

'I can't believe you're here and the family isn't.' She waved her hands. 'You just missed your sister by a few hours. She's gone up to London to meet her fiancé. She's just heard he's being transferred to the Far East.'

'No.' My hand flew to my heart. That explained the sorrow that had been slipping around the edges of my thoughts. I had been pushing it aside because of my own happiness.

'Are you all right? You've gone very pale.' Bobby's glance was full of concern.

'Yes, just worried about Amelia.'

He nodded and Madame Pomfrey took her cocoa and left us. I switched off the kitchen lights and Bobby followed me into the garden. We stood in the darkness letting our eyes adjust and I tried to send love to Amelia. This war was hell, especially on our hearts. The Far East was a lifetime from here. There would be no possibility of seeing Eddie until he returned. If he did return.

Bobby slipped his arm around my shoulders. 'It will be tough on your sister.'

'Yes.' I began walking, not turning on the torch but navigating in the darkness by memory and feel. The landscape had changed and soon we had stumbled into Grandmother's vegetable patch. How I could have forgotten she had dug up the lawn?

I switched on the torch briefly to locate the small path to my secret place. Bobby followed along the narrow way close behind me, with an ever-ready hand to steady me if I stumbled.

I stopped abruptly and Bobby collided with me. He had no idea how close to the cliff edge we were as I teetered on the brink. Then, taking his hand, I turned and found my spot under an outcrop of stone and scrub pine.

It was a tight fit for the two of us, a small place between the rocks and sheltered from the elements. He was pressed against me. The tingling of the whisky on my taste buds vied with the reaction of my body to his. I knew this was just purely chemistry, chemistry of the physical kind. I wanted him and was more and more impatient. The scorn I had poured on my sister had begun to feel like ignorance.

'I can see Orion's Belt.' He pointed then brought his arm back down and placed it around my shoulders, pulling me closer to him. Warmth overtook the cool night air.

'Yes, and the Plough,' I said.

He turned to me. His face was just inches from mine. 'Do you mean the Big Dipper?'

'Dipper?'

'Yes, Dipper.' He kissed me. 'Dipper as in ladle.'

'Ah.' I tasted the whisky on my lips from his. 'Thank you for the translation.'

'Hmmm.' He kissed me again and I forgot the difference in our common language, even the stars above, and simply felt my need for him.

Windward, Mawnan Smith, Falmouth, Cornwall
13 September 2015

The wind hit the house with force. After the glorious day and evening for the wedding, all hell had broken loose, just like in my thoughts. Turning on the light I could see the window frame shaking. Before long rain would follow, persistent and powerful, so I rose to shut it. I hoped everything outside was battened down. Once the window was shut I paced, trying to empty my mind. Sleep had not visited me as I listened to the wedding music into the small hours. Laughter, so much laughter, and sounds of happiness drifted in between the thump of the bass. I was so pleased for Peta and Fred.

But as I looked out on the darkness now, my heart bled. That girl in the dress. I knew she had been real, but standing there alone I felt differently. She had brought everything back, everything that was lost. Did she know? Or was it some cruel twist of fate that had brought her to my door?

Something crashed against the house. I walked downstairs. In the kitchen I grabbed a torch and pulled on my waxed jacket. The back door almost ripped out of my hands as I opened it. With all my strength I managed to push it shut behind me. Both Jack and Eddie must have been sound asleep not to have been woken by the noise.

Reaching the terrace with the bay below, I felt the full force of the wind. Small drops of rain hit my face as I shone the torch into the darkness. The clock in the kitchen had read four in the morning, which meant there was a while before dawn would come and reveal the damage, but I couldn't find anything amiss. Not that I could do anything on my own. Standing out in a howling gale was not sensible, but I felt better in the elements. My hair whipped around my head, echoing my thoughts. Standing where I last saw my sister, I let the tears that had been threatening fall. They mixed with the light rain.

I walked on until I came to the narrow path towards the cove. Halfway down, as the rain changed from small drops to big fat pelting missiles of water, I turned and pushed my way through the wild growths of brambles to my secret spot. A lump formed in my throat. Bobby. My heart called out to him. I couldn't go on. I bent myself down into the small hollow and curled into a ball, holding my memories, hoping death would take me. Trying hard, I could feel his arms around me and his lips on mine. A cry sprang from me. I closed my eyes and waited.

✶ Twenty-Six ✶

Boscawen House Hotel, Constantine, Cornwall
18 September 2015

As Lara passed through the gates of Boscawen, the drive
ahead was longer than she'd expected. She'd always been
intrigued by the set-up process of restaurants. All the ones
she'd worked in had been well established by the time she'd
joined – the last had already earned its first Michelin star and
she had helped it reach its second. She had learned a lot from
the experience, but in return she'd given everything, including
her marriage as it turned out. Would she want to do that again?
Was it worth it? Her chest tightened in sadness not love.

She had spoken to both Demi and Sam at the wedding,
where they had once again issued their invitation to visit; a
quick bit of scheduling and they'd found a morning that suited
all of them. Things were thankfully quiet today at the catering
company as well – Cassie was still with her parents, and her
mother was home and on medication. Life was going to have
to radically change for all of them. Fortunately the business was
quiet enough at the moment that Lara could safely keep an eye
on things and still spare the time for today's trip.

Sunlight fell through the trees and fallen leaves covered the
drive. In the distance Lara saw cattle heading to a gap in the
hedge on the far side of a field. Their meat would taste of the
grass and the fresh air. She imagined a dish made of bresaola
and soft cheese like burrata. Her mouth watered, before she
realised that maybe if she hadn't missed out on breakfast, she
wouldn't be eyeing the livestock with such carnivorous intent.

The drive opened up to reveal a mansion made of what she guessed was granite. It appeared like it had been there forever, rooted to the ground. It was vast, bigger than the word 'boutique' had implied to Lara. Lawns and flowerbeds surrounded it. Its history must be fascinating. She pulled up next to the smart cars in front and walked through the large wooden door. She could hear the hushed tones of conversation and then Demi appeared from out of the shadows beside a sweeping staircase.

'Morning.' Demi came forward. 'Everyone's just finishing their breakfast so this is a good time to slip away to the river.'

'Great.' Lara's head swivelled around, noting the windows and paintings. It looked like something out of a PBS Masterpiece Theatre series except it was a bit more updated, though not modern.

'It's a bit overwhelming at first.' Demi smiled as they walked through the grounds, past a walled garden onto a woodland path. 'We have fixed the old lane down to the quay, but I really prefer walking through the wood.'

Lara nodded, and studied the twisted shapes of the trees and the patches of blue sky visible between the uppermost branches. She couldn't sense that there was water nearby except for the cry of a gull from above. 'What made you think of opening a restaurant here in a remote building?'

'Well, when we saw pictures of the old boathouse it seemed to fit.'

Lara frowned, envisaging access issues and wondering how they would draw enough people to make it viable. She was thinking overheads and staffing problems, but then the path ended abruptly and the river flowed past her with the dense growth of trees on the opposite shore visible. A boat with red sails slipped past and Lara turned to see a wooden and glass structure sitting on a quay that jutted into the river.

'It was used to take away the granite quarried from other parts of the estate at first, and then just for pleasure until it fell into disuse and basically disintegrated.'

'It's beautiful.' The building was deceptive. The structure certainly reflected its industrial roots. It used granite and oak and then lots of glass. Lara could imagine that when the wood had greyed with age it would look as if it had always been there watching the tides.

'Yes, I worked with Mark Triggs. Did you meet him at the wedding?'

Lara shook her head.

'He's a brilliant architect who understands the area, its uniqueness and its history. All of which I'm still learning.'

Big doors were open at the back and light flooded into what Lara assumed was a large kitchen, which faced the woods. Plumbing and electrical bits stuck out from the walls made of rough stone.

'Hey, Sam, Lara's here.'

A head appeared from below a ledge. 'Hello.' He placed the hammer in his hand down. 'What do you think of the boat-house?'

'Amazing.' Lara walked through the large space to the walls of glass that were pushed back to the edges, leaving the sides of the dining room totally open to the river. The setting was fabulous even with the tide out and a stretch of mud flats exposed below. Mussels clung to the rocks at the base of the quay. The only things preventing her from clambering down and reaching them were steel safety wires. The sun hit the surface of the river and the reflected light played off the white ceiling. 'What an incredible set-up.'

'We thought so.' Sam draped his arm loosely over Demi's shoulders.

'I googled you last night.' Demi pulled out her phone. 'And I couldn't find a Lara Pearce.'

Lara sighed. 'Try Lara McNulty.'

Demi frowned. 'Oh.'

'That's me pre-divorce.'

'Ah.' Demi was still frowning as Lara smiled, pulled her hair back tightly then put her most serious face on.

'I see the resemblance now.' Sam smiled, glancing at his phone. 'Would you take a look at the kitchen plans?' He rolled out architect drawings on a table.

Lara studied them, reacting almost instantly. 'It looks good but I think you'd need a larger prep table.' She looked into the kitchen space. 'It might mean shaving a little out of the dining area, but not much.' She frowned. 'But other than that it looks ideal.' She ran a fingertip over the plans, feeling a longing to be back in a kitchen, working, playing with flavours and simply being useful.

'So would a chef of your calibre consider working in the back of beyond . . . or know someone who would?'

Lara took a look at the river then back at the plans. A restaurant of her own. 'It's a tempting idea.'

The tyre was flat. Lara knew the stone she had driven over must have been the cause. Above her a canopy of trees covered the road and the sunlight made patterns on the surface of the tarmac. It was the worst possible place for this to happen – in a dip that was also a blind corner. She opened the trunk and looked for a spare but all she found was a small repair kit. The car was as far to the side of the lane as it could be and she hoped any vehicle that came along could pass, but looking at it again she wasn't too sure. At the least, she didn't think this road had much in the way of traffic. She was lost. Somewhere leaving Boscawen she must have taken a wrong turn.

Checking to make sure her hazard lights were functioning, she moved to the side of the car and went to work. As the canister pumped air into the tyre, she tried to listen out for oncoming vehicles over the noise of the mechanism. Comparing one front tyre with the other, she decided it looked right and was worth a try.

With everything stowed and her fingers crossed, she drove a short distance along the narrow road, finally reaching a wider section that was also the entrance to a field. By then the same thumping sound that had alerted her to the flat in the first place was back, so she pulled in next to the large metal gate across the entrance. At least she was off the road.

She took out her phone and found it dead. Not helpful. With no other option, she locked the car and began walking with the map, hoping to figure out where she was. She had an idea but wasn't certain.

Coming to the end of the lane, she recognised the gates to Windward, and realised she could ask to use their phone. The September sun was warm and the air sweet with the scent of apples. The trees were laden and the wasps were busy with the windfall as she walked down the drive. She paused at the open kitchen door, peering into the darkness inside. 'Hello?'

Out of the shadows a figure emerged, walking towards her. It was Jack. 'If it isn't the cake dropper,' he said.

Lara flinched. He was a fine one with words. 'Um, yes.' She looked around hoping someone else was with him.

He stared at her as if seeing her for the first time. 'You re-made the wedding cake.'

'Yes.'

'It was delicious. I liked how it was different from the normal ones.' He paused. 'You used apples.'

'It is the season.' She hoped she'd hidden her surprise that he'd noticed. 'Look, sorry to trouble you, but my car has a flat and my mobile is dead. May I use your phone?'

'Of course.' He gave her a handset.

'Thanks.' She dialled and placed the map on the kitchen counter. Jack looked over her shoulder. She explained the situation to the person at the roadside assistance call centre, and when it came to directions she fumbled until Jack indicated to hand the phone to him. She did so, and he explained the situation swiftly before giving them the number for Windward and ending the call.

'Their nearest van is in St Agnes,' he said, 'so it will be a while. You're welcome to stay here.'

'Thank you.' That was the rest of her day gone. She wouldn't be able to investigate any further into Grandie's footsteps. She'd picked up a local history book from Falmouth Booksellers and was slowly piecing together what had happened in the area during WWII – the short answer was a very great deal. Now she wanted to find out what role Lt Robert Webster had played. He had always maintained he was just a messenger.

Also, Leo had been in touch giving her the names and numbers of someone called General Tucker and three West Point classmates who were still alive. He'd even spoken to one of them, who confirmed that Grandie had embarked for D-Day from Trebah. Whether the other two were still compos mentis was yet to be discovered, but she'd already written to them.

'Why are you over here?' Jack asked as he put the kettle on. 'It's clear that you don't normally work for Cassie because Peta would know you.'

She started. 'Oh, well …' Right then the phone rang and Jack gave the person on the line a stream of instructions.

Once finished, he looked over at her. 'That was the van driver. According to him, he's going to be at least another three hours.' He picked up two mugs. 'So you were telling me why you were here?'

'I'm here researching my great-grandfather.' Lara looked at her hands, thinking of how little she had actually done since she'd arrived.

'Your roots? A very American thing to do, but I think it's spreading here.'

'Genealogy is not a disease.'

He laughed. 'I'm not so sure about that. But in my experience families can behave like one.' His jaw clenched.

She frowned. 'I happen to like mine.'

He looked away. 'Your great-grandfather came from Cornwall, then?'

'No, he was American, of English and Irish stock.'

'Sounds to me like you already know your family history.' He leaned against the counter. 'So what are you researching then?'

'He died in August and there was a picture of him as a soldier in the Second World War. On the back it said "Helford River".'

'Ah, so he was one of the Yanks that left for D-Day from Trebah.'

'I believe so. The other thing is he clearly fell in love with an English woman whom he married.'

'You think she was local?' He raised an eyebrow.

'Possibly. It's hard to know because all I have to go on is one faded black and white photograph taken on their wedding day. The scenery looks familiar, though – in fact, the house looks like Windward.'

'Odd. But then, there's nothing special about Windward's architecture, or location for that matter.'

'I did think that might be the case. The photo is out of focus so it's hard to tell.' Lara took the mug he offered. 'The only sections that are sharp are the edge of the building and a bit of the bay window.'

'Strange. You would think the couple would be.' He led her out into the garden.

'Maybe the photographer sneezed or something.'

He laughed. 'Possibly, although with the rationing of paper at the time they wouldn't have taken too many pictures.' He bent to pull a weed from the path. 'So you know nothing about your great-grandmother?'

'No.'

'But you have all your great-grandfather's details?'

'I do.' She looked to the bay. The view was mesmerising, with yachts sailing about and the orange hulk of an anchored tanker.

'Surely the wedding information should be easy enough to track down.'

'That's what I thought, but thus far, nothing.'

'Have you checked the records here?'

She nodded.

He indicated to a bench facing the view. 'What was her name?'

'Amelia.'

'Amelia what?'

'That's the problem. We don't know.'

He frowned. 'Your grandparents don't know?'

She shook her head.

'This sounds odd to me.'

'Agreed.' She sighed. 'Amelia died tragically young, only a few years after they were married. My grandmother was four. My great-grandfather loved her. It's clear they had a great love

248

affair.' Lara tried not to blush. 'I have some of her letters to him during the war.'

He raised an eyebrow. 'That good?'

'Umm, yes.' She glanced at her tea. Jack cast her a sidelong glance. He'd made his views on love very clear at the wedding.

'So, you're tracking down an American GI who may have been in the area.'

'In short, yes.'

'Don't you have a job?'

Lara flexed her hand. 'Garden leave.'

'But you're covering for Cassie.'

'Not officially working.'

'This is just a research trip, then.'

She nodded.

'Have you been to Trebah?'

'I visited just before Peta's wedding. It's hard to imagine the boarding craft for D-Day heading off from that beach. It was so peaceful and serene.'

He laughed. 'Yes, this place feels very far away from everywhere, especially from things like World War II. Yet during the war it was a hive of activity.' He stood up. 'My grandmother is of the right age to be able to tell you something about the war in the area.'

'Yes?' Lara's breath caught. Maybe she would finally make some progress.

'She hasn't been well.' He put his mug down on the ground. 'She caught a chill after the wedding and that turned to pneumonia.'

'Oh no.'

'Yes. If you don't mind, I'll just go and check on her.'

Lara watched him walk away and tried not to notice just how attractive he was. Instead she focused on the roses that lined the path. The blooms were finished and had produced big, beautiful hips. She thought of the rosehip syrup recipe in the back of the old *Tante Marie* cookbook. There were enough hips here to make a huge batch.

Jack returned holding the teapot. 'She's sleeping.' He shook his head. 'It's like she's given up.'

'How old is she?'

'Ninety.' He refilled her cup and put the teapot down on the ground.

'Maybe she has.'

He nodded. 'I just wish she'd eat. I've tried tempting her with food but it hasn't worked.' He touched one of the rosehips. 'I know she won't be around for ever but she was in good health right up to the wedding. That seems to have pushed her over the edge.'

'Always a time fraught with emotion.' She kicked herself as she said that.

'True.' His eyes met hers. They held humour and a touch of remorse, she thought.

She turned to look at the rosehips again. 'Have you tried old-fashioned food with your grandmother? I believe you call it nursery food here?'

He gave her a questioning look.

'I'm thinking something like tapioca ...' She turned to the rose bushes. 'Maybe flavoured with a bit of rosehip syrup.' She smiled. 'She may have had it during the war.'

He raised an eyebrow.

'I could help you cook some nourishing things which might build her up. Then maybe when she feels better I could ask her about the war?'

His eyes narrowed. 'I can cook.'

'I'm sure you can but it's what I do for a living.'

'I'll think about it.' His whole face lit up as he smiled. He stared at her as if he was seeing her for the first time. Something stirred in her.

Twenty-Seven

Windward, Mawnan Smith, Falmouth, Cornwall
15 May 1944

The morning sun found the gaps in the blackout protection and the squeal of a gull announced it was later in the day then I'd planned. I stretched in bed, remembering the taste of Bobby's kisses and the feel of his hands on my body. My cheeks warmed and I knew that wasn't just a blush from my memory but the after-effects of Bobby's stubble. We'd come so close to making love last night and I'd wanted him so much, but as before, he had stopped.

Desire still filled me but I pushed it from my mind and went to the window, flinging back the fabric. The sky was cloudless and the bay calm, too still to sail – not that we could. However, to bathe in it would be bliss. There might be a chance of a dip, especially if the day remained this fine. The carriage clock on my dressing table said read ten o'clock. I needed to move quickly.

Downstairs I found Bobby in the kitchen in conversation with Mrs Tonks, which surprised me, but then I suspected Grandmother might have asked her to pop in. No doubt she would expect a full report on her return from London.

It was apparent Bobby was charming Mrs Tonks, and from the aroma, he'd brought real coffee with him. All these little luxuries he slipped into my life, but none of them truly mattered, only him. He turned and his glance met mine. My world stopped and began at the same time.

'Miss Delly,' said Mrs Tonks. 'How lovely to see you and how kind of you to show this charming man our part of the world.' She looked between us and I steadied my features. I had no desire to share my love with the world yet, and simply wanted to hold it close to my heart. Telling people would take it from me. I was only ever good at sharing with Amelia, but things were different now. She was holding Eddie close, and I knew they wouldn't be social in these few days before he shipped out. They would cling to each other, making the most of every moment, and I intended to do the same.

I wasn't here in Cornwall to show him around, although I might have been given leave with such short notice for just that reason. Commander Rowse and First Officer Smith knew where I lived and knew I was Bobby's girlfriend. It wouldn't have taken much to put two and two together.

It was odd how I'd come to accept his frequent departures, never asking because I knew he couldn't say. In fact it would be worse to know, for then I might have to lie to others, either by denying knowledge or fabricating something innocuous. The only thing that felt real in this mad world was Bobby and my love for him.

Mrs Tonks smiled at me. 'There's a rasher of bacon in the pan, Miss Delly, but I'm afraid we finished the coffee.' I saw Bobby's mouth twitch at the use of the names we were known by locally, Melly and Delly. 'But I've made a fresh pot of tea for you.' She put the old brown pot on the table. How things had changed. Not the Georgian silver one, but the one used for the help. Amelia and I always thought the tea tasted better from it. No metallic tang to ruin the flavour. I poured Bobby and myself a cup and added the smallest dash of milk. I'd learned to like it without sugar since the start of rationing.

'It's been wonderful to see you,' said Mrs Tonks, untying her apron and hanging it on the hook on the back of the pantry door. 'I'm so pleased your grandmother asked me to come by.' I smiled as my suspicions were confirmed. 'It's a lovely day to go exploring,' she continued, as she moved to leave. 'The Ferryboat is doing a good lunch, I hear.'

We waved goodbye to her and watched her collect her bike and cycle down the drive.

252

'Alone at last?' Bobby walked towards me.

'For the moment.' I wondered where Madame Pomfrey was as he closed the distance and took me in his arms.

'What are your plans for me today?' A wicked glint lit up his eyes, making them dance with mischief.

A smile hovered on my lips as I glanced out of the window. 'I wish we could take the boat out and I could steal you away to a secret cove. But there's not enough wind, so that can't happen.'

'Shame. I like the sound of another one of your hideaways.'

I blushed. 'I bet you do. Instead we'll walk the coastal path and have lunch at the Ferryboat.'

He frowned. 'Ferryboat?'

'The Ferryboat Inn. The name comes from the ferry that goes between Helford Passage and Helford.'

'A ferry?'

'Not a big one but a passenger one. It's been going for hundreds of years. To reach the south side of Helford by road takes for ever, but crossing the river is short.'

He kissed me then, and suddenly the cup of tea that I'd been trying to keep upright splashed down the front of my shirt. 'Oh,' he gasped, 'I'm so sorry.'

'Not to worry. I'll just go and raid my sister's clothes.'

I bounded upstairs and entered Amelia's room. The scent of her perfume hung in the air. Tabu. It captured her as nothing else could. On her bedside table were photos of Eddie and one of me. I smiled. It was good to have confirmation that she was missing me too. The room was exceedingly tidy, which meant she'd changed – but then so had I. Living in a cabin with five other women had done that for me, but she hadn't had the same motivation living at home.

I opened her cupboard and pulled out a top. A few minutes later I was back downstairs wearing a violet blouse that was Amelia's favourite. I had been jealous when she'd found it and there was only one. It had been a long time since we'd had matching clothes.

We walked down the drive from the house then out onto

the footpath cutting across several fields. The hedges were filled with bluebells. I loved this time of year when the greens were brighter and sharper, and everything had an urgency to it. The lane to the church was strangely quiet, though I wasn't sure what noise I was expecting. Everything was still. I listened for birdsong but there was none. Even the new leaves on the trees were motionless. The heat of the day would build quickly without a breeze.

As we walked up, the old parson was by the lych gate, getting onto his bike and adjusting his glasses. 'Morning.'

I waved back. Bobby smiled at him, then turned to the inscription above the gate. 'What church is this?'

'It's the church of St Mawnan and St Stephen, but it's called Mawnan Church.'

'Mawnan.'

I smiled. 'A saint who settled here in the sixth century.'

He raised an eyebrow.

'There were many religious pilgrims who landed in Cornwall from Ireland and Wales to convert the heathens.'

He chuckled as we walked through the graveyard to the entrance of the church itself. Pushing the door open, I led him inside and sighed, realising how much I had missed it here. Sunlight streamed through the windows and caught the dust in the air. As a child I used to sit and watch the motes, thinking it was God's way to show me He existed.

'This place is important to you,' said Bobby, studying my expression.

'Yes.' I looked around at the familiar stonework. 'It is.' I looked up at him. 'I always dreamed of getting married here.'

His smile faded.

'What's wrong?'

He shook his head. 'It's just that it couldn't happen.'

I grabbed the nearest pew, feeling the grain of the wood beneath my fingers.

'Not that I won't marry you, but it's just ...'

'What?' My mouth dried and I couldn't swallow.

'I'm Catholic.'

I nodded. Conversion. I knew this but hadn't thought about the implications. From his expression, nor had he.

'Falling in love wasn't in my plans and yet …' He smiled. 'I have.'

My heart stopped and started again. 'Me too.'

'But I—' He ran his hand through his hair, messing it. Suddenly he was younger and less sure of himself. 'I can't convert. And seeing you here, I'm realising that I can't expect it of you either.'

I looked to the streams of light then to the altar. Would I give this up for him?

I took him by the hand and walked to the front of the church. We stood facing each other by the altar rail. 'I'll convert.'

His face lit up, but then he frowned. 'I can't ask this of you.'

'You haven't. I have willingly offered it.' I stood on tiptoes and kissed him. 'Robert Webster, I love you and I will do whatever it takes to be with you for the rest of my life.' A tear slipped down his cheek and I wiped it away. 'I love you.'

'You do, and I feel unworthy of that love.'

'No, not unworthy at all.' I took his hand. His fingers tightened on mine as I lifted them to my lips. I loved this American with everything that was in me, and I would prove it to him.

❊ Twenty-Eight ❊

Constantine, Cornwall
18 September 2015

The night was drawing in by the time Lara returned home. Snowy was sitting outside on the terrace looking both angry and hungry. He made his feelings loudly known when she opened the door, meowing and wrapping himself repeatedly around her legs, so she went to the cupboard in the kitchen and grabbed the box of cat food she'd bought last week.

She placed a bowl of dry biscuits on the floor in front of Snowy, but the cat simply looked at it blankly before looking back up at Lara. 'Sorry, old chap,' she said, 'but that's what you've got for dinner tonight. The tin of tuna will be mine.' She opened the fridge, pulled out a bottle of Sauvignon Blanc and poured a glass. The inside revealed little else except one withered pepper and some desolate rocket leaves.

Snowy looked from the tin of tuna and her glass of wine to his bowl of dry cat food, then padded away to stretch out on the sofa. Lara couldn't help imagining that he would use the nearby remote control, turn on a sports programme and snub her totally if he could.

Instead she ignored the fluffy white shape and looked at the photos and letters spread out on the kitchen table. There was so little to go on and only one clue, Helford.

She picked up the wedding photograph. It gave no sign of the time of year. She turned the photo over, hoping she'd missed a vital detail, but all she could see was the same faded pencil marks declaring the year, 1945. Grandie was in uniform, which was logical – he had served in the US Army until 1950.

It was all a bit of a wild goose chase. Still, Leo had been right to get her off the Cape and stop her from festering. She took a large sip of wine and set about making dinner. Cassie was still with her parents in north Cornwall, and by the sound of it their whole lives needed to alter. Lara shook her head. It was all very frightening, and had made her stop and evaluate her own life. She was enjoying the slower pace here.

Her stomach rumbled and she turned to the counter behind her. As soon as she picked up the can opener Snowy was off the sofa and up on the counter. He sat there beautifully with his two big front paws placed delicately as if he were about to plié. His glorious fluffy tail swung wide and then gracefully covered his paws. The look in his eyes said it all: *If you think you're going to have that whole can of tuna on your own, you can abandon that idea right now.* In her mind Snowy had a very upper-class British accent. He was a proper cat and she had let him down terribly by offering those appalling dry nuggets when she was about to feast on tinned tuna fish.

She stroked him and he purred loudly, absorbing the adoration that was his due. She could tell he thought he'd won, and he may well have – guilt was creeping in. The cat watched the tin-opening operation closely, especially when she squeezed the excess water from the can. He did not move, simply continuing with his scrutiny. Taking down a bowl, she threw the rocket into it, then the pepper and finally three quarters of the tuna. She peered at the cat food on the floor, and was tempted to just put the tuna on top. However, her distinguished guest might turn his nose up at that too. Instead, she placed the rest of the tuna into a fresh bowl and put it down next to the original serving of cat food. Snowy hit the floor at the same time and quickly buried his face in the new bowl.

Topping up her glass, she ate at the table and looked over the list of the few facts that she had. Robert Webster had married Amelia sometime during or after the war. They had a daughter, Betty, who was born in England in 1946.

My phone pinged with an email from Deborah, Leo's fiancé.

Hi Lara,

Did a little digging on Amelia's death for you. She drowned on October 5, 1950. It's not clear how. But the ruling was accidental death. The newspaper said her body was found on the beach outside of Eventide by a neighbour and Betty was alone in the house. By all accounts it had been a stormy night. Maybe she went out to stop something blowing away and got swept up.

Leo sends his love.
Dx

She chewed on a piece of rocket, thinking over the contents of the email. Grandie had never remarried after Amelia's tragic death. He left the Army in 1950 and returned home to Massachusetts to look after Betty, continuing his education and becoming a professor of Marine Engineering at Woods Hole.

Lara flipped through his diaries. She had the one for 1945 but there were no entries from one week after VE Day. It was as if his life had ceased to be worthy of recording from that point onward. His last entry was one sentence:

I've been such a fool.

That was it. No more excitement about meeting with A. No more coded entries about where and whom he was with.

Tomorrow she would try calling this General Tucker that Leo had tracked down. Hopefully he would be able to shed some light on Grandie's war, at least, if not on her great-grandmother.

Snowy jumped up on the seat next to her and proceeded to clean his paws while she pushed the chopped pepper around in the bowl, debating what to do next.

Her phone rang three times. Snowy stretched.

'Hi, Lara,' said the voice on the line. 'It's Jack Rowse.'

Lara raised an eyebrow at Snowy, who was watching intently. 'Hi,' she said carefully.

'Just wanted to check that everything was sorted with your car? And were you serious about cooking'

'Of course I was. Sadly, it's a bit worse than they thought. The rim was damaged too.' She tilted her head and gave the cat a surprised look. 'So I'll be without the car tomorrow. But I'm still good to come by and cook, if you want me to. I can borrow Cassie's van.' I frowned.

'No need. I can collect you …' He hesitated. 'I've been thinking. When Gran was running a high temperature, she mumbled "the girl" repeatedly – and I just remembered that when I was talking to Eddie about it, he said she must be referring to the caterer in the pretty sundress.'

Lara pulled the wine bottle out of the fridge. 'I *did* wear a sundress.'

'Yes. And the more I think about it, you do have something of a resemblance to my grandmother when she was young.'

'I do?' She looked at the cat lounging with his back legs out straight behind him. It boggled the mind how he could do it and then manage to walk afterwards, but it appeared to be his favourite position.

'Yes. I only saw a picture of her young for the first time a few months back. This BBC reporter wanted to interview her, and brought along a photo taken of her on VE Day, in 1945. The way she looked back then – you're very similar.'

'Oh.' Lara's skin tingled. Maybe his grandmother was related to Amelia. That could explain the house in the wedding photo.

'Anyway, I don't know how she'll be tomorrow but I think she may be able to help. See you in the morning.'

'Great.' She put the phone down and stared at it for a moment. That had to be the most unexpected conversation she'd had in a while. Her trip to the library tomorrow would have to be put on hold, but hopefully Jack's grandmother would feel well enough to chat.

15 May 1944

The cool air wrapped around us as we walked under the cover of the pine trees. Bobby's silence worried me. I had hoped that my promise to convert would have eased the tension in him, but with each step away from the church towards the coastal path his silence became heavier and he withdrew further from me. As we cleared the trees I stopped and turned from the view towards him. 'What's wrong?'

He looked away from me, towards the view, and then shook his head. 'I'm asking everything of you.'

I took his hand. 'I give it willingly.'

'I know you do.' He scanned the coast and then began to walk again. 'I can't take you from this. You have a wonderful life.'

I grabbed his arm. 'Stop walking and look at me.' The water of Falmouth Bay was glistening like blue diamonds, the hillside was blossoming and all I wanted was slipping from me.

He turned and focused on me. 'I'm sorry.'

'Stop. I love you.' I took a deep breath. 'If this wretched war has taught me nothing else it's taught me how important now is and how we act in the present. It's about us and how we feel about each other.'

His pupils were small pinpricks in the bright sunlight. I searched for some sign that my words were reaching him.

He shook his head. 'I've seen first hand what can happen when people from different worlds marry.'

'No, I will go to the States and no one will know who Adele Seaton was or who her family were. They will simply know I am Adele Webster, English wife of Bobby.'

'I pray that you're right.' He tucked a strand of my hair behind my ear. 'I love you.'

'I love you too and that's all that matters. We can overcome everything else.'

He brought me into his embrace and kissed me. 'Now tell me what I'm seeing.'

'Across the mouth of the Helford is Dennis Head, then Nare.'

'It's so beautiful here.' He scanned the horizon.

'It is.'

He took my hand and we began walking side by side when the path was wide enough. 'That house on the south side is

Pengarrock,' I said, pointing out the landmarks. 'And above us is Porth Sawsen. This is its beach.' The pebbled strand was vast as the tide was out, while the water was clear with pockets of turquoise rimmed with dark cobalt patches. The cool water called to me on this hot day, but we walked past the temptation holding hands.

From behind the boathouse at the end of the cove came Bill Tonks in his Home Guard uniform. 'Hello, Bill,' I said.

'Hello, Adele.' He squinted at me. 'Home on leave?'

I nodded, thinking how quickly the gossip moved around here.

'And your man?'

'Lieutenant Robert Webster.'

Bill looked him up and down. 'Papers, please.'

After reviewing them he looked up. 'Off to the Ferryboat?'

'Yes.'

'Have a pint for me. It's going to be a hot one today.'

'Will do.' We walked behind the pillbox and continued in silence along the path until we came to Durgan, looking sleepy in the noon sunshine. Fishing nets were drying on the foreshore and for a brief moment I could forget that there was a war going on. However that changed by the time we reached Trebah. The beach was unrecognisable with a pier protruding into the river. It was like a foreign land as we were stopped not only by the Home Guard but by American soldiers, who stood like imported plants that had pushed out the native species. The beach had been covered in concrete and the garden was unrecognisable, with many of the plants hidden under equipment.

'Papers?' asked our latest obstacle, a young corporal. We handed them over and I saw Bobby's glance take in the number of men on watch and the barbed wire marking the boundaries.

'Sir.' The corporal saluted him.

As we continued the short distance to the Ferryboat Inn I knew I was the alien now. This was no longer mine and would never be again. I had promised to marry the man beside me, change my faith, my name and my country. Breathing deeply, the smell of salt and seaweed filled my lungs. Amelia would have this place always and I might never return. I stopped walking and stared across the river to Helford. The view was achingly familiar. Part of me would always be here. The noonday sun fell on the cluster of houses at Treath. Lobster pots were drying on the quay. The tide was far out, transforming the landscape. Bar Beach to my right was vast, not as I imagined when I thought of home. I had to burn these views into my mind so that I never forgot them.

I turned to Bobby. 'Tell me about your home.'

He looked at me, his eyes narrowed from the glare. He had altered once we had entered the grounds of Trebah. 'It's beautiful but different.' He glanced across the estuary. 'Mostly though the land is flatter.' He took my hand. 'I'm asking so much of you.'

I sighed. 'Yes.' The water of the river reflected the cloudless sky. The beauty hurt. Maybe it was best not to dwell on what I'd be leaving behind and to focus on what I was going to. 'But you're worth it all.'

He studied me. 'I hope I don't let you down.'

'You won't.' I kissed him then pulled him towards the pub.

✳ Twenty-Nine ✳

Knightsbridge, London
28 May 1944

The tearoom was empty except for an old woman sitting in the corner. I looked up from the teapot in front of me when I heard the bell on the door ring. Amelia was in London and we hadn't seen each other in months. Her letters told me so little but she seemed changed. Gone was the exuberance, no doubt due to Eddie's transfer to the Far East.

Another old woman came slowly through the door and I stared out of the window again, watching the bustle of London life in the street outside. It had been years since our family had fled the city. I didn't miss it but I did miss Cornwall. Those few days with Bobby there had reminded me of what I'd left behind – Amelia, Mother, Grandmother, Windward and simply the land and the sea as they lay together, distinct yet tied. A bit like Amelia and me.

Would Amelia be altered in appearance? I knew that I had changed irrevocably since she had last seen me. Bobby had transformed everything. Today I'd even been to Farm Street Church in Mayfair to speak to a priest. The sooner this obstacle was out of the way the better. Days ago the padre in Weymouth had been helpful but very American. The priest today had been kind and given me a book. It was a beginning.

I poured another cup of tea. She was late. There were so many disruptions these days, which somehow we all took in our stride, but today I had little patience. I longed to see her and hear all her news. Her letters were wonderful but I needed to be with her. Aunt Margaret had become the only person in the family who saw everyone. She'd had a lovely time with Mother and Grandmother and had said Father was well when I had had breakfast with her that morning. She was behaving a little oddly, though, very distracted. But then, so was I.

In fact I hadn't even told Amelia Bobby's name yet. Maybe it was fear that if I spoke it he would disappear. By holding him close and not sharing him with anyone other than those who were with me at HMS *Attack*, he felt more mine and I felt more me and not just a twin. I frowned, realising that I hadn't told Bobby that Amelia was not just my sister but my twin. Maybe the time had come to tell him; after all, we were engaged.

The bell on the door jingled and in walked Amelia. My breath caught. Like me she was in uniform, and as always it startled me to see myself. She looked radiant, happier than I had ever seen her. I leapt to my feet and embraced her. 'Melia, look at you.'

'My God, Del, you are glowing.'

'You're the same.' We let go of each other and collapsed into the seats. People around us stopped talking to stare, but we'd grown used to this reaction. With the matching uniforms we must have looked startling to most people, with our pale blonde hair and amber eyes in duplicate, even down to the matching mole just below our left eyes.

'Tell me all about this mystery American.'

I looked down. 'Nothing much to say.'

'You brought him to Cornwall.'

'He was going anyway. I simply tagged along.' I stirred my tea in my cup.

'I can't believe you were there when I was away. Bloody bad luck.'

'Language,' I said, and looked into her laughing eyes.

'Sorry, I know. It's slipped terribly since I began driving.'

I shook my head then poured my sister a cup of tea. 'I'm so thrilled to see you.'

'Same. I've missed you.'

'Tell me all about Eddie.'

'You always knew, didn't you?' She peered at me over the rim of her cup. If she felt for Eddie half of what I did for Bobby then it was perfect.

'Possibly. But what I can see now is that you're happier than you've ever been.'

'I am. Can't hide it.' She clasped her hands around the cup.

'Why try?' I reached out for her hand. Connection was made and something realigned inside me.

She raised her eyes and looked into mine. A shadow fell across them. 'Because I'm afraid being this happy is wrong.'

My breath caught. 'I know what you mean.'

'I can hear Grandmother's voice saying that too much pleasure is indecent and will never last.'

I laughed. Grandmother had said that years ago, when she'd been talking about a cake that Amelia had made. She'd disapproved of the fact that Amelia could cook at all. The cook would do the cooking, she told us, not the lady of the house – that was the way of things. Poor Grandmother had eventually discovered that knowing how to cook during a war was a key survival skill.

'Come on. Tell me about your American.'

'Nothing to tell.' I glanced away as a soldier and a woman entered. Her face was solemn. I wondered why. Turning back to Amelia I continued, 'He's just been promoted to captain and been transferred, therefore he has less time to spend with me.'

'I'm so sorry.' She grabbed my hand then blurted out, 'Have you seen Father?'

'No. Will you see him?'

'I hope so but it's looking doubtful. I was lucky to have this leave. It coincided with an admiral needing to be in London urgently.'

I frowned. 'You didn't take the train?'

'No, I drove to London and will drive back the day after tomorrow.'

'Ah, leave cut short, yes.' I squeezed her hand. 'I was lucky to receive permission to come to London.'

'I was puzzled when I rang, not daring to hope.'

'Luck was on our side.' I looked at the waitress serving another table. I couldn't tell my sister I had already planned to come to London to visit a priest at Farm Street Church. I'd never kept secrets from her before. Was it the war that made me secretive or was it just part of separating? When I turned back to Amelia I could see that she knew, but she smiled all the same. I'm sure she had things she no longer shared with me. With distance that sense of knowing the other had abated. Although I could tell when she was unhappy, everything else from her felt further away. 'What news of Eddie?'

'Last letter arrived two days ago and all is well. He loves India. His letter was full of the exploits of his navigator's dog, which has become the company mascot. In fact he sent a photo of the dog.' She rifled through her handbag and pulled out two photos and handed them across the table. One was of a small dachshund and beside it its official flying logbook. In the second picture were Eddie and another officer.

'That's the owner of the dog, Gordon George.' She took them back with a smile. 'By all accounts they're having a wonderful time.'

'So pleased all is well.' I thought of Bobby. It was good that he was close at hand, although I only had a letter from him once a week.

'Shall we get another pot of tea?' Amelia looked for the waitress.

'Let's go shopping.'

She laughed. 'There's nothing to buy, but let's anyway.'

I paid the bill and linked my arm through hers. 'I've missed you,' she said as we walked down the pavement towards Harrods.

My breath caught. 'Same.'

'But I can see you're happy with your Yank, even if you won't tell me about it.'

I laughed. 'I am. Just as happy as you.'

She narrowed her eyes at me. 'You're engaged?'

I frowned. 'Yes, but we'll wait to marry until the war is over.' I looked down at my hands. 'I haven't told anyone.'

'I understand.' She peered into a window. 'You're right, there is nothing to buy.' She grinned. 'Let's forget shopping and go and have a drink. We need to celebrate our engagements!'

A few moments later Amelia had flagged down a taxi and we were on our way to the Savoy. On the back seat of the cab, still smiling, she took my hand. 'So you'll be … ?'

'Mrs Robert Webster.'

'And I'll be Mrs Edward Carew.' Her big grin faded, turning to a frown. 'We'll be even further away from each other.' We both sat in silence while this information registered. I looked out the window and away from Amelia. I wanted my own identity separate from her and I'd been achieving that, but the Atlantic was vast. I swallowed. The taxi paused in front of the wreck of a building with only the back wall still upright. How was it still standing unsupported? Rubble filled the hole in front of it – the charred and broken remains of lives. I turned away as we arrived at the Savoy.

Paying the fare, it seemed hard to believe that this was where I had met Bobby for the first time just a few months ago. How my world had changed. Amelia and I waltzed through the doors to the Savoy shoulder to shoulder, smiling at everyone who stopped to take a look at us as we went through the lobby. It had been so long since we'd been together I'd forgotten what a stir we could cause.

'I intend to have a gin and dubonnet!' Amelia walked up and sat on a stool in the American Bar. I held back. 'Don't be a spoilsport. You shall have one too.'

I glanced around looking for anyone who might know us. Surely this would get back to Grandmother? Amelia turned from me and spoke to the bartender. She was flirting again. It was just the way she was. I sighed and slipped onto the empty chair beside her at the bar.

'Delly, you still need to lighten up.' She grinned at the bartender and raised her glass. 'Here's to us and to our men.' She took a big sip. I laughed then joined her. 'I wish they were both with us tonight but we shall go dancing and lift some other poor soul's spirits.'

I pursed my mouth, thinking.

'Come on, Delly. We'll be married and boring soon. Let's paint the town red tonight.'

I laughed. 'Yes, let's.' Our glasses clinked, we both sipped our drinks, and I felt the alcohol and the excitement inside me mingle. I smiled, looking at my sister. We would make it through this war and win. If we could cope with everything that had been thrown at us so far, we had to win. If we didn't, Bobby and I could never be together and that didn't bear thinking about.

✳ Thirty ✳

Constantine, Falmouth, Cornwall
19 September 2015

The doorbell rang and Lara opened the door to Jack. Curled by the fireplace, Snowy put his head back on his paws and watched the newcomer. 'So this is where Mrs Carr's cat ended up,' said Jack.

'You know Snowy?'

'Snowy?' Jack frowned at her. 'You mean Sid.'

Lara eyed the cat. Snowy definitely suited him better than Sid. 'Can I bring him back to her?'

He shook his head. 'She's gone into a care home outside Birmingham near her daughter.'

'Oh.'

'I'll make sure she knows he's found himself a new abode.'

Lara frowned, unsure how Cassie would feel about that. 'How's your grandmother this morning?'

'Awake, and she's reluctantly taking the high-calorie drink recommended to build her up.'

'Yuck.'

'It's not too bad.' He leaned on the doorframe while she collected her jacket and her bag, which was weighed down by the *Tante Marie* cookbook she was bringing along.

'You said she became ill after the wedding?' Lara said, as she locked the front door.

He nodded. 'For some reason she went to check things when the storm blew through. I found her sheltering in the morning, frozen and very wet.' Having walked her to the car, he opened the door for her then got in himself. 'I'd put it down to the hassle of Peta's wedding.'

'Weddings cause a lot of stress.' She cast him a glance and one side of his mouth lifted. 'But are you sure it's that?'

As the car eased out onto the road, she looked out the window at the passing scenery and wondered what Grandie had thought of it here. 'My great-grandfather was ninety-four and his health seemed to decline very quickly. There never seemed to be a cause – simply old age, and I think tiredness as well.'

As they were turning into the drive at Windward, Jack's phone rang. Lara waited in the garden while he took the call, and used the opportunity to once again look at the wedding photo of her great-grandparents. She walked around to the front of the house, pulled the picture from her bag and held it up for comparison. The window matched and the view looked the same. Grandie was obvious, even out of focus, but Amelia was hard to make out, aside from her classic 1940s rolled hairstyle, part hidden under the veil.

Lara thought of the hundreds of shots taken of her own wedding day. All of them perfect and capturing a love that hadn't lasted. At least with Grandie's it was a love that he had held onto all of his life.

Of course she was still puzzled by his last word. *Adele.* Even now she could see the moment clearly. The tide had been about to turn as she and Leo held him and he looked out to the Sound. His eyes had been focused on the horizon to the east and he had sighed and said 'Adele,' not once but twice.

Her phone beeped and she read the text from Cassie.

Mum much improved. Parents send love.
C x

She was still with her parents and would be for a few more weeks. The business was ticking over and the christening party at the weekend didn't need Lara's input, as Cassie had said her team could do the event blindfolded.

The wind blew the lavender below the roses, sending a waft

of scent Lara's way. She pulled out the *Tante Marie* cookbook and looked at the proportions for the rosehip syrup. It wouldn't take too long to harvest a sufficient number.

Jack's voice floated on the breeze and Lara wandered to the edge of the terrace. All evidence of the wedding was gone and on this crisp fall morning the bay in the distance glistened and clouds scudded across the sky. She pictured the beach in front of Eventide and homesickness flooded her. The landscape here was beautiful with the house in grey stone sitting happily above the water. The colour of the granite was almost the shade that the weathered cedar shingle turned after a few seasons in the New England elements.

Her sneakers were damp from the dew. The hum of a lawn-mower in the distance and the smell of cut grass brought her instantly home. She loved the fall, with the turning of the leaves and the less crowded roads.

She stopped. Wasps were busy on the apple trees laden with ripening fruit. In her childhood her family would make an annual pilgrimage north to New Hampshire and return with an abundance of apples, mostly Macintosh but with other varieties thrown into the mix. The trees here in the garden looked close to perfection. After making the rosehip syrup today, they could work with apples. In her experience a bit of apple and cinnamon appealed to all but the most finicky eaters. But of course eating wasn't the only problem for Jack's grandmother. Pneumonia was so dangerous in the elderly.

Jack came towards her and she held the wedding photo out to him. 'Has this house always been in your family?'

He frowned, taking the picture. 'Not sure. My grandmother would be able to tell you.'

She watched his expression while he studied the photo, looking back at her and then down at the black and white image again. 'It definitely looks like Windward, and it's hard to tell but I'd say the woman resembles my grandmother when she was young.' He looked at Lara. 'And like I said, you look a lot like she did back then.'

'I don't quite know what to make of that.'

'Neither do I.' They walked to the kitchen. 'Maybe if she's feeling up to it later, I can introduce you, and show her your photo.' He handed it back to her.

'Thanks. But first we need to harvest the rosehips.'

He raised an eyebrow.

'Yes, let's get to it,' she said, and smiled.

'Rosehips?'

'Trust me.'

He tilted his head to the side and studied her. 'Fine. I'll grab some gloves and the secateurs. Drop your things here, I won't be long.'

As he disappeared she grinned at the thought of a day of cooking, as well as maybe coming a step closer to finding answers.

I looked at Jack's eager face and lifted the spoon to my mouth. The aroma took me back to Christmas 1943. Rosehip syrup. Mrs Tonks. He was trying to build me up when I wanted to let go. I smiled at him and tasted the pudding – tapioca. Nursery food. The sweet yet sharp taste of the rosehips with the creamy sweetness of the pudding was perfection. I ate another spoonful and he smiled.

I frowned. 'Did you make this?' He was a good cook but he didn't do puddings often.

He grinned. 'Well, I had help.'

'Who? Did you pick up the syrup from the WI?'

'No, I harvested the hips with my own fair hands this morning.'

I opened my eyes wide and ate some more. 'What inspired this new type of cooking?'

'Lara.'

I raised an eyebrow. It was a name I hadn't heard before. 'Who?'

'She's a chef.'

I paused with the spoon halfway to my mouth. 'You hired a chef?'

'No, she volunteered after I helped her.'

I frowned. 'And she ...?"

'Offered to help me find ways of making food more enticing than something chemical out of a tin.'

My mouth lifted. It had worked. I'd finished the bowl and the taste of times long past stayed with me. I closed my eyes. 'Thank you.'

'A pleasure, Gran.' He took the bowl and kissed my forehead. 'Get some more rest.'

'I will.' But I wasn't sure if my mind would let me. The taste had taken me back to a summer night in 1944 when Pat had arrived with a bottle of gin and we'd sat by the tennis courts drinking gin mixed with rosehip syrup. The evening had been warm and the sky clear. I had even seen Orion's Belt. I'd slept well that night despite the constant worry about Bobby. It must have been the gin and the taste of Cornwall in the syrup.

HMS *Attack*, Portland, Dorset
30 May 1944

I caressed the envelope, missing Bobby so much. We hadn't taken advantage of being stationed so close together and now I lived letter to letter.

May 23, 1944

Darling Adele,

You know I'm missing you. When the opportunity for sleep comes my thoughts drift to you and I dream of our future. I feel you near me here because I know how much you love it. Are your family well? I had a letter from my mother. All is fine in Massachusetts.

How is Portland? I can imagine it's busy. The men here are restless, so together with the padre, Fr Lynch, and the Mother Superior who runs the school, we have concocted a plan. The men are going to build a shrine to Our Lady of Lourdes. It will be a grotto. Do you know the school run by Les Filles de la Croix at Tremough?

Did I know it? Yes, I did – Amelia and I had nearly attended it when we moved in with Grandmother.

I was at the Ferryboat Inn two nights ago. I cannot be there and not think of you. I feel guilty about taking you away from all of this. Everything is in bloom here. So many rhododendrons it reminds me of home. I wrote and told my parents of our engagement. I hope I will be able to meet your father before long and ask his permission to marry you. I hope you don't mind that I've told my parents. I found that when I was writing all I was doing was talking only about you, so my mother asked directly in her last letter. I couldn't lie. She is delighted.

I love you so much and am counting the hours until this war is over and we can marry.

Yours always,
Bobby xx

Leaning back on my bunk, I thought about his parents. What must they feel with him being away and falling in love with a stranger? I wondered how my parents would react. Grandmother would be livid. I smiled. That shouldn't please me but it did. How far I had fallen. Fortunately Amelia would be marrying well in Grandmother's eyes.

I was due on duty in an hour. Focusing on work was hard when part of my mind was on Bobby, and now like so many others I lived letter to letter. The last one was dated four days ago. But the atmosphere here had changed since then to high alert. All leave had been cancelled. We were all on edge although we had no idea what was going on. One of the girls had come back from the docks yesterday afternoon in shock because she'd been caught in her overalls and headscarf with a wrench in her hand when two cars went past. Inside them were the Prime Minster, the King and General Patton. As she recounted it she said she'd wanted to meet her king but not dressed in grease-spattered blue overalls. We laughed with her but I knew that this meant major events were imminent.

Father's last letter was full of so little. He spoke of the dinner he'd had with Aunt Margaret and not much else. To be honest it was hardly worth wasting the paper for what it said except that he hoped to see me soon. I had no idea when I'd have leave again. I longed to be with Bobby in London so that he could speak with Father. I wanted our plans to be public now and my desire to hold things close felt foolish when so much was at risk. Amelia had been right to rush forward.

Her letters were bursting with news. Her handwriting was minute in order to save paper and tell me everything.

I heard from Eddie last night. He'd been at a do and had to dance with the governor's wife who repeatedly crunched his toes. They were so sore the following day he walked with a limp. I can just see him being so polite, can't you? He's good that way. Do you remember at that house party when he was pigeonholed to dance with every wallflower and we managed to dance with him just once before the band called it a night? He has such a good heart and that is why I love him so much. He spots the wallflower and always makes sure she has one dance. I could not love him more.

Please tell me more about your American. I heard that he is very handsome and has been spotted again in the Ferryboat. You also haven't told me what you thought of all the changes around here. It's strange, isn't it? I can't tell you how much easier it is driving on the widened road. Yes, I still enjoy driving and the admiral I'm looking after is very funny but recently there is a sternness and focus about him. 'Nuff said.

Father called last night. Mother actually spoke to him. She lit up for a while but then came crashing down. I am distracting her by creating new and interesting food with what we have. I have never eaten so much fish and have become very good at adapting French recipes. Madame Pomfrey has given me her **Tante Marie** *cookbook. It keeps my French fresh and my cooking different. Grandmother is happier than I have seen her in years. She is also fitter. I think it's all the exercise she is getting between the fishing and the garden. Her pride in her vegetables is so amusing. I heard her bragging to Lady V.*

Last night I went to the social held for the Yanks in the village hall. I found myself studying all the men wondering if one of them was yours. I don't think he was there because I'm sure I'd know your American. I would feel your love for him. Despite not finding him, I had a good laugh and so enjoyed dancing. It helps to keep my mind off the distance between Eddie and me. I feel your hunger for your Yank and know you understand mine. Who would have thought that we would both be in love and be separated? I pray daily for us both and for our men. Mother is in the same place but Father is here in the UK – at least he is at the moment, although I overheard something that made me think this may not be the case for long.

Stay safe. Keep me in your thoughts and prayers along with our men.

Xxxx

5 June 1944

I was out of breath from racing up the hill. I rushed into my cabin and collapsed on my bunk with my head in my hands. My mind was full of images of what we'd just witnessed – the troops boarding the landing craft. Somewhere Bobby was readying himself too. I tried to pray but no words could express the fear in me, yet at the same time there was hope that we could win this war. I heard footsteps approaching and I looked up. Pat came into the cabin carrying a letter. She smiled. I knew it was from Bobby.

1 June 1944

I don't when I'll be able to write again. I know you will be aware of what is happening. Know that I love you with all my heart.

Pray for us all.
Bobby

I quickly stood, adjusted my uniform and walked to my duty with a heavy heart.

The sky was clear above me and planes flew silhouetted black against the evening sun. Each plane was towing a string of gliders. I knew then that the operation had begun. I waved at them and saw a group of my friends cheering as they flew past. The area was in full operation mode. The invasion was under way. I clutched Bobby's letter in my hands as I watched the landing craft leave the harbour. My fear was beyond words. I looked to heaven and swallowed back tears. I had a job to do.

Stand of the Tide

The tide has turned! The free men of the world are marching together to Victory!
I have full confidence in your courage and devotion to duty and skill in battle.
We will accept nothing less than full Victory! Good luck! And let us beseech the blessing of Almighty God upon this great and noble undertaking.

GENERAL DWIGHT D. EISENHOWER, 2 JUNE 1944

It involves tides, wind, waves, visibility, both from the air and the sea standpoint, and the combined employment of land, air and sea forces in the highest degree of intimacy and in contact with conditions which could not and cannot be fully foreseen.

WINSTON CHURCHILL, 6 JUNE 1944

☀ Thirty-One ☀

HMS *Attack*, Portland, Dorset
11 June 1944

I'd fallen asleep in the sun. It hadn't been my plan and now I could feel the sunburn forming on my skin. Grandmother's voice rang in my head, but the last thing I was worried about at the moment was my complexion. The days were blurring together. Having seen the departure of so many vessels as I went on duty days ago, it broke my heart to find boats returning with the dead and wounded. I didn't know what to do with my feelings so I locked them inside and made my face a mask. Exercise Tiger had taught me what the Allies were up against so I knew when the boats departed that the odds of all these men returning were slim. Pat was becoming more worried by the day. I tried not to think, just to work, eat, drink and sleep.

'Adele,' Dot shouted, 'there's a call for you.'

I raced to the telephone, my heart beating. I knew it wouldn't be Bobby but I couldn't help hoping as I picked up the receiver. 'Hello?'

'Adele, darling.'

'Mother.' I swallowed my disappointment. 'How are you?'

'Fine, fine.' She hiccuped.

'What's wrong?' I could hear her controlling her breathing. She sobbed.

'I just—' She took a deep breath. 'I just wanted you to know that your father is fine.'

I frowned. 'Why wouldn't he be? Father's in London.'

'He's in France, dear. He landed with the Canadians.'

'What?'

'He's a doctor, darling.'

I bit back my response. 'He didn't say,' I said at last.

'I know. He didn't want to worry you.'

I sighed. Didn't want to *worry* me? Just in that moment I realised how little my parents knew me. 'So he's in France now.'

'Yes, darling, but he's fine.'

'Thank God. How's Grandmother, and Amelia?'

'All is well. Amelia's off driving at the moment.'

That was not what I wanted to know. Mother sounded so odd. 'Thank you for letting me know. Are you well?'

'Just fine. But –' she paused '– I must tell you.' Her voice wobbled. 'Reginald is missing presumed dead.'

'Oh Mother, I'm so sorry. Poor Aunt Margaret and Grandmother. How are they taking the news?'

'Not well, but your grandmother has gone to London to be with Margaret.'

'That's good.' I took a deep breath. 'I'll try and ring Aunt Margaret but will write immediately.

'Yes, you do that, dear. Now our three minutes are up. Love you, darling.'

'Love you,' I said, but I don't think she heard me. I placed the receiver down and walked back to my cabin.

I collapsed on my bunk. Uncle Reginald dead. I closed my eyes offering a prayer for him. Father in Europe. With all the casualties, he and all the doctors they could muster would be needed. Surely he might be more useful in a proper theatre rather than in the field? But then, I knew very little of what was happening. Mother's words sounded in my head again: Uncle Reg, dead. I couldn't believe it.

Pat walked in. 'You caught the sun.'

I nodded. 'Yes, silly really. I fell asleep.'

'Good. Then you'll be rested for the dance tonight.'

I made a face. The last thing I wanted was to go dancing.

'None of us feel like it,' said Pat, 'but it will do us good.'

I shook my head.

'We'll all just mope otherwise.' She forced a smile.

282

'True,' I said. Pat hadn't had word about Joe either. Her nails had been bitten down to the quick, but she was nothing if not determined to keep a brave face. I would go with her and do the same.

Windward, Mawnan Smith, Falmouth, Cornwall
20 September 2015

Lara popped her head through the kitchen door. 'Morning.'

'Coffee?' Jack placed some mugs on a tray with the cafetière and milk.

'Wonderful.'

'It's one way to say thank you.' They walked together toward the terrace. The sky was moody today with grey heavy clouds interspersed with spots of blue sky. 'Gran loved the tapioca and ate the tomato soup last night.' He smiled, poured a mug for her.

'I'm so pleased.' She added a bit of milk to her coffee then sat on the nearby bench. 'My great-grandfather had pneumonia last year. All he would eat was good simple food, from tapioca to homemade ice cream.'

'And you lost him in August.'

Lara nodded. 'But not from pneumonia.' She stood. 'I think we should see what we can tempt her with today. Maybe we can up your standard while I'm here, as well,' she said, smiling and turning to take in the view again. In the distance the white column of the lighthouse stood out against the blue-grey water in front.

He laughed while trying to look indignant. She affected a very straight face but she liked the way his eyes crinkled when he smiled. His whole face lit up. 'Shall we begin?' she said in her best teacher's voice.

'Yes, ma'am.' He grinned. 'Follow me.' Jack strode through the large hall to the kitchen. Yesterday Lara had loved the time she'd spent here with him.

'Is it just you and your grandmother here?'

'Yes.' He leaned against the counter, watching her. The

283

bookcase on one wall was stuffed with cookbooks that had been heavily used, the spines creased and dented. She recognised a few of the names, including one by her old boss Stephan who had fired her.

'I didn't ask yesterday – is there anything in particular your grandmother likes to eat?' Lara spoke quietly in case she had the layout of the house wrong and his grandmother could somehow hear her.

'She's not really interested in food or cooking.'

'A challenge then.' She turned back towards Jack. 'What's your speciality?'

His mouth twitched. 'Osso bucco.'

'Anything else?' She opened the big fridge, checking out the contents and beginning to form a plan.

'A few things. What about you? What can you teach me?'

It was her turn to smirk. 'Plenty.'

His eyebrows rose.

'I worked in a two-starred Michelin restaurant as the second chef.'

She watched the information sink in.

'Why the gardening leave then?'

She stuck her head in the pantry. Should she just state the facts or try and make them sound better? Finally, she decided honesty was better. 'I lost my temper with my boss and he fired me.'

'Should I be worried?' He raised an eyebrow. 'Throw anything other than a tantrum?'

'No, I didn't.' She walked to the garden door. 'Let's start with a tarte tatin and see if we can tempt your grandmother with fruit from her garden.'

'That's a good choice. She doesn't normally do French food. Apple crumble is her preferred choice. Good English food with no foreign influences.'

'So you don't do the osso bucco for her?'

'I just call it stew and serve it with potatoes.'

Lara grinned. She liked his way of thinking. 'Well, let's try and entice her with a few foreign dishes that are only partially familiar. Hopefully this will wake up her appetite.'

They stood together and looked at the sky. 'We'd better be quick harvesting the apples because it looks like we're in a for some rain.' Jack handed her a basket and they dashed to the trees.

'What types of apple trees are in the backyard?'

'Yard?' He frowned, then smiled. 'You're in England now. You mean garden. Or even orchard, at a stretch.'

'I guess I do.'

'As far as I'm aware they are mostly eaters, but the furthest ones from the house are cookers.'

'Eaters and cookers. Well, I suppose that tells me something.'

'Oh, you wanted to know variety then?'

She nodded while picking ripe ones off the tree branches as well as windfalls from the ground.

'I believe they're a mix of the local varieties like Rattler, Tommy Knight, Manaccan Primrose and Pig's Snout, to name a few.'

'What fabulous names.'

He laughed. 'I suppose so.'

Jack and the young woman had gone from the terrace. So that was his Lara. Didn't he see the resemblance? I stood and picked up my sister's unopened letters in my unsteady hand. This pile began in late 1946 and the last one was postmarked October 1950. She must have simply stopped writing because I hadn't replied.

How could I? Turning the first letter over, I tried to imagine her life in the United States with their child Elizabeth. I hadn't come home for the christening; in fact I hadn't returned to Windward to look after Mother until Amelia and Elizabeth had been gone a month.

My stomach tightened and the letter dropped from my fingers. I couldn't read them, not now, not after all these years. But part of me was curious, had always been. I slipped the letters into the top drawer of my desk. Those letters would tell me everything I wanted to know and everything I didn't.

My window rattled as the wind picked up. Despite the clear morning, I could see weather coming in from the east. In about an hour the house would be lashed with rain. Opening my bedroom door the smell of cinnamon and cloves drifted up from the kitchen. They were scents of the past – harvesting apples and preserving them with Mrs Tonks. Sitting down, I let the memory fade away while I sipped a glass of water. I didn't need food to tempt me to the past – it was becoming ever present.

The first drops of rain were spitting down, yet in the distance Lara could see sunlight falling on a sloping field filled with cows. She stopped on her way back to the kitchen, noticing particular fruit on a nearby tree. 'You have figs.'

'Brown Turkey.'

'What a lovely name.' She reached up and took several fat figs with raindrops beading on their surface. So many were ripe. Collecting more would be their next task after the apples. But these figs would be perfect for lunch. Lara had noted a selection of cheeses wrapped in paper on the marble counter in the pantry. It showed that Jack had an understanding of food and maximising flavours. It also demonstrated the cool temperature of the pantry, and also how temperate Cornwall was.

As they arrived back at the kitchen, she asked: 'Jack, does your grandmother enjoy her food when well?'

'She does.' He held open the door, studying her, and suddenly laughed.

'What?' She placed the basket on the kitchen counter with unsteady hands.

'You tilt your head at the same angle as she does. And you wave your hands in the same expressive manner.'

'Really?'

'Yes.' He paused, studying me. 'You know, now that I've noticed it, it's difficult *not* to see the resemblance.'

'That picture you mentioned,' she said, carefully, 'of her, on VE Day – may I see it?'

He nodded and placed his basket down. 'I'll just grab it.' He left the kitchen.

Lara went to the fridge and made sure there was sufficient butter before they began the tart.

'Would you like another cup of coffee?' Jack had returned, and was holding up the picture.

'I'd prefer tea,' she said.

'Of course.' He put the photo down on the table and placed the kettle on the Aga. She picked the photograph up, and instantly her hand shook. It was her. It was as if someone had put her in a uniform and posed her.

'The similarities are quite strong, aren't they?' Jack said, watching her staring at the photo. He reached into a cupboard and took out a brown glazed teapot just like Grandie's – and right then, she felt her great-grandfather's presence in the room, and found herself looking over her shoulder as if he might be standing there. Sensing him like this was odd – but maybe if he had had his wedding reception here, there might be a link.

'What's your grandmother's name?'

'It's Elle Rowse now, but her maiden name was Seaton.'

'Elle? That's unusual for a woman who avoids French cooking.'

'Not just French, all foreign cooking. She eyes garlic as suspect, but since we grow our own she tolerates it.'

She laughed.

He poured the tea. 'Milk?'

'A bit, please.'

'So where do we begin?' he said, and leaned against the counter.

'How are you with pastry?'

He tilted his hand back and forth.

'Then let's start there,' she said.

'If you insist. I usually use pre-made.'

She smiled. 'Great if you're short of time, but we're not, are we?'

'Not today. I was up at five and completed what I needed to do so I could give you my full attention.'

She spluttered in surprise as a mouthful of tea nearly went down the wrong way. 'Impressive,' she finally managed.

'That's the plan.'

'A star pupil in the making?'

'I'll do my best.'

'I bet you will.' She grinned. He could be charming, clearly, when it suited him. 'Right, now we come to the great debate.'

'And that is?'

'Do you use puff pastry or shortcrust for a tarte tartin?'

He shrugged. 'I do what the recipe calls for.'

'Personally I prefer shortcrust, but I have to say puff is delicious if you are eating it immediately.'

'Why?'

'It's delicate and melting but can become soggy if left too long.'

'Makes sense.' He grinned. 'Many things do.'

'True.' She laughed, and wondered where this bantering, light-hearted Jack had come from. She pulled a Julia Child cookbook off the shelves to the right of the Aga. 'Are these yours?'

'No, my grandfather's.' He came to her side. 'You need a recipe for the pastry?' He frowned.

'Not at all – but I wanted to show you a few different ones, because they all have their merits.'

'But what is your favourite?' He was standing so close, the scent of his aftershave circled around her. It was fresh and touched with citrus. She sniffed again: lime and sandalwood, with a hint of something she couldn't place.

'Again, this all depends on the ingredients you are using, like the apples themselves. Cookers or eaters, as you mentioned. Their sugar levels, textures and tastes.'

He raised an eyebrow. 'Sounds complicated, which is why I follow the recipe exactly. It makes it simple.'

'Then it takes the joy out of cooking and working with ingredients that are fresh.' She picked up one of the apples, turning it around in her hands. 'Very sweet apples need less sugar and might require lifting with a spice like cinnamon or even salt.' She held it to her nose. 'Earth and rain and a slight musk.'

The texture of the fruit was firm with no give. She looked at Jack and wondered what had turned him from sweet to hard. Those blue eyes were shielded except when he laughed or spoke of his grandmother. What spice would she add to him to make him balanced? The heat of chilli and the warmth of cardamom, maybe.

She flushed. She was supposed to be thinking about apples and not about the attractive man in front of her. A slow smile spread across his face. He might not need the chilli to add fire. It was simmering under the surface already.

It was hard for me to stand still and not make a sound. Jack was practically dancing with this woman in the kitchen. He was interested in her. His glance never left her, as if he was mesmerised. I stood there silently and watched the whole process of them making the pastry. I saw him dust flour from her cheek. The intimacy. I closed my eyes and memories of attraction danced through my veins. Excitement, that hollow feeling in my belly.

The desire in them sparked even if they couldn't see it. She made him taste everything. It fed the old hunger in me. Who knew I could still want? From this distance I could smell the sharp tang of lemon and knew from the expression on Jack's face when the apples she gave him were sour. She asked their names, and he didn't always know, but I did.

It was as if I was watching myself, and that made the longing harder to bear. I wanted Jack to find love, to break out of the cage he'd placed around his heart. Closing my eyes I remembered the stomach-turning anticipation of waiting for Bobby, of just simply watching him breathe.

She placed a piece of apple in her own mouth and the juice ran from the corner of her lips. Jack stared and his fingers moved at his side. He wanted to touch her. If I didn't know better I would swear they were lovers. I knew they weren't, yet it was just a question of how long before they were.

My breath caught and the hall swayed. I reached for the doorjamb and missed.

⁜ Thirty-Two ⁜

Weymouth, Dorset
18 June 1944

We were in the White Hart with a few of the US Army officers. We'd come here because the Golden Lion was too packed, but this wasn't much better. These officers had survived and therefore I had hope, quiet hope, that Bobby had too. Dot knew that her pilot was fine. He'd called her last night. His bombing raid had done its job. Having thought loving a flyboy was the riskiest choice, right now I envied her. We were due to head on to the dance but had stopped to have a drink first. The boys were full of talk about the invasion, but weren't saying anything I hadn't read in the papers. The more they spoke the whiter Pat became. These men were not in the same company as Joe, yet I watched the colour leave her face with each word they uttered.

'Ladies, let's go dance and forget,' said a captain and I looked at the beer in my glass. Pat stood and wobbled and I knew it wasn't from the drink. The tall Texan steadied her and led her out into the beautiful spring evening. I went through the conversation in my mind and tried to figure out what had caused her so much distress. A few more acquaintances came up and joined the group and a major attached himself to Pat and the Texan. As we approached the hall Pat stopped and shook her head.

'I can't do this. I'm heading back to *Attack*.'

I stepped forward. 'I'll take you.'

'No, Tim will. Thanks, Adele.' She took the Texan's arm

and they walked away. Something had been said and it wasn't good. With heavy feet I entered the dance with the others. It was crowded as always and before I could dwell on my own fears I was swept into someone's arms and was dancing to 'Chattanooga Choo Choo'.

I was panting by the time I came off the floor five or six dances later. My head was spinning and I barely noticed the glum faces at our table. Dot sat stony-faced, which was so un-like her. 'Most of the Rangers we knew including Joe are gone,' she whispered.

'Gone?'

'No survivors. None cleared the beach.'

My hand flew to my mouth. I had heard the words of dying men months ago. The Rangers' voices wouldn't have been any different.

Our cabin was in darkness when I returned and I could hear Pat's breathing. It wasn't the regular rhythm of sleep, it was the ragged breath of someone who had been crying. I stopped in the doorway. I might be doing the same any day now. I turned around, saying a prayer as I left her in peace to try and fall asleep.

It was eleven and the brightest stars were beginning to ap-pear. The moon looked translucent against the darkening sky. First I picked out the Plough or Dipper. I smiled and tried to hold onto hope, but as each day of silence passed my worry increased. If he survived – and that was a big 'if' – he wouldn't have time to write. None of the men tonight knew if he had. As we'd left the dance I couldn't hold back my questions any longer, but sadly they had no answers.

Orion's Belt. Could he see it tonight too? Would he sense that I was leaning against the hillside looking up and thinking of him?

Dear God, please keep him safe.

I paused in my prayer to watch a shooting star race across the sky.

Keep Eddie safe too.

A shadow fell across the hillside and I saw someone walking towards me. I sat up when I realised it was Commander Rowse. His shoulders were slightly dipped.

'Evening,' he said. 'Don't stand up.'

I relaxed.

'Enjoying a moment of quiet?'

I couldn't see his features. 'Yes.'

'Me too.'

I heard the exhaustion in his voice. It was his job to keep things running smoothly and with all the activity that was no small task. He nodded then walked on.

He needed his wife right now, someone to help ease the worry even for an instant. But who knew when any of us would have leave? Maybe Mrs Rowse should visit. Or would that make it worse? One moment of being together, then separation. A taste and nothing more.

I walked back to quarters. I would settle for the smallest taste just to know that Bobby was alive. As I entered the cabin, Dot was heading to her shift. She held out something to me – an official-looking envelope. Taking a deep breath, I took it, my hands shaking.

'This was caught under some other papers.' Her voice was quiet. She too thought it was the worst possible news. 'Would you like me to stay?'

I shook my head. I needed to face this alone. 'You have important work to do.'

'I do.' She smiled and gave me a quick hug before she set off. Bless her, she understood.

My hand shook so much it was difficult to rip the envelope open.

Darling,

I won't talk about D-Day. I'm sure you've seen things in Portland. To have left the beauty of the Helford to land on Omaha Beach was like leaving heaven for hell. Everything was

against us including the tide. That is all I will say. Thoughts of
returning to you keep me focused. I am too tired to write more.

I love you
X.x.x

The letter dropped to the floor and I leaned against the wall.
Tears rolled down my cheeks. He was alive.

❧ Thirty-Three ❧

HMS *Attack*, Portland, Dorset
20 August 1944

Having been given permission to swim on the beach below, I hoped the break would clear my mind and refresh me. The heat of the day had caught me off guard. My duty over, all I could focus on was the brilliant blue of the sea. Bobby was in London but I didn't have leave. Somehow this was fine. If he was in London then he wasn't dead.

The path down to the beach was steep and the urge to run down it squealing like a child was enormous. I had spoken to Amelia last night. Eddie was good and Mother wasn't. Father was vague about what his role was now. She wouldn't take heart from the fact that he was no longer on the front line. His surgical skills were needed further back.

I began to hum 'Roll Out the Barrel' once I reached the deserted beach. Scanning the horizon, I noted where the waves were breaking far from the shore. It looked safe. I had put my swimming costume on before I left quarters so I discarded my shorts and my top quickly. The water was clear and cool. A lone crab scuttled along the beach. I couldn't tell if the tide was coming or going as the waves repeatedly hit the same spot.

I wasn't sure how quickly the water would become deep, and suspected the beach under me might drop off sharply. The other girls had already been swimming but I hadn't been able to join them. My feet numbed and once I was up to my knees I dived in, gasping for air as I broke the surface. Everything tingled and I was thankful to be alive. I turned onto my back and gently kicked against the current pulling me away from the beach. It wasn't strong so I was confident my efforts would keep me in one place.

The mackerel sky above me told of a weather change. I was almost glad – much more of this heat would be unbearable. How I missed Amelia and lazy summer days without a care in the world. Flipping over onto my stomach I looked around myself, and back the way I'd come. The shore was further than I'd expected. Much further. Panic surged inside me as I realised that I'd drifted too far.

Even though I was a strong swimmer I knew what must have happened. I was caught in a rip current. I tried to keep calm, and remember what the best thing was to do. These currents happened off the Cornish coast frequently. Swimming as hard as I could, I struggled against the force of the water, but the more I tried the further out I went. Adrenaline and panic impeded any clear thoughts. I glimpsed a figure on the beach. I waved, but then the water pushed me even further out.

My limbs ached as I tried again to fight against the current when I saw the man wave back. He pointed to further along the coast and I knew what he meant. I stopped trying to battle the flow and instead let the water take me out. It felt wrong but I forced myself to allow it to happen. The man ran down the beach.

Slowly the current dropped off, losing its strength, and I regulated my breathing until I felt able to begin a gentle breaststroke parallel to the shore. It was a long way but I knew the man on the beach was swimming out towards me.

I only barely registered him reaching me and helping me back to shore. Once I was back on the sand of the beach, coughing and sputtering, I opened my eyes and finally recognised Commander Rowse looking down at me, dripping wet, his face full of concern. Water drops clung to his long black eyelashes. 'Welcome back,' he said.

'Thank you, sir,' I managed, between dragging in great gasps of air.

'That was all a bit touch and go.'

'Thank you.' My voice was breathless. I wasn't sure I could say anything else. I tried to sit up but everything went out of focus.

'Don't rush.' He pushed my hair off my face and then hesitated for a moment. 'I'm sure you've been told this a thousand times but your eyes are extraordinary.'

I smiled. From anyone but Commander Rowse I would have taken that as a chat-up line, but not him.

'Ah, here come some Yanks. I bet they have a bit of sugar in some form with them. Just the thing.'

'Commander, I see we were too late to be of help.' The man winked. My skin crawled. I didn't know him nor did I want to. However I knew the lieutenant with him.

'Do either of you have any food with you?' asked Commander Rowse. 'Leading Wren Seaton has had a nasty shock and nearly drowned. I think before we tackle the hill, food would help.'

'It so happens we do.' The lieutenant produced a bag and pulled out some sandwiches and a thermos.

The commander helped me to sit up. A chill ran across my skin despite the heat of the sun. With a shaky hand I took the half a sandwich given to me. I could see it included jam but wasn't sure what the other ingredient was. I took a bite. My eyes widened. The saltiness of the peanut butter mixed with the grape of the jam was unexpected to say the least.

'What do you think of the monkey butter and jelly sandwich, ma'am?' asked the American with the leering eyes. He had stripped down to his swimmers and although quite muscled he looked unfit compared to the commander.

'Interesting.'

The commander chuckled. I smiled. The combined flavour wasn't bad but it wasn't good either. I was thankful that Bobby hadn't subjected me to this 'treat' on our outings. The lieutenant poured some lemonade from the thermos and I sipped it.

'Better?' The commander spoke quietly.

'Yes, sir.'

He smiled. 'Good, when you feel ready I'll walk with you up the hill.'

I was about to refuse but knew it would be foolish. My hands were still wobbly. 'Thank you.'

Windward, Mawnan Smith, Falmouth, Cornwall
20 September 2015

I opened my eyes and looked at the sitting room ceiling. Something icy cold was pressed against my head, and Jack was hovering nearby. 'Hello,' he said.

'Yes.' I blinked, trying to pull everything into focus.

He rubbed the back of his neck. 'That was some entrance.'

I must have fallen forward into the kitchen. That explained the pack of peas on my head. Nothing else felt too sore.

'The doctor's on his way.' Jack came closer with a torch in his hands. 'Sorry about this, Gran, but you gave yourself a great knock. Need to check for concussion.'

I closed my eyes.

'Open.'

Obeying, I glared at him, and squinted as he aimed the torchlight at my eyes.

'Your pupils are responding.' I tried to sit up, and he held out a hand and pulled me upright. Things around me seemed to swirl. I held the peas back in place. 'We've made some lunch and I want you to eat it. That's probably why you fell. No energy and being out of bed when you shouldn't be.'

You've no idea. I sighed. Standing watching the two of them for so long without moving had been the problem. Food was not the issue. Jack helped me to my feet and brought me out of the sitting room, into the kitchen. The rain outside was pelting from the south. It was a dismal afternoon and standing in Windward's kitchen was the replica of my youth. Lara.

'Gran, this is Lara Pearce. I mentioned her yesterday.'

I rounded on him, but stopped myself from speaking. My heart told me who she was. It was there in her face, her eyes, even the way she moved. Talking would complicate things. It would encourage more conversation and I didn't want to know any more than what my eyes told me. Bobby. Was he alive? Was my sister alive? What of their daughter, Elizabeth?

'Hi, Mrs Rowse,' she said. 'You have a lovely home. It must be so wonderful to have so many fruit trees.'

I nodded. Jack helped me to a chair. 'Tea?' he asked.

I sighed. He'd used the old brown pot and not the silver one. Spread out on the table were cheeses with figs, a salad and a few slices of the ham that Jack had tried to tempt me with yesterday. He poured tea into a mug, and with two hands I picked it up. Every joint ached.

Lara and Jack sat down. 'You probably didn't know but Lara helped on the day of Peta's wedding. Cassie, the caterer, had a medical emergency with her mother.'

I looked between the two. Lara was buttering a piece of bread, making an open sandwich with ham and a dash of wholegrain mustard. Her hands. They were Amelia's, working so capably in the kitchen. Had she learned to cook from Amelia? I opened my mouth and closed it again. I couldn't take an interest. Silence was the best approach. But Jack wasn't silent. He was more animated than I'd seen him in years, too many years.

He stared at me as if willing me to talk. 'Before coming to Cornwall, Lara was a chef.'

Lara flushed. Her complexion was beautiful. Had I realised how lovely we were then? I don't think so. Youth is wasted on the young, as they say. Jack cut open a fig and handed half of it to Lara. Their fingers touched when she took it. I looked away. As much as I didn't want Lara around, she was good for Jack. The light had come back to his eyes.

HMS *Attack*, Portland, Dorset
30 August 1944

'Adele.'

'Bobby.' I clutched the handset close to my ear. 'Are you in London?'

'No, but I will be next week.'

'I'll see what I can do.' I held my breath, hoping I could get an overnight pass.

'You're fine after your ordeal?' he asked.

He'd obviously received my letter. 'What, the peanut butter and jelly sandwich?'

His laughter ran down my spine. 'It grows on you.'

'I'll pass.'

'Well, you can't have good taste in everything.' I heard voices around him, French ones.

'Don't drink too much champagne.'

He chuckled. 'I'll try not to. Maybe I can bring back a bottle for us.'

'Oh, yes.' I smiled.

'Stay safe.'

'You too.' I sent a kiss and heard him do the same.

'I love you.' The line went dead.

Chelsea, London
19 September 1944

Bobby stood opening a bottle of Pol Roger. I couldn't believe we were together in the spartan flat he used when in London. Alone. I didn't want champagne, I wanted him, but I sat still and took in every detail of him.

'How decadent.' I smiled.

'Yes. It was a present.'

I arched an eyebrow. 'Not from a lady friend, I hope?'

He laughed. 'Far from it. It's from a wily Frenchman.'

'Truly?'

'On the recommendation of a plummy, cigar-smoking Englishman.'

I opened my eyes wide. He touched a finger to his nose.

I stood up. 'Were you in Paris?'

'I might have been.' He poured the champagne into two chunky glasses more suited to holding a toothbrush than fine wine.

'Just what do you do, Captain Webster?' I ran my hand along

his waist. He kissed the tip of my nose. 'So you've become a spy, then?' I laughed. 'Seriously, what do you do in the Army?'

'I'm a paper monkey, a messenger.' He handed me a glass and raised his.

'To us.'

'Yes, us,' he said. The champagne was cold and not too bubbly. Bobby put the gramophone on. 'I Only Have Eyes For You' began to play, and he held out his hand and pulled me close. 'I love you so much,' he whispered in my ear, in between singing the words to me. 'I can't think of anyone but you.'

'Same.' We kissed and as the recording ended we fell onto the sofa. His hands caressed me more openly than in the past. They travelled up my leg and reached the top of my stockings. My breath caught.

'Yes.'

His hands stilled but then moved higher.

'Please.'

He sighed. 'We can't.' He pulled away and picked up his glass, knocking back the contents.

'But—'

'No, we've made it this far, we can make it until we marry.'

I sat up, shifting my skirt down. I knew if I pushed he wouldn't be able to stop. But I loved him and this was what he wanted. The champagne still tasted good but not as good as he did.

He went to his coat. 'It's not a proper ring but I wanted you to have something.' He knelt in front of me and took my hand. 'This is my promise to you. You are the love I never dreamt I would have. When this war is finished we will marry as swiftly as we can. And then I ...' He slid the simple gold ring with small, fine turquoise stones on my finger. 'And then we will make love and it won't be a moment too soon.'

A stillness came over me as I looked in his eyes. There was so much emotion in them that it hurt. I loved this man more than I'd thought was possible. I pulled into him my arms and promised him my love forever.

Stolen Tide

Turning and turning in the widening gyre
The falcon cannot hear the falconer;
Things fall apart, the centre cannot hold;
Mere anarchy is loosed on the world,
The blood-dimmed tide is loosed and everywhere
The ceremony of innocence is drowned;
The best lack all conviction, while the worst
Are full of passionate intensity

W.B. YEATS, THE SECOND COMING, 1920

✳ Thirty-Four ✳

London
8 May 1945 – VE Day

I looked at my watch again. The train was now two hours late and we were sitting just outside Clapham Junction. I sighed, wanting to get out and push the darn thing. Bobby was waiting for me at the Savoy; he'd just have to wait a bit longer. But that didn't matter. We'd have all the time in the world now. The war in Europe was over. Mother had been wrong. The war had taken many of our wonderful men but not all the good ones. Not Bobby and not Angus. I swallowed. Of course it was only over in Europe. Eddie was still at risk in the Far East. I doubted Amelia would be celebrating much tonight. At the least, I did know that she was happy. We'd spoken less than a week ago. I hadn't been able to keep the excitement out of my voice. It had been bubbling since the Nazi forces had surrendered in Italy on 2 May.

By the time the train reached the platform at Waterloo, I'd abandoned my plans to change into evening dress at Aunt Margaret's. I stepped from the station and emerged to a London full of light. After years of darkness it looked wonderful. Not a taxi was in sight so I walked over Waterloo Bridge looking down river towards Parliament, marvelling that its clock tower still stood.

I picked up my pace as best I could through the crowds. *Bobby*. I hadn't seen him for six weeks and my head felt light with anticipation. The war in Europe was over and we'd both survived. We could stop holding our breath and begin to plan our lives together.

Someone knocked into me. 'Sorry, my lover.' The man responsible lifted his hat before walking on, and I rubbed my shoulder where we had collided, rejoicing at his Cornish accent. My thoughts shifted to Cornwall and to my mother. She wasn't well. The confirmation of Uncle Reg's death had hit her badly. That wobble I'd heard in her voice had been just the beginning. She fussed over everything now. Hopefully my engagement news would lift her spirits. Bobby and I planned to see Father soon and then we would go together to see Mother. I prayed that my parents would find their way back to each other. Now I understood how separation could eat away at you. Father had always pulled her from the depths in the past. Surely he would be able to again.

Squinting into the distance, I saw the streets were full of people dancing and singing. The words of 'Roll Out the Barrel' carried on the air and I sang along as I made my way across the bridge. Just as I was approaching the Embankment, two airmen approached, grinning like idiots. I knew the feeling. They linked arms with me and pulled me along with them through the crowds.

'Where are you heading?' I asked as I studied them. One had a scar across his cheek and the other one was ginger-haired.

'Trafalgar Square. Where are you going?'

'The Savoy.'

'It's on the way.' The ginger airman laughed.

'It is indeed.'

'May we have the pleasure of escorting you?' the scarred one smiled.

'I would be delighted.' We moved through the crush carrying Union flags and singing. As we came to the Savoy music spilled out of a window and the scarred airman swung me into his arms to dance. My head rocked back, but I quickly recovered and in the crowds we jived to 'In the Mood'. The last time I had danced to this was with Bobby, and hopefully in a few minutes I would be in his arms again.

Turning with a big smile on my face I saw a photographer take my picture. I could imagine what I looked like, with my hat askew and a grin stretching as wide as my face. The war was over and Bobby was near. The music faded and I stepped away from my partner.

'Must you go?'

'Sorry, but yes.'

He released my hand. The weight of the crowd swept me towards the entrance. Somewhere in this chaos would be Bobby. Glancing at my watch, I saw that I was three hours late. In the busy lobby, I made my way towards the American Bar and searched the hubbub inside. Although I spotted a few American officers, none were familiar. I turned and headed for the Grill, hoping he'd be there. Before I could speak, I was in the arms of a general, twirled around and passed into the arms of another gentleman. It was hard not to be caught up in the happiness, but mine wouldn't be complete until I was with Bobby.

Eventually I ducked through to the Grill but he wasn't there. I could see one of Father's colleagues, who indicated for me to come and join them, but I simply waved back and slipped out into the crowd.

'What brilliant luck,' said a familiar voice, and suddenly I was swept into another man's arms and kissed soundly.

'Angus,' I laughed. 'You devil.'

'God, I've wanted to do that for years,' he said. 'And this time I know which one it is too.' He grinned, looking so like the boy we used to race on the beach, and yet there were lines around his eyes that hadn't been there when we last met.

I laughed. 'Are you sure?'

He squinted at me. 'No – to be honest, I'll never be sure, but I do know that Adele Seaton is in the WRNS. Your uniform is a big help.'

I laughed. 'Amelia's a Wren too.'

'True – but now I come to think of it, I'm sure you are Adele.' He pointed to the sparker's badge.

'Come on, Angus.' A tall airman tugged at Angus's arm. 'We're off to go dancing.'

'Come with us, Adele. We're off to the 400.'

Angus gestured to me with a grin, but I looked around, still searching the crowds.

'Meeting someone?'

'I'm late.' I frowned.

'Tonight everyone's late. Come with us and celebrate.'

'But I'm not dressed for it.

'No one is. Do say yes.'

I looked at my watch. It was now four hours since I was supposed to have met Bobby and he still wasn't here. Angus grinned and I couldn't resist that smile. 'Yes.'

'Shame Melly isn't here too.'

'True.' Amelia would have mixed feelings tonight, being apart from Eddie. A little of my happiness dimmed. Angus linked his arm through mine and we pushed through the crowd out on to the street. I wondered what Amelia was up to tonight, as London celebrated like there was no tomorrow.

Windward, Mawnan Smith, Falmouth, Cornwall
22 September 2015

Left on the tray with the teapot were the remains of the beautifully scrambled eggs on toast that I'd enjoyed. Jack had even plucked a bit of parsley from the garden. A little time with Lara and he was garnishing things. I took a sniff to confirm what I'd tasted. He'd added something to the eggs. Truffle. Dear lord, he was worried about me. That wasn't what I wanted. I simply did not want to talk or be asked questions, and it wouldn't be long before Lara was asking them. They were there in her eyes – I had seen them as she studied me. She looked at me and saw herself, while in her I saw my youth and so much more, so much that had been lost. Why on earth would I want to talk about that? My desk, out of reach opposite the bed, was open and my sister's letters sat tied up. If I opened them, what would they say? I shook my head.

Peta cleared the breakfast tray then came back with a fresh cup of tea. I continued to stare out of the window at the bleak weather and the sudden rain that beat on the panes.

'OK, Gran what's going on?'

I looked at her as she walked to the window the turned about to face me.

'Silence isn't the answer.' Peta smiled. 'I understand that sometimes not talking is the easiest option, but what isn't a good idea is hiding.' She shook her head. 'I know it's Lara. There is something you are avoiding and you are trying to push me out of your head.' She laughed and I sipped the tea.

Peta came to sit beside me, taking my hands in hers. They were warm, while mine were cold. 'Look, Gran. You have got to try. For Jack. Right now he needs you.' She gently rubbed my fingers. All the plumpness had gone. They were nothing but thin skin, blue veins and liver spots.

'I know it's Lara. And I know you're afraid.' She looked up. 'I'm going to be honest here – and believe it or not, it's hard to say this – but you have to forget about yourself. You've seen with your own eyes the transformation in Jack when he's around her. His walls slip. This is the first outsider he's let anywhere near close.' She smiled.

I turned away.

'Be brave, Gran.'

She had no idea.

'But I do,' she said, answering my thought before I could speak it. 'I can't put it into words, but I do.' She kissed my hand and held it to her cheek. Her love flowed through me, trying to strengthen me.

The 400 Club, Leicester Square, London
8 May 1945 – VE Day

Why Angus and his friends thought there would be room to dance on London's smallest dance floor I didn't know. Incredibly, it was dustier than it had been the last time I'd been here with Bobby. He'd laughed at the place and the fact that they would keep his bottle of whisky there for him for his next visit. Peering through the gloom, I wondered where we would sit, let alone dance. But I shouldn't have been concerned. We were soon wedged in with friends of Angus's from Bomber Command.

'I'm so sorry about Eddie,' said a sandy-haired flight lieutenant, leaning forward to me.

'What?' I frowned. What was wrong with Eddie?

Angus put his arm around me. 'This isn't Eddie's fiancée; it's her sister.'

'Looks just like the picture he carried around.'

Angus nodded.

'What's happened to Eddie?' My stomach tightened. The sandy-haired lieutenant looked apologetically at me.

'Missing,' he said, 'presumed ...'

The band struck up and his last words drifted away to the sound of a French horn. My glance flew to Angus. Eddie was his best friend. His jaw clenched as he swallowed. I looked at the champagne in my hand and didn't feel like celebrating. Closing my eyes, I tried to 'feel' Amelia, but the sensation was about as clear as the air around me. I stole Angus's cigarette and took a long drag. Those silly summers messing around in boats in Cornwall seemed a long way from the dark fug around us.

He pulled me close. 'He wouldn't want us to act like this, tonight of all nights.'

I took a deep breath. He was right. Eddie had been the life and soul of the party. I raised my glass, and Angus's lightly touched mine.

'To Eddie.'

'Eddie.'

We knocked our drinks back, glasses were refilled, and before I knew it I was in Angus's arms, swaying to the music, trying not to think of Eddie, or how my sister would be taking this news.

As 'Moonlight Serenade' played, I rested my head on Angus's shoulder. The champagne was making the world soft-edged and it had dulled the pain a bit. What was Amelia going to do? I glanced at Angus. He was a good catch but I knew her heart would not transfer so easily.

The last notes of the song finished and the band rose for their break. We were on the far side of the club, away from our friends. Scanning the tables to distract my thoughts, I wondered how many people were here with someone they shouldn't be.

I froze. My heart stopped. Father was at one of the far tables … and he was in a passionate embrace with Aunt Margaret.

'Who have you spied?' Angus whispered in my ear. He looked in the same direction and then took my hand, tugging me towards the door. 'Make nothing of it. Pretend you haven't seen.'

Father looked up in my direction and our eyes met, just as Angus pulled me away.

✳ Thirty-Five ✳

Kensington, London
9 May 1945

I sat at Aunt Margaret's kitchen table alone. It was midday. My head thumped and I remembered little of the rest of the night after we left the club. In spite of what I had seen, or maybe because of it, I had looked for Bobby in the crowd. I had needed him so much right then. He was a straight American who stuck to his values. No, I was being unfair to the English. I just had to think of Commander Rowse. He was how a man should be; my father was not. My father hadn't even the decency to have an affair with someone outside the family. Dear God, my mother's brother had been dead for less than a year.

Cradling my head in my hands, I wondered what had happened to the world. My mother was depressed and lonely in Cornwall. My father was having it off with my aunt, my sister's fiancé was missing presumed dead and I was in love with an American. I laughed. If I presented that list to my grandmother, out of everything she'd probably still think the worst problem was my American.

The telephone sat a few feet away. I'd picked it up three times and put it back. I couldn't call home to ask if Amelia was there. What if Mother answered? What would I say? There was nothing I *could* say. She knew. She had to, or at least suspect. How long had he and Margaret been carrying on?

Taking my tea, I went up to the room where I slept and had kept a few things. This small bedroom had been my London base and up until last night had felt like home. I took out my suitcase and began putting everything in it. I couldn't stay here now, but wasn't sure where I could go. The trains weren't running today. I would try and reach Bobby, then once my head was functioning properly I would see who else was here in town. Clear thinking was needed but my brain wasn't capable of that.

I opened the wardrobe to retrieve my evening gown, wondering if I really wanted it any more – after all, it had been Margaret's. But it wasn't there. The place it had hung on the wardrobe rail was empty. I tilted my head, as if somehow shaking my brain might make it work. I knew I'd left it here, the last time I'd been in London. I'd only worn it a month ago.

Sinking onto the bed, I took a sip of tea, grateful that my aunt wasn't around. It didn't bear thinking about where she was. The war had changed everything but I hadn't expected this. Maybe I should have done. Father was here and Mother was in Cornwall. They shouldn't have separated – she should have stayed in London with him. But I remembered the Blitz and her nerves. Once she was away in the country and with Grandmother things had improved. Father had the War Office. Aunt Margaret had the Red Cross. But obviously it had not been enough. Yet Mother hadn't taken up with any of the American generals who frequented the Ferryboat Inn, or even the handsome Dutchman with the gammy leg who flirted outrageously with her. Mother was beautiful, quiet, caring. Margaret was . . .

'Hello.'

. . . right in front of me, standing in the doorway, looking sheepish.

'Leaving?' Her voice was husky and her face a little drawn.

I shrugged.

'May I come in?'

I bit back the words I wanted to say – *it's your house* – and nodded.

'Your father said you were at the 400 last night.'

'Yes.'

She took a step into the room. Usually so confident and vivacious, my glamorous aunt now looked unsure.

I stared straight at her. 'Am I the only family member who knows?'

She moistened her red lips. 'I believe your mother may suspect.'

I nodded. 'My grandmother?'

'The same.'

'The whole of London?'

'No. Of course not.'

Her eyes turned from me and she looked out of the window, but from her expression, I could tell. People knew. They would talk. My mother would be the object of pity. Amelia would kill my father.

'He needed someone.' She turned to me. '*I* needed someone.'

'So this was a thing of convenience.' I raised an eyebrow and tried not to sound bitter.

'Honestly, it began that way.' She took a deep breath. 'Your father wasn't my first lover since I became a widow. Or even before.' Walking to the window, she looked down on the large hole at the end of the garden where her neighbour's house used to be. 'I tried to fill the loneliness any way I could.'

'So my father filled the gap in your life.'

She laughed drily. 'No, he returned after D-Day a different man.'

That I could understand.

'He wakes at night screaming.'

I closed my eyes. I didn't want to hear this about my father for so many reasons. But mostly I didn't want to hear it from my aunt, someone I'd looked up to until last night.

'Adele, you're an adult now,' she said.

'That doesn't make things right.' I closed my suitcase with a snap.

'No, but things are never black and white.'

'Do you want him to divorce Mother?'

She crossed her arms. 'Heavens, no.'

I frowned.

'I love your father.' She sat down on the edge of the bed. 'I love your mother and you and Amelia.' She looked hard at me, giving me the same look people did when trying to work out which of the sisters I was. But Father had known it was me last night. My uniform had given me away, the tell-tale badges. This was not how things should be.

My hands were neatly folded on my lap. 'What do you plan to do?' I asked. I didn't really want to know, but hearing it might help somehow.

'Nothing.'

I shook my head. If she loved my father then surely she wanted to be with him. Now that the war was over, Mother would expect him back. I looked down at my fingers twisted together in my lap.

'He'd like to see you.'

I looked up from my hands to the hallway.

'He's not here. He's at his club. He'll be at the Ritz at one o'clock.' She stood. 'I know it's a great deal to take in. I remember my own anger when I discovered my father had taken a mistress.' She laughed. 'In the end I became quite close to her.' She left the room.

That may have been true for you, I thought. *But this is different.*

✷ Thirty-Six ✷

Constantine, Falmouth, Cornwall
23 September 2015

Lara left Cassie's house with a great deal on her mind. It was 11.30 a.m., which made it very early in Boston, but she didn't care. She needed to talk to Leo before she got to Windward. All night long Elle Rowse's face had woven its way through her dreams. Lara had reread Grandie's sparse diaries hoping for a clue. He had mentioned Cornwall, Falmouth and the Helford only during May 1944, when he was on leave with 'A'.

May 15, 1944

Left with A and drove to Cornwall.
  Drank whiskey above a cove. I cannot describe how I feel about her.
  The house is charming. Had lunch at the Ferryboat.

The Ferryboat Inn. She smiled, glad that she could visualise the location now. Grandie had mentioned it a few times in the diary.

May 30, 1944

Strange to be here without A. Am meeting the DQ here. This area reminds me so much of the Cape.

Lara knew that only Grandie would have been able to fully decode his use of initials for people and places. But she was certain Windward and Mrs Rowse were linked to him in some way. A rain squall descended as she pulled into a passing place. Thankfully, her phone had signal, so she dialled.

'Morning.' The voice on the line was Deborah, sounding like she'd been awake for hours.

'It's Lara.'

'I've been thinking about you. Leo's been restless which means you have too.'

'Sorry.'

'No need to apologise. I knew when I started dating a twin that there were certain consequences, other than the chance of having twins of my own. I'll pass you to him.' There was a pause, a brief clatter on the line, and then:

'Hey, you.'

Lara smiled. 'This is really weird, Leo. I feel Grandie all around here like I've told you, but – I met an old woman who looks like me. Well, she did when she was young.' She took a breath. 'But her eyes even now, they're like ours. It's like looking into the future.'

'Is she related?'

'She must be.' Lara sighed. 'I'm dying to ask her a million questions but she's not very well.'

'Not good,' he said.

'No. By the way, I haven't had any luck reaching this General Tucker.'

'Sorry, meant to update you. He's moved into a home. I had a great chat with him.'

'Did he know anything?' She glanced up at a tractor coming towards her but there was enough room for the vehicle to get around her safely. The farmer in the driver's seat waved as he passed.

'In his words, Grandie was in love with a girl called Adele. She was a Wren. A beautiful thing with amber eyes.'

'Adele.' Lara looked out to the field. A gush of wind brought a few leaves down onto the hood of the car.

'Yes, Adele. I did say that he married an Amelia and General Tucker knew that.'

'I don't suppose he knew Amelia's last name?'

'No, he never met Amelia but he knew Adele well, as she worked as a telegraphist in Portland. He and Grandie were stationed in Weymouth, which according to the map was close by.'

'And you didn't call me about that straight away?' She sighed. 'I guess that explains his last words.'

'She must have been his great love.' She heard Leo take a sip of what she presumed was coffee.

'But what about Amelia? He married her.'

'Tucker knew Grandie had married another woman but couldn't remember the details. Although they kept in touch via the odd Christmas card they never saw each other after Grandie left the Army.'

Lara tapped the wheel with her free hand. 'Thanks. It all helps. Adele makes sense if she was the love of his life, but it feels wrong knowing he married Amelia. And knowing him. Why would he have done that?'

'Maybe he made a mistake and did the right thing.'

'Possibly, but does getting a girl pregnant sound like the man who said the rosary on his knees every night?' She pictured Grandie so clearly right then, beside his bed, his head bowed.

'Maybe that's why he did.'

She shook her head. 'True.'

'Keep me posted. Love you. I'm off to the office now.'

'So early?'

'Big case,' he said. 'Bye.'

'Love you too.' Cows had spotted her car and were making their way towards the gate. She ran all the facts she had through her mind then closed her eyes. Were they missing something? Her eyes flew open. Of course they were. 'A' didn't have to be Amelia; it could be Adele. Those passionate letters were from Adele.

She turned the ignition then continued on her way to Windward, wondering if Elle Rowse could be Amelia's cousin, or maybe even her sister. Lara's likeness to the young Elle was too marked to be a fluke.

Turning into the drive carefully so the sourdough starter she'd stowed in a bag on the back seat wouldn't spill, she looked forward to an afternoon of bread, the food of life. Now that Elle was eating a bit more, it was good to keep things varied, plus Lara was enjoying the time spent with Jack in the kitchen. She had forgotten the joys of simply cooking for pleasure. Parking next to his 4x4, she got out of the car just as the rain eased off and breathed in the clear air. The sea in the distance was still and grey, a shade lighter than the sky. More rain would follow shortly, she was sure of it.

Avoiding a series of puddles, she made her way to the kitchen. The back door was wide open and no one was in sight. She put the starter down and wondered if she should call out or prepare things while she waited.

'Hello?' She walked towards the central hallway, glancing into the breakfast room as she passed. The dining room and sitting rooms were empty too. Continuing through the house on tiptoe, feeling like she was trespassing, she searched for more photos of Elle, but those that she saw were of Jack and Peta and another man she assumed had to have been their father.

In the living room she found a photo of Elle with a tall, handsome man. In the picture, she was wearing a hat and holding a bouquet so Lara assumed it was a wedding photo. Elle looked about forty and the style of her dress suggested it was some time in the 1960s.

At the sound of a thump upstairs, she stepped back from the picture. There was a cry and she dashed to the main staircase. 'Hello?' This time she made sure her voice could be heard. 'Mrs Rowse? Jack?'

No response. She ran up the stairs and quickly searched for where she'd heard the noise, towards the front of the house above the sitting room. There she found a door ajar – and beyond it she could see Elle on the floor, clutching a pile of letters.

Lara rushed in and fell to her knees. Elle's breathing was laboured but her eyes opened, focusing on her.

'I know you.'

'Yes, you do. I'm Lara.' She looked for signs of an injury but saw none. 'Are you hurt?'

'I know you.'

Lara smiled and tried to assess Elle's condition. Her pupils were slow to react but responding. In her hands she was still clutching the pile of envelopes. Lara reached for her wrist to check her pulse. The skin was papery white and soft.

'Why are you here?' Elle's words were slow and slightly slurred.

'To cook.' Lara wondered if she had had a stroke. On the bedside table was a phone, so she quickly went over to it and called the emergency services. Once she'd made sure an ambulance was on the way, she went back to sit beside Elle.

'Why are you here?' Elle asked again. Her eyes looked at Lara but she could tell they were seeing something else. 'We were wrong, you know.'

'Why wrong?'

'It seemed right at the time.'

Lara hoped the ambulance would arrive soon. She held Elle's hands, but they were so cold, the fingers long and slender like Lara's own, down to the slightly crooked pinkie.

'Why are you here?' Elle was studying Lara.

'I'm here to find out about my great-grandmother, Amelia.'

Elle gasped and closed her eyes. Lara watched her chest rise and fall. It reminded her of those days with Grandie.

'Amelia.' Elle's voice was very faint.

'Yes. She married my great-grandfather, Robert Webster.'

Lara could hear a clock ticking. Outside, the rain began again with a few gentle taps on the window. Where the hell was Jack? His car was in the drive. They had been due to start cooking twenty minutes ago. She continued to check Elle's vital signs. How long it would take for help to arrive?

'Is he dead?'

Lara nearly jumped out of her skin. Elle's eyes were open again, looking at her and very focused.

'Yes,' she said. 'He died in August, just over a month ago.'

Lara's heart tightened as she thought of him. Back then it had appeared his life had been simple. He'd been a single parent and had mourned his wife for most of his life. Now it was more than possible that he'd mourned his first love for even longer.

Elle's gaze fixed on some point beyond Lara. 'Did he send you?'

'No.'

'Amelia.' She spoke the name so softly Lara wasn't sure if it was intended for her.

'Yes, my great-grandmother was Amelia.' Lara brushed a strand of hair from Elle's face.

'You look just like her.'

'What the hell has happened?' Jack came in, followed immediately by two paramedics. Lara stepped aside and answered their questions quickly, then she and Jack left the room and headed downstairs to leave them to their work.

Jack stood for ages looking out at the rain from the sunroom, not saying a word. Lara lost track of time thinking about the woman upstairs. How did Elle fit? Her words: *You look just like her* ran round in Lara's head. It was clear that she and Elle were related; it was just a question of how.

❊ Thirty-Seven ❊

The Ritz, London
9 May 1945

Everyone was still smiling but looking tired as I hopped off the number 9 bus with my suitcase in hand and headed towards the Ritz. Evidence of the night's revelry was everywhere. I adjusted my hat and straightened my jacket. My uniform was slightly the worse for wear, but when I looked at my other options nothing seemed right. My father would be in uniform. I didn't want to see him but I didn't have any choice. No, I knew that wasn't true – part of me did want to see him. There were so many emotions in me right then. I stepped through the bits of paper and broken glass at my feet. Last night all that paper flying about had seemed joyous, but now, as I watched an old man in the distance sweeping it all away, it was just work.

I almost marched through the Ritz lobby to the restaurant. As I approached the table, my father stood. 'I wondered if you'd come.'

'So did I.' Taking my seat, I looked at my father as if seeing him for the first time. He was handsome, so very handsome. His green eyes lively, intelligent but weary. He must have known that if he was carrying on with my aunt we would find out eventually. But maybe that was what he had wanted, the cheat's way. Now he didn't have to break the news because I had seen it with my own eyes.

'Delly,' he began and I flinched. 'I'm sorry ... you had to find out.'

I blinked. *Find out?* He should have been apologising for

doing all of us a grievous wrong. 'I'm sorry you thought that you could do something like this and I *wouldn't* find out.'

'We have been very discreet.' The word *discreet* gave me images of back alleys and dodgy hotels that I didn't want. 'No one thinks anything of seeing us together for dinner.'

I shook my head, trying to see where my father was heading. 'Last night was an exception then?'

'Exactly. A bit of VE Day madness. And no one talks about what they see in the 400.'

'That's not true. I've heard you talk about the shenanigans of certain people.'

'Yes, but I am below notice.'

'You may be but Aunt Margaret isn't.'

He peered into his whisky. I imagined he'd had a few while he was waiting for me, and now that I looked I could see the signs of drink on him. His face was high in colour and a sheen of perspiration gleamed on his brow. 'Margaret is different.'

'What were you thinking?' I twisted my water glass on the table. A waiter approached, but I waved him away. Food was the last thing I wanted.

'I wasn't ...'

'No, you weren't, were you? Mother, Amelia and me. Don't we count?'

'It's not like that.'

'It wouldn't be like that if it was someone else, maybe, but *Margaret?*'

He looked me in the eyes then down at his hands. I once thought them capable, strong and clever, but now I saw them as the hands of a man who thought only of himself. Margaret could have her pick of men, available men. He hadn't even considered my mother.

I stood up. 'I'm sorry, but I can't condone this.'

He stood up as well, reaching out to me. 'Don't make a scene.'

I smirked. *A scene!* 'Don't worry about that,' I whispered. 'You are doing quite well on your own.'

'Don't tell your mother or Amelia.' He shook his head. 'I

know the two of you communicate without words, but don't tell her.'

'What? You can't bear to fall from the heights she has put you on?' I laughed softly. 'Father, you should have thought about that before you took my aunt to bed.'

I turned and walked away. As I left, I heard a quiet, plaintive 'Please' behind me. But I did not turn back.

Windward, Mawnan Smith, Falmouth, Cornwall
23 September 2015

'I'm so glad you were here.' Jack smoothed the hair on the back of his neck then left his hand there, his shirt riding up, revealing a large patch of taut skin on his waist. Lara tried not to look. 'When I went to give our neighbour Martha a hand with her car, I hadn't realised it would take so long.'

'Well, don't worry. You couldn't have stopped the stroke, if that's what it was, and she'll be fine for now.'

'But not much longer.' He turned to her. 'The pneumonia has accelerated her end, I think.'

She nodded. The doctor was with Elle. It had been decided it was best not to take her in to hospital, despite the belief that it was a mini-stroke. Elle did not want to go and had promised the doctor that she would rest.

'What's going on?' Jack dropped his hand and stuck it into his jeans pocket.

'She's old and tired.'

'True, but it's all happened so quickly.'

Lara walked closer to him. 'It's hard.' She bit her lip, thinking of Grandie. 'But it may be a blessing.'

His eyes filled with unshed tears.

'I know how hard it is to let go,' she said.

He nodded and she reached out and touched his hand. He took hers in his and held it tight.

Chelsea, London
9 May 1945

I'd tried to ring Bobby but there was no answer. So I wrote a note and set out to drop it off where he was staying. The flat in question wasn't far from where Angus's mother, Mrs Lambert, lived in Cadogan Gardens; I'd rung her earlier that morning, asking for a bed without much explanation. I think Angus might have said something because she didn't query my request and was very welcoming.

Knocking on the door of Bobby's flat, I was greeted by a dishevelled officer I didn't recognise. 'Sorry to disturb you – I'm looking for Captain Robert Webster?'

He gave me an odd stare. 'He's gone. He left this morning.'

I glanced at the note in my hand. The captain was looking at me as if he'd seen me before, but I knew I'd never met him. 'Could I leave this for him?'

'You can, but he'll be gone for a while. If it's an important letter then sending it might be best. I can give you the address.'

I frowned. 'I have it already.'

'I hope you enjoyed your night.' He smiled.

'Thank you, I did. It was a wonderful celebration.'

'Yes, it was.' He leered at me and I shivered as I walked away.

Putting the letter in my pocket, I stepped back out onto the pavement. What a peculiar comment that had been.

As I continued, on the road ahead I saw Margaret's long-time friend Lady Hall. This was a meeting I didn't want to take place so I took a right turn and slipped down Moore Street. Thankfully there had been no sign of my aunt when I'd left to meet my father, which was a relief. I had no idea what more I could say to her. No doubt she would hear from Father how I felt.

How could I not tell Amelia what I knew? How could he ask that?

But then I hadn't told her much about Bobby, so I'd kept things from her before. He hadn't entered her sphere. But Father and Aunt Margaret were different, and this had changed everything. We would be left taking care of Mother. Or, truthfully, Amelia would – I would soon be on my way to the States as Mrs Robert Webster, as long as all went to plan.

I was sorry that I had missed Bobby last night, but pleased that he hadn't witnessed my father's betrayal. Angus had handled it well and none of the others with us had known anything was amiss. We had left the 400 and ended up at the Embassy Club. The words to 'Don't Sit Under the Apple Tree (with Anyone Else but Me)' ran through my mind as I made my way to the Lamberts' flat. I thought of that glorious May weekend with Bobby, and him singing to me as we sat under the fading apple blossom. My hunger for him was greater, if that was possible, knowing there was now a future for us.

On the bottom step, a stab to my gut stopped me. Amelia. What of her future? She was in pain right now. I looked around, feeling she must be close, but I was alone on the street. Where was she? I shivered and focused on holding her near. But I sensed she was pushing me away. The front door opened and Mrs Lambert stood there with a beaming smile. 'Adele, do come in!' she said. 'We're about to have tea and then Angus must head back to his unit.'

Windward, Mawnan Smith, Falmouth, Cornwall
23 September 2015

My sister was dead.

She had to be. Bobby was already gone, and now Lara was looking to find out more about Amelia. The letters my sister had written to me sat on the top of the desk, but I had no power to move. The pneumonia had weakened me. From downstairs I smelled the aroma of butter and onions and garlic. I imagined Jack and Lara in the kitchen and smiled. Peta was right – Jack needed Lara. He was beginning to trust and let her in because of me. If she could help him to live then what difference did my secrets make? None at all.

My sister was dead. Bobby was dead. And I would soon join them.

The need to know about my sister's life was awake. It had been forcibly put to sleep by me so many years ago, and now it was like a persistent itch that wouldn't be soothed. I tried to move my legs but they shifted only inches. What would those letters tell me? What was I afraid of now?

'Hey, Gran,' Peta whispered as she came through the door.

'Peta.'

She went straight to the desk and picked up the letters. 'This is what you want.'

I nodded and she came and sat beside me on the edge of the bed. 'OK.' She looked at each letter addressed to me. 'From A. Webster of Falmouth, Massachusetts,' she read. 'Why did you never open these?'

'Simple. I didn't want to know what was in them.'

She laughed. 'But you didn't throw them out.'

'I did, but my mother – who didn't know what day of the week it was by then – fished them out of the bin and saved them in my old suitcase.'

'Dementia?'

'I'm not sure.' I coughed and she handed me a glass of water. 'Certainly a nervous breakdown when my father moved in with my aunt, her sister-in-law.'

'Ouch.'

'Yes, at first they were discreet but that didn't last long.'

'Divorce?'

I shook my head. 'That would have been kinder in the long run but Grandmother wouldn't have it.'

'Why ever not?'

'She told my mother to just turn a blind eye and count her blessings. As a divorcee she would be worse off. Her husband having a mistress would make her an object of pity but not an outcast.'

'Strange times.'

'Very. The war turned our world upside down.' I looked at my sister's letters. A. Webster. She hadn't written Mrs R. Webster. 'People did things they never would have considered before the war.'

'I bet.'

'Even you, Peta, have no idea.' I looked at the letters. What would they tell me? How wonderful life with Bobby was? How delightful the baby was?

'Gran, be brave. We love you.'

I tried to squeeze her hand but mine was too weak.

'You need to rest.' Peta picked up my hand and kissed it. 'I almost couldn't believe what I was seeing.' She grinned. 'In the kitchen Jack was acting as sous chef, cooking without a recipe.'

I raised my eyebrows.

'I know,' said Peta. 'She's making him taste ingredients and make decisions from taste alone!'

'Wonderful.' I smiled. There was hope for him.

'Yes, and now you'll sleep and grow stronger.'

I nodded.

'It will be OK.'

I shook my head.

'Trust me.'

I knew I had no choice. Events were taking their own path, as they had done seventy years ago. But if I died, would these letters tell the story?

✳ Thirty-Eight ✳

10 May 1945

On the train I sat looking out of the window at the Dorset countryside with a blank sheet of paper in front of me. I had so much to say to Bobby but didn't know where to begin. Finally, I started to write:

My dearest love,

I can't believe I missed you on VE Day. I know I said this in my note that I posted to you. I hope you managed to celebrate without me. What did you do?

I pictured him in the crowded streets dancing and celebrating with everyone. My heart stopped. He wouldn't have kissed anyone else, well, at least not seriously. I laughed, thinking of all the men who had kissed me that day – but then I thought about Father. It was twisting my insides. I couldn't write to him about Father and Aunt Margaret yet I needed to talk to someone about it.

I was afraid to call home. It would be there, in Mother's voice – the knowledge of what had happened. Knowing why she was depressed didn't help. Before I knew the reason, I had thought it was because Father was away. Of course, the war was still at fault for his absence from her life. It had made the most of people's weaknesses. Yet many had found strength they hadn't known they had. I never imagined that Father could have landed on the beaches, let alone what else he witnessed in

Europe. His night-time screams were not the surprise; simply the person reporting them. It should have been Mother comforting him.

I missed you. I eventually made it to the Savoy but hours after we'd said. Fortunately I bumped into an old friend, Angus Lambert, and a few of his flyboy friends. It was a good evening, but not truly fun without you.

The landscape was bursting to life outside the window, as if the land itself was rejoicing, and part of me was too. The war was over. There was a future that wasn't bleak. But then I thought of Amelia.

I longed to be in your arms and feel your lips on mine. I know we have waited for this moment. We can now plan. Last night I dreamt that finally we had made love, knowing the future was ours. I know if it had happened it would have been wrong, but it also would have been so right. On my way to Aunt Margaret's

I stopped writing, leaving off in the middle of the sentence, and winced, thinking about the walk back to Aunt Margaret's house, knowing what I'd seen. The fear that she might be there when I arrived.

I saw couples love making and I hungered for you. The ache inside nearly had me crying out. I miss you so much and I know I must be patient. The war isn't over yet. I'm praying they won't transfer you to the Far East now.
  I can barely breathe for wanting to hear from you. All my heart is hoping we can be together soon. I can hear you whispering to me to be patient. I have been patient, darling, and I will try to be a bit longer.

Kisses and hugs and so much more,
Xxxx

As the train pulled into the station, I twisted the ring he had given me. I folded the letter, then sealed it with a kiss.

Mawnan Smith, Falmouth, Cornwall
24 September 2015

The rain had eased and the bread was baking. Peta had arrived at Windward and was sitting with Elle, while Jack and Lara were walking to the nearby farm stand for potatoes. Lara's wellies squelched through the mud on the track, but Jack was silent as they walked. She guessed that his thoughts were with his grandmother. He sighed and she turned to him. 'When did you take up cooking?'

He looked at her, startled. 'When I was in university. Why do you ask?'

'I thought university was all beans on toast over here.'

He smiled. 'It was, but that becomes dull very quickly. When Peta gave me a recipe book my first Christmas at uni, I began to cook.'

'And you followed them to the letter.' She turned and strolled along backwards, facing him.

He smiled. 'Yes.'

'What happened if you didn't have an ingredient?'

'I didn't make it.'

She laughed, then fell into step beside him. 'You're an accountant.'

'Yes, I am.'

'It makes sense then.'

'Why do I feel like you are damning me?' A grin played on his mouth.

'Not at all. It's not anything I could ever do.'

'So by implication I could never cook.'

'Touché, but no.'

They left the track and walked along the road. Leaves were spinning down from the trees and landing in the puddles. Lara jumped in the next one and water splashed Jack. He followed suit and soon they were puddle jumping until they reached the junction. Mud had splattered all the way up her jeans and she was laughing like she hadn't in a long time.

'You're mad,' he said, and looked down at the muck that had made its way up to his shirt.

'Yes, and it feels so good.'

He nodded.

Once they reached the farm stand they bought potatoes and admired the vegetables for sale, then they raced back to Windward just as the heavens opened and the rain started to pelt down.

HMS *Attack*, Portland, Dorset
10 May 1945

It felt like Mary, the new girl in our cabin, would never finish telling me about the VE Day celebrations at HMS *Attack*. It wasn't that I didn't want to hear them, but in my hand I held a letter from Bobby. Our letters must have crossed with each other. I could almost imagine the envelope being red hot, burning my fingers as she went on and on. I kept a smile on my face while all I was thinking of was Bobby. Could he now say where he was and how soon I would be able to see him again? I had leave coming up. I didn't want to go home to Cornwall. I wanted to go away with him. Maybe we could slip off and be married? Surely it could be possible? I would talk to the padre.

'Did you hear a word of what I said?' asked Mary.

I blinked. There was no use lying. 'No.'

'I didn't think so. Is that a letter from your Yank?' She looked at my hand.

I nodded.

'Fine,' she snapped. 'Read it. It'll just be worthless words of passion. He'll let you down, these Yanks always do.' She wandered down the gangway. I'd heard why she felt that way, but Bobby was different. He was the one who had held our passion in check and talked of our future. He wanted to do things the right way around. He had principles, unlike Father.

Turning the letter over, I slipped my nail under the edge to break the seal. Holding it up to my nose as I wedged my finger between the envelope flaps, I sniffed to see if I could smell him, but there was nothing but the dry scent of paper.

My dearest angel,

I don't know where to begin. I don't know if you will ever forgive me. You fled before I woke, before I could apologise, before I could say anything.

I put the letter down. This made no sense. What was he talking about?

After a moment, feeling a twinge of fear, I continued reading.

I was wrong, so wrong to make love to you when we were both so drunk. It's not what I ever wanted for us. I cannot forgive myself and I understand if you can't forgive me for treating you in this way. The first time I touched you that way I wanted to be fully there, not fumbling through a haze of whiskey and beer. I can only begin to imagine what you think of me and what you must think I feel about you to treat you in such a manner.

I understand why you didn't want to wake beside me in the morning but I wish you had. Then I could have begun to repair this. I want to fix this. We can, I know we can. I love you so much and I believe that despite what happened we love each other.

More than anything I didn't want to make the mistakes my father made. And here I have gone and done that. You cannot begin to understand how low I feel. How utterly sorry I am.

I dropped the letter from my shaking hands. He'd slept with someone else on VE night and he was asking me to forgive him. My hands moved to my heart and I looked at the scattered pages on the bed. Could I bear to read the rest?

You looked so beautiful in your green dress and I ruined everything. I wish I could go back to that moment when I spotted you in Trafalgar Square and instead behave how I should have done. I am not proud of what happened at all. I just ask that you forgive me.

I want you to be my wife. I need to see you but I'm not sure when I can get back to London. Please tell me you are well and that you will at least see me.

I love you more than life itself.

Yours forever,
B xxxx

I ran to the loo, making it there just as the dry retching began. My stomach tried to release but nothing emerged aside from a stream of bile.

Bobby thought he had made love to me.

Amelia.

Flood Tide

Just lost when I was saved!
Just felt the world go by!
Just girt me for the onset with eternity,
When breath blew back,
And on the other side
I heard recede the disappointed tide!

Therefore, as one returned, I feel,
Odd secrets of the time to tell!

EMILY DICKINSON, CALLED BACK (LVII)

Time and tide wait for no man.

CHAUCER, THE CLERK'S TALE

❊ Thirty-Nine ❊

Cornwall
14 August 1945

I t was the day before VJ Day and the train was crowded with happy people. This was a journey I'd been avoiding, but I had leave. I didn't know where Bobby was. Today held too many echoes of VE Day, so I watched the scenery and tried to forget. Signs of life returning to normal passed me by. Fields were laden with ripening wheat. It was August and it looked like it might be an early harvest.

I clutched my handbag to my stomach. In it was a letter from him. I hadn't opened it. There had been such a long gap since his last one. I had reread the other over and over until the paper had practically fallen apart. The words were imprinted on my brain. From what he said, I knew what had happened three months ago. He wasn't at fault. I was. He hadn't known that my sister was my twin, my identical twin. I'd never told him. There was no possible way he could have known that he'd made love to my sister in a drunken fumble, but I did.

I had no idea if Amelia would be in Cornwall. I'd shut her out of my head and I refused to care about her pain. She might never have met Bobby until VE Day, but she must have known that someone calling her Adele and knowing so many things about me had to be my Bobby, not just any American captain strolling the streets of London in drunken celebration. She'd known what she was doing and had done it anyway. She could have contacted me but I hadn't had a letter or a telephone call.

As we approached Plymouth, I was confronted with the

remains of the city, its war scars plainly visible. All around summer was in full force, but wrecked buildings covered the landscape surrounding the station, just shells of what they had once been. As the train came into the platform, the rattling of the wheels and the noise of the brakes spoke to me – −••• • − •−• •− −•−− •− •−•• *Betrayal.*

I closed my eyes. Amelia had to have known what she'd done.

The train jerked forward and I opened my eyes, I was amazed that Brunel's bridge across the Tamar had made it through intact. At each stop I watched the reunions taking place on the platforms and beyond. Mother knew I was coming home, but I didn't expect anyone to meet me. I planned to avoid Mother for the whole leave, but I would try talking to Grandmother. She was tricky but she was straight. Maybe I could speak to her about my future. I couldn't talk to Amelia.

I pulled Bobby's letter out of my bag and opened it at last.

My love,

I don't know what to say. I have just received your letter. I am confused. If it wasn't you I was with then who was it that answered to your name, spoke exactly like you and was wearing your dress? Yet your letter says clearly it wasn't you.

The only thing I can say is that she didn't smell like lily of the valley but something far more exotic. I should have known. Please tell me what I have done?

B xxx

I took a deep breath and looked out onto the moor with its bleak beauty. The sky was heavy with the promise of rain but like me it was holding back. Tears wouldn't help things and I didn't know what would. If Bobby could forgive himself then maybe we could move forward. I loved him. He had done no wrong in my eyes but my sister had. We would be moving to America and I wouldn't ever have to see her again.

As the train travelled on I pulled out paper and pen and began to write to Bobby.

My dearest love,

I believe I know what happened and it is my fault. I haven't spoken to her yet but I know the truth. In Trafalgar Square you met my twin sister, Amelia, wearing my dress.

I closed my eyes. I wondered if she still had the dress. Not that I would want to touch it.

'Writing to your sweetheart?' The old woman sitting across from me smiled.

I nodded, not wanting to engage in conversation. Aside from when I had changed trains, I didn't think I had even looked at my fellow travelling companions. Right now the battle in my head was far too important.

'Is he still away, not come home yet?'

Again I nodded, and looked down at what I'd written, wishing it hadn't happened; that I'd told him that Amelia was my identical twin. A continuous circle of what ifs went through my thoughts ... what if the train hadn't been late, what if my sister hadn't worn my dress, what if ...

The train lurched as the conductor announced St Austell. 'That will be me.' The woman stood with her bag. 'Make sure he knows you still love him. Men will be in short supply just like after the last war. Take care.' She left the compartment. I didn't know the woman's history, but my whole war had been spent surrounded by men. The last thing I felt right then was a shortage.

Why hadn't I ever told Bobby that Amelia was my twin? Was it because when I was with him I was simply me for the first time ever? Growing up it had been as if Amelia and I were one. We were dressed alike, spoke alike, did everything alike until it came to school. Only then did differences appear, and even after that the connection was still so strong, so powerful.

I forced myself to concentrate, and finish the letter:

Bobby, I'm so sorry this happened but it doesn't have to affect us. I love you. You love me. I need to see you to make sure you know how I feel. I'm on leave in Cornwall for ten days then I'm back to Attack. *I imagine I shall be demobbed soon.*

I love you with my whole heart,
A xxxx

'Next station Truro. Change for all stations to Falmouth ...' The conductor's voice faded away. I folded the paper and put it in the envelope. All my dreams for the future were caught in this letter. I grabbed my bag and prepared to change trains. I prayed Bobby would forgive himself, the way I was ready to forgive him.

Constantine, Falmouth, Cornwall
24 September 2015

Lara received a filthy look from Snowy as she poured out a measure of dry cat food, but she didn't care. She was bubbling with excitement and couldn't wait to go to Windward today. Elle had eaten all her soup and bread last night. She'd looked much better for the food but still wasn't saying much, which was understandable. Lara knew Elle had the answers she needed, but patience would be required.

The doorbell rang and she found the mailman standing there. 'I have a package for you.'

'Thanks.' She signed for it and quickly ripped it open. The package contained a small cloth-bound book, along with a handwritten letter from her mother.

Darling,

I'd grabbed this collection of poems from the library at Eventide. I thought it would be useful for teaching and hadn't looked at it until the other night. Read the inscription, darling.

Lara put the letter down, carefully took the book from the package and opened it.

To my dearest sister Amelia on our first Christmas apart. I love you and miss you. Adele, December 1943

Her hand shook. Adele was Amelia's sister. Were Adele and Elle one and the same? The need to find out overwhelmed her. What the hell had Grandie done? She couldn't just burst into Windward and accost Elle, especially in her current condition.

She turned on the kettle and tried to think it all through. What had happened all those years ago? How had Grandie ended up married to the wrong sister? A chill went down Lara's spine as she thought of the betrayal involved. Her appearance here would have brought up all that pain again for Elle – if she was indeed Adele, and not another relative.

Dear God, how was she going to ask these questions? *Should* she? She now knew where her great-grandmother had come from, that she had married Grandie at Windward and that he had been in love with Adele. Lara poured boiling water onto the ground coffee, and watched the water consume the powder. She had opened Pandora's box, and she didn't know what to think about Grandie anymore.

Windward, Mawnan Smith, Falmouth, Cornwall
14 August 1945

I waved to Mr Tonks as he drove away down the lane, grateful for the lift he'd given me from the station. Windward looked exactly as it had when I'd last been here with Bobby, which seemed somehow impossible. It would almost have been easier if it *had* changed, along with everything else in my now upside-down world. The gate pillars still stood. Honeysuckle filled the hedges and the scent had already caught me when I'd passed the fruit trees. In the distance, beyond the house, the sea was blue and a merchant ship made its way towards Falmouth. All was as it should be – except it wasn't. Aside from the bees, there was silence. Someone should have been home, the noise of the wireless should have been audible, but instead there was nothing.

Peas were staked on the canes by the kitchen but the door was closed. I frowned, set my bag down and turned the handle. It was locked. The house was *never* locked. Stepping back, I looked up. Windows were open, which was a relief. I hadn't thought that Mother and Grandmother might not be here. I'd only hoped that Amelia wouldn't be.

Strolling to the front, I admired Grandmother's roses, which were still blooming. Her vegetables were doing well. She might not have liked the idea of looking after her own potatoes but it was clear she had a knack for it.

There was a breeze from the east and I hoped the French windows would be open, but as it turned out they were closed too. The journey had been long and I needed a cup of tea or even something stronger. Perching myself on the wall, I looked out at the sea, towards St Anthony's Lighthouse. Aside from the ship movements, everything from this distance looked unchanged, but closer inspection would show that the beaches were still mined. It would take time for life to return to normal, whatever that would be now. My head hurt and my heart was broken. A cup of tea would help the former and being with Bobby would fix the latter.

One thing I knew, my future wouldn't be here but in America with Bobby. Amelia's betrayal had made that decision easy. Before I'd worried about leaving her behind to look after Mother. Now I knew it was the only thing I could do.

The sound of a car in the drive interrupted my thoughts. I jumped up but then sank back down. Neither Mother nor Grandmother could drive so that meant that Amelia was here. My hands clenched and my nails bit into my palms. Taking a deep breath, I pushed myself upright and walked slowly to the back of the house.

In the distance I could see Mother helping Grandmother out of the car while Amelia was removing something from the boot. As she closed it she looked up and saw me. She smiled, and then the smile disappeared along with any colour she had had.

'Adele,' Mother called. 'How wonderful to have you both home. We didn't know you were coming or we would have collected you.'

I frowned. I'd telephoned and spoken with her a few nights ago. As I came closer to her I could see the strain on her delicate features. Grandmother hadn't changed but seemed to have a more pronounced limp.

'Have you been demobbed? Amelia's finished.'

I raised an eyebrow. 'No, not yet.'

'Such a shame. It would be so wonderful to have you both home. Hopefully your father will be returned to us soon.'

My eyes opened wide. I didn't think Father had any thoughts of returning to Mother and life here. She looked away from my surprise while Grandmother glared in my direction.

'Why don't you help your sister?' Mother said as she led the way to the door and unlocked it. Turning, I walked to the back of the car and stood with my arms by my sides. I could sense Amelia's thoughts, and they were everywhere and nowhere. This close to her, I could feel everything – pain, anger, fear and that familiar completeness. I closed my eyes to try and shut the connection but it didn't work. There was no escaping the sense of wholeness that came only when we were together. The years away hadn't diminished the feeling, nor had the betrayal.

'Delly,' she said. 'I—'

'Don't.'

'But—'

'No.' I grabbed a bag and walked to the house. She wouldn't turn this around and make it my fault. We'd been there before but on nothing more important than Grandmother's Ming vase. This was something altogether different.

✳ Forty ✳

Windward, Mawnan Smith, Falmouth, Cornwall
24 September 2015

I could hear the waves and smell toast but I couldn't see anything.

'Morning, Gran.' Peta's voice was close, and I heard her put a tray down. I tried to open my eyes but they wouldn't do it. 'Hold on,' she said. 'Your eyes are covered in gunk.'

I relaxed against the pillow while I listened to Peta as she moved across into the bathroom. It would take a while for the hot water to come through the pipes and reach the sink. It would have been quicker to go to the kitchen and get some from the kettle, which would probably still be warm. It couldn't have been used that long ago – the scent of coffee was still wafting in on the breeze from the open window, along with the distant crash of waves on the beach.

'Hold still while I clean your eyes,' said Peta. Her fingers pressed on my forehead while her other hand carefully cleaned the sleep from my eyes. However, once I had blinked several times and my vision cleared, I saw the questions in Peta's eyes and wondered if maybe I should have stayed asleep. She finished cleaning me up and I blinked again, bringing the room into full focus. A leaden sky hung over the bay, promising more rain. Was this the calm before the storm? Was the storm itself out there at sea, waiting to follow the waves it had sent as an advance party? Did it even matter?

'How are you feeling?' She brought the tray over.

I closed my eyes.

'Gran.'

Opening them, I saw the worry on her face.

'Don't give up now. If you do, so will Jack.'

I frowned.

'He's only playing along with Lara for you,' said Peta.

I shook my head. 'He thinks he's acting but he's not.' A sigh escaped me.

'I know,' said Peta. She buttered the toast, cutting it in half and offering it to me. 'Marmalade?'

'No.' I took it from her and nibbled the corner.

'He's cooking with Lara. He thinks she will help you to talk about the past, which will make you better.'

My eyes opened wide. 'It won't.'

'You've got to play along.' Peta sighed and I could tell she was reading me, seeing my thoughts. Her hand sought mine. 'You know what you need to do. You love him.'

That I couldn't deny, but what she was asking cut right through me.

'He's got to think he's helping you. We need him to keep acting until it isn't an act any more. Until he realises that he can be human, that love is worth the risk.' She squeezed my hand. 'Gran, you know love is good.'

I took a deep breath. Love. I didn't think I had the strength.

14 August 1945

As we sat down to eat, the silence made the empty places at the table more poignant. We should have been buzzing with conversation – it was the first time since my very first leave that I had seen either Mother or Grandmother in person. At the least, the meal was delicious and Grandmother's vegetables were the stars. Her once-unmarked hands were now heavily callused and her nails were ripped in places, yet she still wore her pearls and had changed for dinner. I smiled, pleased that at least one person was the same.

My sister picked at the food in front of her. I still wouldn't let her into my thoughts. It took everything to block her but it wasn't as if I needed to sense her feelings – her face showed enough, with hollow cheeks, and dark circles lining her eyes. She looked so different from when we last met. It was clear she needed to eat but instead she simply moved the food around on her plate.

Was this so I would forgive her? Her heart was broken into a thousand pieces. Eddie was gone. I swallowed. She was looking down at her hands. She still wore his ring. Surely that would make her feel worse. I had taken mine off so I didn't have to face questions to which I had no answers.

Finishing my meal, I stood. I couldn't take any more of the silence. Mother didn't even try to fill the void with chatter, the way she usually did.

'Excuse me.'

I left the room, went to the kitchen and cleared my plate. I felt rude but it was too hard to just sit there. After I had washed my dish and the pans in the sink, I went out of the kitchen door. Why had I come back?

Leaving the house, I walked down the drive, across the fields and eventually made my way to the church. The sky was still a soft blue and the stars had begun to appear. I could just make out the Plough and I longed for Bobby.

Going through the lych gate I strolled among the gravestones. It should have been frightening, being among the stones as the light faded and the shadows lengthened, but I wasn't sure I would ever be scared by the dead again. Years ago, Amelia and I had run out of the churchyard spooked by some jackdaws that we were certain were spirits of the dead, and Mrs Tonks had told us: 'Never worry about the dead, they can't hurt you. But the living can.' Now, years later, I understood what she meant.

24 September 2015

Jack was standing at the sink when Lara tapped on the door. He was soaking wet with puddles at his feet.

'Hi.' Lara stepped in out of the rain and peered over his shoulder. The sink was full of mackerel. 'Been fishing?'

He nodded and moved away, pulling off his shirt and grabbing a towel out of a basket filled with folded items. Lara swallowed. It was hard not to look as he dried himself. His hair ended up in spikes after its treatment from the towel. He took a tee-shirt out of the basket and pulled it over his head before he smoothed his hair. She turned to the fish in the sink, which were equally beautiful in a different way, although they didn't have the same effect on her. And, technically, the fish were better for her.

'What do you plan to do with the fish, smoke them?'

'Not sure.' He turned from her and slipped out of his jeans. She picked up the firm, clear-eyed fish from the sink and started counting them, only turning when she was sure he was fully clothed. He'd hung his wet jeans over the handle of the Aga. From the way he stood she could tell something had changed. If she didn't know better she would think this was a different man standing in front of her with his arms crossed, feet wide and eyes shuttered. There was no sign of the playful puddle-jumper from before.

She bit her lip, debating what to do. She longed to talk to Elle and spend more time at Windward but she was now getting a distinct 'brick wall' vibe from Jack. In fact, maybe a brick wall was too friendly a comparison. 'Is this a bad time?'

He opened his mouth.

'Perfect timing.' Peta stepped out from behind her brother. 'Gran has just finished breakfast and is wondering what delights you two will create for lunch?'

Jack turned swiftly and went up the stairs. Lara sensed that he had been about to tell her to leave but clearly Elle or Peta wanted her to stick around for some reason. Lara always knew when she was not wanted – it was probably the reason why she'd chosen to hit back at her boss. She blinked. Of course. Stephan, her boss, had been vile because she was treading on his heels. She'd done him a favour by quitting. She shook her head.

'Peta, thanks for trying to protect me, but I know when I'm not wanted.'

Peta put the kettle on the Aga. 'Nonsense. Jack is like that sometimes. Ignore him.' She laughed. 'I think it's the accountant in him. He wants everything to work like numbers and pushes back when things don't add up.' She put the kettle on the range. 'Life isn't like that ... it doesn't come with precise instructions. It just throws ingredients at you and sees whether you make a meal or a mess.' She took out three mugs. 'Jack likes to be able to follow a recipe. It's safer and there's a guaranteed result at the end.'

The image of Jack's bare chest flashed in Lara's mind. He was not an easy man to ignore. Peta smiled.

'Have you had a formal job offer from Demi and Sam yet?'

Lara grabbed the chair in front of her. 'No, not yet.'

'It will arrive today.'

'Will it?' Lara knew she would seriously consider it if it did come. 'Look, Peta – I'd love to talk to Elle, to find out if she is my great-grandmother's sister or cousin, but I don't want to upset her.'

Peta poured the water into the old teapot. 'You won't. She just needs a little more time before she can talk.'

'Does she have that time?'

'That I don't know.' She handed Lara a mug. 'But I'm hoping she does.'

✳ Forty-One ✳

Windward, Mawnan Smith, Falmouth, Cornwall
15 August 1945 – VJ Day

Grandmother said the beach in the cove below Windward hadn't been mined but the razor wire and other defences wouldn't be cleared for a while. As I looked down on it from above it appeared the same yet different. The tide was out, revealing the jagged rocks, and the water ranged in colour from a deep, dark blue to turquoise. My back was baking in the heat of the sun, reminding me of the last swim I had taken in Portland. If I swam here and got myself in trouble again, there would be no one around to save me – but there was no risk this time. I knew the currents and the ways of this cove too well.

Climbing over a small stile I joined the main path to the beach, which had remained a mix of pebbles and sand. Why I thought this would have changed I don't know but I found myself looking for differences everywhere and finding none. Falmouth had altered in many obvious ways, but here life had continued virtually the same. I looked up to the field behind when I heard a noise and saw a woman adjusting the collar on a plough horse. She saw me and waved. I didn't know her. She must be one of the girls from the Women's Land Army, doing farm work while the men were away at war. That was one thing that was definitely different.

VJ Day. Japan had surrendered. The war was truly over, and everything had changed as Mother had said – just not as I had expected.

As I reached the beach, I dropped my things below the cliff

face and scrambled over a few large rocks to avoid the wire. It wasn't going to keep me from the sea, not on a day that was meant for swimming and laughter. I knew I wouldn't have the latter so the former would have to do. This place held so many happy memories including my first kiss with Philip. So much goodness and promise lost.

Reaching the finer sand by the water's edge, I winced as the soft skin of my feet felt the edge of each shell. In past summers my soles were tough from barefoot days of freedom, but now they were delicate. I tiptoed into the water, gasping at the temperature, but with a shallow dive I was in and soon clear of the shore in the middle of the cove. My eyes stung from the salt but I finally felt clean for the first time in days, which begged the question of why I had felt dirty. Was I tarnished by my father's actions and the deceit he expected me to maintain? Yes. Listening to Mother wittering on about how wonderful it would be when Father returned had been awful. I'd had to bite my tongue to prevent myself from shouting at her, from telling her to stop lying to herself and to us.

Treading water, I looked back towards Windward. It appeared solid, peaceful and like it had been there forever. From here I couldn't see the lawn filled with cauliflowers or that the windows weren't as sparkling as they had been in the past when full-time help had been on hand. The future for Windward was unclear – but while I still cared what happened to the house, I was going away. They would all be fine without me. Amelia could marry Angus if she was lucky and Mother and Grandmother would muddle through. God knew what Father would do. Aunt Margaret would thrive. She had money, she had connections and she was beautiful.

The icy freshness of the water had cleared my head, but sadness still surrounded me. I felt a stab of sorrow every time I looked at the sights I loved, knowing that I wouldn't be able to bring Bobby back here, to swim and truly enjoy Cornwall. I was sure we would find other places to enjoy together. But I would not come back to Windward. Each stroke I took confirmed this thought and opened the crack in my heart a bit wider. I was resolved, though, and after a few more laps I came ashore – where I found Amelia sitting by my towel and clothes.

Dripping, I stared at her. I had come to the beach for space, especially from her.

'You don't understand,' she said, and wrung her hands.

I picked up the towel and began to briskly dry myself. 'No.'

'You won't even try.'

'You ...' I wrapped myself in the towel. 'You and Bobby.'

'I know.'

'Then what is there to understand?'

'I was drunk.' She looked at me with huge eyes, pleading.

'So?' I slipped my costume off.

'It's not an excuse.' She stood. 'I didn't plan to get drunk. It just happened.'

I pulled my knickers and shorts on, then tied my belt too tightly. 'I know.'

'Eddie.' Her eyes, my eyes, showed me the pain she was feeling. I knew, even understood it, but what about *my* pain? 'A group of us had been celebrating and then the news of Eddie arrived through one of his friends, stumbling across us in Trafalgar Square.' She dragged in a long breath. 'My world went dark. I drank anything I could get my hands on, which was a lot. I lost my friends, I lost myself. I became consumed in the crowd.'

Pulling my bra and shirt on, I could see it as if I had been there with her. Everyone celebrating around her, and Amelia standing alone, her world torn to shreds. Despite what she had done, I still felt for her. 'I'm sorry,' I said.

'Yes.'

With the towel I rubbed the last of the water out of my hair. 'Why?'

She shrugged.

I turned from her. She owed me answers.

'I – I wasn't thinking straight,' she said at last.

'No. You weren't.'

'I wanted to be loved.'

349

'Or to take mine from me.'

'No.' She stepped towards me. 'Never that.'

'Liar.' I twisted my hair and secured it with a clip.

'No, I – I didn't think.'

'You never do.'

I turned away from her and walked back up the hill, leaving Amelia behind. She had known what she was doing, no matter what she said. She knew she couldn't hide those thoughts from me.

24 September 2015

Jack paced the floor at the end of my bed. His hair was wet and in disarray. He would stop for a moment, look at me and then continue wearing out the carpet. How could I make this easier for him? Was Peta right? 'Are you trying to make me sea sick?'

'Sorry.' He turned and sat on the bottom of the bed. 'I want ...'

'Yes, what do you want?'

He shook his head.

'You need to live.' I bit my tongue. He didn't need a lecture from me. Peta was right. I needed to hold on and play a game so that he learned how to let someone into his life again. Lara. Bobby's great-grandchild. Bobby had opened my heart and she was the key to Jack's. No matter what it cost me, I had to help Jack save himself. He needed to see that love didn't lead to death. Yes, his father hadn't coped but it wasn't always that way. We hadn't spoken of it and maybe some things needed to be spoken about.

'Jack?'

He looked up.

'Is Lara here?' My voice croaked.

He frowned.

'After I get some more rest, I would like to see her.'

'Are you sure?' He stood, thrusting his hands into his pockets.

'Yes, yes, I am.' I closed my eyes and prayed as I hadn't in years that this was the right thing to do. That revealing the past would heal the present, or at least open a door for him. I would never be able to make him walk through it but I could give a little push. Or would my interference simply ruin more lives?

15 August 1945 – VJ Day

The walls and ceiling of my room closed in on me. Pulling out my suitcase, I began to pack. My uniform and Bobby's letters were the key to holding me together. They would keep me sane. The people in Windward would not. I flung the rest of my things including my teddy bear into the case and closed it. There was one other item I wanted. Grandmother's wedding veil. I knew where it was. I planned never to return and that was the one thing I would take with me.

I crept out of my room with my suitcase and climbed into the attic. Each creak of the floorboards threatened to give me away. In the darkness I found the old chest. Slowly, trying not to disturb the dust or anything else, I raised the lid and lifted up the veil, which was wrapped so carefully in tissue. Abruptly I sneezed – in my surprise I let go of the lid, and it came crashing down. I held my breath, waiting for the sound of footsteps – I was certain someone must have heard that – but thankfully, none came.

Once I'd packed the veil, I went back down the stairs, taking each step carefully. If I left now I would get to Falmouth in time to make a train that would connect somewhere. I really didn't care where I went, as long as it wasn't here.

Reaching the landing on tiptoes so as not to make a sound, I looked up and found Grandmother standing there, watching me.

'I wondered when you'd leave.' She rested heavily on her cane.

'Excuse me?'

'I knew you'd go.'

I could hardly deny that was what I was doing, thanks to the suitcase in my hand.

'I don't blame you,' she said. 'Your father will be here soon and I imagine it could be unpleasant.' She shook her head. 'Of course it doesn't have to be if your parents can both be reasonable.'

I raised my eyebrows. Was my grandmother saying what I thought she was? 'You know?'

'Of course I do. Are you shocked? Well, you shouldn't be. My father had a mistress. My mother was relieved when it happened.'

I collapsed against the wall.

'She'd done her bit, produced the required heirs and was much more interested in her garden than him. She was quite happy for him to trouble someone else for sex while she kept the house, the title and the money.'

I swallowed.

'Yes, it would be best for you to leave.' She sighed. 'Especially as I suspect your sister is about to announce she's pregnant, and then we will have to ask who the father is, considering her fiancé had not been on English soil for months before he died.'

I felt the colour drain from my face.

'Know who it is, do you?' She shook her head. 'It's a good thing you have enough sense to not behave in the same manner.' She focused on me as if she was trying to see inside. 'Off you go.'

My hands were shaking. Amelia was pregnant, my grandmother was right. That was what I had been sensing but had been unable to place because I didn't understand. She was pregnant with Bobby's child. The bag fell from my grasp and I heard my father's voice downstairs.

'What? Have you changed your mind and decided to stay for the fireworks? It's one thing for your father to behave badly but another for your sister.' My grandmother was half muttering to herself as she moved past me and went down the stairs. 'Men always have it easier.'

I knew I needed to speak to Amelia, but my feet were rooted to the spot as I heard another voice downstairs – Bobby's. Dear God. Why was he here now? Had Amelia contacted him? No, she wouldn't have. He must have received my letter and come straight away.

Amelia opened her bedroom door and looked at me. She'd been crying. Despite my own feelings, I wanted to hold her and tell her it would be all right. But I knew it wouldn't be. There was no possible way that anything would ever be right again.

✳ Forty-Two ✳

Windward, Mawnan Smith, Falmouth, Cornwall
24 September 2015

Lara stood at the kitchen sink, looking in the mackerels' eyes. She knew they would be best filleted – unless Jack was using them as bait, which would be a sin. She didn't know if she was still welcome at Windward, despite what Peta had implied, but she figured doing a little prep work before she left couldn't make things worse. She dampened a dishcloth and placed it on the counter top before putting a white cutting board down. Jack's kitchen really was properly equipped – she quickly found a flexible filleting knife and set to work, pondering as she did so the possibility of staying in the area and having a restaurant of her own. The setting was stunning and she could specialise in seasonal and local produce. The region was surrounded by some of the best fishing waters in the world and it was a short trip from field to plate.

'Lara.'

Startled, she swung around with the knife in her hand, then quickly lowered it while her heart raced.

'Sorry,' said Jack, putting his hands up. 'I didn't mean to scare you.'

'No problem. I had no plans to kill you either.'

'Pleased to hear it.' He stepped closer and she saw that his eyes weren't quite so shuttered now. 'You've done all the work for me, I see.'

'Well, they were there.' She shrugged, trying to discern if he was still cross.

'What was your plan for them?'

'Actually,' she said, 'I was waiting to discover yours.'

'I didn't really have one.' He came to her side and picked up one of the fillets. 'I usually just gut them and then put them on the barbecue.'

'Oh, I'm sorry.' She ran a finger across the sleek skin. 'I find the fillets cook better and it makes them easier to eat and enjoy without the bones.'

'You are right.' He put the fillet down. 'I have a lot to learn.' Putting on an apron, he cocked his head to one side. 'Where do we begin?'

15 August 1945 – VJ Day

Bobby traced each of my fingers with his own, sending shivers through my body to places I was trying to ignore, telling myself they were no longer useful. He'd changed my world by holding my hand and opening my heart. We had come to my hiding spot, the small hollow in the cliff halfway down the path to the cove, and there we sat in silence. I was fighting the urge to flee with him there and then, to keep him from learning the truth of what had happened. The desire was so powerful, but I couldn't do it – it wouldn't be fair.

I could still see the look on his face as he watched Amelia and me walk down the stairs side by side a few hours ago. He hadn't known which was which and that had broken my heart all over again.

I had always wanted to find someone who knew me, really knew me, and I thought Bobby had. But when faced with both of us, he couldn't see which one was me.

And now I had to save my sister. She had few choices but I knew only one of them would work for Bobby. The only one for me would be if we fled. But I would have to lie to him and never be in touch with my family again. He would be suspicious and the lie would be between us, always pushing us apart.

Without saying a word, my twin had asked me for help. She didn't know what to do or where to turn. What could I do?

Screaming *what about me?* wouldn't help any of us. Her fate was in my hands, as was that of Bobby. Did I just break his heart and tell him that I didn't love him any more after what he had done with Amelia? Would he know it was a lie? Yet his heart would still be broken when I told him that my sister was carrying his child. Of course, I knew it was his. Once Amelia had given her heart to Eddie, she hadn't looked at another man until she'd seen mine.

The fir tree above us dropped a few pine needles, and as they fell onto my hand their spikes lightly pricked my skin. He brushed the needles away, sending the warm aroma into the air around us. I leaned my head against him. The last time we'd sat here the sky was black and his breath tasted of whisky. Now it smelt of peppermint and I knew that whatever kisses we shared here would be our last. I swallowed.

'I'm so sorry.' His deep voice went straight through me.

'I know.'

He turned my face to his. 'I wouldn't do anything to hurt you. You mean everything to me.' His lips touched mine almost as if he was asking my permission. Closing my eyes, I kissed him back with all the love inside me. The hunger in both of us brought tears to my eyes. Bobby pulled away and looked closely at me as if he was trying to see a difference that wasn't there. Amelia and I were too alike physically. It was only on the inside that we were different.

'I've made you cry.'

I shook my head.

'I have,' he said.

'No. Something else has.'

He brushed the tears away with his thumb. 'What is it?'

'First, kiss me again.'

I wanted to remember this moment forever, for I knew it would be the last time. I clung to him, wanting to imprint everything into my memory. 'Hold me tight,' I whispered against his neck.

'What's wrong?'

I couldn't keep it from him any longer. I knew Amelia was

telling our parents she was pregnant while I hid away with Bobby. They would be reviewing her options. Grandmother would be giving her thoughts on the matter. Banished to Scotland to have the child then give it up for adoption. Use Father's connections and have an abortion. But mostly they would want to know who the father was, for they knew it wasn't Eddie. I didn't know what she would say. But I understood that Bobby needed to know that Amelia was carrying his child.

'There's no way to say this that will make it any better.'

He frowned.

'Amelia is pregnant.'

He closed his eyes.

'You didn't wear a French letter, did you?'

He shook his head then looked out to the bay. His shoulders fell. The water below us was glass-like, the tide high. Nothing disturbed the picture, not even a ship heading to Falmouth.

'I thought you should know.'

He nodded.

'I don't know what she will do.'

He turned to me. 'What do you mean?' His skin went pale, making his blue eyes stand out. 'You don't mean she would get rid of it?'

'I don't know.' All I could be certain of was that Amelia didn't know what to do.

'She can't.' He grabbed my hand. 'I can't let that happen.'

'I know.' I brought his hand to my lips and kissed it. 'We must go to them and tell them that you will marry her.'

'Oh God.' His eyes filled with tears. 'Why couldn't it have been you? It should have been you.'

'I know.' My gut twisted. I wanted to double over with the pain, but I needed to make this as easy as possible for him.

'I want to do the right thing, but I . . .'

'This is the right thing.' A spasm passed through me. He would never be happy knowing that a child of his was out there somewhere, or that the child had been aborted.

Tears rolled down his cheeks. I wiped them away, then took

his hand in mine and led him out of my hiding place, up the pathway, and back towards the house.

We stopped before heading in. 'I love you.' I kissed him one last time. His glance was so full of love and sorrow that it was hard to separate them. His tears had dried, the soldier returned. We walked in side by side.

✳ Forty-Three ✳

Windward, Mawnan Smith, Falmouth, Cornwall
25 September 2015

Lara didn't register much of the scenery on the journey to Windward. As she drove, her mind couldn't help but go over the events of the previous day. Elle had slept for most of it, but she had at least eaten the grilled mackerel that Lara had served on a bed of chunky salsa, made from ingredients found in the garden. There had been no further discussion or questions yesterday, and Lara hoped that today might be different, especially since the doctor was due to visit.

She didn't want to upset either Elle or Jack, yet her fingers twitched with tension and excitement. She was so close to discovering what had happened. Somehow Grandie had made a huge mistake. The poetry book from Adele to Amelia was on the back seat. She hoped to be able to ask Elle about it today.

A tractor came towards her along the narrow lane, and this time she reversed quickly out of its way without her nerves taking over. Finally, the gates to Windward appeared and as she pulled in she realised with surprise how much she was enjoying spending time with Jack. She parked next to a car she didn't recognise, out of which an old man was clambering. Once upright, the man glanced over at her and smiled. 'Good morning, beautiful,' he said, and bowed slightly to her.

'Good morning,' she replied.

'Allow me to introduce myself. I'm Eddie Carew, and you must be Amelia's great-granddaughter.'

Lara inhaled and stood clutching the handle of the rear door of the car.

'May I assist?'

'Thank you, but no.' She collected the poetry book from the back seat along with her bag. 'I'm Lara.'

'What a delightful name.' They walked toward the house. 'I hear my dear friend isn't well.'

She nodded.

'I'm afraid seeing you throws light onto the past,' he said, and sighed.

'Is that bad?' As they walked together towards the kitchen, she studied his face, creased with lines that told so many stories. Right then, she wanted to hear them all.

He stood back to allow her to enter the house first. 'Not bad, but it certainly hasn't been easy.' He studied her with soft brown eyes that were full of kindness. 'You know, you look so like my love that it hurts.'

'Your love?' She frowned.

'Yes, I was engaged to Amelia.'

She gasped in surprise. He gave a dry laugh in reply. 'Let's take a short stroll before we go in,' he said.

Lara nodded and they headed out to the large sweep of lawn that overlooked the bay.

'That,' he said softly, pointing up to the window of Elle's room, 'is your great-aunt Adele.'

It was what she had suspected but it still surprised her. 'My great-grandfather's first love.'

'Yes, and the twin sister of mine.'

'Oh my God.' Lara stood still for moment, letting the information sink in.

'I don't know the details. Adele has never spoken about it and I can understand that.' He smiled. 'But I came back from the Far East to find that my fiancée had married Adele's American and had given birth to his child.'

Lara reached out to him as he continued to speak. 'You see, she thought I was dead. And, to be honest, when I found out what had happened, I wished I was.'

'I don't know what to say.' Lara couldn't bear to look into his eyes. The pain inside him was plainly too raw, even after seventy years.

'Tell me about Amelia,' he said.

'I'm afraid I can't. She drowned when my grandmother Betty was four.'

He took a breath and looked out to sea.

'That's why I came on this trip. You see, my great-grandfather's last word was "Adele".'

Jack came around the house to where they were standing by the end of the lawn near a footpath heading into the trees. 'I see you've met.'

Lara nodded. 'How is she?'

'Sleeping again, but she ate breakfast.' He stood with his arms across his chest.

'Good. I could use a decent cup of coffee, young man.'

'Follow me.' Jack led the way into the house but Lara didn't follow. She walked to the far wall and sat down, looking out at the sea. There was so much to think about. She opened the poetry book and looked at the inscription. Christmas 1943. She flipped through the pages, trying to see if any of the poems had notations or anything to shed some more light on Amelia.

15 August 1945 – VJ Day

My mother held Amelia's hand, Father paced the sitting room and Grandmother looked out of the window at her roses while Bobby and I stood side by side, his arm making light contact with mine. My fingers itched to hold his hand, but if I did, I knew I wouldn't have the strength to let go. Amelia looked up at me with her hand resting protectively on her abdomen. That told me what my father wanted to do about this. I could see that, in many ways, it would be the easiest solution. It would even mean that I could still have Bobby – but I knew if that happened he would never forgive himself, and would never again be the man I loved.

Father stopped walking and glared at me. 'Now isn't the time for any happy news.'

'Amelia, please take a walk with Bobby.' I looked at them both. I could read the question in my sister's expression but she stood and came towards us. I offered an encouraging smile to Bobby and stepped aside so that they could head out together.

Father waited until they had left the room before turning to me. 'Just what was that about?'

'I have a story to tell.'

'I don't bloody well have time for stories. Amelia has been unforgivably stupid. Right now we need to act and do so swiftly.'

I took a deep breath and looked at Mother. She was a mess, her eyes red and her skin lacking all colour. I knew I could solve this – as long as Amelia said yes to Bobby. 'I don't know how much Amelia has told you.'

Father turned from watching Amelia in the garden. 'She was blind drunk on VE Day and had sex with a stranger.'

I silently thanked my sister for trying to protect Bobby and me, but it wouldn't work. 'She was drunk but it wasn't a stranger.'

Grandmother turned from staring at her roses. 'Don't leave us hanging on that.'

I took a deep breath. 'It was Bobby, my fiancé.'

'Your *what*?' Mother sputtered her words.

'Bobby, like many, was drunk and saw Amelia that day,' I said. 'I'm sure we don't need any more details but he thought she was me.'

'Dear God.' Grandmother rose and went to sit beside Mother.

'Yes.' I sighed.

Father's glance bored into me. 'So your sister is pregnant with your fiancé's spawn.'

I nodded. My legs wobbled but I locked my knees. Someone had to be strong here. Out of the corner of my eye I could see through the window, out to the garden – Bobby was holding one of Amelia's hands. He then put an arm around her shoulders. I looked away.

'So what is happening out there?' said Grandmother, pointing at the window.

'Bobby is proposing marriage.'

'Honourable but unnecessary,' she replied. 'I think your father is right. We need to act quickly. It's best to abort the baby and not ruin three or four lives.' She grabbed her cane and stood.

I glared at her. I understood what she was saying but she was wrong – none of us would walk away from this whole, no matter what steps we took. All I wanted was the least amount of harm to add to what had already been caused.

It wasn't for me to explain. I had done all I could do.

The only thing left for me was to stand there with them, waiting, until Bobby and Amelia re-entered the house and came back into the room.

'Are congratulations in order?' Father clenched his jaw.

Amelia nodded. I could feel her calmness, but I couldn't look at the two of them any more. More than anything else, I needed to leave. 'I'll be off,' I said, and before anyone could reply, I dashed from the room. My sister's voice followed me up the stairs, but I did not falter. My bag was still packed. I pulled the veil out and put it on the bed, then locked my case and was down the back staircase in moments.

25 September 2015

'What's this foolishness of nearly dying on me?' said Eddie as he limped into the room. He wore a tweed jacket, thick corduroys and a checked shirt with a cravat neatly tied at his neck – the image of bygone days. He put the two glasses and the bottle of single malt whisky he was carrying down on the bedside table.

'Come on, Delly, we've lived through too much to go feeble now.' He poured two large measures and handed me a glass. 'This is foolish. Just because Amelia's great-granddaughter has turned up.' He straightened his cravat. 'We should rejoice. She is a beautiful girl and something good came from an unfortunate affair.'

My eyes filled. He pulled out a handkerchief and wiped away my tears. 'You silly old thing.'

'I am.' I touched his hand and he stilled.

'It's all water under the bridge now,' he said gently. 'I'm sure we'd both do things differently if we could.'

'I would but Amelia had little choice.' I swallowed.

'I know. She had such a gentle heart.' A tear slipped down his cheek. 'Wasted lives. The only good that came out of it was the child, and through her Lara.'

'There's so much you don't know.'

He looked into his glass before taking a big swig. 'You don't have to say.'

'But I do. Now, after all these years, I do.' I leaned against the cushions and Eddie sat on the bed holding my hand.

'Then tell me.'

I sipped the whisky, thinking, trying to find the right words.

'Why don't you let me begin?' he said, and stroked my cheek. 'I was a mess and worse when I found out what had happened.' He shook his head. 'I had to go away to be far from our memories together so I moved to France. I didn't come home until I was forced to deal with the house when Mother died in the late sixties.'

'I remember. You came to see me.'

'I did.' He shook his head. 'It was worse than I'd thought, seeing you but seeing her ... if you know what I mean.'

I nodded. 'I imagine we both aged alike.'

He looked up and then away. I frowned.

'How did you cope?' he asked quietly. 'How did you let them marry?'

I took a long sip of the whisky. 'It was the only choice. Amelia had been wrong to sleep with Bobby but then she'd just found out that you were missing presumed dead.' I turned the glass around in my hands. 'Once I told him that she was pregnant, the die was cast.' Eddie held my hand and stroked it. I couldn't stem the tears. 'He was Catholic and honourable and my sister could barely kill a fly.' I wiped my face with Eddie's handkerchief. 'I had to be brave and do the right thing.'

'Oh, my darling girl.'

'What have I done?'

'I don't know, but that beautiful woman downstairs belongs to you. All is not lost.'

I thought of Jack. If she could help save him, then maybe that was true.

❋ Forty-Four ❋

Windward, Mawnan Smith, Falmouth, Cornwall
25 September 2015

A gust of wind lifted Lara's hair and covered her eyes. She tucked it behind her ear and glanced at the bay. White caps were appearing out in the distance. She'd lost track of time sitting in the garden reading poetry. It had been ages since she'd last done so. Looking back at the book, she tried to turn the page but it was stuck. Gently she eased it apart and found an open yellowed envelope. The glue to seal it had attached to the page. It had covered Elizabeth Barrett Browning's 'How do I love thee'. The last line of the poem was underlined in faint pencil: *I shall but love thee better after death.*

Lara's hand shook and she struggled to read the spidery script on the envelope.

Mr Robert Webster
Eventide
Falmouth Heights
Falmouth
Massachusetts

There was no stamp on it. She swallowed the lump in her throat, unsure what the letter would say, but she read it anyway.

Dear Bobby,

I tried. You tried. You look at me and see my sister then you see me and the light in your eyes disappears. I know you being away makes it easier for both of us. We don't have to pretend but Elizabeth needs a father. I can live without a husband, or I thought I could.

My mother has written. Amidst her ramblings about home she dropped in the news that Eddie is alive. He was a prisoner of war, he lost a leg, but she says that none of that matters. She writes that his mother told her that what has destroyed him is my betrayal. Then she goes on to talk about the flower show.

I can't tell you about how I feel. How alone I am. I can't tell anyone. This is all trapped inside me and I can't escape. I want a divorce.

It wasn't signed or really finished, as the handwriting tailed off on the last word. From the look of it, Grandie had never even read it. Lara turned it over, looking for more clues, but found nothing else.

'You've been out here for a while.' Jack handed her a mug of tea. 'Are you OK?'

She nodded.

He sat next to her. 'What's that?'

'I'm not sure.' She gave it to him and watched him scan the contents.

'Is Bobby your great-grandfather?'

'Yes.'

'You think my grandmother is related to Amelia.'

'I know she is.'

He frowned.

'Eddie told me. They were twins.'

He shook his head. 'Maybe we should show this to my grandmother. Eddie's with her.'

'Are you sure?' Lara took a sip of the tea.

He ran a hand through his hair and gave Lara a half-smile. 'No, but I don't know what else to do.'

The door was shut and Jack knocked before entering. Both Eddie and Elle had tears in their eyes.

'What's going on here?' Jack grinned, looking at the whisky bottle. 'Drinking in the bedroom again, Gran? Not sure the doctor would approve.'

Elle looked at Lara. 'I have something to say to Lara and it's not easy.' She held out a hand to her and then her glance fell to the letter still in Lara's hand. 'I recognise that writing.'

Lara gave it to her. 'Does it make sense to you?'

As Elle read the letter, her hand flew to her mouth. Once she had finished reading, she nodded slowly.

'I don't understand,' said Lara. 'Grandie would never divorce.'

'I know.' Elle took a deep breath.

'Be brave.' Eddie walked to the other side of the bed and placed an arm around her. 'It's in the past.'

She nodded. 'There's no way to make this easier.' She took a big sip of whisky. 'I loved Bobby Webster more than I can begin to say.'

Lara went to speak but Elle raised her hand. 'Please hand me those letters,' she said, and pointed to the desk.

Jack gave them to her. 'Gran, is this a good idea?'

'I doubt it, but we have begun. I will open the last letter I received from Amelia first.'

Lara put her hand over Elle's. 'When did it come?'

She nodded at the postmark. 'October 1950.'

'It's her farewell.' Peta's voice had come from nowhere. Lara looked up to find the girl standing in the open doorway, as if she had somehow known what was happening. And right then, Lara understood what she was saying. Amelia's death had not been an accident.

'You may not want to read it aloud, Gran,' said Peta.

'Should we leave you?' Eddie rubbed her shoulder.

Elle shook her head. 'Please stay, all of you. I'm not strong enough to do this alone.' With that, she tore the envelope open, unfolded the letter inside, and started to read. Tears were soon streaming down her face. By the time she reached the end of the letter, she looked somehow even paler. Carefully, she held the letter towards Lara, gesturing for her to take it. 'Read it aloud, please.'

Lara swallowed, took the paper from Elle's hand, and did her best.

15 October 1950

Dearest Half,

He won't look at me. He tries to be a loving father when he's home on leave but it's too hard for him. He can't love me. He looks at me and sees you. He never touches me unless it's necessary. Each day I die a little more. Elizabeth is quite independent. She reminds me of Grandmother. I give her love but she doesn't want it.

Yesterday I received a letter from Mother telling me Eddie was alive. I thought I could carry on but now I can't. Elizabeth doesn't want me. I am so alone here in this place by the sea, Eventide.

Knowing Eddie is alive and broken by the war and by me is too much to bear. I thought I knew what loneliness was before – when I was without Eddie and without you. I know you will not read my letters. I know that giving up Bobby to save me will have broken you. You loved me and I will hold onto that. You thought giving me Bobby would make the wrongs right. But they couldn't be fixed. There was no right.

Goodbye, dearest half, better half,
A xxxx

By the time she had finished reading the words aloud, Lara's voice had cracked and broken several times, and Eddie's head had fallen to his chest.

'Oh my God,' Lara said. 'So much love, and so much sadness.'

'Yes.' Jack took the letter from her.

Lara picked up Elle's hand. 'He loved you to the end. His final word was "Adele".'

Elle closed her eyes and pulled Lara's hand to her heart. 'Thank you.'

Lara stood staring out at Falmouth Bay. The sun had long since set and the easterly breeze was cool. She played with the pearls around her neck. Elle had given her the second string, the mate to the one Betty had given her. They fitted together at the clasp, and Elle had told her that her grandmother had given each twin a strand on Amelia's wedding day. Tears had run down Elle's face as she saw them together again around Lara's neck.

There was a cough behind her. Lara started in surprise, and turned to find Jack standing there.

'Now that you've found out about your great-grandmother, I hope you aren't about to leave just yet.'

She raised an eyebrow. 'Is this because you realised that you don't know how to cook properly yet?

'I can cook.'

'Well ... a bit. But you need to learn to trust the ingredients and your taste buds.'

'Hmmm,' he said, considering the idea. 'Cook without a recipe?'

'Yes, or at least only use it as a guideline.'

'I'm not sure I'm ready yet. I might need more lessons.'

'That's the last thing I would have expected you to say.' She studied him closely.

'Thank you for being so understanding with Gran.' He smiled and touched her hand. 'All these years I thought she was simply tough and sensible. She never indicated that there was such heartbreak in her past.'

Lara took a deep breath. 'Grandie's behaviour makes sense now. He loved her and her alone. That must have been very hard for Amelia to cope with.'

'What are you going to tell your family?'

'That's a good question.' She sat on the wall. 'I don't want to cause more pain, but maybe if my grandmother knew what happened, she could forgive.'

'Forgiving is very hard.' His voice caught as he spoke. He sat beside her. 'I haven't been able to forgive my father for loving my mother so much that he left us.' He stared out at the water.

She touched his arm.

'Love is so powerful it scares me.' He said as he turned to her.

'Me too.' She drew a deep breath. The intensity of his glance unnerved her. 'Maybe ... it's like cooking. It takes time, patience and the right ingredients to make it work.'

Spring Tide

Never give up, for that is just the place and time that the tide will turn.

HARRIET BEECHER STOWE, OLD TOWN FOLKS, CHAPTER 39

Forty-Five

Boat House Restaurant, Boscawen, Constantine, Cornwall
11 March 2016

The river was so high Lara was worried it would climb over the quay and flood the restaurant. Both the architect Mark Triggs and Demi had promised her that they had taken into consideration the spring tides and storm surges when they designed the place, but as Lara peered at the rushing clear water outside, she wasn't so sure. It looked like the grey mullet swimming below in the river would be on the floor and not on the plates if it rose any higher.

The first guests were due in a half-hour. The tables were set – primroses adorned each one and the candles were lit. Tonight was the soft opening of the Boat House and Lara's stomach flipped at the thought. Not only were local friends coming but so were Leo, Deborah, Mom, Gerard, Betty and Kevin, having all made the journey from the States.

Taking a deep breath, she walked back into the kitchen. Everything was ready and her team were prepared. It was a set menu that night, beginning with mussels in Boscawen cider, cream and wild garlic; then a surf and turf of grey mullet – not from the river but the bay – and fillet of beef; this would be followed by a rhubarb sorbet, and finally a selection of local cheeses.

'I can hear them.' Cassie was helping tonight and she popped open a bottle of Pol Roger champagne, Grandie's favourite. Lara leaned out of the window to see the lanterns twinkling on the woodland path and spied the white, fluffy form of Snowy, who had adapted well to his new home with Lara in the Boscawen stables. She could almost imagine that fairies might appear, but instead the first person to emerge into sight was Jack. Her heart beat faster and she touched the pearls at her neck. His arms were full of daffodils.

'Come on, Chef,' Cassie said. 'You need to greet your guests. No hiding in the kitchen tonight.' She picked up a tray of champagne flutes. Lara straightened her apron and nodded to the team before heading to the door.

Jack grinned as he reached her, then bent his head and kissed her deeply. 'Congrats.' His voice dropped to a whisper. 'Dreams do come true.'

Lara closed her eyes for a moment. *They do*, she thought, *but not how I first dreamt them*. 'Yes.' She handed him a glass and took the flowers. 'Thank you.' One of the waitresses quickly put the flowers in water while Lara greeted her family and everyone else she had come to know in the past few months.

Demi tapped a glass. 'Welcome to the Boat House. Thank you for coming.' She smiled and raised her glass. 'This restaurant is the result of hard work and imagination. I know tonight we will be treated to a meal that will thrill our taste buds, so let's hear from our chef.'

Lara smiled. 'Thanks, Demi, and welcome all. Tonight we are featuring local food, hopefully with a slight twist that will surprise and delight you.' She looked into the faces sitting at the tables, knowing all of them. Each one had played some role in making this happen, but it was hard not to feel the absences as well. 'Demi has thanked you all and I do hope you enjoy the meal. I had such pleasure in planning it.' She smiled and lifted a champagne glass. 'Before I slip into the kitchen I'd like to propose a toast to all our friends and family who couldn't be with us tonight, for one reason or another.'

'Hear, hear,' they all said in unison. Lara looked over to Eddie and Betty. Elle would have loved to have been with them but she had died just before the New Year. Taking a sip of the champagne, Lara fled into the kitchen and started work.

The next hour passed in a blur of activity, and Lara barely

stopped moving until the last dessert had left the kitchen. Finally, she was able to return to the main restaurant, and Jack smiled at her as she walked in, standing and pulling out the seat beside him. Everyone clapped as she sank to the chair. She had certainly worked longer shifts in the past, but never before had working meant so much to her.

'The meal was a triumph.' Jack poured her a glass of wine, handed her a piece of Cornish Yarg cheese then placed an arm around her weary shoulders. She closed her eyes, listening to the buzz of conversation and feeling Jack's presence. 'I wish Gran had lived to see today.'

'Me too.' Opening her eyes, she looked towards the shelf by the kitchen door where Amelia's *Tante Marie* cookbook had pride of place. Elle had confirmed it had been her sister's and a French refugee Mme Pomfrey's before that.

He raised a glass. 'As you said, to those not with us.'

She lifted her glass to his and looked him in the eyes. 'And to the future.'

'The future.' Their glasses touched lightly and then his lips met hers.

Acknowledgements

The Returning Tide for me has been a huge step into the dark, the dark of history. It is a subject I have always loved but to actually be writing about it still gives me sleepless nights. In February 2015 my editor Kate Mills asked me for a bigger story and as we brainstormed ideas I thought of my mother-in-law June Fenwick, who served as a Wren telegraphist in WWII, and particularly one incident in her war – Exercise Tiger (see Author's Note below). From this one event *The Returning Tide* grew. Without Kate's unerring belief that I could do it this novel wouldn't have been written. Thank you, Kate.

The upside of writing about WWII is that there are a few wonderful people around who were willing to share their memories with me. Jean Rawson and Val Watson, two Wrens who served at HMS *Attack*, were a delight and an endless source of information. Val entrusted me with her diary for 1944 and this gave me a first-hand glimpse into life during the war. I am so grateful. I wouldn't have found these two women without the help of Twitter. Christine Baker runs the Twitter account for the WRNS Association Weymouth, and not only did she help me find Wrens who served at HMS *Attack* but she also read through early drafts of the book, checking my naval details – any mistakes are mine, not hers. Without her assistance I'm not sure the book would have gone beyond the research stage.

Thanks also go to Gloria Richardson who served as a Wren in Plymouth. She told me of her experiences of exploring Cornwall by catching lifts with the Americans. On the GI front I had the pleasure of interviewing John Salzer, and from him the delights and downfalls of camping in a muddy field in England came

379

alive, as did the reality of the war from a soldier's point of view.

Cornwall played a vital role in the war. I am grateful to Jane Hubbard, who put me in touch with Sylvia Dunstan and Sylvia King, who both provided me with research materials and their recollections of the war on the north side of the Helford. Tiffany Truscott of BBC Cornwall also gave me a hand when I went on her show with a plea for people with wartime recollections.

When you are nothing more than a decent cook, writing about a chef provides a few challenges. In order to showcase Cornwall's fabulous food I ventured to Philleigh Way cookery school, where chef George Pascoe and fish expert Annie Siebert taught me to fillet and cook fish; in particular, Annie proved to me that grey mullet didn't have to taste like blotting paper.

As always my family came to my aid – my sister-in-law Debbie Barton on the intricacies of making wedding cakes and her daughter Philippa Kay on how to have the most beautiful Cornish wedding.

Many thanks go to what I think of as my writing support team – Julia Hayward, Sarah Callejo, John Jackson, Dom Fenwick and Anita Burgh. My wonderful agent Carole Blake died in October 2016. Her wisdom, laughter, and encouragement have guided this novice through the tricky world of publishing with friendship, love and gin. I will miss her sage advice, her wicked laughter and her friendship. Thanks to her belief in my writing – even when I didn't – there are five Liz Fenwick books and one novella out in the world. She is sorely missed. A heartfelt shout of gratitude to Bethan Jones and everyone at Team Orion. Special thanks go to the fabulous Brigid Coady ... sounding board and friend.

No writing would happen without the support of my family. They put up with me being lost in another world, meeting deadlines at inconvenient times and being embarrassing beyond words. Their love and especially that of my husband Chris makes the writing possible.

I lost my wonderful father at the end of September 2016. It's too raw to write about it but I have to say that there is more than a little of Bobby Webster that came from my father.

Finally I wish that my in-laws June and Gordon Fenwick were still with us. The details they shared of their war years have inspired so much of this book.

P.S. Some of you will know we lost our beloved cat Snowy while I was writing this book. Somehow he found his way onto the pages ...

Author's Note

It's hard to know where to begin with the event known as Exercise Tiger, Operation Tiger or the Slapton Sands disaster. Type it into Google and the differing reports begin. How did this event come to be a key part of the novel? My mother-in-law June Fenwick played a role.

Back in 1994 Chris and I were sitting around the dining table in my parents-in-law's house in Cornwall. I can remember so much of the evening clearly except how we came to the point of discussing my mother-in-law's role in the war. I suspect there may have been something in the news. She explained that she had been a telegraphist but insisted that my father-in-law's war was much more interesting, he having served in the Far East.

As usual with family conversations around the table there was much laughter, but suddenly she spoke about the night the E-boats came among the US troops practising for D-Day. Her voice dropped as she explained how she had been working with the Americans that night. The men on the boats had stopped transmitting in code and used plain language in the panic. She said she heard them die. My heart stopped then, and still does when I think about that. Later I pressed her to write down her experiences during the war; she always said she would but sadly that never happened.

Even to this day there are conflicting reports about what exactly happened on 28 April 1944. Those that knew weren't allowed to speak of it and now they are gone. What is clear is that there was a tragic loss of life and it was covered up for many reasons. The biggest one of all being the coming D-Day invasion. I hope someday some historian will be able to shed more light on the tragedy.

I know that the event never left my mother-in-law. For years she could never speak of it because of the Official Secrets Act, and then when she could she didn't. To me that said so much, and was typical of a generation that lived through hardships that seem inconceivable today.

Please know that I had many holes to fill in when writing about this event, but thankfully I'm a novelist and not a historian. The account is fiction not fact. In sewing together a few pieces of information I hope I have conveyed some of the horror of the event, as it might have been experienced by my mother-in-law and those who served. I stand in awe of their bravery, strength and honour.